DARKLING

"The most fulfilling journey of self-discovery to date in the Otherworld series . . . An eclectic blend that works well."
—*Booklist*

"Galenorn does a remarkable job of delving into the psyches and fears of her characters. As this series matures, so do her heroines. The sex sizzles and the danger fascinates."
—*Romantic Times*

"The story is nonstop action and has deep, dark plots that kept me up reading long past my bedtime. Here be Dark Fantasy with a unique twist. YES!"
—*Huntress Book Reviews*

CHANGELING

"The second in Galenorn's D'Artigo Sisters series ratchets up the danger and romantic entanglements. Along with the quirky humor and characters readers have come to expect is a moving tale of a woman more comfortable in her cat skin than in her human form, looking to find her place in the world."
—*Booklist*

"Galenorn's thrilling supernatural series is gritty and dangerous, but it's the tumultuous relationships between all the various characters that give it depth and heart. Vivid, sexy, and mesmerizing, Galenorn's novel hits the paranormal sweet spot."
—*Romantic Times*

"Yasmine Galenorn has created another winner. . . *Changeling* is a can't-miss read destined to hold a special place on your keeper shelf."
—*Romance Reviews Today*

continued . . .

Witchling

continued . . .

"Yasmine Galenorn hits the stars with *Night Huntress*. Urban fantasy at its best!"

—Stella Cameron, *New York Times* bestselling author

"This is an amazing series . . . a great balance of action, mystery, and steamy romance . . . a must-read series for any readers of the genre."   —ParaNormalRomance.org

"Fascinating and eminently enjoyable from the first page to the last, this skillfully written book is populated with unique characters who never bore. *Night Huntress* rocks! Don't miss it!"   —*Romance Reviews Today*

"Love and betrayal play large roles in *Night Huntress*, and as the story unfolds, the action will sweep fans along for this fast-moving ride."   —*Darque Reviews*

Dragon Wytch

"Action and sexy sensuality make this book hot to the touch."   —*Romantic Times* (★★★★)

"Ms. Galenorn has a great gift for spinning a compelling story. The supernatural action is a great blend of both fresh and familiar, the characters are each charming in their own way, the heroine's love life is scorching, and the worlds they all live in are well-defined."   —*Darque Reviews*

"This is the kind of series that even those who do not care for the supernatural will find a very good read."

—*Affaire de Coeur*

"If you're looking for an out-of-this-world enchanting tale of magic and passion, *Dragon Wytch* is the story for you. I will be recommending this wickedly bewitching tale to everyone I know!"   —*Dark Angel Reviews*

BONE MAGIC

YASMINE GALENORN

BERKLEY BOOKS, NEW YORK

THE BERKLEY PUBLISHING GROUP
Published by the Penguin Group
Penguin Group (USA) Inc.
375 Hudson Street, New York, New York 10014, USA
Penguin Group (Canada), 90 Eglinton Avenue East, Suite 700, Toronto, Ontario M4P 2Y3, Canada
(a division of Pearson Penguin Canada Inc.)
Penguin Books Ltd., 80 Strand, London WC2R 0RL, England
Penguin Group Ireland, 25 St. Stephen's Green, Dublin 2, Ireland (a division of Penguin Books Ltd.)
Penguin Group (Australia), 250 Camberwell Road, Camberwell, Victoria 3124, Australia
(a division of Pearson Australia Group Pty. Ltd.)
Penguin Books India Pvt. Ltd., 11 Community Centre, Panchsheel Park, New Delhi—110 017, India
Penguin Group (NZ), 67 Apollo Drive, Rosedale, North Shore 0632, New Zealand
(a division of Pearson New Zealand Ltd.)
Penguin Books (South Africa) (Pty.) Ltd., 24 Sturdee Avenue, Rosebank, Johannesburg 2196,
South Africa

Penguin Books Ltd., Registered Offices: 80 Strand, London WC2R 0RL, England

BONE MAGIC

A Berkley Book / published by arrangement with the author

PRINTING HISTORY
Berkley edition / January 2010

ISBN: 978-0-425-23198-2

BERKLEY®
Berkley Books are published by The Berkley Publishing Group,
a division of Penguin Group (USA) Inc.,
375 Hudson Street, New York, New York 10014.
BERKLEY® is a registered trademark of Penguin Group (USA) Inc.
The "B" design is a trademark of Penguin Group (USA) Inc.

PRINTED IN THE UNITED STATES OF AMERICA

10 9 8 7 6 5 4 3 2 1

Dedicated to
my sister Wanda:
Through hell and high water,
despite all the rattling skeletons in our family's closets,
you and I have come so far that the past is finally a
distant memory.

ACKNOWLEDGMENTS

Thank you to my beloved Samwise—the dragon who holds *my* heart. And my gratitude to my agent, Meredith Bernstein, and to my editor, Kate Seaver: Thank you both for helping me stretch my wings and fly. A salute to Tony Mauro, cover artist extraordinaire. To my Witchy Chicks—a family of wonderful writers. To my "Galenorn Gurlz"—those still with me, those who have come into my life this year, and those who crossed over the Bridge this sad, sad summer—I will always love you, even through the veil. Most reverent devotion to Ukko, Rauni, Mielikki, and Tapio, my spiritual guardians.

And the biggest thank-you of all—to my readers, both old and new. Your support helps keep the series going. You can find me on the net at Galenorn En/Visions at www.galenorn .com, on MySpace at www.myspace.com/yasminegalenorn, on Twitter at www.twitter.com/yasminegalenorn, and on my fan site at www.moonstalkers.com. You can also find the D'Artigo Sisters on Twitter: www.twitter.com/SOTM_Sisters.

If you write to me snail mail (see website for address or write via publisher), please enclose a stamped, self-addressed envelope with your letter if you would like a reply. Promo goodies are available—see my site for info. Fan club information on my site, as well.

The Painted Panther,
Yasmine Galenorn
November 2008

Where there is much light, the shadow is deep.

—JOHANN WOLFGANG VON GOETHE

If you can't get rid of the skeleton in your closet, you'd best teach it to dance.

—GEORGE BERNARD SHAW

CHAPTER 1

"Run! Get the hell out of here!" Morio pushed me toward the iron gates.

I didn't ask why. I just took off for the opening, avoiding the metal as I darted past the wrought-iron spikes. Nearing the steps leading out of the mausoleum, another shout from Morio stopped me and I whirled around. He'd dropped his bag containing his skull familiar and had pulled out a pair of curved daggers, one in each hand. A wedding present from me, but he wasn't taking any time to admire the carved antler handles.

No, it was show-and-tell time.

Two people with long, shuffling strides were headed his way. Or rather, two *bodies*.

"Can you cut off their heads?"

Morio snorted. "Oh sure. I can just zip in and lop off their heads with these babies. *Get real*, woman. We've got our work cut out for us."

"Hey, life would be easier that way," I called out, but he had a point. It wasn't that he couldn't fight. In fact, Morio was an incredible fighter. But we were facing one teensy problem. Our opponents weren't exactly alive. They were already dead. And dangerous.

One of them was just what he looked like—so much dead meat on the hoof. Normally, returning the zombie to the grave wouldn't be much of a problem—they were shambling, brainless monsters. No brains meant for less of a challenge. But we'd made a potentially deadly mistake. His companion was all too aware of our intentions and was whispering something under his breath.

That we'd accidentally chosen a demon's corpse to experiment on didn't help matters. Neither did the fact that we'd summoned a spirit into the body, and that spirit knew how to use magic. Oh yeah, we'd fucked up royally.

As I raced back to his side, Morio leapt into the air, spinning with a kick that landed squarely on the chest of the first corpse, sending the creature reeling back. The zombie thudded against the wall and slid to the floor. It was still moving, though, and if we'd done our job right, would be back in action in a moment. And it looked like we deserved an A+ for attention to detail. The zombie was struggling to push itself up off the ground.

"Cripes. *Now* our magic works," I said, torn between being proud of our work and wishing we weren't so damned good. I ran through my repertoire of spells, trying to think of something to help. We had to reverse the summoning spell but in the meantime, what could freeze an angry spirit waltzing around in a demon's body?

Morio sliced through the air, catching one of the creature's arms. He managed to carve off a long strip of the flesh and I grimaced as the chunk o' demon fell to the floor. The zombie reeled as Morio punched him in the jaw. He knocked him back a few steps, but barely put a dent in the monster's speed.

Oh, this was *so* not how our experiment was supposed to go.

Quick, quick, what could I use? Fire? No, the damn thing was demon and there was a good chance the body was still immune to flame. But what about lightning? I grinned. Electricity just might work.

I thrust my arms into the air and closed my eyes, summoning the Moon Mother, calling down the lightning. A storm was on the way, so the bolts didn't have far to travel.

The lightning instantly responded. I could hear it crackling from about five miles away as the clouds raced in, carrying it to me. As the energy began to swirl around my hands, it thickened, shrouding me like a fog. The power soaked into my pores and entered my lungs with the rising mists.

The energy coiled like a snake at the base of my tailbone and began to ascend through my spine, prickling me like a thousand needles, the pain sharp and exquisitely sensual. A rush of desire rode on the back of the bolt—sex and magic were integrally combined for me. I sucked in a deep breath as the spell took over, then arched my back, arms open wide, and pointed my palms toward the demon's body.

Morio glanced at me and I heard him mutter, "Oh shit," his look one of stark terror. He jumped back, striking the demon with a final kick, and then cartwheeled out of the way. As soon as he'd cleared the zombie, I spread my fingers and let the energy stream out of me. It reared up, taking the shape of a dragon, and dove for the demon, arcing with ten thousand amps.

The spirit we'd invoked shrieked and fled the body as the carcass fell to the ground. I dropped to my knees, my gut aching like a son of a bitch, but when Morio shouted, I glanced up just in time to see the bolt of lightning coil, then reverse direction as it raced straight toward me. I screamed and raised the horn of the Black Unicorn.

"Deflect!"

The Master of Winds residing within the horn rose up and as the bolt came crashing down, he thrust his sword in front of me. The lightning fastened onto the sword and followed the trail leading to the air Elemental's body, harmlessly passing through him as it grounded into the floor. I scrambled back from the blackened spot on the concrete not two feet away as Morio carved up the second zombie into small enough pieces that it couldn't bother us.

"Well," I said, panting as I leaned against the wall, all too aware that I'd barely skipped out on becoming toast. Again. "We can add this one to the list of *thou shalt nots* we've managed to accumulate. Whose bright idea was this, anyway?"

"So we made a mistake in choosing our host. It happens." He shrugged.

"It happens? How on earth did we manage to end up with a demon's body and *not know it*?" I stared at him for a moment and he gave me a sheepish grin. "Oh good gods, *you knew*. You knew we were invoking the spirit into a demon's body and blithely told me to go ahead with it. What the hell were you thinking? Are you insane?"

"I thought you'd figure it out," he said, laughing. He looked like he was enjoying this fiasco just a little too much. "We're still alive so I consider it a success. And if you hadn't chosen a mage's spirit to invoke, we wouldn't have had a problem. If you'd just chosen Joe Schmo's ghost, then he wouldn't have been able to use magic and we could have controlled him. Can you imagine what a demon zombie could do for us on the battlefield? Hard to kill, hard to take down. Goblins, trolls, even other demons would have their hands full fighting him."

I blinked. "So now it's *my* fault?" He laughed again and I sputtered. "You didn't tell me who to call from dial-a-ghost. I just randomly chose somebody. I didn't know he'd been a mage—"

"Camille, babe, it's okay." Morio leaned against me and brushed the side of my face with his hand. His skin felt *oh, so smooth*. "No harm, no foul. We're dealing with it, so it's all good. Now, get a move on, woman. We still have to banish the spirit back to the Netherworld." He pointed toward the wall of the mausoleum.

There, a ghostly white shape hovered almost close enough to touch—the spirit we'd summoned into the demon. But the phantom couldn't do anything now that we'd blasted it out of its host. The mage had practiced earth magic when he was alive, which meant he couldn't attack from beyond the grave unless given a body through which to work. And I'd just blasted his vacation timeshare to smithereens, well beyond what Demons-R-Us could fix.

I dusted off my skirt, which was now beyond the place where anything but a lint roller and a lot of detergent could help.

"Fine. Where to?" I limped over to Morio, my knee aching. I'd bruised myself pretty good when I dove to avoid the blast.

"Are you hurting?" He wrapped his arm around my shoulders and fastened his lips on mine, giving me a long, luxurious kiss, playing lightly over my tongue with his own. Morio might be on the slender side, and he wasn't the tallest of my lovers, but oh Mama, he had one hell of a hot body.

"Not so much that you couldn't kiss it and make it better," I whispered, pressing against him as my fingers traveled to his nether regions. I brushed my hand against the front of his pants, inhaling deeply as I felt him harden behind the loose material.

"Stop that," he whispered with a grin. "We've got work to do."

"I need you," I whispered back. Magic and cheating death were two of my favorite aphrodisiacs. Combine the two and I was ready to rumble, tear off my clothes, break the bed horny.

"Patience. Patience," he said, nibbling my ear. "When we get home, Smoky and I'll give you what you crave, love."

I danced away from him. "Then let's get this wrapped up. The sooner we're done, the sooner the two of you can play a duet on me." I loved both of my husbands. And together, they could do a number on me that sent me into orbit. Sex had become a cornucopia of delights and once Trillian, my alpha lover, returned, I expected to be the happiest woman in both Otherworld and Earthside. *As long as Trillian didn't blow up over finding out I'd married Smoky and Morio*. He knew they were my lovers, but formalizing the relationships might be enough to send him over the edge. Not so much with Morio, but Smoky—big testosterone wars had been looming when Trillian was called away.

"It's a deal," Morio said.

Laughing, I followed him out of the mausoleum. Spirit-dude wasn't tagging along behind us for a change. In fact, he was hanging back, looking right and left as if he was trying to decide which way to vamoose.

"What about the ghost? He's kind of a must-have during the ritual."

Morio shrugged. "Don't worry. He'll be there. He can't refuse."

As he spoke, the spirit slipped around the corner into a narrow hallway that led farther into the Wedgewood Cemetery mausoleum. We watched as he disappeared from view.

I shook my head. "Does he really think he can get away

that easy? He has to know that the only reason he's here is because we summoned him. And *because* we summoned him, he's magically bound to stick near us until we're done with him. Or give him another body to roam around in."

"Maybe he's an optimist," Morio said. "Come on, let's get outside and send him back to where he belongs." He shivered as a blast of cold air hit us. "We can't be expecting a frost yet—it's not even the equinox."

"Autumn's already here," I said. "Trust me. And winter's going to be a doozy."

As we slipped out of the mausoleum, a wash of moonlight splashed across our path. The wind was rising but the wind-chill made it feel colder than it was. The temperature barely kissed forty-five degrees and the scent of moisture hung heavy in the air. The storm was coming in fast, and before the hour was over we'd be facing a downpour as the early autumn rains hit Seattle.

I inhaled a long, slow breath to steady myself as the rich scent of loam and moss washed through me, buoying me with the magic rife within their essences. The Earth Mother had been speaking all evening, the slow, steady pulse of her heart tripping a steady cadence beneath my feet.

We traipsed back to the altar we'd arranged on a stone bench behind a patch of rhododendrons. A few yards from the mausoleum, the rectangular dais rose about eighteen inches off the ground. On the left side of the bench Morio had placed a black pillar candle, and on the right—an ivory one. Their flames flickered in the steady breeze. In our absence, wax had puddled down the sides to form rings at their bases on the granite slab. Oh yeah, that was neat and tidy. *Note to self: Next time, bring candleholders.*

Beside the black candle rested an obsidian dagger, its blade gleaming in the soft glow from the candle flame. The hilt was carved from a yew branch and a nimbus of violet light gently pulsated around the blade.

Next to the ivory candle stood a crystal chalice filled with dark wine. It looked like blood, but was actually a robust merlot.

"Well, well, well, the demon brat and the Faerie slut finally remember me and come waltzing in like queens in a drag show. I thought you'd never get your asses back here." A faint voice echoed from a branch on the rhododendron. "Where the fuck have you two nincompoops been?"

I grimaced. The skeleton was all of twelve inches tall. Perched on the branch, he was holding onto the leaf next to him. Grandmother Coyote had loaned him to Morio. The creature was actually a golem of sorts, created from bits of bone and then animated and given a sense of intelligence. Whether she'd made him, or found him, I didn't know. And I wasn't going to ask. Pry into the private affairs of the Hags of Fate? Not so much.

"Shut up, Rodney." Morio frowned. The miniature miscreant was a smartass. And foul-mouthed at that.

"You want my help or not, you bitches?" Faint bluish lights glimmered in his eye sockets and he sounded a little bit overexcited.

Morio thumped him lightly on the skull, almost knocking him off the bough. "Chill, little bone man. So, did anybody pass by while we were inside?" Morio glanced at me, and by the look on his face, I could see he wasn't all that thrilled about Rodney's help, either.

"Watch it!" Rodney steadied himself. "Nope. You're home free."

Morio grinned. "Good. Back in the box." He held out a carved wooden box that looked for all the world like a miniature coffin. The lid was open and the inside was lined with thick, purple velvet padding.

"Fuck a duck." Rodney let out a long huff. "Do I *have* to?"

"Yes," Morio said.

Rodney slowly lifted his middle finger and flashed it at us, then lithely leapt into the box, lay down, and the light faded from his eyes. Morio flipped the lid shut and locked it.

"I don't like to look a gift horse in the mouth, but I have a feeling Rodney's going to end up on the junk heap before long." I poked the box with my finger. "You think Grandmother Coyote would be offended if we gave him back?"

Morio gave me a long, lazy smile. "You want to be the one to ask her?"

Backtrack and avoid the steely teeth at the end of the road.
"No, no . . . just put him away for now. We'll figure out what
to do about him later." I wondered if we could cast a mute
spell on him. Washing his mouth out with soap wouldn't help.
He didn't have a tongue or taste buds.

As Morio stashed the box in his bag, I stared up at the sky.
The wind was rustling through the leaves, sending a handful
whirling to the ground. They were changing color fast this
year. Autumn was coming in with a heavy heart. I sucked in
another deep breath and felt the rush of graveyard dust fill my
soul. Oh yes, the Harvestmen were on the move.

Morio motioned for me to take my place at the altar. His
dark eyes sparkled with flecks of topaz, even as my own violet
eyes were flecked with silver. We'd been running magic thick
and fast for days now, accelerating our practice, trying to hone
our spells before we came face-to-face with the new demon
general that Shadow Wing had loosed upon Seattle. Once we
found the lamia, we'd have our work cut out for us. She was
lying low, hiding out, and none of our contacts could place
either her *or* the half-demon wizard we suspected had gated
her in, but eventually she'd make her move and we had to be
ready.

As I stared at my husband, I realized that he was looking
older. Not old, but wiser, stronger, and more world-weary than
when we'd first met. Hell, we'd *all* aged, if not in looks, in
spirit.

Morio wore an indigo muslin shirt and a matching pair
of loose pants. His outfit was belted with a silver sash, off of
which hung a sheath protecting a serrated blade. His jet-black
hair was smooth and shiny, loose from its usual ponytail. My
ritual garments complemented his own: an indigo low-cut
gown that swept the floor. It was loose enough to move in,
form-fitting enough not to hinder me. Belted on my right side
hung my silver dagger. On my left—the unicorn's horn.

He paused, finger to the wind, then nodded.

"So we just repeat the Summoning spell, but in the opposite pattern, along with the Chant to Dispel?"

"Right. Go ahead. Since you did the actual summoning,
you should be the one to banish the spirit."

I leaned over the center of the bench, across which was

spread a smooth layer of salt and rosemary needles. Picking up the obsidian blade, I pinpointed the energy and traced the salt-drawn pentagram in reverse, then circled it widdershins to open the pentacle.

"*Suminae banis, suminae banis, mortis mordente, suminae banis.*" I focused on banishing the spirit we'd summoned.

The energy swirled through my body, through the blade, into the salt and herbs. There was a sudden silence as the wind dropped and the air grew thick. Above the center of the altar, the ghostly form appeared and, with a slow shriek, vanished from sight, sucked into a spinning vortex. I sealed the spell with a violent slash, severing the energy that had opened the gate to the Netherworld. There was a swift *pop* and the portal disappeared.

"Nifty! It worked. Not quite as powerful as opening a Demon Gate, but hey, at least this time I didn't set loose a dozen wayward ghosts," I said as the clouds broke wide, loosing thunder and lightning and a flurry of hail. The candle flames sizzled and went out, and rain began to pour, soaking us to the skin.

"Think the universe is trying to tell us something?" I watched as the rain washed away all evidence of the salt and rosemary.

Morio let out a long sigh and picked up the candles, emptying the water that pooled in their centers. "Come on, we've got two zombies to clean up after. And after that I just want to go home, take a hot bath, and then . . ." He paused, giving me a long look.

"And then you're going to jump my bones and make me a happy, happy woman," I finished for him.

He cocked his head to one side and winked. "Oh yeah," he said. "And make myself a happy, happy man."

CHAPTER 2

By the time we cleaned up the zombies and reached the car, I was feeling grungy and in need of a shower. The thought of hot water was my holy grail. I wanted nothing more than to wash off both ectoplasm and the tidbits of rotting flesh that clung to my skin. Gingerly, I slipped behind the wheel as Morio slid into the passenger seat. A glance at the clock showed that it was eleven P.M. We hadn't hit the witching hour yet, but the only magic I wanted for the rest of the night was sex magic. Better yet, skip the magic, just bring on the boys.

I leaned back against the plush leather seat of my Lexus, closing my eyes for just a moment before starting the ignition and glancing over my shoulder to make sure I was clear to back out of the parking lot.

Morio seemed as tired as I was. He yawned. "Death magic really takes a toll on the body, doesn't it?"

"Yeah. Summoning that spirit left me wiped. I'm more exhausted from that than from calling down the lightning." I was about to pull out when my cell phone jangled. I stopped, put the car in park, and motioned to my purse, which was on the floor next to Morio.

"Hand me my phone, would you? That better not be Delilah

asking me to pick up some milk for her. I'm not playing delivery woman tonight."

He fished it out for me.

I glanced at the caller ID. Menolly. My other sister, who just happened to be a vampire. She should be at work, but the number read as her cell phone rather than the bar. Flipping it open, I pressed the receiver to my ear. "What's up?"

"If you're done playing George A. Romero, do you mind helping out in a real emergency?" Her voice was terse. She wasn't teasing.

"What happened? Is Delilah okay? Iris? Maggie?"

"Yeah, yeah—no problem on the home front," she said. "Chase called us in. I'm headed over to help him right now and Delilah's on her way from home. Apparently there's a run on the undead tonight. You know Harold Young's house, or at least, what's left of it?"

I didn't want to think about Harold Young or the scorched remains that had been his mansion. In fact, if I never heard his name again, it would be too soon. He'd been one of the nerds from hell we'd had to take out. Bent on sacrificing female Fae to Shadow Wing, he and his buddies belonged to a secret order called Dante's Hellions. They'd royally fucked up and actually invoked a Karsetii demon—one of the Demons from the Depths. That's depths as in astral depths, not ocean depths.

Their mistake had been the only thing that saved themselves—and us—from total catastrophe. But they'd caused way too much death and mayhem, so we'd taken their entire organization down and trundled those who survived over to Otherworld for incarceration. They knew far too much about Shadow Wing to leave them Earthside.

"I'm putting you on speaker so Morio can hear," I said slowly, punching the button so her voice echoed with an eerie static through the car. "Go ahead."

"According to Chase, something's haunting the tangle that's grown wild around the ruins of Harold's house. A passerby spotted what he thought was a dead body in the bushes before seeing something that scared him spitless. He raced out of there like a bat out of hell and called the cops."

"He know what it was?"

"Nope. And when Chase and Shamas went to check it out,

they encountered the same thing—some sort of spirit that scared the shit out of both of them. Shamas said the energy signature places it as being from the Netherworld, but he's not sure exactly *what* it is. Chase needs to check out the body, but doesn't want to send his men in until he knows what they're facing."

"And that's where we come in." I let out a long sigh. "Oh all right, we'll meet you there." I handed the phone to Morio.

"What is it?" He took the phone, softly stroking my hand in the process.

"There have been far too many reports of ghosts and zombies and ghouls lately. Something's up and I'd like to know what's going on." I frowned as I put the car in reverse and pulled out of the parking lot. The Lexus could go from zero to sixty in the blink of an eye, and as we sped down the street, I kept my internal radar on for cops. I wasn't a speed demon like Morio or my sister Menolly, but right now the thought that we were on the verge of something big and ugly niggled at the back of my brain.

"Yeah, I know. Last week we took four calls about spirits, and three about zombies. Somebody around here is raising the dead and we need to find out who."

"You mean besides us?" I flashed him a grin as he tapped my knee with one finger, sending a shiver of desire up my thigh. His mere touch was enough to set me off when we'd been running magic. "What?"

"Slow down. We're in town. There are women and children about."

Snorting, I eased back on the gas. "You're one to talk. And at this time of night on a wet September evening, the only ones still out are the junkies and the homeless—and the homeless don't usually hang out in the middle of the street." I sighed. "I think we should just dig up every corpse around here and cremate them, seal the portals once and for all, and then take off for a nice, long vacation."

He laughed, the smooth cadence of his voice soothing me like warm honey. "If we went on vacation, you'd be bored and complaining in no time. You want me to drive the rest of the way?"

I shook my head. "Nope . . . just stick by my side, love. Stick by my side."

So, I guess introductions are in order. I'm Camille, the oldest of the D'Artigo sisters. And because of our heritage, we're all a bunch of misfits, in one way or another. Our father is full-blooded Fae, our mother human. With our mixed heritage, the three of us walk between the worlds, belonging neither fully to Otherworld nor to Earthside.

I'm a witch pledged to the Coterie of the Moon Mother, and I'm the oldest of three sisters. Four, technically, if you count Arial, Delilah's twin, who died at birth and who recently showed up to surprise us all. She's a ghost leopard and none of us knew about her until just a few months ago.

I've been called everything from seductress to slut, and when people do the *tsk-tsk* thing about my wardrobe (elegant fetish-noir) or my lovers (multiple and none of them human), I just chalk it up to envy. They don't have to walk in my shoes, so they can take their opinions and shove it. My magic back-fires all too often. I'm addicted to makeup and coffee. And I'm certainly not the most diplomatic person in the world. But as Popeye said, I am who I am, and if people don't like it, fuck 'em.

Delilah, the second born, is the most naïve of the three of us though she's learning too fast what the world is really like. A werecat, she transforms into a long-haired golden tabby cat at all the wrong times. Now she also has to cope with being a Death Maiden, thanks to the Autumn Lord, and the second Were form that's emerged for her—a black panther. She can't control it, either. As I said, Delilah had a twin, but something happened. We don't know what, thanks to our not-so-talkative father, but Arial died at birth. Delilah thinks Jerry Springer is god, and she has two boyfriends—one human, one not so much, though Zachary, the werepuma, was seriously hurt not long ago saving the ass of her FBH boyfriend Chase.

And our youngest sister is Menolly. Menolly used to be a *jian-tu*, a spy who was an incredible acrobat. But once in a while that old half-breed curse hits her and her powers falter.

That's how she ended up a vampire. She was spying on a rogue clan of vamps back in Otherworld when she literally fell into their midst. Dredge, the most horrific vampire alive, raped her, tortured her, bled her dry, and turned her. Menolly spent a year in a black fit of insanity but the OIA helped her learn to control herself and she came home to the family. Not long ago she staked her sire—a revenge long overdue.

We work for the OIA—the Otherworld Intelligence Agency. Of course, back home it's known by another name.

What the OIA *didn't* realize when they parked us Earthside is that Shadow Wing, demon lord in control of the Subterranean Realms, was bent on a plan to break through the portals that divide the realms so he can turn both Earth and Otherworld into his private little mosh pit. To do so, he needs to gather as many of the spirit seals as he can—ancient artifacts that keep the realms separate. We stumbled onto his plan and we're now the frontline defense, trying to collect the spirit seals before he has a chance to. We've got four; the demons have one and that's one too many. Four are still up for grabs. We've been gathering our allies, but they're few and far between given the number of the enemy that we're facing. So far, we've defeated two of his scouting squads and one of his generals—the Rāksasa who managed to get hold of the third spirit seal. But there are thousands of demons just waiting to cross through the portals. And they plan to make life a living hell for anybody who stands in their way.

As we sped through the September night, the rain splashed in fat globules against the windshield. I flipped on the wipers and thanked the gods that I hadn't let the car dealer talk me into a convertible. Morio was busy searching in his bag. He finally pulled out a couple of Snickers bars, opened one and handed it to me.

"Here, you need the energy. So do I."

I bit into the candy. "Thanks—needed that," I said, my words muffled by caramel and nougat. He was so right. I was exhausted, and I knew he wasn't far behind. Being a youkai-kitsune, he was stronger than me and had more endurance.

"Smoky going to get his ass out of bed and show up?" he asked.

"Probably," I mumbled through another mouthful of chocolate. Smoky, also my husband, was—like all dragons—concerned most with his own affairs. But he loved me. Ergo, he helped us. And his help was incredibly welcome. That tall drink of water was a force unto himself. As I finished the candy, the sugar rush hit. "I could use about ten of those, but that definitely hit the spot."

I swung a left onto a side street. Seattle was dead in the middle of the night, all the better for us, and as I slowed to twenty-five miles per hour, Chase's prowl car came into view. As did Menolly's Jag. Delilah's Jeep was nowhere to be seen.

I swung in behind the patrol car and we tumbled out into the dripping night. The storm had settled in for a good drenching and I shivered. Morio noticed and reached in the car to pull out his leather jacket, which he slid around my shoulders.

We sidled up to Chase. The FBH detective was leaning against the cruiser next to my cousin. Though Chase Johnson was a good-looking man, he paled next to Shamas, who was full-blooded Fae. Shamas had that rock-star glam going on and looked a lot like me, but since he was full-blooded, his magnetism radiated stronger and sexier. He knew how to use it, too. I'd seen him bring home a dozen different women in the past two weeks after his shift was over. His mother had recently died and it seemed to unleash something in him—a darker side that I could sense but not put my finger on quite yet.

"Where's Menolly?" I asked, looking around. For all I knew, she could be hovering in the trees, or trying out her bat form again—*not* such a good idea. The last time, she'd lost her concentration and gone tumbling to the ground from a three-story height.

"Over there," Chase said, pointing to a rotting pile of lumber from what had once been a three-story mansion. "She's playing bloodhound. Said she's going to look for any scent of Demonkin or undead."

I nodded, glancing at the detective's face. He looked beat. His suit was wrinkled—a rare sight—he had bags under his eyes, and I noticed the cigarette between his fingers. The stub of his little finger had healed up fully, but as I glanced at his hands, he saw me and I noticed he tried to hide it. Still feeling vulnerable, I thought.

Ignoring his discomfort, I reached out and slapped the cigarette to the ground, grinding it out beneath my heel.

"You know Delilah won't sleep with you if you smell like ashes." I arched my back, trying to get the kinks out. "Smoking's a disgusting habit."

He stared at me, the corner of his lip twitching. "Disgusting? Let me get this straight. My girlfriend turns into a cat and eats mice and bugs and uses a litter box. Menolly drinks blood. And you—you . . ." He wrinkled his nose. "What is that stench? I haven't smelled anything that bad since we exhumed a week-old corpse. Oh no," he said, shaking his head. "Please, don't tell me you've been playing with dead bodies again."

I blushed and scuffed the ground. "Well, sure it sounds bad when you put it that way."

Chase groaned. "You've been grave robbing?" He glanced past me at Morio. "The two of you?" Before I could answer, he held up his hand. "Don't say a word. What I don't know, I can't run you in for. And right now, I'm neck-deep in shit and sinking fast. Just do me a favor when you're out playing your nightmare games?"

"What's that?" Morio said, sauntering up to my side, where he slid an arm around my waist.

"Choose bodies nobody's claimed. Don't raise anyone who might be recognizable. No celebrity zombies, okay?" And with that, he turned back to the taped-off crime scene. "Now, do you mind if I tell you what we're facing?"

"It's your nickel," I said, leaning into Morio's embrace. He smelled musky and sweaty and all those good things that normally set my pulse to racing. But I'd passed horny and was into chilled and exhausted. The night was a little too cold and I was a little too tired, and right now a warm nightgown, some wine, and a soft bed sounded better than anything.

Just then, Menolly returned, her eyes icy gray and her fangs extended. The only sound as she walked up to us was the clicking of the ivory beads in her cornrows. She'd tried her hair down, but said it just didn't feel right, so we'd hired a vamp who used to be a hairstylist to come over one night and rebraid the multitude of tiny braids.

She rubbed her nose. "I wish that blood didn't smell so good."

Chase grimaced. "Yeah, yeah. What did you find out?"

"Nothing. I know there's something in that patch of rhodies and ferns, but if it's Demonkin, I can't put my finger on what kind." She saw us and waved. "Good. You're here. Maybe you can figure it out. Chase, did you tell them what you told me?"

"I was about to," he said. "You see over there, behind that overgrown rhododendron? There's a body behind the shrub, but we can't get to it. When Shamas started to push his way through the undergrowth, we heard a deep growl and then a black . . . thing . . . rushed forward. Even though I had a searchlight trained on the area, it couldn't penetrate the depth of that darkness." Chase motioned to Shamas. "Go ahead. Give them details."

Shamas gave me a lazy smile. "Hey, cuz." He'd acclimated remarkably quick once he was Earthside, picking up the vernacular and customs all too easily. "I know it's from the Netherworld, that much I can tell, but I haven't the faintest idea what it is. And I'm used to mingling with creatures from the darker planes."

The look on his face unsettled me. Shamas had developed some remarkable powers over the past year, but we had no idea where he'd learned them. He certainly hadn't trained for them back in Otherworld. And he'd managed to wrench the power away from one of Jakaris's triad of assassins and use it for himself—an unheard of feat. The more we hung around together, the more I wondered just what his escape from assassination had done to him. He wasn't the Shamas I remembered from childhood.

I stepped past him, Morio at my side. "Is Smoky here?"

"He told Delilah he'd come if we need him. He's waiting by the phone," Chase said. "Delilah's on the way."

I stepped off the sidewalk into the shadowy remains of the frat house. The property had recently been sold and, for the first time in over a hundred years, belonged to someone other than Harold's family. We happened to know that Carter, the man who bought it, was actually a demon. He was on our side, but we kept his nature quiet. What the city didn't know, wouldn't hurt them. At least in this case.

As I slowly approached the weeping willow, Morio at my back, my breath caught in my chest. The energy was thick and dark—almost rancid. There was something here all right, an unfriendly presence that bordered on angry. I paused, uncertain what to do next.

Morio leaned close and whispered, "I know what this is. And Shamas is right—the creature's from the Netherworld, but it's not a ghost."

"What is it?" I kept my voice as low as I could.

"A goshanti devil. They're created by the wrath of scorned or murdered women. There are a lot of these creatures, not just in my homeland but all around the world. With all that's been done to the female sex over the years it's no wonder the spirits begin to take on form and substance."

He placed his hands on my shoulders, bracing me from behind. "They hate men, and they lure women into their midst, then attempt to kill them and absorb their souls. That's how they grow after they're initially formed. Men, they just kill and absorb for minimal sustenance and revenge, but female victims are like a psychic form of steroids. They seem not to make the connection that they're doing to other women what was done to them."

Great. Just great. And it made all too much sense, given the murders that had taken place on this piece of land. "Do you know how to kill them?"

Morio kissed the top of my head. "They thrive on anger and strife. If we create some really good vibes, the goshanti might withdraw back to the Netherworld."

I glanced at him. "Oh please. I am not dropping trou here just to create happy thoughts."

"I wouldn't dream of fucking you out here in the rain and cold unless you're raring to stir up trouble," Morio said. He slid his hand up to caress the back of my neck. "But if you insist, I'll oblige. I'd never refuse you." He leaned around to plant a kiss on my lips, his lip curled in an insolent smile. "I do, however, wish to point out that *you're* the one who thought of it. What *I'm* suggesting is that we perform a cleansing ritual.

Best to do it in the daytime though—these things mainly come out at night, though you can still feel their unsettled energy during the day. Actually, I'm not sure if they ever wake during daylight or not."

I rolled my eyes. "Yeah, yeah. Okay, so we come back tomorrow and clean out the area. What do we do until then?"

"Barricade the lot and keep a few Fae officers here who can resist the lure. Goshantis have it right up on par with sirens in luring FBHs into their traps."

Sighing, I turned toward the sidewalk, just in time to feel something lunge at my back. I whirled around and found myself staring into an inky pit of energy that was oozing etheric drool. Oh boy, somebody else slavering over me! I hadn't felt so desired in . . . in . . . well . . . a night or two but this wasn't exactly the passionate hunger usually aimed in my direction. No, the goshanti was jonesing for munchies all right, but not in any manner I considered healthy—at least for my continued existence.

"She took a swipe at me!" I called on the Moon Mother, wondering if I had enough energy left in me to shoot a nice, bright, shiny bolt of lightning toward the creature.

Morio shoved me behind him, disrupting my concentration. "Stop! She'll just feed on your energy. Let's get out of here and we'll come back tomorrow and clean them out when the shadows aren't so long."

He hustled me back to the sidewalk. I nervously glanced behind us but the goshanti stopped at the edge of the lot, unable—or unwilling—to go farther. Taking a deep breath, I steadied myself on Morio's arm, so tired I could barely think. Death magic sucked energy from the core, and the goshanti's darkness was as cold as the Netherworld itself. I felt like I was standing at the bottom of a pit, looking up.

Chase and Menolly were waiting expectantly, but before we could say a word, Delilah drove up. She jumped out of her Jeep and hurried over.

"Did you find out what it is?" she asked.

Morio slid his arm around my waist, half holding me up. "A goshanti devil, straight out of the Netherworld. We can't do anything until tomorrow. Chase, assign a few full-blood Fae out here to corral the lot, and under no circumstances allow them to enter it. Nor should they be female. The creatures are more dangerous to women than to men."

Chase nodded, motioning to Shamas. "Get on it," he said. Shamas took off for the prowl car. "I guess that's it for now. We'll wait here until everything's set up."

Delilah meandered over to his side. She never put an unprofessional spin on his behavior when he was on duty, but now she settled down on the sidewalk beside him. "I'll wait with you. Can't hurt any to have an extra body here."

Too tired to protest that it might be dangerous for her, I glanced over at Menolly. "You heading back to the bar?"

She nodded. "Luke's on duty but I really need to draw up a few purchase orders. We're almost out of Mindolean brandy and we need another case of vodka." My sister owned the Wayfarer Bar & Grill, an official hangout for both Earthside and OW Fae, as well as Supes, vamps, and Faerie Maids—FBH women looking to get it on with an Otherworldly lover. The Wayfarer originally belonged to the OIA but that had changed over the past six months.

"We're going home," I said. "Morio and I will come back tomorrow morning. We'll cleanse the lot and knock its ugly butt back to the Netherworld."

Chase gave me a two-fingered salute. "Sounds good. Be careful on the drive home. You look too tired to see straight, and I've seen how Fox Boy floors the gas when he's driving."

Morio arched his eyebrows. "Suck me dry, human," he said, but grinned. "I'm a better driver than you are, and you know it."

Chase flipped him a friendly bird and we turned back to my car. I handed Morio the keys and slid into the passenger seat. As he buckled himself in, my gorgeous hunk of fox demon said, "Don't get too comfy over there. We're still on for tonight. And before you protest, trust me—sex will make you sleep better."

Too tired to argue, I leaned back against the leather and breathed in his musky scent. As it blossomed in my lungs, I thought about the goshanti devil and the anger that propelled her.

A lot of young women had died on that land, tortured and sacrificed to evil. In some ways, I felt sorry for the devil and the thought of driving her out bothered me, even though we had no choice. Some demons were markers of the past, there to remind us never to let it happen again. And the goshanti devil, for all her anger and fury, had been formed by great pain. I wished there was some way we could pacify her and lay her to rest without destroying her.

But I had a feeling that it wasn't just the women's deaths that had summoned her. Whatever was causing the current spate of paranormal activity had nourished the conditions for the goshanti's formation. And the energy behind all the ghosties and beasties haunting the Seattle night was growing in power. We had to find out what was causing it and put a stop to it before the city became known as Haunted Seattle. Sure, it might make a great tourist attraction, but living in Spooksville wasn't likely to be conducive to happy, healthy campers.

I stared out the window, watching the bright lights of the city pass as we headed toward the border of the Belles-Faire District where my sisters and I made our home. Morio remained silent, his eyes on the road, but I knew all the way home that he was keeping tabs on me out of the corner of his eye, standing watch to make sure I was all right. And I loved him all the more for it.

CHAPTER 3

Home was a three-story Victorian set on five acres of land on the outskirts of Belles-Faire, a seedy but comfortable district in north Seattle. Our land was filled with wetlands, skirting Birchwater Pond where we held rituals and holidays. I had an herb garden, and Delilah roamed the woods in cat form, playing with her unlikely friend Misha—a mouse—and keeping an eye on the local flora and fauna. She lived on the third floor of the creaky old house, I had the second, and the main floor was the common area for all of us. Menolly nested in the basement, her lair a vision of green toile and elegant ivory.

As Morio and I drove through the wooded suburbs, it occurred to me how much had changed over the past couple years since my sisters and I'd come Earthside, and not all of the change was for the best. But at least home was still safe and welcoming.

In some ways, I missed the privacy we'd had early on, but now our house was truly a thriving home, no longer a temporary sanctuary while we waited out the agency-imposed sabbatical the OIA had thrust on us. No, now our home was a sanctuary against the demon menace, and we were here for as long as it took to put an end to Shadow Wing's plans.

In the beginning, it had just been the three of us. Then came Maggie, our baby calico gargoyle I'd saved from a demon's lunch box. After Maggie came to stay, it was obvious we needed a nanny and housekeeper, so we'd taken in Iris—a Finnish house sprite (or Talon-haltija as her proper title was) who was also a whop-ass kind of woman. She had a lot of secrets, but we'd ferreted out a few, like the fact that she was a pledged Priestess of Undutar, the Finnish goddess of mists and snow. What Iris was doing here, working with us, we still weren't sure, but we knew she was heart-and-soul loyal.

And then the men had come. My ex, Trillian, showed up and once again reentered my life. A Svartan, he was currently missing, but we were due to go home to Otherworld in a few days and bring him back. And then Morio and Smoky had interrupted my life. Rozurial, an incubus, lived with us, too, and Vanzir, a turncoat demon who had defected to our side.

There were others who came and went—Menolly's girl-friend Nerissa and Delilah's other suitor—Zachary—were both werepumas from the Rainier Puma Pride. And our cousin Shamas lived with Roz and Vanzir out in the shed that had become a studio.

Yes, our family had increased multifold. And even though it meant we'd lost some privacy, I liked the feeling of security it provided.

The house was silent when we pushed through the door. Iris had left a note on the bulletin board saying she and her lepre-chaun boyfriend were in bed, and Maggie was sleeping, and would we please avoid disturbing any of them. Rozurial and Vanzir were either out or in the studio.

Morio and I checked the wards to make sure everything was secure, then trudged up the stairs. The only thing I wanted was a hot bath, but both Morio and Smoky had other ideas.

Either Morio had let Smoky know how I was feeling, or the tall drink of glacial water had tuned into my mood, but the six-foot-four dragon was waiting by the bathroom door, his ankle-length silver hair unbound and coiling around him like snakes on a medusa. Without a word, Morio pushed me toward Smoky, who whispered something I couldn't catch. In silence, two thick strands of his hair rose up to wrap themselves around my wrists and gently but firmly spread my arms wide.

I caught my breath as another strand of hair slithered behind me, taking hold of the zipper on the back of my gown and slowly lowering it. As the tendrils of hair slid the dress down my shoulders, over my arms, and to the floor, I stood breathless, naked except for my bra, panties, and stiletto ankle boots and I realized I was at the point where I wanted Smoky and Morio to take over. I didn't want to do anything except let them play me as they would.

Morio unhooked my bra. My breasts jiggled free. Too tired to move, I closed my eyes as his hands slid around from behind to brush my nipples, his long black nails raking over the skin. He was leaving faint marks, but the burn brought me back to life, reminded me that I was still here, still in my body.

He slid his hands down my sides, curving along my waist, over my hips, setting off minor explosions all along the way until he hooked his fingers around the waistband of my panties, and just as slowly, lowered them to the floor, taking hold of my ankles to lift my feet one at a time. Tossing the flimsy silk to the side, he untied my boots and eased them off. I moaned gently as he worked his way back up the inside of my legs, over my calves, running his hands along my inner thighs, his touch exquisite and firm. I started to spread my legs but Morio stopped and gave a soft laugh.

"Not yet," he whispered. "You need your bath."

Smoky stepped forward and swept me up in his arms as Morio slipped into the bathroom. I leaned my head against my dragon's chest, inhaling the familiar scent of his musk as I slowly began to unwind.

The bathroom was dimly lit, violet candles lining the vanity. The oversized tub was filled with bubbles that smelled like lilac and lavender and narcissus.

Smoky nodded to Morio. "Go and take your shower. We'll meet you in the bedroom. I'll bathe her."

He lowered me into the water and I leaned back against the warm porcelain, drawing a deep breath of the fragrant steam and letting it settle in my lungs. Morio silently withdrew as Smoky knelt beside the tub. He picked up the bath sponge and dipped it in the bubbles, softly circling my breasts with the warm soapy water, pressing against my nipples, trailing the loofah down the center of my chest. My breath quickened as he moved the sponge to bathe my arms, then pulled me forward to gently scrub my back.

When I started to speak, he brushed my lips with his finger. "Quiet."

Smoky was the only man alive who could make me obey with a single command. Whether it was because he was a dragon, I didn't know. But when he spoke, I listened. Though I put on a show of arguing with him in public, when we were alone or with Morio, I welcomed the chance to let go, to surrender control, to let someone else make the decisions.

I'd always been dominant, the rock of the family, the anchor for my sisters. And they needed me to be that way still. But with Smoky and Morio, in the seclusion of our bedroom, I could let them take over, trust that they'd protect me and help me forget about demons and battle and blood.

He lifted a snifter of cognac to my lips. I took a few sips and smiled as the liqueur burned a trail down my throat, leaving the taste of honey and wine in its wake. Before I realized what was happening, the cognac was followed by Smoky's tongue as he leaned over the tub and pressed his mouth against mine. I opened my mouth to him as he gathered me to his chest, ignoring the fact that the water and bubbles were soaking his T-shirt and splashing on his white jeans. He gently probed my mouth, his tongue darting quickly between my lips as a strand of his hair rose up to curl around one of my nipples.

Dizzy, I leaned back and he reached for a towel. As I moved to get out of the tub he stopped me and lifted me up, pressing me against him as he wrapped me in the huge bath sheet, then carried me into our bedroom. Morio was waiting, lounging on the bed in a loose black and white silk robe.

As Morio dimmed the lights and pulled down the covers on the king-sized bed, Smoky lowered me into the soft folds of the comforter. He stepped back to pull off his shirt and unbuckle his belt.

I watched, breathless. He slipped out of the butt-hugging jeans and stood there, elegant and muscled, his body a mirror of perfection, his cock hard and erect. Morio laughed with an ever so slight rough edge, and slowly pulled off his robe. He

was naked beneath it. His complexion was golden compared
to Smoky's alabaster, and he wasn't nearly as tall, but he was
fit and no less endowed. I gazed at them. Morio was right—I
needed them tonight. I needed sex. I needed to unwind and let
go of the tension.

I rose up on my knees, my heart thudding. If only Trillian
were here, my circle would be complete, the loves of my life
would all fit in their proper niches. But until then . . . a sudden
streak of hot lust raced through my body and I tossed my hair
back and laughed.

"Come and get me, boys."

"As you will, my love," Smoky said, pouncing on the bed
next to me. He pushed me back so I was lying to his right.

Morio stretched out on my other side, propping himself
up on his elbow, as he leaned down to lick one of my nipples. Smoky ran his fingers down my thigh and slid his hand
between my legs, coaxing his way up toward my inner lips as I
let out a small gasp. My body burned under their hands, sparks
raging like a bonfire lighting up at the touch of a match.

Morio fastened his lips on my breast, nipping me with his
teeth. The pain bordered on pleasure. I reached for his head,
but two silken strands of Smoky's hair caught my wrists, pin-
ning them above my head.

"Give us your control. Give yourself up to us," Smoky
whispered.

I closed my eyes, then opened them again, wanting to see
their faces, wanting to see them bearing down on me. Smoky's
eyes sparkled as he slid his fingers inside me and thrust deep.
Full and yet not full, aching for more, I let out a sharp cry.

"I want you inside me. Or Morio. Or both. It's all good."
My pussy throbbed, aching to be used. "Take me, please."

"She's ripe," Smoky said, glancing at Morio.

"She's hungry," Morio shot back. "Shall we give her what
she wants?"

"I think so, but not *too* quickly."

I groaned as they joked together, ignoring my moans as
they held me down. "Oh for the sake of the gods, just fuck me,
boys."

Smoky's smile vanished and he leaned down to stare at my

face. "On *our* terms, in *our* time. You *will* be silent, my pet, or I'll have to punish you."

I shut up. Smoky's punishments usually didn't hurt, though he had a thing for spanking and I allowed it because he put up with so much from me. But I knew from experience that he could string out sex to last all night, and he knew how to keep me from coming till he was ready. Oh, at times it was glorious—a fuckfest that was divine agony. But right now I wanted release. I wanted to leap over the abyss and go barreling toward the bottom of the ravine.

Morio laughed aloud as Smoky leaned back against the headboards and bent his knees. He encircled my waist, pulling me against him, my back against his chest and groin. He was hard and demanding, and his cock slid between the folds of my ass, testing ever so gently against me. I tensed, but for now he was just making certain I knew he was there.

Morio knelt in front of me, spreading my legs wide. He leaned between my thighs, searching for my core with his tongue. Sucking, biting, and then darting away, he teased me before settling in to fasten his lips on my clit.

The smoldering embers burst into flame and I let out a sharp cry.

Smoky's hair stroked my body, squeezing my breasts together as the dragon held me fast. I thrashed, trying to move, wanting to hold Morio's head as he tongue-bathed me, but Smoky's grip was so strong that I was helpless. Frustrated, I panted raggedly.

"Give it up," he whispered in my ear. "Give in to us. Let us take you down and bathe you in fire."

Tears forming in my eyes, I let out a harsh moan as Morio slid his tongue inside me, darting quickly in and out, curling around the edges of my pussy to set off a trail of fireworks in his wake.

He rose up, then, to stare in my eyes. Feral, primal, the energy rose around him like a silken green veil. Smoky's own aura flamed silver and when the two met they coiled like mating serpents, shrouding me in a cloak of passion that reached far beyond the human part of myself.

Each time this moment occurred, I wondered if I'd be able

to come back, if I could return from the realm into which these men who were not men dragged me. We were bound, on a soul level, and sex had become so much more than just sex. We were soul mates as well as lovers, connected forever by an ancient ritual.

My thoughts went silent again as Smoky trailed a circlet of kisses around the back of my neck. Morio pressed his lips against mine and I tasted myself on him—and yet, it was sweet honey and wine that touched my tongue.

Lifting me gently, Smoky flipped me over so I was on my hands and knees, facing the side of the bed. He slid his fingers inside me, drawing out my juices to bathe his cock, then positioned himself at the center of my ass. Gently, he tested, but I was ready and he slowly began to thrust forward, taking his time to penetrate, letting me rest between each fraction of an inch. I was tight, but he moved slowly and a sweet sensation began to rise through my body. As I squirmed, then gave in, he began to gently pump from behind.

His lip curled in a delicious smirk. Morio stood at the edge of the bed, his cock poised at my mouth. "Taste me," he said, his voice lusty. Smoky's thrusts making me hunger for more, I welcomed Morio in as he slid his girth between my lips, filling my mouth with his warm and salty taste.

Morio grasped my hair with one hand, his fingers tangled so tightly that my scalp ached, but the pain blended with the pleasure and I wanted more. I wanted both of them, inside of me, together. *Now*.

And then Morio was fucking my mouth, plunging just deep enough so that I didn't choke. I sucked hard, licking and teasing him as my own energy rose like a violet shadow to spiral up between the two men.

"That's it. Harder!" Morio's eyes shimmered with topaz flecks and I could see his form shift, mutating ever so slightly. I knew that he wanted to change, but there was no room on the bed for him in demon form, not with Smoky in bed, too, and so he abruptly withdrew from my mouth and slid beneath me, between my legs.

With one swift thrust, he drove himself up and into me, his chest pressing hard against my breasts as he wrapped his arms around my waist and pumped from below. The fire raged like a string of explosions up and down my body as Smoky and Morio began to synchronize rhythms. They filled me up, every inch of me, and the smell of their musk swept around me like the Goat god's perfume. Everything felt so right, so perfectly balanced, and I found myself rocking on the edge, the orgasm building, knotting my stomach.

I raised my head, panting raggedly as Morio raked his nails—now sharp—across my thigh, and I knew he'd left welts across my skin but the pain enhanced the pleasure and I groaned loudly, willing myself to come, to soar, to fly. As he drove harder into me, his expression lost all sense of humanity as his vulpine nature emerged and passion raged across his face.

"My demon," I whispered, tears sliding down my face from the intensity.

"Don't forget me," Smoky whispered behind me.

"How could I, my dragon lord? Tear me down, make me whole again."

And then, Smoky let out a groan as he, too, started to come. His ecstasy merged with my own, our passion reacting like a creature, sentient and vibrating. It exploded in a brilliant blast of light as we shared one incredible, shattering orgasm. With one last cry, I tumbled over the edge, sobbing uncontrollably, dragging both of them into that dark void where we had been bound together forever, three souls into one, connected on all levels, for all time.

We were up with the sun—figuratively speaking since the day was overcast and gray, like most Seattle days. I grabbed a quick shower while the boys dressed, Morio in black jeans and a green tank, Smoky in his usual white jeans and pale gray tee. As I toweled off and glanced out the window, the grass sparkled with dew and a light mist traveled along the ground. I hunted through my closet and found a burgundy velvet bustier and a spidersilk calf-length black skirt. Spidersilk was warmer than any Earthside weave and with a light capelet thrown over my shoulders, I'd be plenty warm.

We clattered down the stairs and into the kitchen. Delilah and Iris looked up from the table. Iris was reading the newspaper and Delilah was making notes on a steno pad. Menolly was, of course, asleep in her lair. A stack of pancakes sat on a plate, along with bacon and a bowl of mixed berries.

I headed over to the cupboard to grab three plates and stopped by Maggie's playpen. She was sitting next to it, beating on one of the big stainless steel pots with a wooden spoon. As she looked up and laughed, her sharp little teeth gleamed. Her wings had grown about an inch over the past month and she wasn't having such a hard time walking now, but she still tumbled over if the slightest thing threw her off balance. As she saw me, she dropped the spoon, unsteadily pushing to her feet.

"Camey! Camey!" She toddled toward me, arms out, eyes bright. I swept her up and nuzzled my face in her soft fur. A woodland gargoyle, she would age slower than we would. She had years of babyhood ahead of her still.

"Hey, pumpkin," I whispered. "How's my girl? How's Maggie doing?"

"'Kay," she lisped, then looking over my shoulder, she said, "Moky! Orio!"

Smoky plucked her out of my arms and gave her a soft noogie on the head while Morio chucked her under the chin. They handed her to Delilah as we sat down at the table. I managed to snag a few pancakes and some bacon before the guys emptied the plates.

"Where are the demon twins this morning?" I asked, looking around for Rozurial and Vanzir. Iris had given them the nickname and it stuck. They hated it, but we teased them with it every chance we got.

"Out. They're talking to Carter," Iris said. "He's been trying to pinpoint any sightings of Stacia for us."

I stopped in mid-bite. The last thing I wanted to think about was the demon general sent to replace Karvanak. We'd had enough trouble getting rid of *him*. And Stacia—also known as the Bonecrusher—was somebody I really didn't want to tangle with. We had to at some point but I was dreading the day.

Morio placed his hand on my shoulder as Smoky handed me the jug of maple syrup. "Eat," the dragon said. "You need your strength."

I glanced up at him, his silver hair tendriling around him

like a cloud of smoke. "Yeah, I know," I said with a smile I didn't really feel. "Henry's watching the store today. After breakfast Morio and I'd better head over to Harold's place and clear out the goshanti devil. Smoky, Delilah, want to come with?"

Smoky shook his head. "If you need me, I'll be there, of course, but I have some pressing business," he said, looking a little distant. In fact, now that I thought about it, he'd been relatively quiet ever since we'd woken up.

"We can take care of it without you." Morio glanced at the calendar. "The full moon is only a day or so away. We need to take care of this before then or the goshanti will use the power of it to lure more women into her trap. The devils can do that."

"Not only that, but I'll be useless when the Moon Mother rides high." Every full moon both Delilah and I were off and running—she in her tabby form, and I, with the Moon Mother's Hunt. The morning after wasn't pretty for either of us. I glanced over at Delilah. "What about you?"

She looked up from her notes. "Sure thing. I haven't got any appointments this morning. Say, remember that tomorrow's the primary."

"Will we know if Nerissa wins her council seat?"

"Nope, not till November," she said.

"That's right." I nodded. "It's not like we can vote. But for Menolly's sake—and the Supe Community Council's—I hope she wins by a landslide."

Nerissa was Menolly's girlfriend. As in lover. She was also one of the Rainier Puma Pride members. And Nerissa was running for city council, fully out of the closet as both a Were and bisexual.

"If she takes the election it could mean great strides for the Earthside Supes toward being accepted by the general populace." Iris placed Maggie in her playpen for a nap and handed her a stuffed penguin. Maggie cuddled it and curled up under her blanket. Iris began to clear the table and load the dishwasher.

"Yeah, but you know that the Freedoms Angels and their Earthborn Brethren are going to stage a protest outside the polling places—" I stopped as the doorbell rang. "I'll get it."

I peeked out the door. Oh, hell. Morgaine, the Queen of Shadow and Dusk, was standing outside the door. She was the last person I felt like seeing. *Person* was a misnomer, actually. Morgaine was one of the three Earthside Fae Queens and she was bad news. She was also one of our long-lost ancestors—half-Fae, half-human like ourselves.

Long story short: I'd been responsible for helping the Earthside Courts of Fae rise again and while it had been part of my destiny, I wasn't so sure it had been a good thing. But what was done was done. Instead of just the Seelie and Unseelie courts, there were now three—the Court of the Three Queens.

I opened the door and knelt into a deep curtsy. "Your Majesty, you honor us with—"

"Cut the crap, Camille, and let me in." She pushed past me and sniffed the air. "Dallying in the kitchen as usual, I suspect?" Without being invited, she swept down the hall and into the kitchen. I heard Iris let out a quick retort before she caught herself and shut up.

As I hurried in behind Morgaine, I saw that Smoky was glaring at her. That he didn't like the Fae Queen was an understatement. Morio stood tense and on guard. Delilah had dropped into an awkward curtsy, and Iris was looking put out, as if her territory had been invaded. And it had, when I thought about it. The kitchen now belonged to Iris.

"I see you're all so *happy* I've dropped by. Don't put yourselves out. I'll get right to the point," the petite sorceress said, ignoring everyone except Delilah and me. "You two—and that vampire sister of yours—need to think long and hard about the wisdom of refusing to join my court. We need you, and you're going to need us. The lines are being drawn between the Earthside Fae and the Otherworld Fae and you'd better choose your side before it's too late."

"Say what? Are you threatening us? And what the hell do you mean—lines being drawn? I haven't heard anything about trouble between the factions." I stared her down.

At first, I'd been starstruck when I met her. Now, I was over her. She was no longer the brilliant light I'd thought, but a shadowy troublemaker who kept trying to coerce us to defect from the OIA, along with our Otherworld heritage. All in order to join her court. Of course, we kept refusing and so she was thoroughly pissed at us.

"Threatening? Of course not. Why would I *threaten* my kin?" But her face was clouded, and she looked ready to smack me a good one. I held her gaze, not backing down. We were similar in looks—violet eyes, raven hair, but I was taller and my Fae heritage was closer to the surface than hers. On the other hand, she had eons of magic under her belt and the cloak of a queen on her shoulders.

"We'll consider your advice." I folded my arms across my chest. "Anything else?"

"Better not be or I'll fry you for breakfast," Smoky said casually, tipping his chair back so that he was balanced against the wall. "No one threatens my wife and gets away alive." He gazed at Morgaine, an impassive look on his face.

She narrowed her eyes and though she didn't look his way, I saw a hint of fear creep across her face. So she was afraid of dragons. Well, she'd better be. Smoky could take her down with one nasty swipe of his claws, and he had his own forms of magic to guard against hers. If it came to a showdown, my money was on Dragon Dude.

Morgaine apparently decided it was not a good day to die. She turned back to me without saying a word to him. "Let me know what you decide, but make it quick. There are currents brewing and I wouldn't want to be caught walking between two worlds when they spill over."

"Consider us warned." I gently motioned to the door.

Morgaine let out a low hiss. "Stupid girls. *Stupid, stupid girls*. You think just because you're fucking dragons and cavorting with demons that you're safe? You think that having the blessing of that ancient husk of an Elfin Queen is going to offer you shelter? Think again, girls. You're playing on the wrong side and when the fire comes bearing down, you're going to get your fingers burned." And with that, she swept past me and stormed out the door, slamming it behind her.

I looked back at the others. Smoky was examining his nails. Morio was finishing up his breakfast. Iris was washing the counter. Only Delilah looked at me, and her expression—a mixture of worry and irritation—mirrored my own.

"So much for that," I finally said. "Okay, let's go bag our-selves a goshanti devil." But inside, I was mulling over the thought that our own kin were proving to be more problematic than the demon menace.

At least there were some things we could still control, I thought as I grabbed my capelet and headed for the car. Give me a fight with a simple demon or devil any day, over the whims of a pissed off Fae Queen.

CHAPTER 4

The air smelled of salt and woodsmoke, cedar and moss as we headed out to the car. Delilah called shotgun, so Morio climbed in the back. I tossed the bag of ritual items into the trunk and slid into the driver's seat. As we pulled out of the driveway, Iris waved to us from the front steps. Her fair face, and the hope in her smile, reminded me once again why we did what we did. Why we stayed here and fought.

"So, you really think Nerissa has a chance of winning the council seat?" I glanced at Delilah.

"I think we've got the odds on our side," she said. My sister was on the recently elected Supe Community Council and had vigorously been campaigning for Nerissa over the past few months. "If people aren't scared off by Taggart Jones. Andy Gambit has been pushing him as the front runner in the *Seattle Tattler*, and all he is, is a mouthpiece for the Freedom's Angels. We've been trying to find the evidence that ties them together but haven't been able to, though we know it's there somewhere. Jones is pushing an agenda to strip away all the rights in King County that the Fae and the Supes have won."

"Andy Gambit has his head up his ass, or he would if I had my way," I mumbled. Gambit was a yellow journalist with a grudge against anybody who wasn't one of the "earthborn"—a loose faction of wacko groups who were all militantly bigoted hate mongers. I'd been on the receiving end of his barbs more than once.

"We should encourage Menolly to have a word with him." Delilah giggled. "Of course, he'd just turn around and use it to fuel the flames."

"And flames like that we do not need," I said. "No, we need a more devious plan to undermine Gambit and his xenophobic pack of cronies. We'll have to think about it for a while."

The thought of actually toppling Gambit from his position as god of yellow journalism tickled me fuchsia. Maybe we could lure him into a compromising position and publish the pictures. Spread the love, so to speak.

Shaking away the thought until a more appropriate time, I said over my shoulder, "So, Morio, what's the plan once we get to Harold's?"

He leaned forward, eyes gleaming in the rearview mirror. "Scour the earth with the salt and your Tygerian well water, then exorcise the hell out of it. I've got the litany to free the dead memorized."

I glanced at him through the mirror. Over the months, I'd come to realize that the youkai actually enjoyed the escalating turmoil. He wasn't one for words, but I could smell him. Not exactly aroused, but a hint of excitement lingered in his scent. He lusted for the chase, especially when it involved magic. What scared me a little was I was beginning to notice the same reaction in myself.

Delilah must have caught his scent, too, because she glanced back at him. "Where did you first learn death magic?"

Morio remained silent for a moment. When he spoke, his words were terse. "I learned it while growing up." He lapsed back into silence and I sidled a look at Delilah, who shrugged and went back to gazing out the window.

As the pavement passed beneath our wheels, fat drops of rain began to splatter down and then the skies opened up and a bone-drenching downpour pounded the road. I slowed, careful to avoid hydroplaning so we didn't go sailing into any other cars. Driving in Seattle was crazy enough, but the rain created hazards I'd never thought of back in OW.

Of course, back home I'd never ridden in a car, either, or had to learn to drive anything more complicated than a cart. Riding horses came second nature to me. And horses and carts didn't usually go fast enough to skid on the roadways there. We didn't do concrete back in Otherworld. Though cobble-stones presented their own problems when wet.

"Wouldn't you know it? We're going to get soaked to the skin." I frowned, wondering if I should try a little weather magic, but a flash of the deluge I might create if my magic backfired nixed any further thought in that direction.

Delilah snorted. "So what? In the past months, we've been covered with demon blood, viro-mortis slime, venidemon guts, mud, sludge, and who knows what else? What's a little rain?"

"Don't forget pixie dust." I grinned at her. "And I'm sure we'll be nose deep in oozing green ichor before we're done with the job. I'm just glad I found a talented dry cleaner."

I turned left onto the street leading to the ruins of Harold's house. The morning had taken on a gloomy presence and the last place I wanted to be was here, but if Morio was right and the goshanti devil usually didn't come out during the day, we'd better use the daylight while we had it.

I pulled next to the curb behind a prowl car. The uni-formed figures of Lethe and Finias, two OW Fae who had been assigned Earthside to help out with the FH-CSI—the Faerie Human Crime Scene Investigation team—were stand-ing guard. As we climbed out of the car, Finias strolled over to greet us.

"You're here to clear the land?" he said, his eyes the most arresting shade of green I'd ever seen. He wasn't particularly tall, but his golden hair glimmered like Delilah's, falling to his shoulders, and the scruff of beard that lightly shaded his jaw made him look rugged. Yet he reminded me of one of the golden boys. An Apollo in training.

I nodded. "Mind if we head in?"

"Be my guest. I'm tired of sitting stakeout on a deserted lot. But be careful. I can sense the devil. She's asleep, but she's hungry." His eyes flashed to gold, then back to green, and he placed a soft hand on my arm. "She's stronger than she looks," he added.

Morio edged in next to me and just as softly removed Finias's hand from my arm. "Thank you for the warning. We'll be cautious." He hoisted the bag of ritual gear over one shoulder and his own bag over the other. "Let's get moving," he said, glancing at the blackening sky. "I don't like the looks of this storm."

Delilah fell in behind me and we followed Morio toward the lot. During the night the place had been spooky, but it wasn't much better during the day. The land held a desolate air, and while we could see everything more clearly—including the dead body that still lay behind the rhododendron—there was a dank atmosphere that made me feel claustrophobic.

I tugged on the collar of my capelet, slipping my finger beneath the material to loosen it a bit. The air was close, and every time I took a breath it felt like I was inhaling a lungful of vapor. When we came to the body, I knelt beside it, not touching anything, just looking.

The man had been out jogging. At least it looked that way, judging by the sweats and sneakers he was wearing. A pedometer was attached to his belt, and I noticed a thin flashlight poking out of the pocket of his sweatshirt. He was short but muscular, and looked like he'd been in good shape. Rigor mortis had taken hold of the body, the chill of the night sustaining it. He was stiff as a board, with a look of terror on his face. I wanted to close his eyes, but knew better than to disturb the evidence even though I knew—and Chase would know—that the goshanti devil had caused the poor man's death.

"I wonder who he was," Delilah said, squatting beside me.

"Someone out for a little exercise," I said. "Maybe somebody's father, or husband, or lover. Chase will find out. At least the weather has kept away the worst of the insects."

There were ants, yes, but not many, and a few beetles and flies swarming around the body, but the chill and the damp had fended off the worst of the bugs. From what I could tell, no animals had crossed through the lot. A thought occurred to me and I stood up and hurried to Morio's side. He was setting out the gear on the trunk of a fallen fir tree.

"Do the goshanti devils suck out the life force from animals, too? It seems awfully quiet here today. Nothing—no cats or dogs or raccoons—seem to have disturbed the body."

He frowned as he fit a white candle into a tall silver

candlestick. "I honestly don't know, but it wouldn't surprise me. Here, can you create a ring of salt around us, about ten feet in diameter?"

I nodded, accepting the bag of kosher salt. Kosher salt was purer than iodized, and we used it exclusively in our magic unless we needed sea salt. For cooking, too, I thought with a grin, remembering Iris's insistence on certain brands when we went shopping.

"What can I do?" Delilah asked, glancing around. She frowned at the weeping willow. "I do not like that tree. It has a nasty feel to it."

"I think that's where the goshanti has made her home," Morio said, but then stopped as Delilah knelt by the roots and began sifting through the leaf detritus at the base of the trunk. "What are you looking for?"

"I just have a feeling," she said, clawing away the moldy leaves and twigs and mushrooms that had grown up thick around the tree. "I smell something . . ."

Curious, I sat the salt down and joined her, kneeling to one side as she clawed at the dirt with Lysanthra, her long silver dagger. I had my own matching dagger with me but since I'd be using mine for magic today, I didn't want to get it dirty. Delilah's dagger had a soul and had contacted her. Mine—well, if my dagger was sentient in any way, it sure hadn't shown any interest in striking up a conversation with me.

After a moment, Morio joined us, using a stick to pry at the dirt. I sighed, not wanting to be a shirker, so setting my capelet aside where it wouldn't get caught by the flying dirt, I grasped at the soil with my fingers, digging out clods and pungent toadstools and weeds that were wilting from the moisture.

We dug in silence for a couple of minutes and then Delilah held up her hand. Morio and I pulled back as she began to scrape away a final layer from something that was about the size of a shoe box, buried seven or eight inches deep. After a moment, she sat back on her heels and we peeked in the hole.

A box—a metal strongbox by the look of it—was at the bottom of the hole. On the top were runes painted in a brilliant lemon yellow.

I glanced over at Morio. "I recognize the runes. They're warding symbols, and one looks like it might be a hex symbol."

"A curse," Morio said softly. "But for which—opening the box or disturbing the land?"

"It would only make sense that they warded the land." I leaned over the box and held my fingers a few inches above the runes. "They're powerful but erratic. The uncle—what was his name? Whatever it was, Harold's uncle was a necromancer, albeit a lousy one. I'll bet you he put this together."

"The question is . . . Camille, don't touch it! It might be dangerous." Morio motioned for me to move my hand. I quickly obeyed. He was more adept at Earthside magic than I was. "As I was saying, the question is, will the thing backfire on us if we remove it? Is the curse valid or just as screwed up as the Demon Gate he opened?"

Delilah scrunched her lip, biting the edge of it. I wondered how she avoided puncturing herself at times, given her non-retractable fangs. They weren't as long as a vampire's, but they were there and they'd caused plenty of damage to Chase's private parts during a few ill-chosen blow job attempts. We'd *all* heard about the upshot of that activity.

"Do you recognize the curse? What's the worst that can happen?" She wiped her hands on her jeans and stood. Six foot one, she was lean and muscled, but sometimes I wondered just where she stored her common sense.

"To answer your questions: No, and we could die. And not necessarily in that order," I said. Then, a brilliant thought struck me. "I know! Let's make Rodney drag it out. Then, whatever happens will happen to *him*."

Morio gave me a crazy look but laughed, his lips curling into a devilish grin. "I knew that little bastard had to be good for something. And if it blows up in his face, then we don't have to come up with an excuse so we can give him back to Grandmother Coyote." He rummaged through his bag and pulled out the wooden box in which our skeletal jackass made his home.

Delilah stared at the box. "Who the hell is Rodney?"

Oops. This was going to be fun. I hadn't gotten around to telling Delilah and Menolly about our bony-butted compatriot. Not yet.

I knew they'd want to meet him. And if *that* happened,

there was no doubt in my mind that Delilah would end up in puddy-tat form and Menolly would end up crushing Rodney into bonemeal. Then we'd have to pay some enormously nasty debt to Grandmother Coyote for breaking her toy. The scenario was all too real in my mind and I just didn't even want to go there.

I sighed. "Rodney is a gift. Actually, he's an albatross. Grandmother Coyote gave him to Morio. He's rude, he's crude, he's lewd, and we're stuck with him. Just ignore him if he starts in badgering you, okay?"

Her cat instinct took over and Delilah perked up her ears, looking more curious than was good for her. "Let me see."

Morio cleared his throat. "Remember, we warned you. Don't start whining if he gives you the finger." He opened the box and whispered a low incantation over the miniature skeleton. Within seconds, Rodney sat up, looking around. I shivered. The fire in his eye sockets gave me the creeps. *Everything* about him gave me the creeps.

Rodney fastened his gaze on Delilah and let out a long whistle. "Hot damn! Another broad! Well, fuck me with a swizzle stick. You're a scorcher, *bay-bee*. Anytime you need a boner, just call on me. I may be small but I can travel to places no man can reach. At least not with his entire body—"

"What did you say?" Delilah gaped at him, a bright flush running up her neck to spread across her face.

"I told you," I muttered. "Just ignore him or he'll get worse."

"I've got a thing for the schwing—" And Rodney was off, humming and dancing a rather twisted version of the "Time Warp," his focus being the pelvic thrust, of course. Which was just *so* wrong. I felt like we'd been forced into some nightmare vaudeville of the damned.

"Enough!" Morio glared at him as I resisted the urge to backhand the little creep right into the hole we'd just dug.

"Why the hell do you keep him around?" Delilah sniffed, looking away. I saw a faint shimmer in her aura, which could mean only one thing.

"Curb it, Delilah. You need to stick with us and not go—"

But I was too late. The next minute a lively golden tabby

stood in her place and before either Morio or I could stop her, she gathered herself and leapt, knocking Rodney out of Morio's hand as she threw him off balance.

Rodney hit the dirt running. Apparently the creep had enough sense to know when he'd pushed it too far. Delilah was hot on his heels, her tail swishing from side to side, with a suspiciously happy look on her face.

Uh-huh, I thought. Her transformation wasn't really an accident. She'd never 'fess up if I pressed her on it, though. I knew her well enough for that. *Accidental* shapeshifting had become an easy excuse over the years. When she wanted to get out of doing housework, when she wanted a nap and we were busy, when she wanted somebody to give her a good rubdown . . . oh yeah, my sister wasn't above using her faulty powers for her own gain.

"Delilah! You come back here! Don't you—oh cripes, stop her!"

Delilah had managed to leap over Rodney's head and land on the other side, and now she swatted him a good one with a big old furry paw. Rodney went flying into a pile of dirt.

He leapt up and motioned to her with one bony finger. "Come on, baby, come on—you just try it again, you goddamned fleabag."

Morio was closer to her than I. He took one quick leap and stood towering over the pair. His eyes flashed with flecks of topaz and he suddenly started to grow, morphing into his fox demon shape.

I caught my breath. Even when he was in full demon form, he was hot as hell. At least in *my* eyes. At eight feet tall when he was fully transformed, Morio was huge—in *all* ways. I knew *that* from a very personal and pleasurable vantage point. As his face began to lengthen, his muzzle appeared and his long black nails grew into long black claws.

Before he'd finished shifting, he leaned over the squabbling pair and let out a low growl. "Stop now or I'll eat you both."

Delilah and Rodney froze in their tracks and stared up at him. Delilah slowly backed away, hissing with her tail fluffed up, but she made no move to run or fight back. Rodney glared at Morio, hands on his pelvis, looking put out. Morio waited till

Delilah had moved out of range, then scooped up the skeleton. Within another moment, he'd shifted back.

I stared at all three of them, shaking my head. "Good gods, we might as well slap signs on our backs that read KICK ME. Delilah, turn your fluffy butt back into your normal form. Rodney . . . you're just a stupid ass."

"I'd like to make close personal friends with *your* stupid ass—" he started to say but stopped when Morio began to squeeze.

"Talk to my wife like that once more and I'll break you in two. I no longer give a rat's ass that you're a gift from Grandmother Coyote." His voice was dangerously low and I knew that he'd reached his breaking point. It took a lot to push Morio into a corner but the moment he got there, he lost it and all hell broke loose. In a way, he was more dangerous than Smoky because Morio was more unpredictable.

Rodney squeaked and shut up. Delilah chose that moment to shift back to herself. I gave her a withering look. She scuffed the ground and muttered, "Sorry," and looked the other way.

"Can we *puh-leeze* get on with this?" I wanted to launch into a diatribe but it was useless. "Rodney, get your bony butt in that hole and drag out the box."

Morio set him down on the ground and, as the skeleton flashed me the finger and headed for the hole, the three of us began to back up.

Rodney noticed our retreat. "Where you bitches going? Why—" He stopped, peered in the hole, and groaned. "You can't be serious? You want me to drag a cursed box out of the ground? I get it! You think I'm expendable! Let the bony guy get it. If anybody's going to fry, it's me, is it? Well, I tell you bitches, I'm not—"

Morio's voice ran a timbre lower than scary. "You *are* expendable. At any time, whenever I choose."

Rodney shut up. It was only for a moment, but right then I knew that, beneath the surface, he was terrified of Morio.

"Yeah, yeah, I get it. You're the big bad youkai and I'm just your pip-squeak love bitch. Fine, leave it to me. But if you blow me up, I'm quitting!" Still muttering, he climbed down in the hole and after a couple of minutes, he huffed and puffed his way out, dragging the box behind him. We all took a simultaneous step back.

"What now, boss?" Rodney edged away from the box as he glanced up at Morio. Even without skin and flesh to cover his skull, I could see the worry on his face. Or what would have been his face.

Morio crossed his arms. "Open it."

"But—but—" Rodney was serious now. "It's cursed. I could be killed."

"You can't die because you aren't alive. You're a golem who happens to have some sentience attached to you. I guarantee you, I am far more dangerous than anything attached to that box. *Open it.*" Morio took one step forward.

Rodney let out a shriek and raced back to the box. As the skeleton flipped open the lid and jumped back, I covered my eyes and waited for a moment, then peeked from behind my hands when there was no immediate flash or explosion.

"Nothing happened." Rodney sounded confused.

"Faulty hex," I said, edging my way forward again.

"What's inside the box?" Delilah asked, coming out from behind the tree where she'd been hiding.

"A couple of crystals and a pouch. That's all. You want I should open this thing? It's pretty full." He held up a black felt pouch.

"Do it," Morio said.

I decided to let my suddenly badass lover handle this. That way, if Rodney got smashed to smithereens, he'd be the one answering to Grandmother Coyote, not me. And seeing that they were related in a weird kind of extended family way, she might be nicer to him if he screwed up.

Rodney opened the pouch. Nothing happened again. He slowly upended the contents into the box and I heard the clink of metal on metal.

"Well, well, well," the skeleton said. "Lookie what we have here!" He held up a necklace.

I edged forward another step and peeked in the box. A scattering of jewelry littered the tray. But there were other things in the pouch, as well. Not so happy things. Bones, to be precise, intermingled with the rings and pendants and earrings. Finger bones. Knuckle bones. Despair radiated off them in concentric waves, rippling out of the box, hitting me in the gut and making me queasy.

"These belong to women. To the women who disappeared here. Holy fucking hell," I whispered. "Harold and his pervs were keeping souvenirs from their kills."

Morio and Delilah joined me and we stared into the box, at the macabre treasure that lay scattered before us.

"No wonder a goshanti formed here," Morio said, squatting to poke through the items. "The quartz spikes amplified the energy surrounding the trinkets and bones, rather than protecting them from discovery. Once again, Dante's Hellions fucked up. I'll bet you anything the rune for hexing is actually a rune to ground the energy and keep it right here. We aren't going to be able to cleanse the goshanti devil from this lot until we disperse the items and put these bones to rest."

I nodded. Harold's group had managed to summon a goshanti. Could they have other surprises that might account for the increase in spirit activity from the Netherworld that we'd been seeing? And if so, how the hell were we going to figure out all of the damage they'd caused?

Shaking off the speculation, I looked back at the box, a wave of sadness rushing through me. "Let's start by sorting out the bones. We can purify and bury them."

Rodney reached down and started separating the bones to one side. For once, he remained quiet.

I stared at him. "What? No wisecracks? No dirty jokes up your sleeve?" My voice had a bitter edge to it and I realized I was looking for someone to take my anger out on.

The skeleton looked up at me for a moment, then shook his head. Still silent, he returned to his work.

CHAPTER 5

"So we have to bury the bones first?" Delilah asked.

Morio nodded. "If we don't, they'll just keep infusing her with energy." He stood up, taking the box from Rodney, who had put the jewelry back in the pouch, leaving the bones out. "We need to bury and salt the bones, then sanctify the ground and cast a spell to calm the spirits. I wonder what happened to the rest of the bodies?"

"Other than Sabele, I have no idea." I looked around, not entirely sure I wanted to know. "I just hope that they were dead when Harold chopped off their fingers. Those are pretty severe hack marks and they weren't done with a surgeon's skill. I doubt he'd use anesthesia."

Even as I spoke, I knew the fear they'd felt had fueled the Hellions—fueled their rituals and their sadistic pleasures. And then, without warning, I could hear them. Whispering screams on the wind. Women begging, *Please stop, please let me go, please don't hurt me anymore.*

"I wish we'd let Menolly kill the whole lot of those pricks," I said softly. "If they were here now, I'd do it myself."

Delilah shook her head. "Not if I got to them first. I can hear them, too," she said, pale and somber.

Surprised, I glanced up at her. Her eyes were cool, flashing emerald, and I caught the scent of bonfire smoke that suddenly whipped up around her. Her tattoo—the black crescent scythe on her forehead—flashed with gold specks. The Autumn Lord must be riding her soul today.

We were all changing, evolving into freaks. But if we had to live out on the fringe, at least we were going off the deep end on the right side.

A year earlier, we'd been softer. Now, we were as bloodthirsty as those we fought. What would we be like by the end of the war? Or would we even be alive? My thoughts spiraled into a pit as black as the clouds and I tried to stave off the mood but it was as entrenched as the rain soaking us to the skin.

But even as the water trickled down my face, making my makeup run, I could tell the downpour was letting up. We'd have at least a few minutes free from the deluge.

"Where do we bury the bones?" I looked around for a suitable place. "Does it matter that the land is butt-ugly with turmoil from the crap that went down here?"

Morio shook his head. "No, because we're going to calm some of that turmoil."

And then I saw it. The perfect place—a yew tree. The tree of eternity, the yew was a sentinel of death and rebirth. As I headed over to examine it, I heard Morio grunt with approval. The evergreen sighed as I knelt beside its gnarled, ancient roots and leaned against the trunk. As I pressed my head to the roughened wood, I felt the tree take a deep breath and shudder ever so lightly.

"We have need for your protection, Ancient One," I whispered, sending my words to dig deep, to touch the roots. One of my abilities as a Moon Witch was that I could talk to plants and herbs, though I tended to steer clear of doing so in the woodlands over here Earthside. There were too many angry plants who feared and distrusted humanity, and anyone who was kin to FBHs. And I was half-human.

"What do you want?" The thought was so strong it almost blew me back, and I glanced up at the tree, half expecting to see a face there. But the burls and knots remained fixed in place.

I rested my hands against the trunk and focused my attention again. "Have you felt the unsettled spirits on this land? The women who were murdered?"

"Yesssssss . . ." The answer was drawn out on the breeze, a long susurration that ruffled my hair.

"We have bones that need to be purified and buried in sanctified ground. May we bury them beneath your branches?"

Part of me didn't want to ask, I wanted to just bury the bones and hope for the best. But the tree might say no. So I decided not to take the chance because if we didn't have permission, we ran the risk of not being able to quiet the ghosts.

I enjoyed communing with herbs and flowers, but tree devas scared the hell out of me. They were powerful and old and they had a subtle magic all their own that no one—be they witch or wizard or necromancer—could harness. Only the dryads and floraeds and wood sprites could truly embody the power of the forests.

Morio settled on one knee behind me, but kept his hands to himself. He was proficient enough to know I was in a trance and wouldn't disturb me. After a long, long pause, the yew stirred again.

"Cleanse and bury them and I will keep them safe. But there are other spirits here who still walk the earth, restless and searching. The thread of energy that runs through this land has been awakened and sings strong and vibrant, but off-key, summoning ghosts to journey its length."

The yew fell silent again and I sat back.

"She'll guard them," I said. "But she said there are more spirits around this lot, and she mentioned a thread of energy that's attracting ghosts here. I'm thinking of the ley line? We know one connects Harold's house to the Wedgewood Cemetery. The same ley line runs through the Wayfarer—where the portal is—and two of the rogue portals."

Morio stroked his goatee. After a moment, he nodded. "That sounds right, but what do we do about it?"

"We'll figure that out later, but for now, let's get these bones buried while there's a lull in the rain." I motioned to Delilah. "Can you start digging a hole at the base of the tree? Try to position it in the shelter of the roots. Meanwhile, I'll get the salt and Morio—will you set up the candles?"

As I scattered a ring of salt around the yew, Delilah dug away at a hole for the bones. Morio settled a black pillar candle at one side of the hole, a white one at the other.

Rodney, who had been watching us silently, let out a loud huff. "You bitches forgetting something?"

Great. The jackass was back in action. "What do you want now?"

"You didn't mix rosemary into the salt. Any necromancer worth his nuts knows you have to mix rosemary into the salt."

Gritting my teeth, I exhaled a thin stream of air as I tried to keep my cool. "For one thing, we aren't necromancers, although we're working death magic—"

"Smart, real smart." He made a dinging sound. "A headstone for the broad with the high beams!"

I reached over and thunked him one with my forefinger and thumb. "Will you just shut the fuck up and listen? Rosemary is for *summoning*. We need *sage* for purification, but only inside the grave. Now keep your mouth shut and let us work."

Rodney gazed at me for a moment and then, with a baleful fire burning in his eye sockets, he started to grow. I stumbled back as he rose to the height of a good-sized man within seconds.

"Holy hell!" I stopped as he started toward me. A wreath of fire surrounded him, glowing like a thin nimbus in his aura, burning brightly around his pelvis bones, and he laughed softly. I jumped back a step. A super-sized Rodney was not on my list of must-haves.

"You're one fine bitch, all right, and I'm going to have myself a field day," he said.

I squeaked and went scrambling toward Morio, who looked up from arranging the candles.

"Ooph," Morio grunted as I knocked him over in my haste to get away from the advancing Rodney. He leapt up, stopping short as he took in Rodney's new and not-so-improved size. "What the—knock it off! Enough!" He jumped up and grabbed Rodney's wooden box.

Rodney paused in mid-step. "Oh please, let me have her. Just for an hour. You two are the most kinky pervs I know. Let me play with the Faerie slut? Pretty please? You can watch—"

Morio pushed me out of the way and strode over to Rodney. He didn't look happy. "Why didn't you tell us you could grow like that?"

Rodney shrugged. "You never asked."

"How often can you do it?"

"All night long. Want to find out, youkai bitch?" the skeleton said, snorting. "Oh, this." He swept one bony hand over his body. "Like it? The things I can do with these fingers . . ."

At Morio's scowl, he cleared his throat and said, "Okay, okay. When I'm recharged enough, I can hold this size for an hour or two. Then I revert."

"Good enough. Now get your ass back in the box." Morio held out Rodney's home. "Or I'll take you apart bone by bone."

Rodney sounded aggrieved. "Don't be that way—"

"Now." Morio's voice was too calm. Apparently, Rodney thought so, too, because, without another word, he shrank to his normal size and climbed in the box. Morio slapped the lid shut and stared at the box. "Motherfucking piece of trash. Where the hell did Grandmother Coyote get this thing?" He slid it into his bag and turned back to me. "You okay?"

I nodded. "Yeah, but don't ever leave me alone with him when he's off his leash, okay?" The thought of being at Rodney's mercy, especially when he was my size, was too nauseating to consider.

Delilah was staring at the two of us like we were crazy. "I feel like I'm watching some bad B-grade horror flick. I'd like to know just what you guys have been up to over the past two months."

Grinning, I started to speak but she hastily waved me away.

"On the other hand, don't bother. You might give me nightmares."

I shook my head. "Let's get on with it, or it will be night before we're done and the goshanti will be out and about."

"So why can't Chase come in here during the day since she's at rest?" Delilah asked.

Morio fielded that one. "Because even if the goshanti is asleep, there's still the chance she'll wake up. Or that there are other spirits here with her. Sometimes they run in packs with other creatures from the Netherworld."

I stared at him. "You didn't tell me that."

"You didn't ask," he said, grinning.

While Delilah finished digging the hole, I ringed the yew with salt and then prepared a cup of salt for the grave, mixing in a generous dose of sage and, for good measure, I added a few of the yew needles.

As I took out my dagger and sat on the wet ground in the lotus position, Morio knelt behind me, his hands on my shoulders. I could feel the warmth of his hands through the chill that enveloped my skin, and it traveled down through my breasts, down into my stomach.

When his energy hit my tailbone, it merged with my own and I felt our conjoined essences begin to rise, to cycle through both of us—through me, into his hands, through him, into the earth, then they were spiraling through dirt and soil and rock to root deeply within my legs and travel up through my tailbone again. A circle—a Möbius strip of power, we were joined by both magic and soul.

Since we'd undergone the Soul Symbiont ritual, our rituals had become stronger. Now, we seldom needed words to know what the other was going to do. Morio couldn't reinforce my Moon magic—that came from the Moon Mother herself and was solely mine, and he couldn't strengthen my work with the unicorn horn, as far as I knew. But the death magic had taken on a force of its own and together we were far more powerful than either of us alone.

As the magic cycled through our bodies, I began to force it outward, to send a ripple of energy out to encircle the yew tree, to ride on the wind and soak into the very land. Morio backed me up and the ripple became a cleansing wave as he fed me the energy and I directed it. The wave splashed over the aching souls and wounded bones and I heard a chorus of cries begging for release.

Inhale deeply . . . another long breath as Morio infuses me with the power to guide the spirits to their path . . .

Exhale slowly, as the magic reaches out to scatter the souls, to free them from their shackles to the bones . . .

Inhale again . . . the energy flares and everything within the circle shines with a brilliant golden light. So many people think white is the color of purity but white is the color of death. Gold purifies, silver protects . . .

And exhale . . . feel the souls fleeing the land, racing off to rest and return to their ancestors. The anguish is diminishing . . . and there—there is the goshanti, asleep, for it is her time to sleep, but she knows something's wrong and seeks to wake . . .

"Camille! Camille! Snap out of it. We have to hurry," Morio said, shaking my shoulders.

I blinked, the vibrant colors of the magic blinding me until they settled into the surrounding area, sinking into the land without so much as a whisper. The yew tree let out a long, contented sigh and I quickly poured the sage and salt mixture over the bones. Then, Morio, Delilah, and I stood beside the tiny grave and chanted the litany for the dead.

"What was life has crumbled. What was form now falls away. Mortal chains unbind, and the soul is lifted free. May you find your way to the ancestors. May you find your path to the gods. May your bravery and courage be remembered in song and story. May your parents be proud, and may your children carry your birthright. Sleep, and wander no more."

When we were done, there was another soft hush as a gust of wind rushed by and carried the last vestiges of the souls to their destiny. I arched my back and watched as Delilah filled in the hole and we drew a binding rune on top, that nothing might disturb their slumber.

"Now, we take care of the goshanti," Morio said. He motioned to me and I picked up the bag of salt. "Delilah, would you keep watch for us? Stand right at the edge of the sidewalk."

She took her place and I glanced at Morio. He nodded, and I began to slowly circle the lot, casting handfuls of salt to form a ring of white, a circle of clarity. The salt sizzled as it hit the ground, smoking in some places. The land was hot with turbulence. I closed my eyes, guiding the energy that trailed from my body to form a barrier left in my wake that shimmered and glistened. It, too, was white—white and red. Death and power.

And then, I came back to the beginning and Morio met me,

escorting me into the center. I would be the focal point, the lens, and he would use me to focus the energy. I went down on my knees, arms spread out to the side. Morio stood behind me, legs firmly planted to either side of me, his hands raised to the sky. I waited, feeling for the energy, and there it was—the cord spiraling from him to me. Attaching to my aura, the cord slid into place and I shivered, anticipating the flow of power to come.

Death magic was sensual, passionate, addictive, and yet the process was cool and aloof, taking us to the edge of that stark barrier through which every mortal creature eventually had to pass. Even the gods died, at some point. As Morio and I merged into the same channel, I gasped and my head dropped back. I could feel him, alert, magnificent in his pose.

He wavered for a moment and then—as quickly as the energy caught us up—it grounded us deep into the shadows of the trees, the shadows of life, and we were walking on the outskirts of the Netherworld, between realms, in the wash of spirits that passed by us silently. They did not see us, nor did they realize we had slipped into their domain.

I inhaled, letting Morio lead me. He grabbed the threads of magic that ran rife at the gates to the Netherworld and whispered something, and then they were attached to him, and through him—attached to me. We were ready.

"Open your eyes," he said softly.

I opened my eyes. The lot had taken on a vastly different look. Everywhere I looked, I could see by their auras which plants were dying, and which were thriving. I could feel the bones we'd planted at the base of the yew tree. I could see the aura of the yew itself, glowing like the Blue Light Special at Kmart. And I could see the blood that had fed this ground—long ago soaking deep and drying, but still here, still attached to the land.

"Do you see?" Morio asked.

"I see."

"Then seek the goshanti." His arms were still raised above his head. Mine were wide at my sides still, and I directed the energy to spread from my fingertips, to search and find the devil. It trailed out like smoke, swirling through the trees, seeking, probing, searching for the signature of the goshanti.

Like a mist, the vapor carried my vision with it and through a haze I could see a cat hiding under a fern, a garter snake gliding through the foliage, insects and birds looking for food. And then, the mist stopped in a patch of Scotch broom. There. Behind the thick-branched weeds. The swirl of color that marked the goshanti. During the day she showed as a ball of energy, at night she could take form.

"Found her," I whispered. "Use me."

Morio drew on the threads from the Netherworld, mixing the energy and binding it to his own, forming the spell to send the devil back to the realm from which she'd come. The power darted along the cords, sparkling like lights. Morio swayed to the music of the realm that pulsated along with the magic. As it hit his hands, he channeled it down through me, sweeping his arms down to fasten his grasp on my shoulders.

The sudden flush caught me up in the dance. Together we soared in the astral, our bodies still firmly grounded Earthside. We spun around each other, mating snakes entwining. Morio laughed, throaty and raw, and his joy raced out to include me. The power of the dead, the power of that dark realm was *so much more* than it appeared. A fire raced through my body, sending me into an orgasm.

Morio stroked my chin and whispered, "I love you. I love you more than I love life, Camille."

I traced his lips. "You are one of my chosen," I said, feeling his tongue curl around my finger. "You are one of my great loves and we'll always be together. We're bound for eternity, my youkai, and I would do it all again in a heartbeat. And when it's our turn to cross over, we'll pound down these gates together, and you will enter the Land of the Silver Falls with me."

"We should take care of the goshanti," he said, his thoughts curling around me like a warm embrace.

"Use me, direct me, guide me." I reluctantly turned back to the land, wanting nothing more than to hang out on the astral. But we had work to do.

As we settled into the rhythm of the energy, Morio tapped me on the shoulder and I stood, guiding him toward the goshanti. I could barely see the land around me, the colors were so brilliant and amplified. There was a definite disconnect between my feet and my mind, but Morio steadied me. Something slithered over my shoes but it was just a snake, and I paid no attention.

And then we were there, next to the goshanti. She was asleep, and in her slumber I felt sorry for her. I could see how she'd come to be born. Her body, her essence, was a swirl of pain, of anger, of heartbreak and torture. Tears began to slide down my cheeks as I watched her, curled in a ball like a cat.

"You poor thing," I whispered. "The world can be so fucked up, and you're just as much a victim as those you prey on."

Morio squeezed my shoulder in agreement. "We have no choice, Camille. She'll hurt other innocents if we leave her be. When we send her back to the Netherworld, she'll be with others of her own kind."

"Can't we kill her? Put her out of her misery? It's no life, to live in hatred and bitterness like this. No matter where you are."

I didn't like hearing myself talk like this, but if it were me, I'd rather be dead than live my life a shell, acting out of pain condensed drop by drop from women who'd succumbed to horrendous deaths.

With a slow sigh, Morio nodded. "We can. Are you sure?"

I bit my lip, thinking again that death magic was a nebulous path, a thin line between the power to repel, and the abuse of power.

"I'm not sure of anything anymore." I shrugged. "But if we kill her, the energy is free to disperse, to be cleansed and renewed. We freed spirits earlier, this will just be ridding the world of another trapped memory of pain."

"Then we use the Mordente spell, but rather than the *banis*, we use the *despera* chant." He held out his hand and I took it, closing my eyes.

The power filled my lungs with the taste of graveyard soil and dust, of the hand of glory and the hand of might. I licked my lips and joined in as he began the incantation. Again, I would be the focus for the energy as it traveled through him, through me, toward the goshanti.

"Mordente reto, mordente reto, mordente reto despera."

The goshanti opened her eyes, still in her energetic form rather than physical. She lifted her head and gazed at us, her glowing eyes curious.

"Mordente reto, mordente reto, mordente reto despera."

I could feel the energy quake through me as a breeze sprang up. The rain began to fall again, the sky dark with threatening thunderheads. The goshanti opened her mouth and let out a whimper.

"Mordente reto, mordente reto, mordente reto despera."

Morio's will was strong, and mine as well. The spell raced through us now, alive and aware on its own, affixed to its target. I focused on the goshanti, willing her to go quietly, willing her to accept that if she allowed us to release her, the pain she felt would cycle back to the universe, cleansed and renewed in joy.

"Mordente reto, mordente reto, mordente reto despera."

Morio's voice thundered above mine, and his direction was absolute. I hesitated a moment, but remembered how the devil had come to be and steeled myself. Together, our voices danced on the breeze, spun in a whirlwind of autumn leaves, blotted out the life force of the goshanti.

"Mordente reto, mordente reto, mordente reto despera." As Morio continued with the incantation, I took up the counter-rhythm.

"Go to peace, go to rest, go to slumber, go to your ancestors, go to the dark depths of the world and let go your body, go back to the realm from which you came, disperse on the wind, disperse on the rain, disperse to the flames, disperse to the soil—"

The goshanti screamed as she woke fully. She reared up, still on the astral, staring at me with hatred and lust. But her powers were wavering. We were making an impact.

"Mordente reto, mordente reto, mordente reto despera," Morio commanded, forcing the energy through me at a tremendous rate, so fast and hard that I could barely stand against the astral tidal wave crashing through my body.

"Return to the elements, return to the void, return to the core of the universe to be cleansed and renewed. Go now, let the life force drain from you, let the power of breath flow out of you, may your sight dim, may your passion fade, may you rest in the arms of your ancestors—"

Lunging at me, the goshanti was a whirl of claws and energy. She could hurt me since I was partially linked on the astral, but I dodged her attack and she overshot, spinning around when she realized she'd missed me. She took stock of the situation, eyeing Morio, but shying away from another attempt. I could see the fear in her eyes but there was no place for her to run.

"Mordente reto, mordente reto, mordente reto despera."

I raised my voice to match his, holding fast against the onslaught of energy that poured out of the Netherworld, through him, through me. A whirlwind of black and white, a vortex of death and annihilation, it shook me to the core.

"Rest now, sleep forever, dream deep and do not awake. Venture to the sweetness of oblivion, sink into the darkness, join the brilliance of the stars—to the void we cast you, to the void we send you, to the abyss we guide you, give over—let go, be one with the world and *be no more*!" As I forced out the last three words, the goshanti shrieked and then slowly coiled in on herself, the colors fading as she grew smaller and smaller and then, with one last whimper, vanished.

"It's done." Morio sucked in a deep breath. "She's gone."

I stared at the spot where she'd been. There was no room for remorse, no room to wonder if we'd done the right thing. I turned back to him and placed my hand on his chest. He lifted it to his lips and kissed each finger softly.

"She's gone," I said, exhausted and wanting only to rest in a warm chair, with a blanket and a cup of tea.

I motioned for Delilah to join us. Wide-eyed, she edged over in our direction, holding up her cell phone.

"You can tell Chase that he and his men can get in here now. We'll purify the rest of it later, but they should be okay for now."

"Good. There's a call for you. It's Iris. She said she'd wait until you were done, so it must be important."

Immediately thinking that something had happened with Trillian, I grabbed the phone and answered. "Iris? Camille. What's up?"

She was whispering, which was strange enough in itself, but she also sounded like she'd swallowed some sort of frog. "You need to come home. *Now.* We have visitors."

"Who? Trillian?" My heart leapt in my throat. Had he gotten away early and come home without warning me to surprise me?

"No," she said, sounding both amused and wary. "Smoky's father is here. And he's brought someone with him."

Smoky's father? I paled, dropping to the ground, not paying attention to the fact that I ended up in a mud puddle. "And just what the hell does Smoky's father want?" I asked in a low voice. If Smoky was powerful and ancient, his father had to be terrifying.

"Apparently Smoky . . . well . . . there's someone else here, too. A woman—a female dragon. She says she's Smoky's fiancée and he's not disputing her claim."

I stared blankly at the phone, unable to comprehend what I was hearing. Standing, I motioned toward the car. "We have to go home. Get the stuff and let's go. *Now*."

Iris heard me and whispered a quick good-bye. I flipped the phone shut and tossed Delilah the keys. "You drive. You're never going to believe what I'm about to tell you. Hell, *I* don't know what the fuck to think."

But as we packed up everything and headed out toward the Belles-Faire District, I knew exactly what I was thinking. Smoky was *mine*. He belonged to me and to Morio.

Like it or not, a jealous streak rose up—a feeling I wasn't all that acquainted with, and one I didn't like. But I was seeing red, and the only thing I could think about was that I needed to get my ass home so I could beat the crap out of the bitch trying to lay claim to my husband, to *my soul mate*. Trouble was, how the hell was I going to convince a *dragon* to get her claws off my man?

"Very carefully," a little voice inside me said. "Very carefully."

CHAPTER 6

As I burst in the door, Iris took one look at my face and hustled me off to the kitchen where she pushed me into a chair.

"You cannot go in there half-cocked. I know you," she said. "I know what your mouth is capable of and you do *not* want to make a mistake right now. We have three *dragons* sitting in our living room, and none of them seem happy. That should be enough to scare the hell out of you, but I can see that you're beyond reason."

Beyond reason was right. All the way home, all I could think about was why the hell Smoky hadn't told me he was engaged, and how that was going to affect the Soul Symbiont ritual we'd performed. I had never been jealous, never been one to worry about my lovers having other partners. I just wanted to be their primary. But knowing there was a female dragon in my living room who had come to sink her hooks into my husband, well, that little fact had triggered off a latent tendency. Embarrassed at my feelings, and angry, I tried to calm down.

A moment later Smoky entered the kitchen. I glanced at him, not saying a word. He motioned to Iris and Delilah and they withdrew with Maggie to Iris's room. I didn't know what to say so I did the next best thing for once. I kept my mouth shut and mutely stared at him. Morio knelt beside me, holding my hand. He knew better than to interfere but I was relieved that he wasn't in a hurry to leave me alone with this mess.

Smoky let out a long sigh and pulled a chair over to my side. "Camille . . . are you all right?"

I shrugged, still not trusting myself to speak.

"I'm sorry you had to find out this way. I meant to tell you at some point, but with everything that's gone on, there never seemed to be the right time." His voice was silken, caressing me even as a strand of his hair slowly reached up to gently stroke my face. I thought about brushing it away, but decided to wait.

"So . . . you're engaged? How long have you been seeing her?" I swallowed my pride. Might as well get the truth out and know where I stand.

He shook his head. "It isn't like that. It's an arranged marriage that I never agreed to. Among my kind, our parents arrange the match. It's more political and financial than anything else. I've been engaged since birth, but I didn't think . . . I didn't think that this would be an issue for a long time to come. I've never dated her, in human terms, never even touched her beyond a simple handshake." His eyes flashed but—as deceitful as dragons can be—I had the gut feeling he was telling me the truth.

"So, what happens next? Why did your father come? And why is *she* here?" The thought that he hadn't been the one to propose, that the marriage was arranged and he had no say about it made me feel better. The question was: What were we going to do about it? Or rather, was there anything we *could* do about it?

"My father found out I'm married, that I performed the Soul Symbiont ritual with someone who isn't a dragon. I warn you, he's not happy. We've never gotten along. I'm the ninth son of a ninth son and I'm expected to carry on tradition and have nine sons of my own. I can't tell you why, at least right now, but the fact that I came Earthside from the Northlands and stayed had everything to do with my father." He frowned, staring at the floor.

Morio stood, moving his hand to rest on my shoulder. "So

your father came to force you to do your duty and marry the woman?"

"That's essentially the picture." Smoky shoved himself out of his chair and paced over to the counter. By the look on his face, I wouldn't want to be his bride-to-be—at least not one being foisted on him. "I'm not ready to return to my kin. Not enough time has passed for me to forgive—" He paused, staring blankly at the wall.

"Forgive what?" There was something he'd left unsaid, something that had driven him from his home. I could see it, could feel it from our connection and Morio could, too.

Smoky blanched, turning a whiter shade of pale. "I can't talk about it. Not now. Not here. Leave it that I have choices to make and I have to make them now, sooner than I thought I would. Either I return home and marry her, or I return home and relinquish my birthright. I can't see any other option."

A wave of dread swept over me. I clutched at the table. "If you leave . . ."

He stared at me, his eyes meeting mine squarely. "Then the bond will be stretched too far, and tear at both of us. All three of us."

"And if you stay . . ."

"I turn my back on my heritage and chance being excommunicated from the realm of dragons." He shook his head. "If you could only come with me. If you could live with me there. My only duty to her is in name only, and to father her children. She would have claim as my lawful wife, but she wouldn't be able to object to you. It's common in dragon society to take paramours and second wives or husbands."

I didn't like the sound of being second place, but no matter— the thought was out of the question. "I can't come with you. You know that. My duty is here, my obligation is to my family and the war we're fighting." And then, because I couldn't help myself, I added, "You said you loved me."

In two strides, Smoky was back at my side. He pulled me out of my chair and held me by the shoulders, staring straight into my eyes. "I do love you. I love you more than you think possible. My Witchling, *you* are my wife."

"But I won't live as long as you. How can I ask you to give up thousands of years with your own kind just to spend perhaps a thousand . . . with me?" I burst into tears, more out of frustration than anything else. "Can't you marry her and then go back to her after I . . . after I'm . . ."

"Sshh . . . hush, my love." Smoky pulled me into his arms and kissed me gently. "This is not your concern. Please don't worry yourself. I'll take care of matters. I'm not leaving you. I'll figure out some way to smooth things over."

I blinked hard at the tears, angry that I'd broken down in front of him. "If you need to stay there, maybe you can come back every month for a few days when the link weakens . . . just to keep us all from going nuts." I didn't want to sound hysterical. His fiancée probably never got hysterical. In fact, being a dragon, she was probably in the living room listening in, laughing at me.

Smoky shook his head again. "Camille. Stop crying. I'm not going to let anything happen to our connection. You are my wife and that's just the way things are."

"My wife, too," Morio spoke up, his eyes twinkling.

Smoky gave him a guarded look, then let out a low growl. "Yes, well, there's no helping that. But I think it's best that you stay in here while I introduce Camille to my father. The less confusion, the better. I'm lenient with mortals but my father isn't . . . so friendly. As for . . . *her* . . . I have no idea and I'm not that interested."

Morio shrugged. "I'm a demon. I doubt either one of them can do me too much damage if I shift, but you're right. Things are skewed enough as it is. I'll wait here. But I warn you—if either of them hurts Camille—"

"Enough," Smoky said, glowering dangerously. "If either of them even attempts to hurt her, I'll put a stop to it. No matter what the cost." He wrapped his arm around my shoulder. "Wash your face, now, and then I suppose you'd better meet your father-in-law."

Since I couldn't get upstairs without passing by Smoky's father and fiancée, I slipped into the laundry room and found a skirt and bustier that were nearly dry. I hurried into Iris's room and quickly used her shower, then touched up my makeup and made sure my eyes didn't look puffy. Both Delilah and Iris stared at me, waiting, but I just shrugged as I slipped into the clean clothes.

"I'll tell you everything later. I don't know what's going to happen, but I can tell you this: Next time one of us gets married, be sure you ask if they have some fiancée or girlfriend hidden out somewhere."

Delilah colored, blushing like a bruised peach. "Yeah, I found that out the hard way, too. But at least I wasn't married to Chase."

I grimaced. "Smoky says he's never even touched this . . . dragon . . . before. It's an arranged marriage. I don't know whether to believe him or not, but with the Soul Symbiont ritual, it's hard for him to lie to me. Or me to him. Same thing with Morio. Anyway, do I look ready to meet my father-in-law?"

Iris gave me a strong smile. "Cheer up. How can anybody resist you?" She leaned up on tiptoe to kiss me on the cheek. "You look beautiful. Now go in there and wow them. Just watch that mouth of yours, and whatever you do, don't let on you have the unicorn horn."

Cripes. She was right. Smoky was good about not swiping it from me but other dragons might not be so circumspect. I lifted up my skirt and unbuckled the garter that held it strapped to my leg. "Hide this. Please. I don't want to take any chances."

Delilah took it and gave me a nod. "I guess you'd better get in there."

I steeled myself and marched back into the kitchen. Smoky gave me a nod of approval as he cast an eye over the clean clothes and my tearless face.

"You're so beautiful," he whispered, as I looped my arm through his. Morio patted me on the butt as I passed by and I tossed him a wan smile. This wasn't the way I'd envisioned meeting the in-laws, but then again, nothing in our lives ever seemed easy. Taking a deep breath, I allowed Smoky to lead me into the living room, right into the dragons' lair.

I had no idea what to expect, and my first impression was one of sensation rather than sight. As we entered the living room, the power struck me like a sledgehammer, almost knocking me down. It was as if I were looking at two pillars of fire—one white, one golden. And they all but blinded me. When I blinked, in their place stood a tall—*so very tall*—man, and a woman whose beauty was so brilliant that it almost made me crash to my knees.

The man looked a lot like Smoky, but his hair was pure white instead of silver, and his face was craggy and far more rugged. He didn't look *old*, but he felt ancient beyond counting. I had no idea how long this dragon had roamed the earth, but Smoky felt positively youthful compared to him.

He was at least seven feet tall, and broad-shouldered. His face was stubbled with whiskers the color of fallen snow, and his skin was even more translucent and milky than Smoky's. The dragon's shoulders were broad, and he wore a flowing robe made of what looked like silk. Silver embroidery adorned the crest on his pocket. I could barely look into his eyes, they swirled with pale blue and hoarfrost and the sparkle of snow.

Catching my breath, I turned to the woman. She felt about Smoky's age, but her skin was warm and tanned and she stood a good six foot three. Her hair was the color of spun gold and fell to her waist, and she was built like a brick house. Sturdy, muscled, firm large boobs, narrow waist, thighs that could crush me like a coconut . . . oh yeah, she was fine. Her eyes gleamed as golden as the rest of her, and she let out a hearty laugh with full, luxurious lips. She was wearing a red robe that revealed as much as it covered, and had belted it with what looked like a gold-plated waist cincher. Nope, not even our most incredible beauty back home in Y'Elestrial could have competed with this nightmare of fantasy.

Smoky felt me waver and steadied me with a discreet hand. I sucked in a deep breath and waited for his cue.

"Father, may I present my wife, Camille te Maria." He used my surname as it was known in Otherworld. "Camille, this is my father. Sir, what name shall I give her to use for you?"

Of course. I still didn't know Smoky's real name. And I sure as hell wasn't going to be offered up his father's name.

His father gave me a look that froze my blood. Nope, he wasn't happy. So *not* a happy camper. Big Bad Mean Dragon. And I was suddenly afraid that the big bad mean dragon might eat me. And not in the good way. I didn't even want to *think* about him eating me any other way.

"I share my name with no human. None are worth even a throwaway name." The man's voice was cold and, in my gut, I knew his heart was frozen against me. I scooted closer to Smoky, who wrapped his arm around my shoulders. "You dishonor your true fiancée by bringing this woman into our presence."

I took a shuddering breath and tried to keep my mouth shut. The female dragon laughed aloud—her voice rough and unpleasant. She took a step forward and leaned toward me.

"You dare to call yourself the wife of Iampaatar? How terribly amusing, but how terribly forward. You can't even bear children for my fiancé." She spit out the words as though she found speaking to me distasteful.

Iampaatar? I glanced up at Smoky, who looked ready to kill. "Is that your name?" I whispered.

"No," he said evenly. "It's my name to the world of the Northlands. I left it behind when I left the family dreyerie behind. My name is Smoky." He gazed at the woman. "You assume far, far too much, Hotlips."

Hotlips? Oh great, the perfect name for the perfect man-stealer. But by the sound of his voice, he wasn't complimenting her.

"*Hotlips?* Lovely, but at least you give me the respect of not mentioning my Northlands name in front of the slut." She snorted. "And just what do I assume wrong? Looks to me like you picked a fairly ordinary trollop, my husband-to-be."

"You'd best rein in that nose of yours before someone chops it off." Smoky was glaring now, and I knew he was pissed because a cold breeze right off the Ionyc Sea bore down on us, chill and bone-numbing.

I tried to edge out of the way. The last thing I needed was to be caught between dueling dragons, but Smoky didn't give me that option; he pulled me tighter to his side.

"Camille is my *wife*. We've undergone the Soul Symbiont ritual, so this woman is also my *soul mate*. She is not fully human, but half-Fae. But be she mortal or immortal does not matter. The fact is that I love her and I've chosen her to be my mate. That's all either of you need to know."

Smoky's father let out a low growl and strode forward. He grabbed me by the wrist and flung me to the side, his touch rough and angry. I tripped over the footstool and scrambled out of the way as he raised his hand and landed a blow across Smoky's cheek that left a red weal. The slap would have broken my neck.

"That's for your back talk." He backhanded Smoky again, and I stared as Smoky stood, taking it, not raising his hand in retaliation. "The second is for insulting your fiancée. She's one of your betters."

Blood, stark against the pallor of Smoky's skin, trickled down from one nostril but my lover ignored it. He stood there, shoulders back, and slowly shook his head. "She may be *your* better but she is not one of *mine*. You're a white wing, but I am born of a *silver* mother, and I bear her status. The golden wings are of worthy caste, but not of *my* stature."

Hotlips's eyes flared, but she said nothing, bowing her head in accordance.

"You dare to contradict me in front of a human? What a failure of a son you are! Have you forgotten every duty you owe your family?" Smoky's father hit him once again, this time hard enough to leave a small gash on Smoky's cheek from a silver ring the dragon wore. It looked like a wedding ring.

Again, Smoky took it, not raising his hand in return. But his eyes were swirling. "I no longer recognize your dominion over me. I would willingly serve my family *if* my family listened to me. But you have no idea what's going on down here. You care only for your own gain through this . . . this . . ." He gestured toward Hotlips. ". . . this political alliance."

He turned to the golden dragon and said, "You are being used, my lady. I will not demean you, but know this: I am not the husband you seek. An alliance with me may increase your family's holdings as well as my own, and yes, it will increase my father's honor and the honor of any children *you* bear. But the fact is, I do not love you. Like my grandfather before me, I refuse to marry out of duty. Beyond all of these issues, there stands another brooding matter. War is coming, and you have no idea just what we're up against."

I fully expected Smoky's father to throttle him, but he stopped and cocked his head. "War? What sort of war?"

Smoky relaxed just enough for me to notice. "If you thought Grandfather's war was bad, what we face here is ten times worse. The demons are breaking through the portals and all worlds will be at risk. If they overrun the Earth and Otherworld, they will overrun the Northlands eventually."

The elder dragon narrowed his eyes and glanced at me. "What does she have to do with this?"

"More than you realize," Smoky said, nodding to me. "Camille and her sisters are our primary hope. The last thing I need to think about is a marriage I'm not interested in, children at this early age, and kowtowing so you can move up the social ladder. And if Mother were here, she'd agree with me."

Smoky's father scowled but he said nothing. Then, he slowly walked over to me, looking me up and down like I was a prize cow. I steeled myself, ready to make tracks if he decided to land a fist on me like he had his son.

"*Camille*, is it? So you've enchanted my son. You must have some incredible talents to pluck his heartstrings thusly." A slow, lecherous smile crept over his face and he leaned too close, crowding me. "Or perhaps it's not so much his heartstrings that you pluck, but another part of his body. Your Fae blood may give you something worth tasting, after all. You are comely enough, for your kind."

His gaze fastened on my boobs. He reached out with one hand and stroked my chin. I shivered. His touch was covetous and grasping, not smooth and caressing like Smoky's. A touch that promised to overpower, to take what he wanted with—or without—permission. Yeah, the old rape-and-pillage mentality, but he had the force to back it up. I steeled myself and looked him straight in the eye as he leaned down and planted a kiss on my lips. His tongue played against them, but I refused to open my mouth and he let out a soft grunt.

"Welcome to the family . . . for as long as we decide to humor my son's whims," he whispered in my ear. "But remember, as Iampaatar's father, I have the right to demand access to anything he possesses and it is his sworn duty to hand it over, to use or abuse as I wish."

I did stumble then, and he caught me up, his fingers too eager to rub against me as he deposited me on the sofa. I wanted nothing more than to crawl away and take a shower to wash the feel of his hands off of me.

Turning to Smoky, who looked as close to pure rage as I'd

ever seen him, he said, "We have much to discuss. Whether I will allow you to pay the release fee for the marriage is still to be determined. But we must talk to the council about this war. You will tell us what you know, my son. And then, we will discuss your nuptials."

Hotlips looked pissed. Arms folded across her chest, she tapped one gorgeous clawed nail against her skin. "You're a fool if you let him talk you out of this marriage, Hyto. This will strengthen your position in the council chambers." Apparently, she had no qualms about revealing the elder dragon's common name in front of me.

Hyto merely shrugged. "The final decision will be up to my wife, of course, since she bears the higher ranking. Meanwhile, we shall return to the Northlands and explore this warfare my son speaks of. Iampaatar, come." The word was definite and even I knew that Smoky couldn't get out of the trip.

He nodded, bowing ever so slightly to his father, and walked over to me; he picked me up, bundling me in his arms. His gaze fastened on mine, he carried me out of the room, into the parlor. There, he shut the door and pulled me over to the far corner, into his arms.

"I am so sorry about my father. If he had tried to actually harm you, I'd have fought him off. Please, never think anything else. But this is such a delicate balancing act . . ."

I sought his lips, and he kissed me long, slow, his tongue coiling around mine, his hands holding me firmly, reminding me I was his. I relaxed finally. The difference between him and his father was as huge as the Grand Canyon. The apple fell far, far from the tree in this case.

I melted into the kiss, afraid that when he left, I'd never see him again. "Come back to me," I whispered. "Don't let them keep you there. Come back to me . . . to us. We need you. *I need you.*"

Smoky leaned down and placed his forehead against mine. "Camille, I promise you on my word of honor. By my smoke-stacks and whiskers, I won't let them separate us. I will return to you and your sisters. Your family is now my family, and if it ends up being the only family I have, then I can accept that. You belong to me. I belong to you. Nothing—not demons, not dragons, not promises made before I was born—can ever change that."

Tears were streaking down my cheeks now and I clung to him, my arms tight around his neck. "I lost Trillian," I whispered. "And though I know he's coming back, what if something goes wrong? I can't lose you, too. I can't lose any of you. You and Morio and Trillian are my loves, my life. You make me whole. You keep me sane."

He pressed his finger against my lips. "Sshhh . . . everything will work out. I promise you. I am not like my father. My mother has honor, though she's haughty and stern as is her birthright. My father has the white dragon's grasping nature. He comes from a lower caste and married into his position, and he's always seeking something higher. My grandfather, though . . . is more like me. You'd like him and he'd like you."

"I doubt I'll ever get the chance to meet him," I said, unaccountably sad.

"Never say never, my love." Smoky kissed me again. "I am not going to marry Hotlips, regardless of whether it gets me thrown out of my dreyerie." He paused, then slowly said, "I mean it when I say we're soul mates. The ritual bound us together forever. Camille—before I go, I have to tell you something. I think I've discovered a way that we can have a child."

I stared up at him, the meaning of his words crashing in on me. "What? That isn't possible!"

"Yes, it *is*. I know of a magical ritual that can pave the way. The child would be a true shifter—a dragon shifter, though not fully dragon."

"I don't know what to say." I stared at him, terrified. He wanted me to have a child. *His* child. A *dragon* child. Thoughts of C-sections and movies like *It's Alive* raced through my head.

"Just think about it," he whispered. "If we were to have a child, this would cement you into my family. And it would take care of one of my duties to pass on my heritage. Please don't say no without thinking about it." He swallowed, looking more nervous than I'd ever seen him.

I let the possibility settle in my heart. Then softly, so softly

I was barely speaking aloud, I said, "You know I have no maternal instincts. But I . . . I'll think about it. I can't make you any promises, though."

"We have plenty of time, and your promise to think about it is good enough for me," he said, wrapping his arms around me. "Remember—there are nannies who can look after the children. And now, I must go."

I stepped back, my eyes dry but inside my heart was aching, wanting to cry, wanting this to all just go away. So much stress, so much worry, and now coping with angry dragons on top of the demon threat . . . it was just too much. "Smoky, go and get this over and done with. I'll be waiting for you."

He reluctantly let go of me. I followed him out into the living room where his father was impatiently tapping one foot on the floor. Hotlips gave me a triumphant grin like she'd won some major victory over me, and Hyto grabbed my ass and pinched so hard I knew it would leave a bruise. Smoky wasn't watching and I decided to keep my mouth shut. No use starting World War III right here in the house.

"Let's get this over," Smoky said.

Without another word, Hyto reached for his son with one hand, and for Hotlips with the other, and they vanished, out of the living room into the Ionyc Sea. I watched as they faded from sight, wondering if I'd ever see my beloved dragon again.

CHAPTER 7

As I stared at the spot where the three dragons had been standing, Morio, Iris, and Delilah filed into the room. I took a long, shuddering breath and turned to them. "You heard?"

"We couldn't help hearing," Iris said. She motioned to the tea tray that Morio was holding. "I made you some Sweet Blossom tea. I thought it might calm your nerves. The gods only know, *my* nerves are on edge and I was only in the room with them for a bit, and neither his father nor the fiancée spoke to me."

Delilah slid onto the arm of the sofa. "What will you do if they don't let him come back?"

I jerked my head around to stare at her. "Don't even go there. Smoky will come back. I know it. He has to." I sank into the rocking chair, cradling my head in my hands. "This is just too much. And that father of his is a freak. The way he touched me—I felt two seconds away from being raped. Or being dinner. Or both, in that order. He hates humans. And I get the feeling he lumps all Fae into the same category. The way he looked at me . . ." I shuddered, remembering those cold, lecherous eyes. He could fuck me, kill me, use my bones for toothpicks, and not feel a shred of remorse or concern.

"If he'd made one move to hurt you, I would have been in there. And you know Smoky wouldn't have let it go that far." Morio stood behind me, rubbing my shoulders. "He loves you. He's bound to us and he won't let us down."

"Well, Hotlips sure doesn't love me, and she wants Smoky to herself. I gather she's a golden dragon and that means . . . well, I don't know what it means but it's obviously important to Hyto." I grimaced. Even saying his name made me feel dirty.

"Relax," Iris said. "I'll pour the tea. And yes, you're right. She's a golden dragon and they are second rung at the top of the hierarchy. Silvers are the most powerful of all the dragon lords."

I must have looked confused because she let out a little sigh. "Did Smoky tell you nothing over the past months?" She handed round the tea, then settled on the ottoman, teacup in hand.

"I never thought to ask," I said.

"Dragons live within a strict caste system. You can marry up or down, but if you're on a lower rung, even if you marry up you retain less stature than your mate. However, the more sons and daughters who marry higher than your station, the more brownie points you accrue with the council. It's terribly complex, but then again, they have eons to figure out everything. Anyway, what it boils down to is this: Smoky is part of the highest echelon, among the Emperor Dragons. He can't move any higher. But his *father* can gain stature if Smoky marries someone above a white dragon, because that's the caste his father belongs to."

"Smoky is part of the Emperor caste?" If silver dragons were among the highest echelon of dragon society, then what he'd said about taking his mother's status since he was mixed blood made sense.

"Yes, because of his mother's blood. Children take on the caste of the higher parent's bloodline. Smoky and any of his siblings through his mother belong to the highest ruling caste. His father hangs out a few rungs lower on the pole. The only dragons to live outside the caste system are the black dragons, and they exist within a hierarchy all their own because of their special abilities."

I tried to sort out all this information.

"I should have asked before, but it never occurred to me that they'd have such a complicated social system." I sipped the steaming brew. The fragrance and delicate blush of the Sweet Blossom plant immediately went to work, calming me down. "I guess my mind has been on the demons, not dragon etiquette."

Iris snorted. "Trust me, girl, you haven't heard the tip of it, yet. When I lived in the Northlands, I learned more about dragons than I ever wanted to, especially white dragons. They're thick as thieves there, and it pays to know just who you might run up against. Now silvers—like Smoky's mother—have a sense of honor and generally keep their promises. They're not as dangerous—at least not until you do something to piss them off. Come to think of it, even though they don't live in the Northlands, the golden wings and the greenbacks are like that, too. But whites—and the indigos and reds—happen to be another matter."

"So not all dragons live in the Northlands," Delilah said, pulling the basket of fruit over to her and pawing through it. Iris was on a health kick, trying to curb my sister's frantic junk food habit, but it wasn't going to take. Sure enough, Delilah wrinkled her nose and shoved it away. "I guess we're out of cookies?"

Iris let out a long sigh. "I'll make some later. Girl . . . oh, never mind. But to answer your question, no—redbacks and golden wings live in the Southlands, and the indigos and greenbacks—well, I'm not sure where they harken from. Black dragons exist mainly on the astral."

"And white dragons are dangerous," I said, grinning at Delilah's dejected look as she gave the fruit basket another once-over and shook her head.

"White dragons are the most volatile, that's for sure, and the most grasping," Iris continued. "That's why I took my time to assess Smoky's demeanor when I first met him. Mixed bloods can favor either—or both—parents, just like the Fae. But Smoky has proved himself time and again. His mother's blood shines through, even if he has a roguish way and tends to be self-centered."

"He told me that he'd found a way for me to have his child," I blurted out.

Morio and Delilah stared at me like I was crazy.

Iris swallowed her tea, set down the cup, and folded her arms. "I *so* need to hear more about this."

I could tell they were all waiting for me to continue, but having burst out my little secret, I had no idea what else to say. For one thing, I was clueless as to what I was planning to do about the matter.

Just as the silence was getting a bit thick, the door burst open and Vanzir rushed in, followed by Roz. They both looked like they hadn't slept in days.

"Yo, dudes, where have you been?" I jumped up, eager to change the subject. Right now the whole Smoky-dragon-father-fiancée-children conversation was starting to give me a headache, and the demon twins provided a handy excuse to exit the subject, stage left.

"Where else? Looking for clues to Stacia's whereabouts." Vanzir dropped onto the sofa next to Delilah and leaned back, his legs spread wide. Why did all guys have to act like their nuts were the size of tennis balls?

But he was cute, in a David-Bowie-as-Jareth-the-Goblin-King sort of way. His hair was short and spiky, bleached so blonde it was jarring, and he wore leather pants tight enough to show off every curve of his goodies. I blinked. Maybe he did need to sit with his legs that far apart. Whatever woman—or man—Vanzir set his sights on, was going to be a very happy camper, all right.

Roz was wearing his duster cum armory. The flasher from hell, I thought, as he slid off the heavy coat and hung it carefully over the back of a chair. Considering the firepower—both magical and technological—he had in there, I was grateful he took pains not to make anything go boom by accident.

He sprawled out in the chair next to mine, jeans black as night, mesh tank showing off nicely defined abs. Oh yeah, leave it to an incubus to find the perfect bad-boy look. He noticed me staring and slowly winked, then glanced around nervously. "Where's Smoky?"

I grinned. "Why, afraid he's going to beat the crap out of you again?"

Roz growled, but I wasn't going to let him live down his claim to fame. A few months before, Smoky had made Roz his whipping boy and the incubus spent two weeks with bruises that covered his body. But most of all, he'd nursed a wounded ego and learned a severe lesson in restraining his wandering hands. At least around me.

"You're setting me up, aren't you?" He gave me one of those pleading basset-hound looks and I relented.

"Don't sweat it. Smoky was called away for a while." As quickly as I'd smiled, I sobered. "His father came to get him. Apparently there's some unfinished business Smoky ran out on. His father is a freak of nature and not to be trusted. Smoky had no choice. He had to go. He'll be back as soon as he can."

"The lizard has parents? Parents who can make him behave?" Roz shuddered. "I wouldn't want to end up on their shit list."

"I already am," I muttered. "So, what news on the Bonecrusher?"

"Not much more than we had before. The information we had was correct. She can shift into human shape, meaning she could pass for a very tall, muscled FBH woman. She's obviously passing right now, keeping out of sight and we can't seem to get a lead on her."

I had the feeling when we actually ferreted her out, we were going to be facing her natural form. And her natural form was truly creepshow fodder. *Tales from the Crypt* scary. Otherworld scary. When she was in natural form, her torso and head were female—very human, but her body was that of a twenty-foot-long anaconda, with all the crushing power of the giant snake.

Vanzir accepted a cuppa from Iris. He balanced the saucer on one knee and took a slow sip from the steaming tea. "Carter has feelers out everywhere. He seems to think we're getting closer, but so far she's managed to elude us. She's either got one hell of a safe house going, or some innate ability to cloak against anybody scrying for her. And none of the scouts has been able to ferret her out."

I bit my lip. "Not good. And nothing on the half-demon wizard who gated her in?"

"Again, a dead end. All the demons who've come over

are accounted for—at least the ones who run in the network. Somewhere out there is a half-demon who managed to sneak Earthside and set this all up. Carter's got scouts on that trail, too."

Frustrated, I set down my cup. "We *have* to know where she is and what she's up to. If she's allowed to run around loose too long, we're going to see a body count rack up."

"Do you think she might have something to do with the ley line energy that's been shifting?" Iris asked, sitting next to Roz, who gave her a long, slow wink. The incubus had tried getting every one of us women in bed. He'd only succeeded with Menolly at this point.

"I think it's a possibility." Morio paced over to the window, staring out. "Stacia Bonecrusher is a lamia, which means she's more powerful than Karvanak was. And we know what a chore it was to bring him down. We almost lost Chase and Zach to that skirmish."

"Does anybody know what kind of magic she wields? Or does she even wield magic, other than whatever she has up her sleeve naturally?" Delilah hopped up and dashed into the kitchen, and we heard the sound of cupboard doors quickly slamming open and shut. She returned with a bag of Cheetos and settled down on the sofa with her treasure.

Roz shrugged. "That's another thing we don't know." He turned to Vanzir. "Do you think Carter has anything on her magical abilities?"

"I imagine he would have told us if he has, but I'll give him a call. Wait here," the demon said and headed into the kitchen.

Delilah, whose fingers were already orange from the cheese crisps, glanced at the clock. "When are you leaving for Dahnsburg?"

I closed my eyes, resting my head against Morio's shoulder as he settled back down next to me in the overstuffed chair. "I want to leave tonight, after Menolly's awake. Delilah, you're in charge here until we get back, and I'm not sure how long it will take. We'll portal hop once we're there. We certainly don't have the time to travel by ground."

The thought of making a trip back to Otherworld both thrilled and terrified me. We didn't have time for vacations, not with the lamia in town. And now with Smoky off in the

Northlands, I was worried about being a man down. But I'd been instructed to go to OW near the equinox to meet Trillian, and I desperately wanted to bring him home.

"You'll be in charge of Maggie," Iris told Delilah. "You and Menolly. I've got some things to attend to in OW and I might as well go with Camille and Morio. It's just safer that way. Roz and Vanzir will be here. Shamas, too, and Chase if you can get him free of that job of his."

"I wish Zachary was out of that wheelchair," Delilah said. "I can't believe how long he's been laid up. Karvanak almost broke his back."

"Karvanak may not have broken his spine, but he did break enough bones to keep Zach out of commission for a while, and that's not easy when you're dealing with a werepuma. I'm just grateful he survived," I said.

Weary, I glanced at the others. "Okay, we'll leave shortly after sundown, as soon as Menolly wakes up. I'm hoping we'll be back before the Moon Mother goes ripe, but I have a feeling we may not be, so tell Menolly to take the next couple of nights off and stay home because you'll be out catting around in your tabby form. There's no getting around the pull of the moon on us." I glanced over at Morio, tired and sleepy. "We'd better get changed and pull together our packs. I'd like to get in a short nap before we head out."

As we stood, Vanzir returned. His subdued look worried me. Something was up. Iris noticed it, too.

"What's going on?" she asked. "Was Carter able to tell you anything?"

He nodded. "Yeah, he managed to dig up a little more on her, but I guarantee you, you don't want to hear it. The information was hidden between the lines in her dossier. Shadow Wing's kept a tight wrap on her history because she's one of his generals, but Carter found what we're looking for, all right. The bitch is a necromancer."

"*A necromancer*?" I blinked, resisting the urge to just fall on the sofa in a stupor. "*Motherfucking son of a bitch*. No wonder we've had such a problem with creatures coming in from the Netherworld."

This was not good. So not good. Toss in the fact that she was a demon general meant Stacia wouldn't be just any ordinary bring-out-your-dead warped puppy. No, she'd be packing one hell of an arsenal in terms of spells and firepower, and could probably wipe out Morio and me with one easy conjuration.

"What the hell do we do now?" Roz leaned forward, resting his elbows on his knees and clasping his hands. "This is bad news. I wish Smoky was around."

"Should we still go?" I turned to Morio. "This puts a different spin on things."

"You have to—Trillian's waiting for you," Delilah said. "And it will only be for a couple of days. We've been hunting for Stacia for weeks now. Two or three days aren't going to make any difference."

"I hope you're right." I hesitated, then looked at Iris. "What do you think? Your instincts are usually right on the nose."

Iris pursed her lips together and motioned for us to be quiet. She sat down on the edge of the ottoman and I could tell she was drifting into a trance. As the Talon-haltija sank lower into her meditation, the ebb and flow of her aura beckoned me in and I hesitantly reached out to touch her energy with my own.

The moment our energies met, she gasped and yanked me into her world.

We were standing in the snows, high on a mountainside, in the middle of a snowstorm. Iris was bundled in a long, thick coat that was midnight blue, her hair hidden beneath the fur-trimmed hood. In the center of her forehead, a brilliant cobalt star glistened—whether it was inset or affixed, I didn't know, but it gleamed with power, pulsing gently to her heartbeat.

She raised her eyes to meet mine and I found myself gazing into a swirl of mist and fog and ice. Iris's power came sweeping over me, knocking me to my knees. I dropped into the packed snow. It was wet, dense, and would harden to ice before long. Soaked through to the skin, I couldn't take my eyes off the woman who was suddenly much more than a sprite.

Iris held out her hands, and in the palms rested a crystal ball, the color of blue topaz. Aqualine, the crystal she'd asked for from Otherworld. As I struggled to stand, she cupped her fingers around it and closed her eyes, murmuring something under her breath that I couldn't catch.

At that moment, a great shadow began to cover the mountain, creeping like inky fingers across the snow-blanketed landscape. The shadow clouded my vision and something told me to run from it, but I couldn't move. As it approached the outskirts of where we were standing, Iris's eyes flew open again and she raised one hand toward the approaching murk.

"Pysäyttää!" Her voice was strong and clear and the shadow stopped where it was. Iris stepped forward and her words thundered through the snow. "Retreat. Return to your cavern, creature of the dark. It is not yet our hour to meet."

As I watched, the shadow slowly began to retreat, a long, fluttering sigh lingering as it rolled back up the mountain. I turned to ask Iris what was going on but she was focused on the crystal ball again, and then, as big fat snowflakes began to fall in earnest, I blinked and found myself back in the living room, lying on the sofa.

"Camille, are you all right?" Delilah was leaning over me as I struggled to sit up. "You fainted."

I swung my feet onto the floor and scooted forward, looking for Iris. She was still sitting on the ottoman, eyes closed, but as I watched her she stirred and stretched, yawning. She gave me a long look, pleading for my silence. What had happened out there—wherever we were—she wanted to keep secret for now.

"I'm fine," I said. Iris was our friend and if she wanted to keep this quiet, then I'd play along, unless it looked like it was going to affect us or the war against the demons. "I guess I'm just tired. Iris, what did you see?"

A look of relief swept over the Talon-haltija's face and she smoothed the skirt of her dress. "We must go. There are things afoot in Otherworld that will have an impact on what we're doing here. We need to bring Trillian back—we can't afford to lose him. And . . . there's something waiting for you in OW, Camille. For both you and Morio. You *must* make this journey. Major changes are afoot and we'll all be caught up in them."

"I guess that answers that," I said. "All right, we'll leave after we talk to Menolly. Delilah, can you fix dinner? The three of us should rest if we're jumping portals tonight."

Delilah nodded, helping me up. As Morio and I climbed the stairs to take a nap, I couldn't help but think about the shadow that had come racing after Iris and me. But had it really been after *me*? When I really thought about it, I sensed the creature had been aiming directly for Iris. And what was it she'd said? *"Retreat. Return to your cavern, creature of the dark. It is not yet our hour to meet."*

What did it want with her? And why did I have the feeling she'd already met the creature? Trying to push thoughts of the Bonecrusher, and of the shadow on the mountain to the side, I focused on Trillian. He was coming home, he was coming back to me. But through the joy, a little voice inside began to whisper doubts. What if he freaked when he found out I'd married both Morio and Smoky? What would he do? And what would I do if he decided he didn't want to put up with the situation?

Unable to shake my worries, I set the alarm for just after sunset and climbed into bed. Morio seemed to sense my discomfort and slid his arms around me, holding me gently as we both drifted off to sleep.

CHAPTER 8

~∽∽~

"Camille, Morio? Time to get up." Her voice was soft, almost a hiss in the dim light of my bedroom.

I blinked and opened my eyes to find Menolly leaning over me, a toothy grin on her face. A couple tiny drops of blood on her chin told me she'd had her nightly drink and I smelled chicken soup on her breath.

Morio had left several charmed bottles of blood in the fridge for her to drink while we were gone. Though she never asked, he went out of his way to make sure she had a variety of choices available, giving her a break from the unending taste of blood on her tongue. Through some sort of illusion/alchemical magic, Morio had managed to alter the structure of the taste.

He'd even managed a good substitute for pizza. I knew, because I'd tasted a few drops, wondering if Menolly had just forgotten what food tasted like or if he'd really discovered a talent for blood cuisine. It gave me a weird sense of relief. If it ever came to it—being a vampire with Morio around wouldn't be quite so bad.

She backed away as I slid from beneath the covers. I was naked, but she'd seen my goodies before. Morio yawned and pushed himself up to lean against the headboard as I stretched. Even though we'd only slept for about three hours, the nap had done me a world of good.

I scratched my stomach and sniffed the air. "Delilah cooking dinner?"

Menolly grinned. "Nope. Roz is."

"Roz? I didn't know he knew which end was which on a skillet."

"Apparently so, or it looks that way to me. He's frying up some sausage links and eggs, and has Vanzir making fruit cups and toast. Iris stumbled in on them, offered to help, and they chased her out of the kitchen. I will grant you this: The boys come through when we need them," she said, her fangs beginning to recede.

"That they do," I murmured. I picked up a towel and slung it over my shoulder. "I need to hit the shower. Can you hunt through the closet and lay out my traveling clothes?"

Menolly nodded. "Yes, but Camille . . . please, be careful. I have a feeling something could go horribly wrong over there, and you know that I'm not prone to premonitions." She sat on the bed, glancing at Morio as he slipped from beneath the covers—naked as a jaybird and standing full at attention. "Down boy, unless you're pointing that thing Camille's way. Don't wave your freak flag in my face."

I snorted. "Don't worry. I'm happy to say he always wakes up bright and perky like that."

"I bet you are," she countered with a laugh. "Get in the shower, both of you, and I'll lay out your things. Morio, I assume that your clothes are in one of these dresser drawers around here?"

"I'll be wearing jeans and a sweater," he said, blowing her an air kiss as he wandered past and joined me on the way to the bathroom.

Once I had the water running full tilt, we climbed in and quickly lathered up. Morio reached around from behind me, soaping my breasts and belly. His hair fell forward, tickling my shoulders. He let out a low grunt and slid his fingers down my stomach to rest against my clit. I moaned, leaning back against him.

"Do we have time?" I asked.

"We always have time," he said, then quick as heat lightning, stroked me with that featherlight touch that sent me into orbit every time. "Besides, it may be a few days before we can find privacy for this again."

I moaned softly and spread my legs, and he slipped deep into my pussy from behind, his cock slick from the soap and water, his girth widening me with a delicious stretch. He reached around to finger me with one hand, and with the other, caressed my breasts.

I braced myself against the wall of the tub, making sure my footing was steady, as he began to thrust, taking long, smooth strokes that kindled the fire growing in my belly. The shower rained down on us like a waterfall and the drops trickled between my breasts, trailing down to where his hands played against my skin.

Pulling away, I stepped out of the tub, Morio following. He grabbed me and shoved me against the wall, rattling the shelves as he forced his knee between my legs. His hands traveled over my breasts, my belly, and he buried his face in my neck, nuzzling, nipping, sucking deeply. I knew he was leaving marks, but we always played rough.

"Fuck me," he said with a low growl. "Let me inside you."

I broke away and grabbed a bath sheet, throwing it over the mat on the floor, which was plush and thick. Morio lay down, quick as a fox.

"Come to me," he said, a willful smile curling the edge of his lip. "Come *with* me, Camille. Ride me."

I obeyed, straddling him, sinking down on his cock as he thrust upward to meet me, his hands gripping my waist.

"Touch yourself," he whispered hoarsely, and so I did, sliding two fingers down to stroke myself gently while I cupped my breast with the other hand and squeezed hard. I leaned back, reveling in the fire raging between us, in the feel of Morio watching me with an eager glint.

He tightened his grip on my waist, then flipped me over and as I rolled beneath him, his breathing grew harder and his eyes took on the edge that I recognized so well by now. As he hovered over me, trapping me between his knees, he began to change and grow.

In his full demon form, Morio was eight feet tall, and his

face lengthened into a muzzle. He was also as flexible as a gymnast. I found myself staring into the eyes of my demon fox man. His arms and legs took on thick waving fur, and black taloned claws replaced black nails.

As my lover shifted form, my hunger for him increased. When we were alone, we didn't play easy unless the mood called for it. No, he was demon and demon he acted. He leaned his head back and let out a yip of lust and joy and I grinned, delighted, at him.

"Come on, take me, show me how much you want me," I dared him.

"Never start anything you aren't willing to finish," he said. And then he grabbed my wrists, bruising them gently as he pressed them against the floor above my head. A knot flared in my stomach as he held me fast and spread my legs wide with his knees as he forced his way between them.

"Tell me what to do," I whispered.

"Wrap your legs around my waist," he ordered, and I whimpered as he let out a guttural sound from the back of his throat. I entwined my legs around his stomach, and his cock hovered inches away from me, fully erect and smooth.

"You want me?" he said, leaning down to nip at my breast. I caught my breath as he demanded again, "Do you want me?"

"Yes, oh yes, please." I couldn't stand it anymore. His energy flared, reaching out with long tendrils to tease me on. I swallowed the lump forming in my throat.

"What do you want me to do to you?"

My heart racing, I let out a long sob. "Fuck me, fuck me hard."

"Ask politely," he said, playing me like a fine-tuned violin.

"*Please*, will you *please* fuck me?" I squirmed under his hold; the only thing I could think about was how much I wanted him to screw my brains out.

"As is your pleasure, my sweet," he said. And then, with one slow, sinuous motion, he drove himself deep into my core, stretching me to the point where I could only let out little screams.

The feel of Morio's weight against my breasts, the cold steam that rose from his flared nostrils, the gentle touch of his

silken fur against my skin—everything was so alien, so deca-
dent that all I could do was give myself up to the passion. And
yet it was all so right.

I met him, thrusting in return as he plunged into me. He was
a demon, Morio was, with glowing topaz eyes and razor-sharp
teeth and a face not wholly human. And yet, he was still my
lover, my husband. Feral and wild, but all him. And then we
were caught on the slipstream of energy, riding it as it raced so
high and so far I wondered if we'd ever be free.

After Morio shifted back and I managed to stand on my own
without turning into a mound of Jell-O, we jumped back in
the shower for a quick rinse and hurried back to my room.
Menolly had laid out our clothes and filled our packs, and we
dressed and headed downstairs.

Menolly and Delilah were watching *Jeopardy*. Chase had
shown up, and he was sitting next to Delilah, holding her hand.
Maggie was on Menolly's lap, playing with a Barbie doll
wearing a ballerina outfit. She'd torn off the head and Menolly
had replaced it with a head from a Yoda action figure. The look
was so wrong, but somehow so right.

"Yobie, Yobie!" Maggie waved the doll at me.

I snickered. "Strong with the pink tutus, we are?"

Roz didn't even bother to look up from the video game he
was playing with Vanzir. They'd conned us into buying them
an Xbox and were hooked on Halo. "I packed you some sandwiches when we figured out you weren't going to be down for
dinner. You can eat them on the way."

But Vanzir shot a glance our way. "You guys sound like a
herd of elephants. What the hell kind of freak show do you put
on when you fuck and where can I get tickets?" His eyes were
luminous and hard to read, but I could sense an edge of arousal
behind the look. He flashed me that snarky grin that I didn't
trust, even though I knew it was just part of his nature. His
demonic heritage was a lot darker than Morio's.

I shook my head. "I'm not a roses-and-candy type of
woman."

"Didn't think so." He leapt on an opening Roz had left him

and dusted their enemy. "More like handcuffs and whips. Next you'll be ordering me into a ball-gag and have me begging, 'Please whip my ass, Mistress Camille.'"

I so didn't want to go there, for more reasons than one.

First, the thought of him crawling nekkid at my feet in a ball-gag so made me cringe. Submissive men were not my cup of coffee. Even more daunting was the thought that Vanzir's life hung on a whim. If my sisters and I or Iris ordered him to crawl on the floor and bark like a dog, he'd have to obey or the soul binder living right below the skin of his neck that bound him to us would kill him immediately. None of us were comfortable with the idea that his life—in fact, every action he made—was entirely within our control. But the cold truth was that Vanzir might as well be our slave. We owned him, body and soul, and we could kill him with the whisper of an order.

I shook my head. "Dude, just wear earplugs next time."

Chase arched one eyebrow as he glanced up at Morio and me. "In Vanzir's defense, you *were* really loud. It sounded like you were having a knock-down, drag-out fight up there."

"And this bothers you because. . . ?" As Chase's ears began to turn bright red, I relented. "Eh, get used to it, Johnson. And be happy you weren't in there with us. If the worst we get are a few bruises, we're happy." Though I had to admit, there'd been a few times Morio had gotten a little too excited and I'd ended up with some nasty bites.

Chase grunted and took another sip from the beer he was holding. "Klingon sex."

"Say what?" I must have looked confused because Delilah burst into giggles.

"Klingons—on *Star Trek*. They're pretty much tear-it-up in the sex department, like you and Morio."

"Not to interrupt this lovely discussion, but are you ready?" Menolly glanced at the clock. It was quarter of eight. "Iris is in the kitchen making a list of chores for us to do while she's gone."

Delilah grimaced. "I forgot to clean out my cat box again and she carried it up to my room and dumped it on my bed."

Ugh. "Kitten, face it, you've become a professional slob. Not so nice. Not so appealing. And I've seen that room of yours—it's no spring clean fling. Whatever happened to the idea that cats are supposed to be clean?"

Delilah shrugged. "I dunno—maybe it's the human side of me."

Chase cleared his throat. "Don't go blaming your human blood. I'm an FBH and I'm not a slob." He turned to me. "I tell her to clean up when she stays at my apartment and she does it." Delilah started to protest but just then, Iris poked her head around the corner.

"I'm ready. The list is on the refrigerator. Don't just look at it, okay? Actually get your butts in gear and *do* some of the chores. And take care of our little Maggie girl," she added, leaning over to give the baby gargoyle a big fat kiss on the head.

"Iss . . . Iss . . . kiss me." Maggie held her arms up for another, then looked at me. Her wings fluttered gently and I could tell she was worried. She'd gotten very clingy over the past couple of months and according to the book we'd been using on the care and feeding of woodland gargoyles, this was a phase she'd be in for some time. As in several years. "Camey—kiss?"

I joined Iris and planted a soft kiss on the Magster's cheek. She giggled and gave me a wet smooch on the nose.

"Be good, little one. Be safe."

Menolly grinned. "We'll treat her like fine china."

Suddenly near tears, I nodded, biting back the fear that rose in my throat. I wanted to go home, I desperately wanted to see Trillian and bring him back, but with all the danger in our lives, I was terrified that something would happen while I was gone. Something I might be able to prevent if I were here.

Iris patted me on the hand. "I know, girl. I feel it, too. These are uncertain times. The potential paths are merging at a rapid rate. Life is becoming a blur of possibilities and so many of them dark. But we must take this trip. I know it in my bones. You and Morio are headed toward another leg of Fate's journey, and I . . . I have to confront something I left behind long, long ago, if I'm to be free of my past and able to move on with my future."

We all gazed at her, but she fell silent—the silence that said, "Do not ask, I will not speak." When Iris didn't want to talk about something, nothing would pry the info out of her.

"Not to mention the most important thing: We need to bring Trillian home." Morio wrapped his arm around my shoulder.

We were dressed for the road. I was wearing a spidersilk skirt that skimmed the tops of my granny boots, and a burgundy leather corset under my unicorn's-hide cloak. The cloak had come with the horn of the Black Unicorn when I earned the right to use it. Now, against all common sense, my instincts urged me to wear it back to Otherworld, and to take the horn with me. The items would put me in danger from any number of mages and wizards who'd sell their grandmother's pussy to own the artifact and cloak.

Morio was wearing black jeans and a turtleneck, and he'd slipped on a hip-length gray buccaneer's jacket with silver buckles. His motorcycle boots came up over the legs of his jeans.

Iris had changed into a walking skirt, indigo blue in color, and a matching long-sleeved top. Over the sweater, she'd donned a thin chain tunic. The links weren't steel, but some bespelled silver, and it radiated with a faint white light. Over that, she'd draped a short capelet with hood, and her ankle-length blond hair was woven into braids that were wrapped around her head.

"Have your weapons?" Delilah asked, suddenly serious. "I wish we were coming with you."

"I wish you were, too, but you have to stay here and keep guard. We'll give Father your love." I parted the side-slit in my skirt to show her my dagger, strapped to my thigh by a leather garter. "I've got my dagger right here, and the horn is in its secret pocket."

Morio winked at her. "I never go anywhere without my daggers, throwing knives, and various goodies."

"I like your goodies," I said, sidling up to him.

Roz stood up and rummaged through his coat, then handed us each a Ziploc bag. Within each pouch were several assorted magical bombs. One, I recognized as a firebomb, a couple garlic bombs, and several others that I wasn't entirely familiar with.

"Here," he said. "You're going in short a few bodies, you might as well have some backup firepower."

As I gazed at him, I realized that they were all scared for us—really, truly frightened. I brushed his cheek with a kiss. "For luck. For all of us. If Smoky returns while we're gone, tell him we had to leave." *If,* not *when.* I still wasn't sure how long Smoky could resist his father's demands.

"And you, golden priestess?" Roz dropped to Iris's side, kneeling to stare her in the face. "Do you have the weapons you need?"

She slowly nodded. "I have my wand and my daggers, and my charms and spells. But do me a favor. If Bruce calls, please tell him that I'm going to . . . to check on the obstacles that face us. He'll understand what I mean."

Menolly gave Iris a steady look, but Iris wouldn't meet her eyes, and Menolly didn't press the issue. "Come, I'll drive you to the portal" was all she said, grabbing her keys.

We followed her out to her four-seater Jag. As we sped toward the woods where Grandmother Coyote lived, a volley of raindrops spattered the windshield. I glanced at Morio, and he took my hand, squeezing tightly. But the mood had shifted from excitement to foreboding, and as we silently waved good-bye to Menolly and began our trek through the copse toward Grandmother Coyote's portal, I wondered what we'd be coming home to.

I looked up in vain, hoping to catch a glimpse of the Moon Mother, but she was hiding behind the clouds. I whispered a silent prayer to her that Stacia Bonecrusher would remain cloaked. At least until we returned home to help with the impending battle.

The portals were an interdimensional elevator, shifting us sideways through time and space. No "Beam me up, Scotty" buttons or gadgets needed, but still, the theory seemed to be the same. What Arthur C. Clarke had said about any sufficiently advanced technology being indistinguishable from magic held true, only it played the other way, too. Magic could mimic tech, even as technology mimicked magic.

The portals were set up to keep the demons where they belonged, and they were fueled by the power of the spirit seals—at least the artificial portals—but now they were breaking down. The unnatural division between the realms, which had been forged during the Great Divide when the Fae had sundered the mortal realm from Otherworld and ripped the worlds apart, was wearing thin. Even though the spirit seals were still functioning, their magic was warping, mutating, and rogue portals had been opening up all over the place.

Queen Asteria—the Elfin Queen to whom we delivered the spirit seals as we found them—and Queen Tanaquar—the new Court and Crown of Y'Elestrial, our home city-state—had set a contingent of techno-mages to try to repair the rifts that were forming, but so far, they weren't having much luck. And so the best they could do was to set guards at each portal.

One or two of the portals had imploded with their efforts. It was dangerous work and last we'd heard, one of the break-downs had worsened the rip in the fabric of space. And the fact that Shadow Wing had one of the spirit seals didn't help matters any.

As we approached the portal, Grandmother Coyote was waiting for us. She gazed at us implacably and I swallowed, trying to wrap my mind around the fact that Morio's father had spent time living with her when he was a child.

She motioned to me and I stepped forward. Hell, what had I done now? The steel-tooth crone had a certain magnetism that made her alluring in a run-to-your-death kind of way. Her face was a topographical map, ridged with the ravines and val-leys and mountains that time forged in flesh.

And in truth, no one but the other Hags of Fate would ever know if Grandmother Coyote had ever *been* young. Or if she'd been *born* at all. The Hags, along with the Elemental Lords and the Harvestmen, just *were*. The only true immortals, they'd existed long before the planet was formed, and they'd live on after the Great Mother turned to ashes in the flare of the sun's death throes.

I knelt. She tweaked her finger, motioning for me to join her. "Camille, my child, you wear a cloak of heavy magic into your homeland."

With an inward groan, I trotted over to her side. Grand-mother Coyote had a habit of handing out unasked for advice that came with a steep price, but no one in their right mind skipped town on the payment.

Sighing, I decided to skip the small talk. "I know. The unicorn horn and the cloak, but my gut warned me to take them."

"You are right to heed your intuition," she said. "But no. I'm speaking of your connection to my grandson here. The Soul Symbiont ritual. It was in your destiny to bind yourself to him and the dragon, but now the ritual will be strengthened, and so will you. Be cautious."

Oh great. Warnings. *Danger, danger, Will Robinson.* "Is there anything else I should know?" I finally asked. She'd extract payment regardless of the number of questions, so I might as well learn all I could.

Grandmother Coyote smiled softly—or as softly as the steel-toothed seer could. "Yes, as a matter of fact. There is. Illusions—both bred of magic and bred of your own fears— surround you. When you get to your home, remember this: What seems born of shadow and fire may turn to brilliance and become the path to your future. And what appears lovely and fair and wise on the outside might just be harboring dark secrets that could be your undoing."

She paused, then added, "On a separate note from the rest, walk softly, Camille. You have made an enemy and he will not easily forget you, nor what he sees as a betrayal that was inspired by you."

My heart skipped a beat. This was sounding worse and worse. The more I thought about it, the less I was looking forward to the coming trip. The Hags of Fate were seldom wrong. "Not Trillian?"

She flashed me a cagey smile, her teeth gleaming under the ripening Moon. "No, my dear, not your beloved Svartan. But I fear there will be much danger in the approaching months for you, and not all coming from the demons. There are several ways the Wheel can turn, and one of them holds an ugly and painful future for you. Be on your guard. Don't discount what has been—or what will be—threatened. You and your loves are powerful, but there are crafty agents at work who have lived far longer than you and who have no scruples."

That was the longest and clearest warning Grandmother Coyote had ever given me, other than the first time we met. I swallowed the gorge rising in my throat, not wanting to think about yet another enemy on my tail. I waited to see if she'd say more but she fell silent.

"Okay, what do you want for the information?" The cost would likely be as steep as Everest, and almost as daunting.

But she surprised me again when she shook her head. "This was a freely given gift. Because I truly fear for you, girl.

Morio, watch over her well, especially when you return from Y'Eírialiastar."

The fact that she hadn't asked for a price, and that she'd used the formal name for Otherworld sent a river of ice careening through my blood. The Hags of Fate didn't always see the complete picture, or if they did they kept it quiet, but they were never mistaken about the possibilities that lay ahead.

I said nothing, just gazed into her luminous eyes. And in the whirling reflection that gazed back at me, I saw myself careening into a treacherous cycle. I tried to look away, but it was too late. A catalyst had been set in motion and, whatever it was, was aimed directly at me. Wondering if there was a way to get off the not-so-merry-go-round, I opened my mouth to ask her for specific guidance, but she turned away and blended into the shadows.

Morio pressed his hand against my lower back and motioned to the portal, which was hidden within a large cedar. As we approached the trunk, the bark wavered and vanished and we were facing the brilliant static that surrounded the energy of the portal. It was time. Time to see my father again. Time to reunite with Trillian. Time to find out what Iris's vision was all about.

I glanced back at Iris and Morio. "Are you ready?"

They nodded. The Talon-haltija had remained silent throughout most of the journey and when Grandmother Coyote had been talking, her face had gone white as a sheet. She still looked scared spitless, but I had a feeling it wasn't for herself. And yet—she herself was traveling to face something from her past, something dark that she couldn't yet talk about.

So many secrets. So many paths that might be. So many dangers.

Taking a deep breath, I stared at the crackling sparks that would whisk us back to my homeland, and then, without a word, stepped into the maelstrom that tore apart body and soul and renewed them on the other end.

CHAPTER 9

Grandmother Coyote's portal was linked to a large cavern near the Barrow Mounds that bordered Elqaneve, the elfin city. There were several portals in the cave, and a few outside the Barrow Mounds. I looked around for one of the guards. We were to portal jump to Y'Elestrial to meet my father, then we'd jump again to Dahnsburg. Not many people could afford to take the portals. Prices were steep, and some were strictly reserved for government usage, but there were a handful open to the public and one of those in Y'Elestrial was hooked up to the Wayfarer Bar & Grill.

Near the front of the cave, I caught sight of someone we knew. Trenyth—Queen Asteria's personal assistant. I waved to him and, looking surprised to see us, he hurried over.

"Is something wrong?" he asked, his ageless gaze taking in the three of us.

"No. Well, nothing a good demon repellant couldn't take care of. But we're not here because of that. We're meeting my father, then heading to Dahnsburg where Trillian's waiting for me."

Trenyth gave me a gentle smile. "Ah, Trillian, is it? I'm so glad that he came through this alive. I felt so bad for you when we had to hide the fact that he was on a secret mission and we told you he'd vanished."

I sighed. I still hadn't forgiven them for scaring me to death, but then again, being a member of the OIA, I understood the nature of top-secret missions. "I know you did, Trenyth. You're a good man, and the Queen is lucky to have you in her service."

He blushed. "My thanks, Lady Camille. At least Trillian's free to go home with you now. With Tanaquar in control of your city, he can remove himself from the war. There are still skirmishes going on but nothing the new regime can't take care of." He flipped through a sheaf of papers. "But stay for a moment. I believe the Queen was going to send someone over to talk to you. She may prefer to do so while you're here in Elqaneve."

"But we aren't all here—" I started to say, then stopped. When the Elfin Queen called, we jumped. She was far more powerful than she looked and she was our ally. "We can spare an hour or so."

Trenyth motioned for us to take a seat while he headed over to the Whispering Mirror that was set up near the entrance of the barrow.

A thousand years ago, the Barrow Mounds had been the home of an oracle to the elves and protector of the portal. She walked in shadow. Half-Svartan, half-elf, her ability to read the future was uncanny. But she'd been killed during a skirmish with bandits and ever since, the Barrow Mounds had been haunted. The mound over the cavern was barren—no grass grew atop it, nor any plants. It was a stark hillock in the center of the lush fields of Kelvashan—the elfin lands.

As we settled down on a bench to wait, Iris tapped my arm. "Can you feel it? Spirits walk these mounds. They're here, watching us."

I glanced at Morio. He took my hand in his and we closed our eyes as we slowly breathed our way into a trance. The air was so clear and fine compared to over Earthside, and the hairs on the back of my neck began to stand. Iris was right. Spirits walked these ancient halls.

As I opened my eyes, I could see them—faint outlines of knights, wounded in battle, of elfin women so translucent I knew they must be far older than most of the Fae I'd met. They didn't notice us, didn't look at us, just wandered along their paths. I wondered why they hadn't returned to their ancestors. What kept them bound to the mortal world?

As Trenyth returned, I let out a long sigh. "Who are they? The ghosts who haunt this area? Why can't they rest?"

Looking a little startled, he glanced at Morio and then at Iris. "So you can sense them? I should have known you would, especially with the magic you two are mucking about with." He nodded to Morio and me, then turned to Iris. "And of course you would feel them, Priestess Ar'jant d'tel."

Her face clouded over. "Priestess I am, yes. But that title was stripped from my name long ago. I've no right to use it," she said, her voice strained. "Please do not call me that again."

Ar'jant d'tel . . . Ar'jant d'tel . . . The word was familiar and I struggled to remember my dialects. And then it came to me. *Ar'jant d'tel* was of the ancient tongue and meant "chosen by the gods." It usually referred to someone who had accorded an extreme honor. I sidled a glance at Iris but her face was pale and her lips were pressed tight.

Trenyth stared at her for a moment, his eyes gentle. He put one hand on her shoulder and softly said, "I did not mean to offend. Some paths are closed by chance and some by fate. And some, by the gods themselves for reasons that are beyond our ken. Rest easy, Lady Iris. You are not what you were accused of being." At her startled glance, he added, "I have many gifts and one is to read the past. Come now, all of you." He nodded to Morio and me. "Queen Asteria awaits you in the palace. She promised this won't take long."

Wanting nothing more than to corner him in a room and ask him about Iris, I managed to keep my mouth shut. As we followed him, Iris walked in front, her shoulders back and her face once again impassive.

The Barrow Mounds were on the outskirts of Elqaneve. Trenyth and two guards led us through the cobblestone streets. It was evening and the seasons were turning just as they were over Earthside. The air was chill and crisp; the stars shone brilliantly overhead without the glare of light pollution. The flower boxes that lined the houses and shops were decked with herbs rather than the spring and summer flowers, ready to harvest and dry for the winter. Soft lights glimmered from within the shrouded windows.

The few elves who were out and about gave us little notice, most just bowing as Trenyth passed by.

As I inhaled a long breath of clear, clean air, I realized how glad I was to be home again. Elqaneve might be the elfin city, but it was part of Otherworld. But even though the thought of staying here appealed to me, I knew it would never be that simple. Earthside had become home, too, and I was pulled by both sides of my heritage.

As if he could sense my conflicting feelings, Morio closed ranks and took my hand, holding it tightly as we walked, but even his touch led to more confusion. Soul-bound as I was to him and Smoky, that meant that they would have to be near me. Wherever I chose to make my home had to be a place they would be comfortable, too. Frustrated, I pushed away the yammering thoughts. Under Shadow Wing's threat, all thoughts of the future were on hold anyway.

Up ahead, the alabaster façade adorning Queen Asteria's palace shone in the evening light. The stones were quarried from the Tygerian Mountains to the west. Surrounded by gardens and stands of ancient oaks, the palace was far simpler in design than the one in Y'Elestrial. Yet, the power here was stronger.

Of all the rulers in Y'Eírialiastar—Otherworld—the Elfin Queen was among the oldest and her presence permeated the grounds of the royal court as if she, herself, were part of the land upon which it was built. Perhaps she was. Perhaps she'd become so enmeshed with her city over the millennia that one could not stand without the other.

Trenyth led us into a great hall, the throne room. Carved from oak and holly, the Queen's throne reminded me of the throne belonging to the High Priestess of the Moon Mother, but this one was more polished, not quite so wild. I glanced around for Queen Asteria, but she was nowhere in sight.

"Follow me," Trenyth said. He led us into a closed chamber that I remembered from the first time I'd stood before the Elfin Queen when Smoky, Delilah, and I had delivered the first spirit seal to her. Had it really only been a month shy of a year since we'd discovered Shadow Wing's plans and entered the war? So much had changed since then.

Thoughtful, I said nothing. Queen Asteria was staring at a map of Otherworld. She turned at our entrance, a troubled smile on her face. Motioning to the chairs, she indicated we were to take our seats at the polished table.

"Welcome, my young Moon Witch," she said, her face crinkling. Though she didn't look anywhere near as ancient as Grandmother Coyote, Queen Asteria had her own map of roads and valleys carved in her face. She turned to Morio. "And good meeting to you, youkai. Iris, I'm pleased to see you looking so well. Trenyth tells me you are making your journey to retrieve Trillian."

"Yes, we're meeting him in Dahnsburg, after we stop to see my father in Y'Elestrial. I haven't seen the city since the war," I murmured. "I'm almost afraid to see how bad it got munched."

"There was widespread destruction." Trenyth winced. "You should be prepared. The spires of Queen Tanaquar's palace will gleam again, though—so don't be too disheartened by what the war has wrought upon your homeland."

"I won't keep you long," the Queen said. "But I must tell you something. I was going to send Trenyth over to speak with you but when he said you were here already . . . Do you know why you are to meet Trillian in Dahnsburg?"

I shook my head. To be honest, I'd been wondering that myself. Dahnsburg was a port city on the western banks of the Silofel Plains, which were part of the Windwillow Valley. The Dahns Unicorns made their royal court there, but the city was comprised of many differing races of Fae and Crypto. Just what Trillian was doing there, I had no idea.

"Feddrah-Dahns's father—the King of the Dahns Unicorns—wants to speak to you. I will not tell you why, that is his concern. But I shall tell you that this meeting is vital, given the treasure you carry. I can sense that you brought the horn with you?" Her face clouded over.

A little knot of worry began to churn in my stomach. I'd gotten used to being a pawn of the Hags of Fate, and perhaps even the gods, but now the unicorns were sticking their hooves in the mix?

"If you won't tell me why the Dahns King wants to see me, then perhaps you can give me some advice for when I meet him? I don't want to piss him off, and I'm not up to snuff on my unicorn etiquette. In fact, even after meeting Feddrah-Dahns, I'm a little shaky on just how one greets four-footed royalty."

Feddrah-Dahns was the Crown Prince to the throne of the Dahns Unicorns, and he'd been the one to bring me the horn of the Black Unicorn. I liked him. A lot. But the thought of facing his father was daunting. Cryptos could be dangerous, and if Feddrah-Dahns's father had a yearbook from his younger days, he'd probably be the one voted most likely to impale. I'd heard he was stern. Fair, but stern.

Queen Asteria let out a little snort, then covered her mouth as if she'd been caught belching, but her eyes twinkled above those aged fingers. "Oh, Camille. Don't worry. You are—and always will be—a woman who plays by her own rules. My dear, you did just fine with Feddrah-Dahns. What makes you think his father won't be just as charmed?"

I grimaced, thinking of Smoky and Hyto. "I haven't had much luck lately charming fathers. And not every son is a chip off the old block." I tried to force a smile into my words, but given I was still a long way from sure that we'd be okay in that little corner of the mess that was my life, it must have come out strained, for the Queen's smile faded into concern.

"What's wrong, Camille? Has something happened? Is your father angry with you for some reason?"

I shrugged, still both embarrassed and angry by the whole affair. "No, not my father. Smoky's father. We met. He didn't care for his son's choice in brides. He's not happy. And that's not the end of the story."

Queen Asteria sat down, staring at me hard. "Be cautious, young one. Dragons can be treacherous, especially white wings and redbacks. Don't anger him if you can help it. Smoky is a fine young beast, but as you say, sons don't always take after their fathers, and if his father is truly full-blood white dragon—"

"He is," I said flatly.

"Then do not trust him. Keep an eye on your back, my dear. And Morio, keep an eye on her as well."

Great. That was the second time today Morio had been

warned to play bodyguard. I was beginning to feel like I had a big red bull's-eye painted on my back and I didn't like it. Not one bit.

Morio nodded. "I plan on it, Your Majesty."

She gave him a silent smile of approval. "Good. Back to the subject at hand. Camille, King Upala-Dahns will be offering you an opportunity, and some information. You must accept it. I promised I would say no more for now, but please—do not shirk the offer he extends to you, even though it may lead you into some danger. The potential reward is far too great."

Oh great, *more* riddles. I was used to it with Grandmother Coyote, but now Queen Asteria was playing the game, too? And "danger"—when applied to me—was code for: *You are going to get your ass hurt during this fiasco, and hurt bad.*

But I did what was expected of me. I smiled and said, "Thank you."

Morio grunted, but kept his peace. Iris just gave me one of those *you're so fucked* looks she was especially good at.

But Queen Asteria wasn't done with me yet. "I see through you, Camille. I see that partially horrified, partially skeptical look in your eyes." She leaned close. "Believe me when I tell you that you *need* to go through with this. Will you trust me?"

Something about her manner scared me. She meant business but I just didn't feel all that confident. Although come to think of it, Grandmother Coyote had echoed the sentiment. "I don't mean to offend you. I'm just tired of riddles and bumping around in the dark."

As she stood, we jumped to our feet. She nodded as Morio bowed and Iris and I curtsied. "My dear, sometimes the darkness is our friend. If Shadow Wing breaks through, trust me: The fires will rage so bright that you'll beg for the velvet womb of the night." And with that, she swept out of the room.

Trenyth motioned for us to follow him back out through the Great Hall. Along the way, I filled him in on what we'd found out—as little as it was—about Stacia Bonecrusher. He jotted down the information.

"Thank you," he said. "I'm sorry, Camille. I know it feels like you are being kept out of the loop at times, but trust me, the Queen has her reasons for it and more will be made clear in the near future."

"It's not your fault," I said, shrugging. "Sometimes I guess we're all pawns in the hands of the gods."

"And some of us just try to keep the pawns out of trouble," he retorted, an impish grin on his face. "Go and be at peace, and may your journey be smooth." He escorted us back to the portals and paid our fee to jump through to Y'Elestrial. As we entered the portal, hand-in-hand, the only thing I could think about was that I was going to see my home again, for the first time in a couple of years. I just hoped there was a *home* to go home to.

CHAPTER 10

~◦⊱~

Y'Elestrial was like no other city in Otherworld.

Located on the southern shores of Lake Y'Leveshan, the city was the last stop before the long trek south to Terial, the eastern port, and southwest to Aladril, the City of Seers.

Caravans left daily, boarded by the majority who couldn't afford to use the portals. Great lumbering wagon trains, they were pulled by teams of the *nobla stedas*, horses that had been forgotten among the mists of legend over Earthside. But in OW the breed had been cultivated for strength and skill until, over the eons, they came to outclass any other equine. Menolly, Delilah, and I'd been required to take riding lessons when we entered the OIA, and I always felt like royalty when I was astride one.

As we emerged from the portal, which rested between two great oaks next to the city gates, I took a deep breath and gazed up at the towering walls surrounding Y'Elestrial. Lethesanar had spared no expense on upkeep. The gates were forged of bronze and they had been polished to a mirrored surface. Guards lined the walls, watching the flow of traffic in and out of the city.

Unlike Aladril, Y'Elestrial wasn't closed to strangers, but it was obvious we'd been expected. One of the guards stepped out, his hand up to halt our approach. Dressed in the royal blue with gold epaulets, his blond hair waved gently in the wind. Though it was hard to tell the age of any of the Fae, except for the very old or the very young, there was a raw feeling to this man. Probably a new recruit.

I handed him my OIA badge. He glanced at it, then held it over one of the scanners the techno-mages had rigged up. A pale blue light flashed and he handed it back.

"Advisor Sephreh ob Tanu is waiting for you at the palace. Let me call a guard to escort you." He started to turn but I reached out and gently laid my hand on his arm.

"That's all right. I know the way."

He glanced at my fingers and a warm flush raced up his face. "I'm sorry, *Mish'ya*, but I have strict orders to give you a full escort. I can't allow you to enter the city without one."

I blinked. *Mish'ya* was a royal title for women of nobility. But then it hit me—Father was an advisor to the Crown. We *were* nobility now.

"We'll be fine," I started to say.

He held up one hand and shook his head, looking alarmed. "Please, don't argue. There are factions about that would still have your head. We're routing them out, but it's impossible to trace all of them at this time. The city is a dangerous place for agents who stood against Lethesanar."

And then I understood. The Opium Eater had nearly destroyed Y'Elestrial in the battle to keep the throne before she fled to the Southern Wastes. Apparently she still had bounties out on the heads of my family with her sympathizers.

"Fuck. That sucks rocks." I let out a loud sigh and the guard broke into a snicker, sobering quickly when he saw my smile.

"I'm so sorry. I didn't mean to laugh," he said, his eyes wide.

Even though I knew his worry was only because my father was the advisor to the throne now, it still felt good to wield a little clout. My sisters and I hadn't been accorded much respect when we served in the OIA over here.

"Don't sweat it. Call our escort. And don't worry, I won't report you for laughing at me. Not my style," I said, giving him a warm smile. "Just watch yourself among the commanding officers. My father being one of them."

Relief flooded across his face and he hurried off to one side, cautioning us to stay where we were.

I glanced at Morio and Iris. "You guys are in danger because you're with me. You do realize that, don't you?"

Iris cocked her head, staring at me like I'd lost my mind. "Oh, really now? And since when has anything about that little fact changed? Camille, we've been in danger every moment of every day ever since you and your sisters stumbled on Bad Ass Luke. Whether we're in Otherworld or over Earthside, it makes no difference. We're used to the thought."

"Iris is right." Morio grinned. "Get a grip, babe. You and your sisters are trouble magnets and we're all along for the ride. We're not going anywhere."

Feeling like an idiot, I shrugged. "Hey, it's late, I'm tired, and portal lag is getting to me." I'd barely finished speaking when the nice young guard returned, an official OIA carriage behind him.

"Wow, we rate the royal treatment," I whispered to Iris. "I guess my sisters and I really *aren't* considered expendable anymore."

As the guard helped me in, his fingers lingered on my arm and I gave him a long smile. As cute as he was, he seemed so young and so vulnerable. My guess was that he'd never seen battle.

And right then, I realized that I'd never be young again. Perhaps I'd never been. Not since the first time a schoolmate had shoved me in the mud because I was half-human. Not since I'd rescued Delilah from boys trying to tease her into her tabby form. Not since Mother died and I took over running the household. And not since the night Menolly broke into the house, fresh from Dredge's torture. Over the last year I'd lost my belief that everything would be okay. But in that void, I'd gained strength, resilience, and a resignation that Fate had unswerving, undeniable plans for me.

The palace seemed gaudy compared to Queen Asteria's citadel. Almost a little tawdry. I remembered the maze of outer and inner courts, and statues that stood two and three stories tall. But there had been a subtle change. As I stepped out of the carriage, I noticed that Tanaquar was renovating parts of the palace that had been destroyed during the siege. And they weren't being rebuilt the same as before. No, there were more gardens, more walkways and fountains . . . more natural elements being added. The shattered gilded columns were being replaced with subtle marble and elegant, hand-carved wood.

Our escorts guided us up the steps. Shining light from eye-catchers sparkled along the path. As a child, I'd chased the glistening orbs, trying to catch them as they zipped just out of range. But now they were a comfort, with their soft pulsating glow in shades of pink and green and blue.

As we entered the great archway that led into the main hall of the palace, someone yelled, "Camille!"

As I swung around, my father stood there, his arms open wide.

"Father!" I raced over to him and he enfolded me in his embrace, kissing my forehead. He was handsome, and I mirrored his looks. Delilah took after Mother, and nobody knew where Menolly had gotten her copper hair. But father and I were two of a kind. His hair was caught back in a braid plaited with gold and blue ribbons, and his pale skin and violet eyes were stark and silken. He held me tight, rocking gently.

After a moment, he pushed me back, holding me by the shoulders. As he looked me up and down, his voice was firm. "You're looking well. Your sisters, I trust they're in good health?"

I nodded. "They're both fine. You remember my husband Morio? And Iris?" They'd met, but I didn't know how much he'd remember of them considering the meeting had been brief and in a crowded room.

Sephreh nodded to Morio and bowed to Iris. "Lady Iris, Master Morio, good meet and welcome to Y'Elestrial. We'll be traveling to Dahnsburg tomorrow morning. Tonight, you will stay with us as our guests in our home." He stopped for a moment and turned to Morio. "And you, sir, I trust my daughter will have no complaints about the way you and the dragon are treating her?" Though he was smiling, there was an undertone of threat there, and I flushed. Fathers would be fathers, even among the Fae.

Morio cleared his throat. "If she had a complaint, she'd

bring it to us. *Sir*," he said, his eyes flashing topaz. Oops, the question had pissed him off.

Time to step in. With haste.

"Smoky and Morio are wonderful, Father. I have no complaints." Other than that Smoky was off with some bitch who claimed to be his fiancée, I thought, but I decided to keep that under wraps. Not unless I wanted Father to rush off on a fool's mission.

"And yet you go in search of Trillian." Sephreh's eyes flashed dangerously and I realized what he was so on edge about. Even with all Trillian had done for us and for the war, Father still didn't like him.

I let out a long sigh. "You know that Trillian will always be a part of my life. We forged—"

"A bond. Yes, I know. The two of you performed the Eleshinar ritual and you foolishly bound yourself to him for life. The fact that it happened doesn't mean I have to like it."

Father had never liked Trillian. In fact, when he found out that I'd given myself over to a Svartan, he'd practically thrown me out on my ass. Delilah convinced him to relent, but he'd always begrudged the relationship. Some prejudices were hard to shake. And harder still when he didn't *want* to let go of the grudge.

"Trillian helped in the war more than most. The least you can do is offer him some respect. Now, can we just go home and have a nice dinner and catch up?" As much as I loved my father, I was beginning to remember why I'd decided going Earthside might not be such a bad idea. Though I didn't want to admit it, the truth was we were too much alike. We butted heads over just about everything.

"Oh, I *respect* the man," my father said. "I just don't *trust* him. Especially when it comes to you. Anytime you give someone power over you, you become vulnerable. As a Guardsman's daughter, I thought I taught you that."

I wanted to point out that Trillian and I had power over each other. And that Father had given the Court and Crown power over him when he signed up for the Guard. But I decided to forego the debate. I'd never win, even when I was right.

"I'm hungry. Can we go home and eat?"

He smiled then. "Of course. I'm being an ungracious host."

Motioning toward the door, he added, "The carriage is waiting, but we have a stop to make first."

"So our home survived the war?" Anxious, I followed him, with Morio and Iris right behind me.

He looked crestfallen. "You're going to see a big change in the streets of our city. And at home, too, Camille, and I apologize for that. When Lethesanar placed a bounty on our heads, she pillaged our house. I managed to get all our souvenirs out in time but the furniture, all the tapestries, were destroyed or looted. Everything is new. Your aunt Rythwar helped me decorate, after she helped me retrieve the goods we put into hiding."

We swept through the halls of the palace until we came to a set of silver double doors. A contingent of guards stood at attention beside the entrance. They bowed to my father. Two attendants opened the doors for us and we filed through.

The room was windowless, and an ornate desk and chair sat toward the back. Sitting in the chair was a woman who looked familiar, and yet I knew I'd never seen her before. And then it hit me. *Tanaquar. The Queen.* She looked a lot like Lethesanar, the Opium Eater. Only, instead of hair the color of spun gold, tresses of flaming burgundy fell to her waist. Her skin was tan and her eyes gleamed with golden light. As she stood, her dress crinkled, the long folds of it gathering at her waist. She wore a golden tiara with a sparkling diamond in the center.

Father knelt at her feet, and instinctively, I curtsied. My knees were sure getting a workout today. Morio bowed low and Iris dropped to one knee.

"Rise," the woman said. Her voice rippled through the room, melodic and enticing. "Sephreh, introduce me. This would be your daughter, I presume?"

"By Your Majesty's will." My father rose, his eyes fastened on Queen Tanaquar. "May I present Camille, my eldest? And this is Lady Iris, and one of my daughter's husbands, Morio."

We waited for her to speak.

The Queen stepped out from behind her desk. She circled me, her gaze then locking with my own. "So you are the leader in our war against Shadow Wing," she said lightly. "Surely a great and horrible task for such a young woman to bear. And half-human, on top of the matter."

The leader of the war? That was news to me, but I had sense enough not to correct her.

She tapped one finger against her chin, still gazing at me. She was tall, taller than my father, almost as tall as Smoky, and she'd obviously been bred from royal stock. Her heritage was in every move she made, every gesture, every nuance of look. Tanaquar embodied everything her sister should have. The Court and Crown of Y'Elestrial would become a true monarchy, instead of a farce led by a demented dictator.

"So tell me, Camille, how goes the war?"

I flinched, wishing she'd asked any question but that one.

"Your Majesty . . . to be honest, I have no idea," I said. "We're doing our best to find the spirit seals and return them to Queen Asteria. That is our first priority. We're on the track of the new demon general that Shadow Wing smuggled over Earthside. We've kept the director of the OIA apprised. The new general is known as Stacia Bonecrusher. She's a lamia."

Tanaquar's eyes flashed and the crash of thunder echoed outside the palace. I had the uneasy feeling that there was some connection there. Just who was this Queen? We'd heard little about her when Lethesanar was on the throne, of course, but now—looking at the imposing figure who stood before me—I had the distinct feeling that our new Queen was packing more than royal blood on her side.

"You have allies in strange places, so I have heard. You mingle freely with demons and vampires and humans . . ." She paused, then her lips crinkled into a smile and I felt like the sun had come out. "You and your sisters have learned one of the most difficult lessons. Not all who appear to be our enemies are truly our enemies, and not all who claim friendship are to be trusted."

"You haven't heard anything about the sixth spirit seal, have you?" I asked impulsively. The minute the words were out of my mouth, I wondered if I'd overstepped my boundaries, but she laughed.

"I will see if we can pinpoint a location on the sixth spirit seal for you. In the meantime, focus on the Bonecrusher. Find her and destroy her. She is far, far more dangerous than you suspect." She lowered her voice. "Shadow Wing bred the Bonecrusher with one purpose: to destroy. You will find no

soft spot in her heart, no compassion. If she catches you, you
will die most horribly. Karvanak was the boy next door compared to her."

And with that, she dismissed us. We made our good-byes
and followed Father out into the hallway again.

On the way to the carriage, I thought about what the Queen
had said. If the Bonecrusher was truly that ruthless, we'd have
to develop a plan to seek and destroy. There would be no room
for errors like we'd made with Karvanak. He'd meant to kill us
but failed. Stacia wouldn't make the same mistake.

As the carriage lumbered down the streets of Y'Elestrial, I
leaned back against the seat, deep in thought. Though I barely
noticed the destruction that had been wrought on the city, it
was there, even through the veil of night. The silhouette of
mangled buildings rose into the night sky. Some were fully
collapsed, along with piles of rubble that had been blasted off
of their fronts. Y'Elestrial was one of the most beautiful cities
there was, but it had taken a beating. Tanaquar had not been
gentle in her siege.

We approached the outer circle of the city, then turned onto
a long dirt path. We were heading home. I shook myself out of
my silence and began peering eagerly out the window.

Father patted my knee. "Most of the damage to our house
has been repaired. Tanaquar paid for it to be renovated when
she appointed me her advisor. I'm just grateful your mother
didn't have to see what happened to her home. She loved this
house so much." His voice was wistful, and I leaned over and
kissed his cheek.

"Mother loved you. She may have loved the house, but
she would have gone anywhere with you. She did, in fact—
she gave up her world for you. And she never regretted it." I
noticed a strange glint in his eyes, and he whisked his gaze
away from mine. "What? What is it?"

With a shake of the head, he said, "Nothing for you to
worry yourself over. Look—we're almost home." He pointed
out the window. Nope, he wasn't going to talk, at least not
until we were alone.

I gave up and gazed out at the faint outline of the sprawling home in which I'd grown up. While it was only two stories, the house was larger than my home over Earthside, and

it sprawled across the lawn, surrounded by gardens. Father had commissioned it to be built for Mother when he'd brought her back to Otherworld, and every brick that had gone into the building of it, he'd hand-selected. A soft glow illuminated one of the windows.

"Is Leethe still with you?" I suddenly asked, hoping that our housekeeper had made it through the war. She'd guided me in learning how to run a household and pay bills and manage the staff. We only employed four or five people, most for taking care of the grounds, but Leethe and her assistant, Kayla, had been in charge of cleaning the house and cooking.

While she was alive, Mother had always insisted on cooking dinner. And we girls had learned to do our chores. If we were short with the help, we were punished. Father's relatives frowned on Mother's methods and whispered behind her back, but she didn't care, and Father stood behind her decisions in childrearing. Our family might not have been among the nobility but there was enough of the upper-crust syndrome going on that my cousins had it easy compared to us, and now I understood why Mother had been so insistent that we learn to take care of ourselves. It was truly a gift in disguise.

Father smiled softly. "Leethe and Kayla are still with me, yes. They'll have dinner on the table when we go in. But walk softly with your questions. Kayla lost her husband in the war. Lethesanar's guards killed him when he insisted on trying to protect the house. I told him to leave, to hide, but he refused. And Leethe is still pining over the good china and the antiques."

As Iris started to clamber out of the carriage, Sephreh reached up to lift her down. She blushed but thanked him, and—followed by Morio—we headed toward the house.

A cluster of eye-catchers floated up the cobblestone path that led to the entrance, and even in their dim light, I could tell that the door was new. Gone were the glorious glass panels Father had commissioned for my mother, with their intricate roses and vine work, and in their place, there was now a sturdy door of solid oak with a smaller pane of clear glass.

My heart sank. Mother had loved the stained glass. Unbidden, images of smashed windows and scarred wood flooded my thoughts. I glanced at Sephreh, but he shook his head sadly.

"I told you, there was much damage" was all he said as he opened the door and waved us through.

I walked into the foyer, breathing deeply. I was home. I had come home again, after over two years of being away.

As I looked around, everything seemed alien. Even the walls, which had been freshly repaired and whitewashed. The furniture was all new, although a number of the knickknacks had survived the siege. There was Mother's anniversary clock, and over there, the carefully crocheted afghan she'd made for the living room. Delilah had peed on it when she was a kitten and Mother had laughingly washed it by hand, taking the entire morning to spread it out *just so*, so it would keep its shape when it dried. Delilah was too little to do anything but cry when she realized how much work she'd caused.

Beneath the new furniture and fresh paint were memories of my childhood. The silver dragon box Father had given Mother for her birthday. The clay candy dish I'd made for her when I was barely three. The framed poem Menolly had written for both our parents when she first learned how to use a pencil. A wave of nostalgia swept over me and I longed for a simpler time when the worst hurts were the taunts of our classmates, when Menolly still ran under the sun, and Mother's smile radiated over all of us.

I leaned on the back of the rocking chair to steady myself, and sucked in a long, deep breath.

"Are you okay?" Morio said, slipping up to lightly rest his hand against the small of my back.

Nodding, I forced a smile. "It's just been a while. So much is the same, and so very much . . . is different."

Different not just with the house and furnishings, but with me, and with my sisters. And most of all—with the world. I tried to shake off the mood as we went into the dining room for dinner. The fire was crackling in the hearth as Leethe and I hugged and kissed, and Kayla, too. They both looked a little worn: Kayla's eyes had lost some of the sparkle they'd had before the civil war.

After dinner, which had been a thick venison stew and fresh bread, Iris and Morio gracefully withdrew to sleep, leaving my father and me alone to talk. I curled up in the overstuffed loveseat, resting my head on his shoulder as he gently patted my hand.

"Every day, I wonder if we'll come out of this alive," I said. "Every night, I go to bed, tired and worried and dreaming about demons."

"You are my daughter," he said. "You share my inability to let go of your duties, but Camille, I never, ever envisioned this life for you. Fighting demons, living among your mother's people. I hoped you would all marry and have families of your own. Of course, Menolly's . . . accident . . . changed all that."

"It wasn't an accident, Father. She was raped, and tortured, and killed, and then Dredge turned her into a vampire. Can't you bring yourself to admit what happened, even now?"

He sighed. "I know what happened, my girl. All too well. I don't like to dwell on it. But Camille, I fear for *you*. Death magic is a heavy yoke to wear. What says the Moon Mother about your studies?"

"I think she likes it," I said softly.

He shook his head. "So much death. Delilah a Death Maiden, my Menolly a vampire . . . I was proud of all of you when you chose to join the bureau of Intelligence, but I never wanted you to face the dangers you now fight. I truly do wish you'd all just married young and moved into peaceful lives."

I gave him a sad smile. "And how long would that have lasted? Until Shadow Wing found the spirit seals and ripped open the worlds? Then we'd all be dead. Or worse. Instead, because we happened to be in the right place at the right time, both Earthside and Y'Eírialiastar have a fighting chance. If we have to sacrifice our lives to grab that chance, then so be it. We are all willing."

As I stood, so tired I ached to the core, Father took hold of my shoulders. "Do you know how proud I am of you? Of all three of you?"

And then, I saw it. There in his eyes—love and pride and honor behind a wash of tears. "And we, of you. Father, please, look for love again. You deserve to be happy. We wouldn't feel badly if you found someone new to share your life with, as long as she accepted us."

He stared at me like there was something he wanted to tell

me, but then softly said, "I don't forsake women. But your mother . . . there was something about her, something I cannot forget. You and your sisters inherited that quality. A radiance that comes not from your Fae charm, but from the core of your hearts. Your mother knew who she was, and knew what she was worth. As you would say, she's a tough act to follow. But thank you for caring."

As he kissed me on the forehead and sent me off to bed, I thought about what it meant to be back here. And then, as I crawled under the covers next to Morio, I realized that no matter how much I loved this house, it was no longer my home. My anchor rested within three men, and my two sisters and Iris. And no matter where we were, as long as we were together, I would be home.

CHAPTER 11

The next morning as we waited for clearance to use the portals inside the palace, we wandered around the Great Hall and I saw just how much of the palace was under renovation. Lethesanar had apparently decided if she couldn't hold the throne and the city, she'd destroy it before her sister took control. She'd done a damned good job of tearing up the joint, as well as ripping a swath of destruction through the streets. From what I gathered, she'd also managed to kill over a thousand citizens who had switched sides on her.

Houses stood in ruins, buildings gutted from magic, fire, and ramrods. Entire stretches of the city were destroyed and there were a lot of people living on the streets and long lines of the hungry lined up at the temples begging for food.

A stone formed in my heart when I saw that the park stretching around the southern border of Lake Y'Leveshan had been thoroughly trashed. Trees were uprooted and burned, the fountains were in rubble, and the rose gardens and arbors that had been so beautiful every midsummer were shredded. Some of my happiest memories from childhood had taken place in that park, and I cried as we passed. Father patted my shoulder, but said nothing.

Sephreh was going with us. He had some sort of meeting to attend in Dahnsburg. Now, as we waited for word that the portal was ready, he wandered through the hall with Morio by his side. They were chatting about Morio's connection with Grandmother Coyote.

I glanced around, looking for Iris. She was pacing the left side of the hall, her eyes focused on the ground. I caught up with her.

"Something wrong? You seem awfully quiet this morning."

She glanced up at me, a haunted look on her face. "I've been debating on when—or even whether—to tell you this. You've seen more of my past than the others, through the inadvertent glimpse you caught of my shadow the other day."

Was she ready to talk? I leaned against the wall. "What was that thing? When you ordered it to retreat, you said it wasn't time yet. Time yet for what?"

A stricken look washed across her face and one tear slid down her cheek. "Camille, what I'm going to tell you must remain secret for now. Please, tell no one else. It doesn't involve the demons so I'm not asking you to hide anything from your sisters that would concern them."

I hated keeping secrets, but at times hiding something was a necessary evil. "Sure. I promise, as long as this doesn't involve our fight."

She cleared her throat. "The shadow is . . . was . . . my betrothed. That *thing* was once a noble snow sprite named Vikkommin. He and I were to be married, until something went horribly wrong."

I stared at her, my disbelief warring with the pain in her eyes. "Your *fiancé?* But what happened? How did he . . . How could he . . ."

She let out a low moan. "He was a priest in the order of Undutar, and I was in line to be High Priestess. We were to be married. But one night, about a month before our wedding, he called me to his room. I went, of course, and when I got there . . ." Iris's eyes filled with tears and she covered her face with her hands.

I knelt beside her, my hand on her shoulder. "What happened? Tell me."

"That's the trouble! I don't know what happened. I opened

the door, and the next thing I knew, I was bound, behind bars, waking up. They said I tortured him and turned him into that shadow creature. They said that when they found me, I was gibbering like a madwoman, that I told them I hated him. *But I loved him*! And I couldn't have done that—ripped away his body and left his spirit embedded in shadow."

I pulled her close, hugging her, holding her as she shuddered against my shoulder. Her heart was breaking. "You've never told anyone this story before, have you?"

She shook her head, wiping her eyes on her sleeve. "No," she said, staring at the floor. "I'm too ashamed."

After a moment, I gently coaxed her to look at me. "Iris, do you even have the power to do something like that?"

She sniffled. "Oh, girl, I *had* the power, all right."

"What happened after you told them you couldn't remember?"

Iris dashed at the tears but they kept coming. "I protested my innocence. They couldn't prove beyond doubt that I'd done it. For one thing, Vikkommin—or the creature he had become—disappeared that night, after they dragged me away. But he's been following me on the astral ever since. I think he believes that I actually hurt him. He never lets me forget it. He wants to kill me and drag me into the shadows with him. Maybe he's gone mad. I don't know."

"Holy hell. Are you in danger?"

"No," she said, staring at her feet. "Not at the moment. Vikkommin can't hurt me unless . . . until I return to the Northlands where he's trapped in body."

I wanted to be tactful but decided that Iris would prefer me to be myself—blunt and undiplomatic. Someone who gave a damn. "What did the temple elders do to you?"

She closed her eyes, trying to keep her composure. "They tortured me, looking for a confession. I can't talk about it—it was too painful. And like your sister Menolly, I bear scars both physical and emotional. Mine just aren't quite so apparent. When I wouldn't admit guilt, they stripped me of my title and my strongest powers, then sent me back to Finland under a curse. I can never carry a child to term until Vikkommin is avenged. That means either I find out who *did* hurt him and claim vengeance in his name, or I'll never have children, never become one of the sacred mothers, never be able to set foot in a temple to my goddess again."

The Finns were wild about motherhood, that much I knew. In fact, the mothers of their heroes were more important than the actual heroes themselves. To be stripped of her ability to carry a child was a cruel punishment. And to be cast out of her temple, even worse.

Angry that anyone would ever believe she'd ever do something that terrible, I clenched my fists. "Why did you come with us today? What are you going to do? Does this have anything to do with Bruce?"

She nodded. "Bruce asked me to marry him and I'd like to. I've grown to love him, Camille. He's a good man, and he's good to me. But I know he wants children. He's the last of his family line. He must carry on the family name. Unless I can lift the curse, I can't—in good conscience—accept his offer. I'm headed to Dahnsburg to look up the Great Winter Wolf Spirit, who spends his summers in the city. He winters in the upper Northlands, high in the mountains near the place where Vikkommin's shadow retreated. He might be able to help me track down Vikkommin and find out the truth somehow. I've tried everything else and this is the only thing I can think of."

Silently, I took her hand in mine and squeezed gently. "Does Bruce know any of this?"

Looking at me as if I was a candidate for *The Jerry Springer Show*, she shook her head. "How can I tell him what happened when I don't even know myself? I have no proof that I'm innocent. My memory seems permanently sealed from the moment I walked into Vikkommin's room until I woke up in the cell. I've tried everything I can to break through the wall but nothing works. The fact that they stripped my title and my strongest powers from me and cursed me effectively brands me as a pariah. And . . ." she paused, her lower lip trembling.

"And what?"

"What if I *did* do it?" she whispered. "What if some horrible part of me—buried deep inside—took over and tore him inside out? What if I turned him into a shadow? What if I *am* the one who destroyed both our lives? If I find out that I'm truly a monster, then I couldn't live with the knowledge. No, best I try to uncover the truth before Bruce knows anything. If I didn't do it, I'll be free to tell him everything. And if I did . . ."

I gave her a long look as she stood there, staring ahead at the wall. "Then, what? What would you do?"

"I don't know," she said in a strangled voice. "I can't think that far ahead. The thoughts are too frightening."

At that moment, my father called to us and Iris quickly wiped away all signs of the tears. I forced a smile as we headed over to the men, but inside all I could think about was what Iris might do if she discovered that she'd been responsible for destroying the man she had loved.

The portal jump to Dahnsburg was like most of the others, but the city was a world apart from Y'Elestrial. For one thing, Dahnsburg was a port city—the western port, to be exact. The smell of brine and seaweed hung heavy in the air.

I sucked in a deep breath, closing my eyes as a crisp breeze swept past. That was one thing I'd loved about moving Earthside to Seattle. We were near the ocean. There was nothing quite as mesmerizing as standing on the pier, watching as the waves of the inlet ebbed and flowed, feeling the call of the Ocean Mother as she filtered into the channels and rivulets that formed Puget Sound.

And here, instead of the Pacific, we stood on the edge of the Wyvern Ocean, a vast body of water that led to the mythic lands of Finnish and Norse repute—the wide woodlands of Tapiola, and beyond that, the fjords of Valhalla and Asgard. And in the far, far north—the lands of Pohjola, which were rumored to contain natural portals leading into the realm of the Northlands.

As we stepped out of the portal, we found ourselves on a butte overlooking the water. The portal itself was set between two standing stones guarded by three Dahns Unicorns. At least, I assumed they were of Dahns descent. Their manes streamed along their backs, and I was surprised to see one of them wasn't silken as snow, but instead dappled gray on white. All three had silver horns, which meant they were female. Males bore golden horns.

One of the unicorns stepped forward and tossed her head, snorting.

"My name is Sheran-Dahns. You are the Moon Witch, Camille. Correct?" She spoke in Melosealfôr, a beautiful and rare dialect of Crypto that all Moon Witches learned, and that the Dahns Unicorns had perfected over the years.

I inclined my head and gave a quick curtsy. "I am. This is my father, Sephreh ob Tanu, Advisor to Her Royal Highness Queen Tanaquar of Y'Elestrial. And this is my mate and husband Morio, and my friend Iris."

The unicorn blinked and her long lashes fluttered in the wind. She had the most lovely eyes—brilliant green against the dappled coat, and they were like twin pools of a verdant pond. With a soft whinny, she dipped her head in my father's direction and spoke in the common tongue. "Your Excellence, we welcome you and your party to Dahnsburg. King Upala-Dahns awaits you in the palace. Please to follow me."

Morio looked at me, slightly confused. He spoke a few words of the common tongue—I'd taught him enough to squeak by, but he wasn't fluent in it yet. I whispered a quick translation to him.

We swung in behind the unicorn as she lightly picked her way down a sloping path. The gentle decline ran four or five hundred yards from the city proper, parallel to the shore below before swinging inland. There were few trees on the butte, or near the shore. The city was situated in the Silofel Plains, a long, narrow stretch of land that was dotted with tall grasses and egg-sized pebbles and sandy soil. The Plains buttressed up against the Windwillow Valley. Dahnsburg itself was positioned on the Bay of Tides.

The morning was overcast and by the looks of the water, a storm was coming in from the ocean. Gray thunderheads swept in from across the sea, driving a force of wind before them that churned the breakers, sending a frothy surge of waves crashing to shore. Electricity crackled through the clouds, saturating the air.

I sucked in a deep breath of the supercharged air as a ripple of sparks surged through my body. At times like these, I missed this world, where everything was so vibrant and alive. Oh, the clouds and the land were alive over Earthside, to be sure, but here they were right in your face, and there was no denying the sentience of the elements.

Morio reached for my hand and I squeezed his fingers. He flashed me a giddy grin.

"You can feel it, too," I said, delighted.

He nodded. "The first time I was here, it wasn't so present. Perhaps because we were in Aladril. But here . . . on the edge of the ocean . . . I feel if I just closed my eyes I could see the Elementals dancing around one another. Everything is so vivid."

"Vivid is good," I said.

Father glanced at us. He'd caught what we were saying and now he winked at me and smiled. In that brief moment, I could tell that he was glad I was home. He must be lonely. Right then I decided that—war or no war—my sisters and I had to find him a wife. He needed someone, and though I cherished my mother's memory, Father needed to move on. To open his heart and his life again.

At that moment, we reached the gates of the city. Dahnsburg was well-fortified. To the north, it faced the Wyvern Ocean. The other three sides were surrounded by large stone walls, with turrets evenly spaced around the top of the walk wall. Each of the three walls had its own gatehouse with a portcullis ready to drop in case of invasion.

"Do you get many threats here? You aren't very close to Darkynwyrd or Guilyoton."

Sheran-Dahns glanced back at me.

"No," she said, her voice lightly trilling over the words. "But there are plenty of Cryptos who roam the Windwillow Valley with nothing but darkness in their hearts. And there are trolls in the Nebulvuori Mountains who travel this way. Thistlewyd Deep lies to the east, and while not as dangerous as Darkynwyrd, the blessed woodland harbors those both good and ill. The ill-tempered often come to see what trouble they can stir up in the city. And then there are the Meré who attempt raids from the ocean."

I nodded, catching up to walk by her side. "True enough. No place is safe, not really."

Sheran-Dahns glanced down at me. Her eyes glowed with a soft light and I wanted to fall into that brilliant green and lose myself. She snorted, just a little, and then reached down and lightly pressed against my arm with her muzzle. The hair was velvety soft, and her nose was damp. I looked up into her eyes.

"All of the Dahns Unicorns know about the demons, Camille. Remember this: You can only do your best, young Windwalker. Don't fret, and don't second-guess yourself." The way she said *Windwalker* didn't make my skin crawl. In fact, it felt almost like a compliment.

"Thanks," I said, impulsively reaching up to pat her side. "It's hard not to worry, but you're right. We can't always win the day. I just hope we win in the long run, because the alternative isn't such a hunky-dory deal."

She snorted again and shook her head, her mane billowing out like a woman on a shampoo commercial. Damn, whatever she used for hair care, I wanted some. Just then, our path forked onto the main road leading in through the west gate of Dahnsburg.

Sheran-Dahns led us to the gate, where a carriage waited, hooked to a team of *nobla stedas*. Once again, it seemed we were to ride through the streets in luxury. I'd gotten used to the cars over Earthside, but when we'd lived in Y'Elestrial, most of the city population walked wherever they went. As my father reached for my hand to give me a boost up, I glanced back at the unicorn.

"Thank you," I said, smiling at her. "And please, if you ever come Earthside, you're welcome at our house. Always."

She dipped her head. "I will remember the invitation. You never know what's going to happen, Camille." Turning to gaze at my father, she added, "Advisor Sephreh, I trust your visit will be a pleasant one. The guard will take you to the palace in safety. Good day." And just like that, she was gone.

The guard in question was Fae, that much I could tell, but it was hard to peg which branch of the racial tree he'd fallen from. Pale to the point of gray, his hair was slicked back into a ponytail. The color was the faintest of blues amidst a silver wash. He looked old, or at least as old as just about any Fae I'd ever met, and he waited for us to seat ourselves in the carriage before climbing atop and picking up the reins. As the horses began to move, I leaned forward, wanting to peek through the window at the city as we passed.

Dahnsburg reminded me of Terial. And, in some ways, of Seattle. All port cities seemed to have a sensation of openness— an expansive air to them. Maybe it was the fact that they bordered coastlines, with wide, unending stretches of water lapping at their shores. Maybe there was an international feel to the air—with peoples of all races and countries journeying in through the shipping lines. Whatever the case, Dahnsburg gave the impression of being vast and roomy. I also sensed there would be more than one escape route should we need one.

The architecture was light; the buildings large and made of stone and adobe. They were whitewashed, though, and throughout the city, I noticed that the streets were clean and litter-free. The roads were wide, too—wider than those in Y'Elestrial. I noticed the number of unicorns wandering through the streets, along with a few centaurs and a handful of giants, and realized that the city had to be built to a larger scale to accommodate the size of the Cryptos.

Trees were rare, but we saw a few. They were similar to the palm trees over Earthside, but I knew them as trehavé—hardier and more suited toward cooler climates than the date palm. The trehavé bore fruit that made wonderful mixed drinks. At the thought of a drink, my stomach rumbled. We'd eaten breakfast but portal jumping sucked the energy right out of me.

The open market was jumping, but even amid the chaos of the street fair, there seemed to be an organization to the venue. We passed by hagglers arguing with vendors, and odd-looking creatures that I couldn't identify. But amidst all the fluttering awnings of the stalls of food and fish, the carts of rugs and clothing, a sense of lawfulness permeated the crowd.

I tapped my father on the arm. "What's going on? I've never seen people in an open market so well behaved."

He laughed. "Camille, you forget your social science studies. The Dahns Unicorns are extremely harsh on rule breakers. Thieves, brawlers, all the petty assaults are harshly punished. It's far worse for murderers and rapists, of course, but crime simply doesn't pay here. It's not worth the risk of getting caught. King Upala-Dahns is reputed to be a severe leader. He keeps a tight rein on his people, if you'll forgive the pun."

Oh great, and I was scheduled to have a nice long chat with him. I just hoped Feddrah-Dahns would be there. I liked Feddrah-Dahns. Feddrah-Dahns liked *me*. He knew what to expect out of me. But first . . . before facing the unicorn king, I wanted more than anything to see Trillian. Although, while I wouldn't admit it to anybody, I was a little worried about what he would say once he found out I was married. To Dragon Dude and Fox Boy, as he'd put it.

But beyond the worry over my love life, I couldn't help but wonder how Trillian's months caught up in the war had affected him. Would he be suffering from some post-traumatic stress disorder? Had he been in active combat all this time? Or hiding, spying his way through the months? I still had no idea what he'd been doing for Tanaquar.

Trillian was not an easy man. He could just as soon slit a throat as kiss it, but when he was devoted to someone, his loyalty came with the promise of his life, should need be. I loved that he was blunt, that he was direct, refusing to pussyfoot around. He didn't like women who shied away, who refused to stand up for themselves and be who they were.

Morio leaned over and whispered in my ear. "Are you all right? I can smell you. You're aroused and yet . . . there's fear on your scent."

I shook my head. I didn't want to talk about my concerns over Trillian in front of my father. He'd only snipe against my lover. As caring and fair as Father could be, he wore his prejudices like a cop wears his gun—as a warning to keep away. The fact that he'd apologized to Menolly for pushing her away when she was turned into a vampire still amazed me. And she had confided in me that she wasn't sure he fully meant it.

"I'm fine," I whispered back. "I'll tell you later."

Morio lowered his voice even more. "Trillian?"

I nodded.

"As you wish. We'll talk later." Morio wrapped his arm around my shoulders.

Iris glanced at us, a wash of worry beneath her smile. She caught my gaze and shrugged, shaking her head with a "what can you do" look in her eyes.

"How far to the palace?" She adjusted her skirt and slid her hand in the pocket, pulling out a box of Milk Duds. I held out my hand, putting on a sad-puppy face. Morio did the same. "Oh for heaven's sake, you two are hopeless. Here, you may have a few but next time bring your own snacks."

Father looked at the box. "What are those?"

"Candy," I said.

"Your mother used to love chocolate, but I never understood why," he said, shaking his head when Iris offered him some. "Thank you, Lady Iris, but no, I'm not fond of sweets."

I popped one of the chocolate caramel drops in my mouth and chewed. "I never understood that about you. Though Delilah's more of a sweet freak than I am. Oh, Morio managed to find a way to flavor the blood Menolly buys to drink while she's hanging out at home—he can enchant it to other flavors now." I watched Father's face, wondering what he would say.

A shadow passed across him, but then he smiled. "I'm glad she has some comfort. There's so little we can give to her, with all that's happened. After you told me what she'd been through, I spent some time in penance for treating her as harshly as I had. I have a surprise for her, but it's in the making and I don't trust you to keep a secret."

When I started to protest, he held up his hand. "I love you, my dear, but you and your sisters always did share secrets. Your mother and I couldn't tell any of you something without the others knowing before we'd turned our backs."

Laughing, I swallowed the candy and peeked out the window as we entered the gate to the inner courtyard of the palace. "That doesn't look like any palace I've ever seen."

King Upala-Dahns had a court fit for a unicorn king. Or a horse. Situated within a series of sprawling gardens, the entire court was surrounded by a series of golden canopies to shelter against the rain. Heavy ivory panels hung from the canopies and formed the roofs. Embroidered with golden silk, they were held back by burgundy sashes, ready to close when the storms arrived. The palace looked mobile, as if it could be packed and moved within hours. *Like the hospital on M*A*S*H*, I thought. *Only much nicer.*

The inner court was surrounded by a wall, with permanent dwellings within for all the two-legged courtiers.

The carriage pulled to a stop and we made sure we looked presentable while waiting for the coachman to open the door. But when the door swung wide, the face staring up at me was not that of the driver. Instead, his skin gleaming jet in the shimmer of the overcast skies, his hair as silver as the dagger attached to my thigh, with hints of cerulean flowing through the long strands, his eyes as blue as the ocean herself . . . there stood my Trillian.

CHAPTER 12

❦

"Trillian!" I flew out of the carriage, landing hard in his arms as I covered him with kisses.

He held me tight, then pushed me back a moment, cupping my face in his hands. His eyes were cool, but behind that cold arrogance I knew so well lurked a whisper of ghosts, a skittering that told me he was haunted by something. Whatever it was had to have happened in the past six months since he'd disappeared, because it had never been present before.

"Camille, my Camille." His voice was steady, but then he pulled me to him and his lips were fastened on mine, and I burned with the fire his touch always set off in me. Trillian, not my first lover, but my first *love*. Trillian, my first heartbreak. Soul-bound as I was with Morio and Smoky, I'd long before given myself over to this man in a ritual older than the Elfin Queen herself. No matter what else happened, he was my alpha.

I pressed against him, aching to drag him to the ground right there, to feel him in me again, to know for sure that he was safe and back with me. His fingers slid along my back, the gleaming jet of his skin glowing under the morning light. He'd always been trim and muscled, but now I could tell that he'd buffed up as my hands roamed his body, and the sexual tension that had been present between us since the first day we met kicked itself into high gear.

Panting raggedly, I pulled away as Father joined us. He sighed.

As I gazed into Trillian's eyes, they took on a gleam of victory, and the edge of his lip quirked into a sardonic smile as he inclined his head in a polite nod.

"Advisor Sephreh, how good to see you again," he said, his arm snaking around my waist as he pulled me close to him.

Father cleared his throat. "Trillian, as always, I'm glad you're well. Don't feel you have to stand on ceremony with me. I won't. But then, you know my feelings about you and my daughter."

Whoops, we were being blunt here, so it seemed.

Trillian dismissed the comment with a wave of the hand. "Over the years, you've made your disapproval abundantly clear. I don't expect that to change. So I accept your greeting for what it is." He reached out with one hand and my father let out a long huff, but took it, rolling his eyes.

Just then, Morio and Iris joined us, and Trillian let out a short cry. He leaned down to hug Iris. "My lady," he said, gently. "I did not expect you to be joining us but I'm happy to see you."

Iris had always been able to tame Trillian—just like she was able to keep Smoky in line. Whatever charm the woman had, I envied her. She could stop an argument with a soft-spoken word. Nobody ever laughed at her when she complained. Now, she broke out of her gloom and kissed him on the cheek.

"Trillian, I'm so glad you're well. We've missed you sorely."

"I'm sure some more than others," Trillian said, turning to Morio. The two men stood for a moment, then Morio clasped Trillian in an embrace and Trillian returned the hug, clapping Morio on the back. "Fox Boy, it's good to see you. Have you been taking care of my woman for me?"

Uh-oh. Now was so *not* the time to spill the fact that I'd married Morio. Or Smoky. I prayed that Morio would keep his mouth shut, but where men and testosterone were concerned, there was no telling whether the big brain in their skull would override the little brain in their pants.

Morio glanced at me, a teasing grin on his face, then nodded. "Smoky and I have kept her safe, but truly, you have been missed."

"So, now that the reunion's over, when do we see the King?" My father interrupted us, still looking put out as his gaze fell on Trillian. I let out a low growl. He didn't like him just because he was Svartan. That was the *only* reason, and it was getting on my nerves.

"Give it a break, Father. Trillian's been missing for six months—"

"It's all right, Camille." Trillian kissed my forehead.

"No, it's *not* all right."

"Your father is more concerned with matters of state than our love life. In fact, I'm here to take you to King Upala-Dahns. I've been working with the Dahns Unicorns for the past couple of months. Your father knows all about it."

That stopped me cold. Working with the unicorns? Tanaquar sent Trillian on some odd missions, all right. I was dying to know what he'd been up to during the time he'd been missing. I'd finally accepted that his disappearance had to go unquestioned, but now surely he could tell me what had been going on.

Father let out a short laugh. "Yes, I know and that's why I'm so anxious. Camille, Trillian's correct. While I make no pretenses to liking the fact that you are a couple, the subject is moot and has been for a long time."

"Then what is it?"

"I'm impatient because I must discuss certain matters with the King. There are still renegades supporting Lethesanar roaming the land, as well as other concerns that affect both Dahnsburg and Y'Elestrial, the demon menace among them. As a member of the Intelligence Agency, you should understand how fatal it can be to jump to conclusions."

I let out a long breath. "Right. Okay then. So will we see Feddrah-Dahns today? I'd like to pay my respects to him. I miss him." I'd grown fond of the Crown Prince during his brief stay over Earthside and thought about him every time I used the horn of the Black Unicorn.

"Oh yes, you'll see him. But first, the King wishes to speak with your father." Trillian motioned to two Dahns Unicorns

standing nearby and they loped over. They wore sashes desig-
nating them as members of the royal guard. "His Excellence,
Advisor Sephreh ob Tanu from Y'Elestrial is ready for his
audience with His Highness. Please escort him into the throne
room."

One of them whinnied, tossing his mane, and turned to
canter toward the central tent. Father followed, speaking in
soft tones to the other guard who walked by his side.

I watched them go, wondering what was up, but it wasn't
my place to ask. By the time I spoke my first word, I'd learned
that state secrets were just that. Many times Father had come
home burdened with information that he couldn't share with
us. As the daughter of a Guardsman, I'd grown up accepting
hierarchy and protocol as a matter of fact.

Turning back to the others, my gaze fastened on Trillian.
The tension between us was palpable, a hunger that throbbed.
Morio looked at the two of us, then motioned to Iris.

"Let's explore the surrounding gardens," he said.

She gave him a brief smile. "You mean, let's give them
some privacy? Good idea. Meanwhile, I'm looking for someone in the city and you might be able to help me find him. The
Great Winter Wolf Spirit, to be precise."

"Who's that?" Morio asked. He glanced back at me and
blew me a kiss, then followed Iris to the outer gardens.

I turned to Trillian, one thing on my mind. "Is there a
place?" My voice was husky, and I tried to calm the trembling
in my stomach. I'd tell him about Smoky and Morio in a while
but right now all I could think about was how much I needed
him. "Do we have time?"

Trillian gazed at me, his lips so full and luscious I wanted
to bite them. "Come." He held out his hand.

We hurried down a side street so small it might be an alley
until we came to a door leading into a two-story building. Trillian pulled out a key and unlocked the door, and I followed
him into a narrow foyer. The hallway led into a spacious
apartment.

"Who lives here?" I asked, gazing at the finely crafted furniture and antiques that littered the room.

"I do," Trillian said. "The King furnished me with this
place during my stay." He turned then, dropping all pretense.

"Get your ass over here," he said, opening his arms. "I need you, woman."

With a gleeful cry, I threw my arms around his neck as his lips began to trail hot kisses down my chest. He walked me backward, still kissing me, into a bedroom, all the while working at the zipper of my bustier. By the time we neared the bed, my breasts were free and he pushed me down to land on the feather mattress covered with a linen bedspread.

I let out a long moan as his lips sought my nipple and his hand snaked under my skirt. He slid his fingers under the silk of my panties, fingering my clit, tweaking it with soft flicks as he buried his face in my breasts.

"I've missed you so much," he growled. "I've missed your breasts and your body and your pussy and your lips . . . Camille, I've missed *you*, more than I ever thought I could."

I reached for his trousers, tugging on the belt. He leaned back on the bed, letting me unbuckle him and slide the material down over his hips. His cock was rigid, dark, and pulsing. I remembered it all *oh so well*, the smooth skin, the salty taste of him. Slipping out of my skirt and panties, I started at his feet, crawling up him, rubbing against him as he laughed in delight, low and throaty. I pressed my breasts against his legs, trailed my nipples up over his hips.

He let out a low grunt as I pulled him to his feet. I sat on the edge of the bed, my legs spread as he pressed his shaft against me. It nestled between my breasts and I squeezed them together, holding him tightly as he began to thrust. My breath came heavily as I gazed at the tip of his cock rubbing between my breasts. Drops of pre-cum clung to the tip, tantalizing and smelling of salt and musk and fresh sea breezes.

"Damn it, Camille, you make me hornier than any other woman ever has," he said, his voice ragged. "How did I get so lucky?"

"Thank the Fates," I murmured, unable to stand it another minute. I bent down to tickle the head of his penis. He let out a shout as I began to work him, my tongue sliding up and down his length, swirling around the smooth skin, then fluttering lightly against the head.

He thrust up to meet my waiting lips and I pursed them tightly, so he had to slowly force himself inside my mouth, offering the resistance that I knew drove both of us wild. He inched his way in, my teeth lightly grazing the skin as he filled me full with the taste of him. He braced his hands on my shoulders and I began to suck, softly at first, then hard, sliding my mouth up and down his shaft as I encircled the base with one hand and cupped his balls in my other, squeezing just enough to make him gasp.

"Stop," he thundered, pulsing so hard I thought he was going to come right there, but he managed to keep control as I broke away.

Feeling heady with power, I leaned back on the bed as he slipped his head between my legs, bracing my knees over his shoulders as his mouth sought my center. Now it was my turn to cry out as he laved tongue against clit, sending me along an ocean of pleasure, each wave higher than the last.

I let out a series of sharp cries as the orgasms began, a string of minor explosions rocketing through me, but before they ended, he rolled over and pulled me on top of him. His touch sent me into another tailspin of hunger as I straddled his body, aching to feel him inside me.

With a triumphant shout, I plunged down as he held his cock rigid and upright for me. I slid down the length, reveling in the feel of his penis. As I sank onto his balls, he reached down and began to finger me and I ran my fingers over my nipples, then pressed my breasts hard, rubbing them with abandon.

One hand on my waist to steady me, with the other he played at my clit, stroking me as we synchronized movements. As he began to thrust, I rode him hard as my breath came in ragged pants. He clasped my waist with both hands and rolled me over again, this time onto my back while he was still inside, then hammered against me, his balls bouncing as he thrust himself into my core, hard and fast.

Then, with one last thrust, he drove down, impaling me. I let out a sharp cry as the orgasm rocketed through me. Trillian arched his back, his arms pressed on the bed to either side of me, and I felt his warm explosion as he came with a loud groan, so deep within me it felt as though he were trying to reach my center core with his cock.

Limp, exhausted, he slowly rolled off of me and I curled

up in his arms, his semen trickling down my leg. There were no words for sex like that. Nothing save the warm afterglow of being thoroughly, totally, wrung out.

After a moment, he stroked my face and kissed my nose. "You like fucking me, baby?"

"Oh hell, yes." I let out a contented sigh.

"You love riding my cock?" he asked gently.

"I love *you*, and your cock."

"So when were you going to tell me?" he whispered.

"Tell you what?"

His eyes narrowed as he leaned up against the headboard. "That you married Fox Boy and the lizard?"

Oh crap, he already knew! And one look at his face told me that he wasn't a happy camper. I scrambled to sit up. "Trillian, I—"

He slowly stood. Even when he was naked, he wore his power and charm like a pro. He could stand in front of a crowd without his clothes and nobody would ever think to point it out to him.

"You what? I knew you wanted the lizard, and I accepted it. You're a woman with lusty needs, but to go behind my back and bind yourself to him? Fox Boy I can somewhat understand. I accept that you have a connection with him. But the lizard only had claim to you for one week. You want to tell me what the fuck happened, my little heartbreaker?"

I slowly slid off the bed. Trillian was angrier than I ever remembered seeing him. "You vanished and I thought you'd been captured by the goblins. The only hope we had of finding you was to home in on your energy and there was one way of doing that. I had to increase my ability to sense where you were. And the best option I had was to bond with Morio and Smoky to give me that extra boost in power."

"Give me a break. You couldn't wait to pull Smoky into the mix. Fox Boy I can live with, but the lizard?" His eyes were blazing now, and he threw my clothes at me. "Get dressed. The King's going to want to see you soon."

"How can you be such an ass? You know I'm telling you the truth. You know that I was worried sick about you." Now furious myself, I glanced around the room for a washbasin. "Do you at least have a bath so I can wash up a little?"

"Why, traitor? Don't like the memory of me in your pussy? Worried that your reptilian lover will smell me on you? Worried that he might be offended I fucked you? Why didn't he come with you today? Does he have better things to do than guard the woman he's married to when she journeys to a dangerous land? At least Morio had the guts to come with you. I'll have to hand it to him, he's got a sense of honor." His face was clouded with jealousy. I couldn't believe he'd gone from being so caring to such a butthead in under a minute.

"Record time, dude," I said, yanking on my clothes. "Go ahead and fly off the handle before you know what the hell's going on, you idiot! *You're* the one who told me to turn to Smoky if something happened to you. Well, as far as I knew, something *did* happen to you and I was beating my head against the wall trying to figure out how to rescue you!"

"I told you not to try! I told you not to come after me if something happened. I had to stop you from trying to find me because I knew this was going to be a long, dangerous undercover mission and I couldn't let you blow it for me. I couldn't let you put yourself in danger!"

We were both shouting now, once again back to the hate part of our love-hate relationship. In a weird way, it felt all too familiar and comfortable.

"Oh for the sake of the gods. Cover yourself up. You're bouncing like a pair of jingle balls." I threw his pants and belt at him. "Why the hell did you tell me to turn to Smoky if you knew what was going to happen? Good gods, man, are you really that stupid? I was crazy to ever get involved with you, but fat lot of good hindsight does me now."

Trillian let his clothes fall without trying to catch them. He leapt forward, trembling as he stood there, his fists clenched. "Camille, I told you to turn to Smoky if something happened to me because . . . because . . ."

"Because *you knew he could protect me*. That's what you said back then." I wanted to cry but I was too angry. "And now that I did what you told me to, you're jumping down my throat, calling me a traitor. Don't you realize how terrified we all were? How terrified I was?"

He said nothing, just stared at me. I couldn't read the look on his face now. He just waited for me to continue.

"I thought the goblins had you. I thought you were being *tortured*. I thought you were going to *die*. So I married Smoky, yes. And Morio. And we worked on tracing you—unsuccessfully, I might add. You're damned good at hiding your signature. There were times that—in my heart—I was ready to give up. To accept that you were never coming back."

"Why didn't you?" His voice had gone scary quiet.

"Because I love you, damn it. I couldn't give up hope. And then I ran into Darynal on a trip to Darkynwyrd and he told us he'd seen you. You don't know how incredibly happy I was, even though I was furious. But at least I knew you were alive and on a secret mission, even though I didn't know if you were ever coming back to me. Morio and Smoky kept me going during the past six months, you moron. Because without them, I would have been lost, thinking you might never return."

And then I ran out of steam as the worry and stress of the past few months caught up with me. I dropped to the bed, staring numbly at my feet.

"Camille?" Trillian's voice was low, the accusation as suddenly gone as it had come. "Camille, are you okay?"

I shrugged. "How the hell should I know? I'm just a pawn in this goddamn game the Fates have going on. I'm just here for them to use and abuse, to steal the phrase a certain creep recently used on me." I cocked my head to one side and stared up at him. "You want to hate me? Fine. Go ahead, get in line. I love you, but I can't do this. I can't play these testosterone games. We're in this together, Trillian. Delilah and Menolly, Morio and Smoky and Iris and Vanzir—"

"Vanzir? Who's that?" He frowned.

"Why? Worried I'm fucking somebody else? Don't be, he's not really my type, but he's on our side and that's what counts." A bitter taste settled on my tongue. What the fuck had I expected? I knew Trillian wouldn't be happy with the situation. I should have anticipated him setting me up like this, though I never thought he'd do it right after we had sex. And speaking of sex . . .

"While we're on the subject, why did you fuck me if you already knew about Morio and Smoky? You just want to get in one good last screw before you kick me out of your life?"

That did it. Trillian dropped to his knees beside me, his eyes downcast. He reached for my hand and I yanked it away.

"I'm sorry, Camille. I apologize. I just get so . . . you do something to me that no other woman does. You always have, from the first time I set eyes on you in the Collequia. Svartans aren't supposed to mate for life, not like this. But from the first time you told me off . . . the first time you kissed me . . . the first time I took you to bed and tasted just how sweet you are. I knew from the beginning I'd never be able to forget you."

Hello, this was new. Trillian detested sentimentality. What the hell was going on? "Are you okay? You aren't sick or anything, are you?" I gazed into his eyes, trying to read him.

He reached for me again and this time I let him take my hand. He stroked my palm gently, then wrapped his fingers over my own.

"No, I'm not sick. The past months while I've been on assignment, I saw more death and torture than I ever wanted to. Up close and personal. You weren't far off base in your worries. There was a point where Lethesanar's men caught me. They decided to teach me a lesson before handing me over to the Opium Eater. They . . ."

He choked, his words thick in his throat as he stared hard at the floor. My gut told me that something horrible had happened. I put my other hand on his.

"Whatever it is, you can tell me. We're two of a kind, Trillian. I won't turn away from you." And I meant every word.

Slowly, he met my gaze. "One of the guards was a big bruiser. They caught me in the forests of Darkynwyrd, a couple of days after I stopped at Darynal's. Camille, you know I'm no lover of men. It's not in my nature."

Oh hell. I knew what was coming and I didn't want to hear it. It would kill his ego to admit it, but as the words began to spill out, I realized that he needed to talk. To tell me his horrible secret.

"Strall. That was the guard's name. The night they caught me, they dragged me over next to the fire where he was waiting. The men held me down, pushed me onto my knees in front of him, and he forced me to blow him. And then, when I was done, the men turned me over and held me down while he reamed me up the ass."

Trillian stared at the wall as he spoke, his voice clear and unwavering, but the control he was exerting over his emotions was so tremendous that I could actually feel it vibrate through him.

I didn't know what to say. I wanted to pull him into my arms but I knew that it wasn't the right time. He wasn't done talking, so I just squeezed his hand, bringing it up to my lips where I gently kissed his palm.

Trillian's mouth tightened. "This went on for three nights. The fourth night, I'd had enough. I figured it was better to die than let them abuse me any further. But when Strall came to me that night, the other men weren't with him. I suppose they were off gathering firewood. They'd gotten lazy, complacent out there. Stupid motherfuckers."

"Maybe they thought they'd broken you," I whispered.

He shrugged. "Perhaps. But it never pays to take chances in Darkynwyrd. Or with a Svartan. Or a mercenary. Anyway, Strall had to untie me in order to get what he wanted. I waited for the right moment. When he grabbed me by the hair and was forcing his cock toward my mouth, I took one big bite and spit it out on the ground. While he was screaming, I took his knife and eviscerated him."

His voice was deadly calm. Trillian could be ruthless. I knew right there that none of the men had made it out alive, and that they'd all died with fear in their eyes.

"As the other men came back one by one," he continued, "I surprised them. They were carrying firewood. They'd gone a ways into the forest and apparently hadn't heard him scream. Either that or they thought it was me. They paid the price for their lack of caution."

"Did you make them hurt, love?" I whispered, leaning close to his face.

He nodded.

"Good. I hope they knew you were going to kill them."

Lethesanar was famous for her tortures, and she'd taught her most fawning guards well. My father had stayed on the perimeter of the Guard Des'Estar as things grew worse and the men grew more violent. Had he ever witnessed events like this? Had he been forced to stand by and watch? I didn't know. But then again, Father had been cross-posted, working with both the Guard and the OIA. Everyone had known how strict he was, so chances were any raping and pillaging had been done well out of his sight.

Trillian sat on the bed next to me, his shoulders slumped. "I didn't want to tell you. I didn't want you to know how bad things were. After I escaped, I managed to catch up with some of Tanaquar's forces and they guided me safely back to her camp. I'd been searching for your father, but apparently he managed to escape on his own. After that incident, I spent some time helping out with interrogations, but I'd lost my appetite for it. I'm a mercenary, yes, but I'm not a sadist. Not unless the situation demands it."

I shook my head. "I know you're not." I paused, then said, "Chase was captured by the Rākṣasa. We're not sure just what went on, but at best, he lost part of his little finger. At worst . . . we don't know. We saved him, but the experience changed him. How could it not? Delilah doesn't talk about it much and he won't talk about it at all, but I can see it in his eyes."

"Fucking demon spawn," Trillian said, hitting the wall next to us. "Chase is human. He isn't cut out to withstand that sort of torture. What else has happened, my love? I knew about Smoky and Morio and you. Your father forewarned me. Now I'm thinking he hoped it would chase me off your tail, but the truth is, Camille, as angry as I was—as much as I hate sharing you with that lizard—you and I are forever bound."

I filled him in on everything from Karvanak to losing the third spirit seal to the Karsetii demon that had almost devoured Delilah's soul, to the nerds from hell and what we were up against now.

"We've been busy," I said softly. "Trillian, now that we've talked, I want to ask you something."

He gazed at me, then lifted my hand to his lips and kissed it gently. "What?"

"Will you marry me? I want you to join us in the Soul Symbiont ritual. You and I are bound by the Eleshinar ritual, but if we're going to be bound by body, why not just go all the way and be bound by soul? I would be honored to take you as my mate and to call you husband."

My heart skipped a beat. What if he said no? What if he couldn't face being around Smoky when I had sex with the dragon? What if he was too angry because of the attack to even think of returning to our relationship?

But Trillian just gazed in my eyes with those icy baby-blues, and a slow, cynical grin spread across his face. "You have a penchant for dangerous and damaged men, my love. Your tastes run to the dark, and now you are practicing death magic with Fox Boy? Camille, there's only one person I'd ever consider marrying, especially through that ritual. So, yes, my love . . . if you'll forgive me for calling you a traitor, I will join your harem and be your husband. But never, ever forget, I always have been—*and will always be*—your alpha lover."

"I know," I whispered as he laid me down in his arms again. "Oh, believe me, I know. But you aren't damaged, Trillian. You are wild and passionate and free. We've all been at the mercy of our enemies, and chances are, we'll all be dancing with the devil again. But as long as we have our dignity, then walking wounded or not, we remain strong. And as long as we're together, nothing—not even death—can tear us apart."

And then Trillian began to make slow, passionate love to me, and all my worries vanished in the wash of his arms, in the taste of his lips, and the feel of his skin gliding against mine.

CHAPTER 13

By the time we'd washed and dressed, a messenger was at the door requesting our presence in the King's chamber. I did my best to smooth out my clothes and Trillian handed me his brush, so my hair wasn't flying wild with after-sex frizz. All in all, according to the mirror on the wall, I washed up pretty good.

Trillian slapped a starberry muffin in my hand. Munching on it, I followed him through the streets, back to the palace. I didn't have time to look around, but I knew that I wanted to return when we had more time. Dahnsburg was clean, and it felt old, with mysterious doorways and curious shops that promised adventure and damned good shopping.

We reached the outer courts just in time to see my father coming down the path. He looked at Trillian, then at me, then rolled his eyes.

"You two have been busy," he said softly.

It occurred to me that although Father was full-blooded Fae, he might actually have a problem with his daughters actually sleeping with men. Or women. But it wasn't something I could ask him, especially in front of Trillian.

I flashed him a slap-happy grin. "Don't worry, I'm not

going to make you a grandpa." *Yet.* Smoky's little bomb about fathering a child on me was still exploding in the back of my mind. I had to find some way out of that one. Delilah could have a litter of young ones and I'd love them all—cat or Were—but babies weren't my style.

"I certainly hope not," Father said. "You've got enough problems as it is." But then he relented and held out his hand to Trillian. "I have an errand to run. I'll be back in a bit." He paused. "Trillian, look out for my daughter."

Trillian stared at Father's hand, then slowly took it. "As always, Sephreh. As her lover, her life comes before mine. And—" He crooked his lip into that damned arrogant smile that was both so appealing and so irritating. "—as her husband-to-be, I'll do everything in my power to make certain she's happy."

Father stopped in mid-step. "*Husband?* So you're actually going to marry Camille?" He reminded me of a flipbook, going from disbelief to distress in a single leap.

"I will join her harem, yes," Trillian said, repressing a grin. I wanted to give him a good kick, but Father had been on his case for so long that I couldn't really blame him.

"So, is this happy news true, Camille?" Father looked anything but happy.

I sucked in a deep breath. "I know you told Trillian that I married Smoky and Morio because you wanted to try to break us up, but it won't work. I love Trillian. He's my alpha lover and he's willing to undergo the Soul Symbiont ritual with us. So yes, he will be my third—and, I sincerely hope, last—husband. Let it go, it's a done deal, it's going to happen, and there's nothing you can say to change it. I should have never left him in the first place."

Trillian wrapped his arm around my shoulder. "And I should have never let you go. We're fated to be together, and there's nothing you can do when the Hags take an interest in your life."

Father looked us up and down and then, sounding the most human I'd ever heard, uttered one word. "Crap."

I sputtered. "Excuse me, but shouldn't that be *congratulations?*"

"Yeah, Dad," Trillian said, making it worse. "Maybe you

can come visit us Earthside and we'll take in a few holes of golf."

Sephreh blinked. Without another word, he marched over, kissed me on the forehead, shook his head disgustedly at Trillian, then stomped off. But as he climbed in the carriage, he turned to wave good-bye and he was smiling.

Trillian kissed my cheek. "I think he's coming around. We'll be best buddies in no time."

"You wish," I muttered. "Come on, I've got an audience with the King."

"As do I," Morio said, coming up behind us. Iris was nowhere in sight.

"What?" I twirled.

"A messenger found me in the marketplace and told me to join you in the throne room." He held up a cloth bag. "I found some fascinating spell components there."

"Come on, woman." Trillian gave me a little shove forward. "We'd better get our butts in gear."

He led us through the maze of gardens toward the central tent. As we passed close to the cloth panels, the material brushed against my arm. Basket weave, it was durable, and yet finely crafted.

"What's this made of?" I reached out to touch the panel. Soft under my fingers, it tingled with a faint buzz. "There's magic woven into the cloth."

"You think?" Trillian arched his eyebrows. "These are the walls of the palace. Unlike stone or mortar or brick or marble, cloth isn't quite as effective in stopping little things like cannons or fireballs. *Of course* the material is enchanted. The tents that make up the palace have protective energy woven into every strand, every thread."

And then we were at the door leading into the throne room. Trillian stood to the side, waiting for us outside as one of the Dahns guards led us on. We followed the unicorn, who looked dangerously large and powerful, up the cobbled path that separated twin courts cushioned with moss and an occasional stone bench. The walls of the tent were a good twenty feet high, held up by an intricate system of cross-bars and I wondered how the unicorns had erected them.

Then, I saw exactly how they had managed the task. Around

the perimeter, manning the guylines and counterweights, stood several large centaurs. Male centaurs. Very well-endowed centaurs. Suddenly blushing, I looked away. I didn't need any new fantasy fodder—I had plenty of it in reality, but man, oh man, the women of their race had a lot to be thankful for.

We followed the guard along the path until we came to a large grass-covered knoll. Atop the knoll rested the King of the Dahns Unicorns. I could see the resemblance between him and his son and as I knelt into a low curtsy a whinny to my left caught my attention. I raised my head and saw Feddrah-Dahns enter the courtyard. He lumbered over toward us and, without thinking, I leapt up and went racing across the grass, laughing.

"Feddrah-Dahns! It's so good to see you again!" I threw my arms around his neck and his velvet coat tickled my skin.

He let out a snort, then a soft chuckle. "Lady Camille, it's good to see you again. How fare you and your sisters?"

I suddenly realized that I'd turned my back on the King and quickly stumbled back a few steps, whirling to face the larger unicorn. Feddrah-Dahns wasn't fully grown, that much was evident, but his father was, and the sire was staring at me with a look of amusement in his eyes.

"You were right," King Upala-Dahns said to his son. "She's impulsive and unpredictable. But also charming, as you said."

"I'm sorry," I stuttered. "I meant no disrespect. I was just so happy to see your son again—"

"No matter, nothing harmed. Not even my sensibilities," the King said in Melosealfôr. Switching back to the common tongue, he included Trillian and Morio in his gaze. "We must talk about the unicorn horn. And about the magic you are learning from this young fox."

Morio looked confused.

"Excuse me, Your Highness, but Morio doesn't speak any of the Otherworld dialects. Do you, by chance, speak English?" I couldn't fathom why the King of the Dahns Unicorns would have bothered to learn an Earthside language, so it was a real shot in the dark.

King Upala-Dahns whinnied softly. "Yes, to some degree. William Butler taught us when he stayed with us for several years."

I smiled softly. "Yes, Feddrah-Dahns and Mistletoe explained about him when they visited Earthside." Glancing around, I added, "Speaking of pixies, is Mistletoe around? I'd like to say hello to him." One of the few pixies I could ever imagine liking, he was Feddrah-Dahns's assistant.

"He's off on an errand, but he should be back soon." As the King switched to English, his voice took on an archaic air. "We haven't much time, so I'll be brief." He paused. "Are you understanding me now?" he asked Morio.

Morio nodded. "Clear as a bell."

"Bell? What should be clear about a bell?" With a shake of the head, Upala-Dahns snorted. "No matter. While it may have seemed foolhardy for you to bring the horn of the Black Beast with you, it was actually a wise decision. The Black Unicorn himself awaits you in the forests of Thistlewyd Deep. He traveled up from his lair in Darkynwyrd and has sent for you."

A cold chill raced down my spine. What the hell did the Black Beast want with me? It was an honor—and a pain in the ass—to be given his horn, but to actually meet him, a creature straight out of dark legend? Not fun . . . not fun *at all*. A vision of a huge stallion with a crystal horn, rearing up as he breathed flame from his nostrils, filled my mind.

"Crap." The word was out of my mouth before I could help it. I blushed as everybody stared at me.

"Excuse me?" the King said.

Stammering, I tried to gracefully backpedal. "I mean, it's just . . . the thought is rather intimidating."

"It should be," Upala-Dahns said, not helping matters any. "The Black Unicorn is the father of the Dahns Unicorns. For him to summon a mortal to meet him—one who is not of his race—is almost unheard of. Most think he's legend, though the Dahns Unicorns know better. As far as I know, the only Fae or elf he's had truck with in the past hundred years is Queen Asteria."

On one hand, I felt flattered. How could I help but be? Big Black Beast wanted to see little ol' me? On the other hand, I was scared spitless.

I glanced at Morio, who shrugged, keeping his mouth shut. He was more taciturn than I. Probably a good thing, considering how lacking in diplomacy I could be at times.

King Upala-Dahns waited as if he expected an answer, but when I didn't speak, he added, "He not only wants to see you, Camille, but your mate Morio."

Now Morio jumped. His eyes grew wide and he nervously glanced over at me. "Me? Why me?" Though his voice was steady, I could sense the rush of fear beneath it.

I repressed a smile and whispered, "Now you know how I feel."

"Because you and Camille are working death magic together."

The King had a gleam in his eye that told me he'd gotten the reaction he wanted. Yeah, Upala-Dahns liked to make people jump. He'd be a bear to work for, but fair.

Dreading any further explosive revelations, I jumped when something landed on my shoulder. I jerked to brush whatever it was away when a voice near my ear said, "Watch it!"

"Mistletoe!" I held out my hand and he stepped onto it. The pixie was nearly translucent and his wings glimmered in the daylight, but when he touched my palm, he was as solid as I was.

"My lady," he said, bowing low. Mistletoe was far more courteous than other pixies. Most were a pain in the ass.

"Mistletoe," Feddrah-Dahns said, "you will go with Rejah-Dahns and escort them to Thistlewyd Deep to meet the Black Beast."

"Can we portal jump there?" I asked.

Mistletoe shook his head. "We can take the portal to the edge of the wood, but no portals ever have been able to penetrate the Deep, and so we will go on foot from the tree line. The place we seek isn't far from the border and we will reach there before midnight tonight."

I glanced at the sky. The full moon was tonight and I'd be caught up in the Hunt. But one look at the King told me arguing would be of no use, so I sucked it up. "Trillian will come with us. I'm not leaving him here."

Upala-Dahns didn't look happy, but all he said was, "As you wish. He will accompany you. From there, after you've spoken to the Black Beast, you may return Earthside."

Feddrah-Dahns stepped up and nudged my shoulder with his muzzle. "I wish I could go with you, but Father forbids it."

I gazed into those luminous eyes and once again felt teary. I always did around the unicorn and I had no idea why. "Feddrah-Dahns, you are a good friend, and I thank you for the guidance and trust you've shown us. We'll try not to let you down." I leaned my head against his downy nose.

A moment later, Trillian's voice echoed through the chamber. "Camille? Is everything all right?"

I glanced over my shoulder. Mistletoe had ushered Trillian into the throne room. "For now," I said, then quickly filled him in.

Trillian stared at the King. "You're serious? You're sending her to face the Black Beast?"

"Not alone," Upala-Dahns said. "She goes with you. And the fox demon will face the Great Father by her side."

By his reverent tone, it struck me that the Dahns Unicorns actually worshipped the Black Unicorn as a living god. After all, he was the father of their race, a living legend. He was the phoenix of their culture, shedding his horn and hide every thousand years to be reborn anew.

And the Black Beast had requested that I face him. He'd given me—a half-Fae, half-human woman—one of his horns and a cloak made from his hide in order to fight the demons. And it wasn't every day that I got invited to pay a house visit to the home of the gods.

I rested my hand on Trillian's arm. "This is an honor, love, and we should remember that." And if we could get out of here without anybody making a scene, so much the better. The last thing I wanted to do was to offend the Dahns unicorns.

Trillian caught my thought and bowed to the King. "Your Highness, when should we leave? Are there any warnings or cautions we should be aware of?"

King Upala-Dahns glanced around the room, then motioned with a toss of the head that we should follow him. "Come, let us walk in the garden."

The clouds had opened up and it was raining as we followed the King into one of the empty gardens. Mistletoe rode on my shoulder, and Feddrah-Dahns walked to my right. Morio and Trillian kept close, a few steps behind me.

The smell of rain-washed grass and hearth smoke filled the air and I pulled my cloak tightly around me.

"What about Iris?" I asked. "Will she be coming with us, too?"

"Yes," Feddrah-Dahns said. "Though I don't think the Deep is a good place for her to be right now." But he wouldn't explain why.

The afternoon was wearing away and even though I couldn't see the Moon Mother, I could feel her gearing up for the Hunt. It had been a good two years since I'd leapt onto the astral to run at her side here in Otherworld, rather than Earthside. Although the Moon Mother was the same goddess in both worlds, the energy of the Hunt ran a little different depending on where you were.

We came to a low hedge trimmed in the shape of a spiral, and followed Upala-Dahns into the center. The labyrinth was simple, but as we walked it, my mind settled. There was deep magic in this place. We were tracing a ley line, and it was singing to me, reassuring me that from here, no one could overhear us. Here, we were safe.

Once we were at the center, the King paused and we formed a semi-circle around him. "I brought you here because this is the one place I know harbors no spies, no prying eyes and ears. Listen to me, and listen well. We've been doing what research we can into the demon threat, and we've uncovered some interesting information that you need to put to use."

I perked up. Any help we could get was welcome, especially when it came from the Cryptozoid Alliance.

"As you know, the fabric separating the worlds is ripping. Together with the elves—and now Tanaquar's magicians— we've been searching for a way to fix what has been broken."

"Is that possible, though? I thought the Great Divide created an unnatural state of affairs and that's why everything is breaking down. The world is trying to right the balance again." I frowned, trying to remember what I'd been told by the Earthside Fae Queens and Grandmother Coyote.

"You're right. There's no way to fix the rip tearing the fabric of space. However, we believe that we can use the spirit seals, along with magic developed since their creation."

What? How could they do that without risking exactly what we were trying to prevent?

"The original spirit seal was specifically created in order

to rip apart the worlds, then it was broken and the pieces hidden. If you bring them together—even with one or two pieces missing—won't that just reconnect the worlds? That's why Shadow Wing is looking for them in the first place." Either I was extremely dense or I didn't have all the pieces to the puzzle.

The King shook his head, his mane fluttering in the rain.

"That's not exactly what we're planning," he said softly. "I'll let Queen Asteria tell you herself."

"Camille, it's good to see you again."

I jumped as the Elfin Queen slipped from behind a well-trimmed tree. Her elderly stature seemed to have disappeared and now she stood straight and ancient, her power radiating through every pore. The woman practically glowed. Behind her walked Titania's old lover—Tom Lane, or rather, Tam Lin. Beside him was Benjamin Welter, a young man with the faintest hints of Fae blood who we'd rescued from a mental institution over Earthside. And behind them . . . Venus the Moon Child? What the hell was the shaman of the Rainier Puma Pride doing here?

"Your Majesty! Tom . . . Ben? Venus?" I started to say, but then fell silent as another figure moved from behind yet another tree. Queen Tanaquar, and at her side, my father. As it sank in that I was standing in the midst of three of the major ruling powers of the Otherworld Fae, I didn't know whether to fall groveling to the ground, or to break out in nervous giggles.

Morio poked me in the side. As he and Trillian began to bow and I started to curtsy, Queen Asteria waved her hand.

"We aren't standing on formality here." She motioned for us all to take a seat on the grassy circle comprising the center of the labyrinth. The grass was wet, but I ignored the chill. Feddrah-Dahns and his father remained standing.

After a moment, Queen Asteria said, "While the seals cannot repair the rifts, we've discovered that they can be used and if used correctly, we might be able to stabilize the portals."

Open-mouthed, I stared at her. "And just *who* will be using them?" I finally managed to squeak out.

"The Keraastar Knights. The Knights of the Portals. I knew there was something special about Tam Lin, and then

Benjamin, when I met them, and so I brought them here. My seers are searching for others with the same qualities. We looked into Venus the Moon Child and he, too, possesses the energy signature we're looking for. These three have touched the hearts of three of the seals. They are now integrally connected to the gems."

I began to breathe a little faster. "But they're all human—well, Venus is a werepuma but . . ."

"And so shall be every one of the nine knights—or ladies. Or rather, they will all be from Earthside. Apparently, the imprinting forges a connection that cannot be broken. Very few possess the ability to imprint with the seals, but there are a few out there . . . And we need them here, to be trained as guardians."

A thousand questions flashed through my mind. "Do they all have to have touched the seals at some point in their lives? Why can they wield them without worrying about corruption? What about the seal that Karvanak stole from us?"

"Patience, patience," Tanaquar said. "What we've learned is this: Not all of the Keraastar will have had contact with the seals, but they all share the same energy signature in their auras."

"They can touch them without corruption because they've faced quests for power before, and they chose not to act on that power. Even if they don't realize it." Queen Asteria let out a sigh. "But we must have at least seven of the seals for this to work correctly. Any fewer and the balance will be upset. We have only four. Shadow Wing has one. That leaves four in play. We must find at least three of them before the demons get there first."

I stared at her. In the core of my gut, I knew they were treading on dangerous ground, but what could I say? I opened my mouth to ask another question but a sharp jab from Morio stopped me.

Feddrah-Dahns's gaze flickered over to me, and as I stared back, I saw concern and doubt in his eyes, too. And in Mistletoe's, also, although pixies could be very misleading. But both of them warned me with their gaze to keep my mouth shut. I glanced over at Trillian, who was staring coolly at Queen Asteria.

At that moment, Queen Tanaquar gave me a narrow smile and said, "The OIA is placing the authority in your hands to do whatever is necessary to find the rest of the spirit seals. You have full license and we'll supply all the manpower you need. Fail, and we all fail."

As I nodded, not trusting myself to speak, the royalty fell to talking. I took the opportunity to glance around. Feddrah-Dahns, Trillian, and Morio were all worried as hell but concealing it rather well. I could see the concern rolling off their auras in waves. My father, on the other hand, was gazing at Queen Tanaquar. Suddenly I saw it—a cord that held them together.

Hot damn! Daddy was *doing* the Queen of Y'Elestrial, and he hadn't said a word about it.

Totally thrown for a loop, I busied myself with smelling the flowers on a nearby tribarb bush. Like a cross between a rose and a dahlia, they were autumn flowers and had an earthy, spicy scent. After a few minutes, King Upala-Dahns adjourned the meeting and he and the two queens headed back to the palace.

Eager to get out of earshot and discuss just what the hell Asteria and Tanaquar were up to with the spirit seals, and to ask why Morio had stopped me from questioning the plan, I urged my companions to hurry away from the gardens. I had a bad feeling about what was coming, and I really didn't want to be standing in the middle of the road whenever it barreled my way.

CHAPTER 14

The minute we were out of earshot, I turned to the others.

"Okay, what the fuck is going on? We agreed the spirit seals should be kept in a secret place, safe from the world. So what happened? What the hell are they thinking? The power in those seals can warp those who wield them."

Furious—and not quite sure who at—I sputtered as Trillian and Morio hurried me along behind Feddrah-Dahns. I glanced over at the unicorn. "How long have you known about this?"

"Only today, Lady Camille. My father didn't tell me anything about this—I swear on my honor to you." He looked as upset as I felt.

Morio glanced over his shoulder to make sure nobody was following us. "I stopped you from questioning their wisdom because if they know you disapprove, they may decide to just keep you out of the loop. And that would be bad. Very bad." He let out a long sigh. "I think we need to find out what Grandmother Coyote has to say about this."

"The price for that one's going to be steep," I muttered. "You're right, though. We'll head for Thistlewyd Deep immediately. They didn't say whether the Black Unicorn knows about their plans but we can find out when we're there. And as soon as we're done, we'll head home and talk to Grandmother Coyote. Getting home has just become a priority."

I glanced at Feddrah-Dahns. "I wish you were going with us." Everything had shifted with the revelation that Queen Asteria was mucking around with the spirit seals. It felt like we were on quicksand. I didn't know who to trust, except I knew that I trusted the Crown Prince.

Feddrah-Dahns let out a snort. "Me, too. Let me see what I can do. The three of you stay together while I'm gone. Don't split up. Go sit in the courtyard out front, in plain sight, and talk about anything except what we learned." He glanced at Mistletoe, who was hovering near his ear. "Find Iris and bring her here. Then go to my quarters, my friend, and get my traveling gear ready."

"My honor, my liege." The pixie darted out of sight.

We split off and headed for the courtyard. I fiddled with the hem of my cloak, wishing to hell I could relax. But the news had me so worried that all I could think about was getting home. It hadn't escaped my notice that none of the Earthside Fae Queens had been present. I wondered if they'd been invited, or conveniently overlooked. Immersed in thought, I sat on the grass a few yards away from the bench where Morio and Trillian sat, and played with the flowers, trying to quiet my mind.

Morio and Trillian made polite conversation, catching up on everything and anything except the demons. Morio had just launched into an exhaustively boring discussion about the problems he was having with his Subaru when a shadow crossed my path.

I glanced up to see a tall man in tunic and trousers staring down at me with a guarded look. There was something off-putting about him, and I was about to ask what he wanted when two other men stepped out from behind a nearby bush, daggers in their hands. They were aiming for me, that much was obvious.

Trillian and Morio were on their feet instantly, but before they could reach me, the two men intercepted them. I leapt to my feet and stumbled back from my attacker. The look in his eyes changed from guarded to dangerous and he brought his hands up. The crackle of magic raced between his fingers. Oh shit, he was some sort of mage.

Instinctively, I grabbed the horn inside my cloak. The Elementals within were awake. I could feel them waiting for my command as I circled with the sorcerer in a slow, wary dance.

I tried to key in on where he sourced its power from. If I tried to deflect the wrong energy, chances were I'd be a goner.

And then, my opponent shot a spell dead center for me. The energy roared like a cannon, an arrow of fire, aiming true and clear. I brought up the horn and summoned the Mistress of Flames. A force field came up, a wall of flame to meet the fiery arrow, and there was an explosion as the flames collided and cancelled one another.

No time to think. I summoned the Lady of the Land and focused on the ground beneath his feet. The soil shrieked as it ripped apart, splitting as the garden quaked, the ground rolling in waves. A crevasse opened below him, big enough to unbalance his footing. He fell into the hole. The ground rippled again and slammed shut.

Pancake, I thought. As in *flatter than a . . .*

My stomach lurched and I stumbled back as Feddrah-Dahns cantered up the walkway on one side, his father from the other direction. They stared at the ground and then over at me. In turn, I whirled around to check on Morio and Trillian. One of the men lay on the ground, dead, and Morio's dagger was bloody. The other was nowhere to be seen.

"I munched your garden," I said, shaking.

"No matter," Feddrah-Dahns said. "What happened? What did they want?"

"What do you think he wanted? He was after the horn." I turned back to stare at the spot where the magician had fallen. Whether he'd been crushed or suffocated, I didn't know. I wasn't sure I wanted to.

"You'd best make your way to the Black Beast without delay," the King said. He turned to the Crown Prince. "Do as you wish and take Rejah-Dahns's place. They need more protection than she can offer, and you have magic at your disposal." Upala-Dahns paused, then spoke to one of his bodyguards. "Get someone in here to tend to that mess." He nodded to the ground. "Make certain the sorcerer is dead. Find the other assailant and execute him. Burn the bodies." With that grim order, the King turned and trotted away.

Feddrah-Dahns tossed his head, motioning for us to follow him. We hurried to a spot near the palace entrance. There stood Iris, next to a willow tree. She gave me a worried look, but said nothing as the unicorn let out a loud nicker.

"Have you everything you need for the journey?" he asked.

I nodded. "I have my bag with me, and I believe Morio does, too."

"Right here," he said, patting the bag he was never without.

"Good. Iris? Trillian?"

Iris held up her traveling gear.

Trillian shrugged. "There's nothing I can't do without. I always carry money and weapons with me."

"Then we should make tracks and get the hell out of Dodge," I said.

"Oddly put, but yes, we must leave now," Feddrah-Dahns said. "I'm not taking bodyguards. We don't know who we can trust, and there are things we must discuss in private. Hurry, follow me." He led us out the western gate and back up the hill, occasionally looking over his shoulder. "We aren't being followed. I don't think my father realizes how concerned I am about the situation, which is a good thing."

We kept quiet until we reached the portal and Feddrah-Dahns ordered our trip to the outskirts of Thistlewyd Deep. The jump was like most of the others, and when we emerged from between two gigantic cedars, I stopped to take a good look at the forest we were about to go charging into. I didn't know much about this woodland. Most of what I knew about the great forests of Otherworld focused on Darkynwyrd.

"What kind of place is this?" I asked as we headed down the grassy slope toward the path leading into the forest.

"What do you mean? Cedar, fir—mostly coniferous woodlands here." The unicorn glanced at me, puzzled.

"No, no. I can *see* that. I mean . . . Darkynwyrd is wild and primal, and filled with shadow-folk. What's the nature of Thistlewyd Deep? I don't remember hearing much about it when I was in school."

Mistletoe, who was riding on Feddrah-Dahns's shoulder, let out a snort. "You're in for a surprise, my lady. This is far more dangerous than Darkynwyrd. This forest is ruled by Raven Mother—one of the Elemental Lords. *Ladies?* She's cunning and devious, and delights in deceiving others to do her bidding."

"Sounds like Morgaine," Morio said, pressing his hand to my back.

"Delightful. I wonder if they know each other. Morgaine travels with a murder of crows . . . She probably gets into ravens, too." I let out a loud sigh. "Can't we ever go any-place where the welcome mat isn't set with spikes or traps or deadfalls?"

Iris clucked sympathetically. "I know. I know."

We plowed through the knee-high grass as the afternoon slipped away. The Windwillow Valley was predominantly comprised of grassy plains, and the long blades waved in the wind like a verdant current, rippling with each gust. The susur-ration of their movement whispered on the wind.

Away from the forest's edge, there were few trees through the wide valley, only small scrub and occasional lakes or ponds that offered animals and travelers a place to rest and refresh. The valley plains went on for days if you were afoot, bordered on the west by the Nebulvuori Mountains of the dwarves. They opened into the Sandwhistle Desert due south.

A gust blasted past, and I could smell rain on the horizon. The clouds hadn't journeyed inland from Dahnsburg yet. The air smelled sweet and mossy from the forest, and I had a sudden longing to just park it right here and forget about everything. Maybe just build a little house on the edge of the wood, set up shop, let Smoky give me babies, and pretend that Shadow Wing was all a bad dream. But after a few minutes spent in daydreaming, I shook my head.

"How did your visit go?" I asked Iris. "With the Great Winter Wolf Spirit? Did you find him?" The others were a little ways ahead of us. I lowered my voice so they couldn't hear me.

She gave me a pained look. "Yes, I did. I'm not sure if it was the right thing to do. I'll tell you later, but things don't look hopeful. I have options, but none of them are promising, nor easy."

Just about then, Morio stopped. "There—ahead. We're almost to the path."

"And how long after we enter the wood until we meet the Black Unicorn?"

Feddrah-Dahns blinked those long lashes at me. "We will be at his doorstep before the evening's over and the Moon is up. We should rest for a moment now, because once we enter the Deep, we shouldn't stop. It can be dangerous for travelers, especially after the sun goes down."

I glanced at the sky. The sun was low on the horizon. We had perhaps another half-hour before dusk would hit and we'd be at the mercy of Morio's light spell.

"Anybody bring food?" I asked, slipping my bag off my shoulder and dropping to the ground to stretch my legs. Trillian and Morio followed suit. Iris opened one of her satchels and pulled out a packet of sandwiches. I laughed. "I should have known. You always come through in the comfort department."

As she passed the food around—thick slabs of turkey on sourdough, with freshly churned butter and slivered almonds and cinnamon cranberry sauce—she smiled ever so faintly.

"Don't get used to it," she said. "Who knows what the future holds? For any of us."

"Fuck the future," Trillian said, lifting his sandwich high. "The only thing we can be sure of is this moment, right here, right now. So eat, drink, and be merry, for tomorrow we—"

"Don't," I said as a goose walked over my grave. "Don't say it."

He acquiesced, leaving the sentiment unspoken. As we settled into our meal, with Feddrah-Dahns munching on grass nearby, I gazed at the tree line leading into Thistlewyd Deep.

The Black Beast was waiting for us—ancient and ominous—and I wasn't sure what the hell would happen when we met him. But our date with destiny wouldn't take no for an answer.

I bit into my sandwich and chewed slowly as a flutter of wings rose from the nearest cedar and three ravens went winging past. It felt like a sign, but just what they were trying to tell me, I had no idea. And for once, I really, really wished I could see into the future.

Thistlewyd Deep was more than a magical forest. It was magic *incarnate*. As we stepped onto the path, a deep resonance hummed through the ground, singing a song as old as the world. I closed my eyes and answered, embracing the welcome that bid us enter the woodland. Wild—yes, and feral— definitely, but Thistlewyd Deep embodied the nature of the Hunt.

The path was narrow, flanked on both sides by thick undergrowth shrouding the trunks of the trees. As we journeyed under the canopy of branches and limbs, I understood what Feddrah-Dahns had meant. Darkynwyrd would meet its match in Thistlewyd Deep. This forest rocked with energy, the ground shifting beneath my feet with every step. Oh, it wasn't a tangible shift like a quake, but every time I put my foot down, the ground seemed to roll in waves.

I bit my lip, wondering how the hell we were supposed to keep moving, with every movement shaking reality. Glancing around, I asked, "Does anybody else feel that?"

"Feel what?" Iris asked.

"The ground. Moving. Everything swirls every time I take a step."

I glanced at the trees. The bark covering their trunks squirmed, shifting patterns. The bushes and ferns nestled at their bases shook as if a powerful wind was gusting through, but I couldn't feel any currents against my skin that were strong enough to move the leaves and branches.

"Camille, are you okay?" Iris looked worried. She motioned to Morio. "Feel her forehead."

As he moved to obey, I brushed his hand aside. "I'm not sick, and I haven't lost my mind. At least, I don't think I have. But don't you see? All the plants are swaying to the pulse that's racing under my feet. Like a hard-core drumbeat. Hell, I feel like I'm in the middle of one of Big Mama's natural raves."

They looked around, confused, then Morio closed his eyes and fell silent. Iris did the same. Feddrah-Dahns whinnied nervously. After a moment, both the sprite and the youkai nodded.

"I'm beginning to sense what you're talking about," Iris said. "It's fainter for me—these are not the far northern climes that call to my blood. But I can feel the vibration of this forest."

Morio let out a long, slow breath. "Got it. Caught hold of it and rode it for just a moment. The soul of this woodland is fluid, existing within every plant and tree, every inch of dirt, every breath of air that sweeps through. You're not going crazy, Camille. You're feeling the heartbeat of the Deep. You've connected with the wood on a soul level."

Oh joy. Why me? Better yet, I should ask: Could I use it to my advantage? I looked around at the vibrant colors that whirled like paint splatters. I felt about three sheets to the wind on Captain Morgan, all right.

"It's hard for me to see anything clearly through the brilliance—all the colors are running together in one giant orgasm of patterns. I'll need help getting to . . . well, wherever the hell we're going."

Feddrah-Dahns stepped forward. His horn glowed with golden light and he looked like an airbrushed fantasy off of some fashion magazine ad. "Lift her onto my back and she can ride the rest of the way."

I stared at the unicorn. *Ride on his back?*

"Don't you know who you are?" I asked. The thought of climbing aboard the back of a Crown Prince seemed too ridiculous to even contemplate. Even if he was shaped like a horse.

"Most certainly. And I know who you are, and I know where we're going. If you'll excuse the abruptness, Lady Camille, quit gawking and get your derriere on my back." He blinked and I started to laugh.

"Even when you're abrupt, you're still proper. Well, fine, if you don't mind being ridden, I'll be grateful for the help, but I need a boost. I'm not quite as athletic as Delilah."

Trillian and Morio helped me sling myself over the unicorn's back. He shuddered as the hem of my cape dragged across his hindquarters and I realized it must strike some resonance within him. The cape was made from unicorn hide, and the hide of the Black Beast at that. I firmly grasped his mane in my hands and hoped I wasn't holding on too tight.

As we pushed ahead, the gentle loping of his cadence lulled me into a Technicolor wonderland ride. Everything was so vivid and the feel of his luxurious coat against my bare legs warmed me through. I drifted off, nursing a growing headache from the overstimulation, wondering what it would be like meeting the Black Unicorn. At least Morio had been able to tap into the energy and knew it wasn't just me reacting to a bad piece of meat or spiked wine. I just hoped this carousel ride would stop before we got there or I'd be off on a Hunt that led straight down the rabbit hole.

Dusk had come and we were well into the Deep when Feddrah-Dahns abruptly stopped. The respite from the colors of the woodland during daylight had mitigated my headache and the grays and blacks of night proved a welcome relief. I was starting to be able to think again, no longer buffeted by the kaleidoscope of the forest, except now it was the Moon pulling on me, calling for me to get ready. The Hunt would be riding out soon.

"Up ahead, we turn left, and then another half mile and we're there," Feddrah-Dahns said. "Can you feel him?"

I sucked in a long breath and slowly exhaled. The night had an energy all its own, and it wasn't altogether pleasant. I wasn't so much frightened of nasty creatures like in Darkynwyrd, but in the Deep dwelt great power and a buttload of chaos. It swirled everywhere, like dew on a raven's wing, the bubbles of mayhem threatening to burst against the darkening sky.

The Moon Mother was rising full, but she was only visible for short periods between the clouds that swept over the forest. They were headed east, off the Wyvern Ocean. Dahnsburg must be having a tidy little storm, I thought. The ocean waves were bound to be cresting high tonight.

And then, with a flutter of wind out of the west, I felt *him*. Or rather: *heard* him. The cloak around my shoulders began to resonate with a low hum, and the horn within the inner pocket vibrated like silver wind chimes or shattering glass. They were answering the call of their master who, in another lifetime, had worn both hide and horn as part of his body.

Since the night I'd pledged myself to the Moon Mother, no summoning had beckoned me so strongly, and like her magic this call was tinged with the hot fire of molten silver, the diamond chill of frost on an autumn night. I leaned my head back and gazed at the clouds as they parted and let the Mother's light shine down, glowing with *her* fire, singing out her name. The Moon Mother watched over me; she was at her zenith and tonight I would run with the Hunt.

As we plunged forward and turned to the left onto a shadowed path, I knew, absolutely and without doubt, that the Black Beast was well acquainted with the Moon Mother. They were of a kind, connected and linked in a way I didn't understand, but a voice in the back of my mind whispered to me that they were kin.

I let out a strangled sob as the full power of my Lady's beauty broke through the clouds and splashed across the woodland, lighting our path as we moved forward. She was my everything, my all, above and beyond my own life. My heart swelled with longing as the summons to join the Hunt began to grow.

Morio reached up and took my left hand and I squeezed hard. He squeezed back. Trillian walked to the right, with Iris beside him, and he glanced up at me as I rode astride Feddrah-Dahns's back. His expression was lost in the night. But I could see the sparkle of his eyes and I breathed a silent prayer of thanks that he was back by my side.

Another short distance. Then, up ahead, I saw a glowing light coming from within a ring of trees. The glade was difficult to see from here, but the lights emanated from a ring of waist-high mushrooms, fly agaric by their looks. The path leading into the glen crackled with energy.

A Fae circle? No, this was more powerful than any I'd ever come across. To cross it without welcome would be to put our lives on the line.

A low voice echoed from the center of the glen, rumbling

through every blade of grass, every rock and pebble and shrub and tree.

"Enter my grove, if you so dare."

And right there, on that spot, I knew that the Black Beast waited for us. I slid off Feddrah-Dahns's back, and without a second thought, marched forward between the mushrooms, to enter the lair of the Black Unicorn.

CHAPTER 15

As I stepped into the ring of mushrooms, the world shifted beneath my feet yet again. What the hell? Losing my balance, I went stumbling to the side, landing hard on my knees. The ground rolled in waves beneath me.

The others entered the circle, but my attention was fastened on a dark patch against the line of cedars, across the lea. It was as if there was a swath of jet painted across the tree trunks. A tangible abyss. A portal, perhaps?

Whatever it was, something waited within. Something terrible. Something beautiful. Something ancient beyond counting. As I watched, a pair of golden eyes gleamed out from the darker-than-ink void.

Then, through the shadowy arch, stepped the Lord of the Dahns Unicorns. As his hooves touched the grass, a ripple of sparks tattooed their way through the ground, the current sending a shock wave through me. I crouched, fear warring with awe.

He was tall. Far taller than any unicorn or horse I'd ever seen. A giant could barely have ridden him, or an ogre. His haunches were sleek and muscled, his fur as dark as Trillian's skin, but patches of gray shone through the ebony hide. His eyes shone like twin golden suns. My gaze rose to the spiral crystalline horn jutting out from his head—and the horn in my pocket set up a keening as if recognizing its true master.

"He's real—"

"The Black Unicorn—"

"Girl, are you all right—"

The voices of the others whispered behind me, but I scarcely heard them. I remained where I was, bewitched by the sight of the great beast. A noise to my side startled me. Feddrah-Dahns was beside me now, kneeling on his two front legs, his head bowed.

"Master of Masters, Lord of the Dahns, I bring you the girl and her mate." His voice was hushed and as awestricken as I felt.

I decided to keep my mouth shut. For one thing, I wasn't sure of protocol and there was no way in hell I was going to fuck this up. For another thing, my voice seemed to have deserted me as I gazed upon this living legend. Between the call of the Hunt and the power of this beast, I couldn't muster even a squeak.

The Black Beast moved forward and stopped about three yards in front of us. I cautiously raised my head, afraid to look into those gleaming eyes. If I looked, would I lose myself?

"On your feet, woman," a voice echoed in my head. "All of you, stand."

I blinked. He hadn't spoken aloud, but I heard him loud and clear. Apparently, I wasn't the only one because Morio, Trillian, and Iris rose from where they'd dropped to the ground. With a small whinny, Feddrah-Dahns pushed me forward with his nose.

I steadied myself, noticing that the ground had quit shifting. One thing to be thankful for. As I sucked in a deep breath and stared up at the creature, I saw that yes—indeed—steam was rising from his nostrils.

Slowly, not knowing why, but feeling it was the only thing to do, I reached in my pocket and pulled out the horn of the Black Unicorn and shaking, lifted my arm and thrust it upward under the quaking moon.

The Black Beast let out a low laugh that echoed through the glade. "I have not seen that part of myself in many years.

Nor the hide you wear around your shoulders." He lowered his muzzle to sniff my cloak. "Yes, this was a far earlier life, an earlier day and age when the spirit seal was first created and then divided. I told them it was a grave mistake, but they would not listen, so I retreated to Darkynwyrd, and from there, to the Deep. Tell me: You wear the mark of the Moon Mother. Have you seen her face?"

I suddenly found my tongue and blurted out, "Yes, I run with the Hunt. I am one of her witches."

"But not her priestess?" His eyes were like golden fire and I couldn't look away.

"No," I said softly. "Nor do I know if I'll ever be worthy. But it's enough for me to be her servant, to be her daughter and work her magic."

Then, the Black Beast stepped forward so his muzzle was staring right into my face, and he bathed me in the steam flowing from his nostrils. "Priestess, though, you would joyfully carry the title if given. Do you know who rides me? There is one, and one alone whom I allow to embrace my back with her thighs."

Shivering, wondering just where this conversation was going, I shook my head. "No, can't say I've ever thought about it." I just prayed it wasn't going to be me.

There was a movement from the shadows behind him, and a raven flew forth from the darkness. A vortex of swirling blood obscured the bird and I shaded my eyes against the waves of incandescent heat that flared out like a sunburst. The air twisted back on itself, rippling reality like the ocean tides. Then, ever so slowly, the magic dissipated.

As the flare faded away, a tall, pale woman stood there, her velvet gaze trailing over us. Her eyes were cunning, sparkled with flecks of gold amidst the obsidian and with a dread so deep I didn't even realize it had been there, I knew who this was.

Raven Mother.

Raven Mother, one of the Elemental Queens who ruled in the dark woods. Raven Mother, of whom I'd only heard rumors over the years. Raven Mother, who was known for cunning and deception and her violent lust after the Moon Mother's possessions.

Her breasts crested in a full curve above the neckline of her sheer black dress. Her lips, stained ebony, glistened when she spoke, and her eyes were masked with black like a raccoon. When she smiled, her teeth gleamed, not fangs but more like jutting arrowheads of bone, serrated and sharp.

"And who are these lovelies? Yes, who are they?" she asked, circling around the Black Beast, laying a lazy hand on his side. He let out a soft nicker and for some reason, it scared me so bad I thought I was going to wet my pants. Well, skirt.

Raven Mother and the Black Unicorn were paired, two of a kind, both as primal and feral as the wild wood in which they lived.

The Lord of the Dahns let out a sharp cough, and once again, his voice filled my head. "They are here for the Hunt. At least the girl is, and her fox demon. She possesses one of my horns, and so she must experience its most powerful use before she can trust herself to use it fully."

"And her lover?" Raven Mother whispered, but her words echoed through the glen, almost like the shrill cawing of her namesake.

"They are soul bound, and death magic they weave. Therefore, he must participate, for the horn will respond to their combined forces in this, and may backfire if he is not aware of its magnitude."

I gasped. So that's why we were here. I turned to Morio, shaking. His face had gone pale, and he quickly took his place beside me.

"Are you sure you want to do this?" he asked.

I paused, thinking about what could happen. Very bad things, no doubt. But then the words of Iris, and Grandmother Coyote, and the Elfin Queen floated through my mind. They had all pointed me on the path and I knew better than to fight destiny. But there was one last thing I had to do before I committed myself.

I walked out under the moonlight and knelt before my Lady. The Moon Mother was near. I could feel her in the tattoo throbbing on my shoulder blade, in the blood flowing through my veins, in the silver fire that wreathed my aura.

"Moon Mother, guide me. Raven Mother is your nemesis— this I remember from training. She seeks to take that which you have. But you have handed me over to the Black Beast and she walks by his side. Should I undergo this ritual? Should I place my trust in him?"

As I fell silent, listening with every fiber that made up my being, a slow mist began to rise around me. It whirled like a vortex, a tornado of smoke and fog, and then all I could see were the twirling mists that surrounded me.

My pulse began to race—the energy within the cone was building and I was at the center. Dizzy, I swayed under the power of the winds buffeting me from the swirling storm. At the top of the vortex, all I could see was the brilliant orb that was my Lady's sign and sigil. And then, the Moon Mother appeared, clad in silver and black, ready to lead the Hunt. She stood a hundred feet tall, towering over the land, a feral smile on her face.

I leapt to my feet.

The goddess leaned down and said to me, "Run with the Beast this night. You will both join me in the Hunt, where you—my daughter—will find your true place in my service."

With a single wave of one finger, the mist evaporated and the night shone through, brilliant and beautiful, and her laughter echoed through the forest as she vanished and I stood there, staring up at the star-studded sky, grateful for every trial she'd put me through.

As the glow from her presence faded, I turned to Morio, surprised to find he was still holding my hand. He looked at me gravely, and I could see my reflection in his eyes. The light of the Moon Mother cloaked me in silver, and for just a moment, I saw myself as he saw me: as more than a fuckup. More than a Windwalker. More than just a pawn in a war I didn't want and hadn't started. I saw myself as the Moon Witch I was, brilliant and beautiful and one of the thousand faces of the lady of the night.

"I'm positive," I said. "We have to go through with this. Whatever it is."

He nodded. "As you wish. I'd walk into the fire with you, if need be."

Trillian silently crossed over to the two of us. "Camille—I love you," he said simply. "Do what you need to. I trust you."

Startled, because Trillian usually didn't talk about love, I opened my mouth but he pressed two fingers to it, then turned to Morio. "Keep her safe, Morio. And . . . yourself as well." And then, he returned to Iris's side.

The sprite stared into my eyes. She didn't say anything. She didn't have to.

I summoned up my courage and said, "If something happens . . ."

She nodded. "I will make certain they know. But you'll come through this. I know it in my heart and center."

I turned back to the Black Beast. "We're ready."

Raven Mother laughed and her laughter was like the cawing of crows. She reminded me too much of Morgaine and I wondered if there was a connection.

"She's with you, my love," she said and leaned over to kiss the muzzle of the Beast. He nuzzled her neck with his nose and she languorously tipped her head to the side, her eyes closing at his touch. She reached up and lightly brushed her hand across her breast. The thought, *Get a room, why don't you,* crossed my mind but I managed to stop myself before my mouth made mincemeat of this meeting.

After a moment, Raven Mother dropped her hand and slithered up to me. She paused, then cupped my chin in her hands. "You are delicious, my beauty, yes you are." Her eyes glinted like steel beads as she cocked her head. I tensed as she leaned down, her face inches from mine. With her brilliant ebony lips, she brushed my own. I tried to pull away, but she held me fast, her fingers grasping my chin so tightly that it felt like she could break my neck with a simple twist of the head if she wanted.

"Don't be so coy, my lovely. I could kiss you all over, you are so precious. That glorious orb you call your goddess better not take you for granted, because I'd be happy to take you off her hands. Think about it. You could spend your days running in my forests and playing with my toys, and I would treat you like the lovely you are."

"Enough," the Black Beast said. "You can entice her later. For now, she has lessons to learn and demons to fight."

Raven Mother turned to him, her eyes narrowing as the smile left her face. I liked her better without it. She wasn't nearly so creepy.

"Very well, my love." To me, she added, "Go now, but don't forget me. I can gift you with marvelous favors and my price . . . is worth paying." And then she backed away and with another flash of red, turned into a raven and winged her way into the top of a nearby fir.

Scared out of my wits, I stared up at her. Elemental Lords were dangerous and wild, and they didn't play by our rules. It paid to avoid their notice, as Delilah had learned the hard way. The fact that Raven Mother was interested in me was *so* not a good thing. She delighted in trying to woo away the Moon Mother's followers, and she coveted the glowing orb in the sky, wanting to rule the night from a brilliant throne instead of a treetop.

I moved closer to Morio and he protectively slid his arm around my waist. The Black Beast turned toward the dark shadow from which he'd emerged. When we hesitated, he let out a snort of impatience.

"Follow me," he said. "The others will wait here."

And so, we did.

The inky blackness wasn't really a portal, but an entrance into a circular, foliage-shrouded tunnel that stood a good fifteen feet in diameter. The walls of the tunnel were a latticework of thorns and briars, except on the bottom, where a path of compacted dirt ran through. The tunnel was lit with eye-catchers in shades of brilliant fuchsia and violet, of neon yellow and soul-shattering green.

I hesitated. I hated small, enclosed places and didn't like being underground, but Morio took my hand and led me into the tunnel. Like the first time we'd gone exploring together, when we first met Smoky—I followed him into the labyrinth.

The Black Beast picked his way through the passage ahead of us, never looking back. I reached out, searching for the Moon Mother to reassure me that she was still with me in this serpentine maze, and after a moment, I felt the gentle touch of her presence, softly reassuring me.

How long we were in the tunnel was hard to tell. I focused on my breathing, trying to keep from freaking out. Even staying at Smoky's barrow was problematic at times. I'd rather be out under the sky, especially on the night of the Hunt. My shoulders began to ache and I realized how tense I was. I tried to relax, but the tension just crept into my neck and scalp. As a headache threatened to explode, the Black Unicorn stopped. We were near another dark, inky patch.

"What you are about to see," he said without turning around, "is something few humans, Fae, or elves have ever laid sight on. Never forget, you are being accorded an honor. Privilege can easily turn into punishment if your actions fail to warrant the gift."

Punishment? What punishment? Where were we going?

My question was answered as we stepped through the darkness and entered another small grove. But this one was no mere meadow, nor faerie ring. No, this was a sacred place. The energy sang loud and clear, a somber melody that echoed in the evening air.

A ring of baiyn cypress stood in the center of the field, an Otherworld hybrid of the Mediterranean cypress, bred for their magical nature. The ring of trees stood two hundred feet tall and had been pruned so the trunks were bare for twenty feet upward. With gnarled bark that had split in places, and faces that formed when you looked too closely at the knots and burls, eight of the trees held dark niches near the ground. Whether they had been carved, or formed naturally, was hard to tell.

Morio touched me lightly on the arm and pointed. It was then that I caught a glimpse of ivory within the hollows of the trees. We were in a cemetery. I slowly crossed over to the trees, the Black Beast saying nothing, but standing to the side, watching me closely.

I made my way through the waist-high saw grass, brushing aside the sharp blades that left little cuts along my bare skin. The Moon Mother was rising and the Hunt was near. I could feel the trail of predators preparing for the chase.

As I knelt by the first baiyn cypress and peered into the hollow, the gleaming bones of a horse sparkled in the moonlight. And yet, it was no horse. It was obvious that the horn once affixed to its head had been severed. This was no ordinary cemetery, but the resting place of all the incarnations of the Black Beast. Eight trees with hollows—eight bodies from over the eons. Eight horns, all but three now lost in the mists of time.

My cloak echoed the vibration of the trees and a faint keening rose through the glade. The horn, one moment in my pocket but now in my hand, began to vibrate and I could feel the power building as the urge to Hunt, to seek, to chase, to strike, flooded through my heart.

I slowly stood and turned, feeling poised on the edge of a chasm. The father of the Dahns Unicorns watched me closely. Morio silently glided to my side. We stood, silent, caught in a tableau of anticipation.

A flurry of images began to race through my mind and, horrified, I tried to push them away.

Blood and pain and loss, hunger and passion and a silver fire overriding everything. The lust of the Hunt, the drive to destroy and renew . . .

The cycle of the Moon Mother. She rose from the ashes, growing brilliant into ripeness, then the darkness ate away at her, destroying her, and she shriveled into the Crone, leading the pack into the depths to rest and be reborn again . . .

Maiden, Mother, Crone, the ever-turning cycle, and her cycle was my cycle, and it was also the cycle of the Black Unicorn . . .

As I stood there, terrified by what I now knew destiny had planned for me, the Black Beast nuzzled me gently. I looked up into the fiery eyes and shuddered.

"I can't . . . do . . . this," I whispered, rubbing his muzzle.

He let out a soft nicker. "You *must* do this. The Hags of Fate have decreed it. This cycle is near its end. You must accept your destiny and I must accept mine."

"I don't want to hurt you." Tears slowly ran down my cheeks, trailing rivulets through my makeup and the dust from the journey. Heartsick, I wanted to run out of the glen, back Earthside.

"The pain that comes with my sacrifice allows the cycle to continue. If you do not help me, then you will never understand the full power of the horn, and you will also put an end to my reign. You have a journey to make as well—this will lead you into a new realm. Can you deny us both our futures?"

Morio let out a gasp and understanding filled his eyes. "But why am I here?"

The Black Beast gazed at him. "The priestess must have a consort. A priest must attend her during the ritual. You understand the nature of death magic, youkai. For you are more than you seem, more than you've let on to even your wife. Tonight, you wear the cloak of priest. And tonight, the cloak Camille wears will change. You must be part of that transformation. You are souls bound together, and after tonight, you will be bound intrinsically by your magic."

Still crying, I allowed the Black Beast to nudge me into the center of the glen. "But why me? Why not Raven Mother? She's your consort."

"And she will continue to be. But she cannot do the deed. She is not mortal, and by mortal—albeit long-lived—hand, my rebirth must take place."

He stood before me, towering and dark, steam rising from his nostrils, his sleek black coat as brilliant and shining as obsidian. I wanted to run screaming, but then I looked into his eyes. There, amidst the fire and shadows I found compassion, and mercy, and understanding. Our gazes locked for what seemed like forever, and I willed the moment never to end. I wanted to lose myself in the depths of the eons this creature had seen.

But then he shuffled, and nosed me out of my reverie. "It's time, Daughter of the Moon. You know what to do." He glanced over at Morio. "Be ready for when she sweeps you up. You will run with her, and you will offer her the strength she needs when the time has come. You will hand her the power of death that she cannot yet fully wield."

Then, with a cry from above, the Moon Mother came streaking across the sky, followed by a legion of bears and panthers, elk and fox and hawks and Moon Witches and priestesses, and warriors long dead. She was beautiful, clad in her hunting outfit of silver and black, her face a mask of brilliant light, while her hands carried the bow and arrows of the Hunt. They raced through the air, pausing overhead.

"Come, Camille," she whispered. "Come to me. It's time

for you to join me at the helm of the Hunt. Come race like the wind to catch your quarry. And then, strike the blow and bring him into the Hunt with us."

A sudden wind shook the trees, howling with gale force and I felt myself slip onto the astral. I grabbed Morio's hand and he let out a sharp gasp as we stepped into the slipstream of energy, catching our breath as we landed next to the Moon Mother, looking down at the ground far below.

"You know what you have to do?" she asked, giving me a stern look.

"I do." I swallowed my fear and pulled out the unicorn horn, thrusting it into the sky.

"Tonight you lead the Hunt with me. Your quarry is great and wise and powerful. He must be caught—his sacrifice must be met this night." She grabbed me by the shoulders, her gaze piercing my soul. "Do not fail me. Do not falter. Show no mercy, for truly—mercy tonight will not be the compassion you wish it to be. Sometimes, to heal means to die. And if you fail to catch the prey, you will take his place."

My voice catching in my throat, I could only let out a strangled cry of assent. She dropped her hand and stepped back. My skin burned from the cold fire of her touch, and I wanted nothing more than to make my Lady happy.

"You took an oath when you pledged yourself to me, Camille. Tonight I ask you to repeat it. Camille Sepharial te Maria, will you live for me?"

The words were familiar on my tongue. I'd sworn them the night the Moon Mother accepted me into her fold. "I do swear . . ."

"Will you heal for me?"

"I do swear . . ."

"Will you kill for me?"

"I do swear . . ."

"Will you die for me?"

"I do swear . . ."

"Then lead on, lead on. Let the Hunt begin, and if you catch your quarry, my priestess you shall become!"

With a loud cry, she pushed me forward and, holding Morio with one hand, I sprang to action, racing across the sky. My Lady ran by my side. Her laughter spurred me on. All I could think of was catching my prey as the cries of the Hunters echoed behind us.

Then I saw him—my quarry, down below. The Black Beast stared as I spiraled down toward him, leading the frothing hounds and huntsmen. He leapt onto the astral and began to race ahead of me, his hooves beating a cadence against the stars and the clouds as we gave chase.

Across the night we pursued our quarry, the glowing moon shining her light on us as the Moon Mother sang her battle song. Lost in her glamour, lost in the brilliant delight of the Hunt, I scarcely noticed the waning night. Morio kept pace with me, his eyes glazed, shifting into his demonic form as we ran.

And then, sometime shortly before dawn, but long, long past midnight, the Black Beast slowed and turned. He was panting, his breath coming in rough, jagged gasps. I slowed, and my Lady slowed beside me. She motioned for the train of hunters to wait as I stepped forward, Morio close behind.

All my doubts fell by the wayside, all my sorrow vanished. This was a time of joy, a time of triumph. The Hunt was nearly over; only there was no solitary victor. We would *all* win. Morio began a low chant—the Chant of the Dead. A necromancer's spell I had just begun to learn, the chant was exactly the magic I needed.

I unfastened my cape and let it drop, then slipped out of my clothes. Naked, holding only the unicorn horn, I stepped forward, the astral breeze caressing my body, brushing over me like a hundred light fingertips.

The Black Beast raised his head, showing his chest to me.

"The day is done, night comes to the soul."

Morio's voice rang clear behind me, his magic buoying me up and giving me strength. I lifted the horn and gazed into those ancient eyes. They were begging for release, rebirth. The cycle was nearly complete, a new cycle ready to begin.

"The forest dims, the light fades into dusk."

"Priestess, do not fail me," the Beast commanded.

"What once was fractured will now be made whole."

And I felt it—he was tired, he was old beyond counting, and this body was wearing out. The phoenix needed his fire. I stepped forward.

"What is left, but a shallow and empty husk."

I gauged my target, searching for his beating pulse. There, against his chest. A mark no larger than a coin, brilliant gold circled with silver.

"There is no room for grief nor for doubt."

"Blessed is the Mother of the Moon and all who walk her paths," the Lord of the Dahns whispered. "Blessed is she who gives me release in the Rite of Renewal."

How could I do this? And yet, my hand was steady and I felt the power of the four Elementals within the horn harken to my silent call. Wind, Water, Flame, the Land—they rose up and combined their powers. Eriskel, the jindasel of the horn, who had once been a part of the Black Beast himself, added his own strength, focusing all of the energy through me.

"Release is sweet, the heart must fly free."

I bit my lip, but didn't waver. There was no going back. This was a one-way ticket and I was driving the train. I inhaled a sharp breath and gazed at my quarry.

"This life is over, the light fades out."

"Join the Hunt! Ride with the Moon! Give yourself over to shadow and joy and passion and the magic that is the glowing Mother who watches over every one of us. I release you from your physical bonds. I release you from your shackles. Run with the Hunt this night by my side, run free, and run wild!" I lifted the horn and aimed.

"Renew and transform, the soul's alchemy."

As Morio chanted the last line, I drew his spell through me, combined it with the energy of the Elementals, and let it fly as I plunged the horn into the target on the Black Beast's chest.

A shroud of icy fire rose forth, as cold as Hel's domain.

The unicorn screamed, a terrifying shriek that echoed in the heart of every creature living in the Deep. Smoke began to rise from his body. As I stumbled back, the crystalline horn burning my hands, the Black Beast let out another piercing cry and turned. As he galloped away, the flesh began to melt away from his body and the Moon Mother cried out in joy.

"Run! Lead the Hunt, for you are my newest priestess, and it is only fitting you and your sacrifice are honored this night at the helm of the Pack!"

The Moon Mother slapped her hand against my right shoulder

and a cutting pain sliced through me as her touch ate into my flesh. Something was happening to my back, but I didn't have time to figure out what it was because she shoved Morio up beside me and we took off, chasing the now-skeletal unicorn who plunged through the early dawn. Followed by my Lady and the pack, we ran until the stars burnt themselves out of the sky. We ran until the sun threatened to creep over the horizon. We ran until the madness left us.

CHAPTER 16

Groggy, I opened my eyes and struggled to sit up. My shoulder burned. Actually, both shoulders burned like a fury, and I was warm with a light fever. I squinted in the morning light, trying to figure out where I was. I wasn't still in the Deep, that much I knew. No, I was in a bed, under a thick quilt. I shifted, pushing myself to a sitting position, and heard someone stir beside me. Morio was just waking, under the covers by my side.

"Camille, how do you feel?" Trillian's voice cut through the fog as he sat down by my side, pressing a cup of dark coffee into my hands. Iris stood near the door, carrying another cup that I assumed was for Morio.

"Like Hel warmed over. Where are we?" I glanced around the room. It was tidy and looked too cozy to be anywhere I was familiar with.

"At an inn. We're in the Dryfor Village." He held my hands to steady the hot drink and I slurped it down.

"Where the hell did you find coffee over here?" Otherworld had its pleasures but coffee wasn't one of them. We'd grown up with it as a treat, because Father used to slip over Earthside and bring it back for our mother, but most Fae had never heard of it.

"I never go anywhere without a stash," Trillian said, grinning. "So, what do you remember about this morning?"

"Not much," I said, turning to Morio, who had greedily accepted the mug of steaming java from Iris. "You?"

He frowned. "Vague events, but nothing after . . ." His voice dropped and I knew what he was thinking.

I glanced around the room again. "How secure is this place?"

Trillian motioned to Iris, who checked the door to make sure no one was outside. "Secure enough. Feddrah-Dahns is downstairs, though. They won't let him up the steps."

"That's fine, because I'm not sure how much to tell him or what he knows." I hesitated for a moment, then just blurted it out. "Last night I sacrificed the Black Unicorn to the Moon Mother."

Pursing his lips, Trillian let loose a low whistle. "So that's what the commotion was about."

"What commotion?"

"When you and Fox Boy came tumbling off the astral, so did another woman—a priestess of the Moon Mother. She hustled us up and told us to get you out of the Deep before dawn broke. In fact, she paved the way by bringing horses with her. If you could call them that."

Iris cleared her throat. "They were skeletal beasts, terrifying, really, but they ran as fast as the wind and stopped on the outskirts of Dryfor Village. Then, before we could say a word, they vanished. The priestess said someone would be in touch with you once you return Earthside. She suggested strongly that the moment you two are fit to travel, we get the hell out of here."

"Camille, look," Trillian said.

"Look at what?"

"Your back." He held up a small hand mirror sitting on the chest of drawers. I glanced over my shoulder at my reflection.

On the right shoulder blade a new tattoo had emblazoned itself in my skin. Opposite the silver spiral on my left shoulder marking me as Moon Witch was the outline of a black owl flying over an elaborate crescent moon with horns pointed up. The crescent sat atop a dark orb.

The emblem all priestesses of the Moon Mother were tattooed with.

I caught my breath and watched as the tattoo shimmered and glistened. The spiral on my left shoulder mirrored its brilliance and it looked like my back was inset with diamonds and onyx rather than the ink of the Moon Mother.

"I'm a priestess," I whispered.

Iris nodded, her face serious. "So you are, Camille. And someone will be coming to visit you to help you adjust, but now we have to hurry."

"Should we tell Feddrah-Dahns?" Morio asked.

The moment the words hit my ears I shook my head. "I don't know. Ignorance may ensure our safety . . . maybe we shouldn't. I feel it's important we keep this under wraps and just get the fuck back home. The priestess was right. Help us get dressed and let's get out of here now."

"What about portal jumping? How will we manage it?"

"I suppose we should sneak back to Dahnsburg and jump from there. We aren't that far away from the portal near the Deep. We'll return the same route we came and pray they don't catch us."

I started to pull on my skirt, but stopped. All my clothes were soaked through with mud and grass and blood. "Lovely. I can't wear this," I said, looking at the sodden mess. "I'd look like a reject from *Satan's School for Girls*. I was naked when I killed him but my clothes still caught the worst of it."

Iris laughed. "I can take care of that. Both of you were a sight when we brought you in here. I washed you up the best I could," she added, blushing as she glanced at Morio. "You, too."

"Thanks, Iris," he said, winking at her. "You're a peach."

She blushed again, then brought out a bag. "While you slept, I did a little shopping at the early market. I couldn't find much but . . . here." She drew out a simple robe in a brilliant blue shade and handed it to me, along with a finely made leather belt. And for Morio, she held out a pair of brown trousers and a green tunic. "I was able to clean your shoes, and they're over there in the corner."

We dressed quickly and shoved our filthy clothes in the bag, then—eating bread and cheese on the run—hurried downstairs.

Feddrah-Dahns and Mistletoe were waiting. The unicorn

surprised me by motioning me aside with a wave of the head. "Priestess Camille, rest assured, my father will not find out what transpired from me. Revealing that information will be up to the new Lord of the Dahns Unicorns."

Priestess? I stared at him. "You know what happened?"

He bobbed his head. "Of course. I felt his death. All of the Dahns Unicorns did—it rocked through every one of us. But none except for myself know exactly how it happened. Each time he is reborn, the herd feels the passing."

"I should have known," I said. "What will your people think? Will they hate me?"

Feddrah-Dahns shook his head. "No. At least not my people. Others may not see the matter so clearly." He paused as if he were wondering how much to say. "Understand: The Black Beast chose *you*, Lady Camille. His command is sacred among the Dahns Unicorns."

"Then is there a problem?"

"To some degree. There are rites and rituals my father would demand you undergo, and you do not have time. I have a premonition there are things afoot Earthside that you must take care of. So I will make sure you get back through the portals without any questions."

Impulsively, I threw my arms around his neck and kissed his cheek. "You are a true friend, Feddrah-Dahns. Please, take care of yourself. I couldn't bear it if anything happened to you. You're the unicorn every little girl envisions walking by her side. You're the unicorn of legends, and on the day you ascend to the throne, your people will have gained the most noble leader they could ever hope for."

The morning flew by in a rush of portal jumping and avoiding the unicorns and elves. At noon, we stepped through the portal leading into Grandmother Coyote's forest, and I took a deep breath. We were home, safely, but nothing would ever be the same. The marks on my back foretold that.

Grandmother Coyote was nowhere to be seen. For once, I was disappointed rather than relieved. I wanted to ask her advice about the spirit seals. The feeling in my gut was that Tanaquar and Asteria were going to make a mess of things, albeit unwittingly, and I was willing to pay the price to get some expert advice. But when we stepped out of the portal, she wasn't there.

I glanced around, looking, but nada. After a moment, I sighed and pulled out my cell phone. Delilah answered.

"We're back. Can you pick us up?"

"Thank the gods you're home," she said, her voice tense. "Chase has been asking where the hell you and Morio are. Apparently the Wedgewood Cemetery has become the liveliest place in town and there's not much Menolly and I can do about it. I'll be there in ten minutes."

As we made our way through the woods to the road, I closed my eyes, readjusting to the presence of power lines and airplane noises and passing traffic. It was so much noisier than Otherworld, but this time, I felt a sense of relief being back. And Trillian was with me. I glanced over at him and he gave me a soft smile, one of those that reminded me both just how passionate and just how dangerous he could be.

By the time we reached the road, the rain was pouring again. Seattle definitely had it all over most of Otherworld in terms of rain. Actually, now that I thought about it, Dahnsburg's climate was surprisingly similar to that of western Washington's. As I drifted into a comfortable silence, Delilah pulled up in Morio's Subaru. He'd left the keys with her. Now, he got in the driver's seat and I climbed in the back with Trillian and Delilah. Iris rode shotgun.

"Welcome home, Trillian," she said. "I'm so glad you're back."

He stared at her, a smirk on his face. "Do tell? That's a change."

She stuck her tongue out at him, but instead of a comeback, said, "So, you guys have the energy to head out to the cemetery tonight? We've got a whole lot of shaking going on. You'd think it was near Samhain."

Halloween and Samhain—the festival of the dead—were celebrated in Otherworld a bit differently than by the humans over Earthside.

For one thing, on Samhain Eve, our dead dropped in for a visit—visibly. They were loud, sometimes obnoxious, and left no room for speculation as to whether they were there or not.

But Halloween itself was moot. In OW, we didn't do the costume party dress-up thing, and candy might be dandy, except we left the big sweet bash until Yule. Santa Claus—aka the Holly King—was a big hit at parties because of his stash.

I shook my head. "We're still over a month from the holiday, and the dead don't usually walk on the equinox. At least not like this. Okay, let's get our butts home so we can tell you all the crap going down back over in OW. You aren't going to believe what happened."

By the time we walked through the door, it was a little after one. I decided to wait to spill all the news until Menolly was awake. Iris headed to her room for a shower, and I aimed myself toward the stairs, also desperately in need of a shower and change of clothing. I wasn't sure what I was going to say once I was alone with Trillian and Morio, but they saved me the trouble.

"I'm hungry for a big, thick sandwich with mustard and mayo," Trillian said, his eyes lighting up when he glanced down the hall at the kitchen.

"Me, too," Morio said. As I dashed up to my room, they were hauling out supplies for what threatened to be towering sandwiches.

I was toweling off when my phone rang. I spread my towel on the bed, sat down, and picked up the phone, once again appreciating my mother's world. Earthside had its advantages and no way would I dispute them.

It was Henry Jeffries on the line. Henry had been a regular at the Indigo Crescent since the OIA first opened it as my Earthside cover. Once I took over the bookstore for real, we'd gotten to know each other better.

A somewhat older gentleman—by FBH years—in his mid-sixties, he loved golden-age science fiction and fantasy. A few months back, I'd hired him on part-time. He made the perfect employee: He didn't need the money, he loved the work, and he was polite and fun to talk to.

"Hey, Henry, what's up?" I expected him to give me a run-down on what was going on at the bookstore.

"My mother died, Camille." He didn't sound choked up

about it—his mother had been a harridan who ruled his life and kept him locked into his perpetual bachelor existence—but I could sense an underlying melancholy.

"I'm sorry. I imagine you need some time off to attend to affairs?"

Surprise number two.

"No, thank you. Mother wanted a simple service, and to be truthful, since she had no friends, there isn't anybody to contact. I buried her this morning. The lawyers will attend to the will but it's fairly straightforward. My mother was a wealthy woman, you know."

"No, I didn't know that."

"In fact, that's what I wanted to talk to you about. I'm her sole beneficiary. I'm going to be a rich man, Camille. Very rich. I've got nothing to occupy my time—I'm not a traveler. I don't want to go adventuring. So I thought of buying the shop next to yours. You know, the bakery that went under?"

"Um-hmm," I murmured, wondering where he was going with this. I was getting chilly sitting in my birthday suit. The second floor was drafty and we hadn't gotten around to having the house insulated yet.

"I thought I'd turn it into a coffee shop and hire someone to manage it. Then I could focus on helping you run the bookstore more. We could put a door inside, between the two shops—really tie them together. That should bring in more business for you. Sort of like me buying into your business without really buying into it." His words came out in a rush and I could hear the excitement behind them.

Touched that he cared so much about the bookstore and wanted to help increase sales, I said, "What a lovely idea. We'll talk about it in a couple of days, but I'm interested. Are you sure you don't need some time off?"

"No," he said softly. "The work is good for me. My mother lived a long life. And you know what she was like. I'm not going to play hypocrite. She was overbearing and sharp-tongued. I'll miss her, of course, but she never gave me the room to love her. She pushed everybody away."

"Okay. Well, if you're up to working this afternoon, that would be great. Iris and I just got back from Otherworld. We had to talk to my father for a bit. So we're both a little tired."

He laughed. "Now there's one adventure I'd love to take. Someday, promise you'll take me on a trip to your home-world?"

I smiled. Henry was a sweetheart and in his own, gentle way, he brought a grace and good manners into our lives. "Henry, I promise I will do my best to make sure you get to visit Y'Eírialiastar. You'd love it."

As I hung up the phone, I thought that if anybody deserved to see their fantasies come true, it was Henry. Though he'd never see the fantasy of marrying Iris come to light. Our man had a bad case of unrequited love, but as much as Iris liked him, she didn't return the affection. And there's never been a way to force love where it won't blossom.

I finished drying my hair and slid into clean, comfortable clothes, then headed downstairs to see if the boys had thought to leave me a sandwich, or if I'd have to lick the crumbs off their plates.

By the time I got downstairs, Chase was there. He had his arm draped around Delilah and they were snuggling in the living room. Trillian and Morio glanced up as I entered the room. I leaned down to plant a kiss on Trillian's lips, then Morio's, but drew the line at sitting between them.

"You both need showers. I'm not going to curl up with you now that I'm all squeaky clean."

Trillian grumbled, but then laughed. "I'm not taking a bub-ble bath with Fox Boy, but I'll head up for a shower now."

Morio let out a snort. "I'll use the shower in Iris's bath-room. I think she's done with her bath."

"Just don't barge in without knocking," I said. As they both left the room, I claimed their spot on the sofa. "Chase, how's it hanging?"

He let out a long sigh. "You be the judge. The Wedgewood Cemetery seems to be *the* place to hang out and party. At least, it is if you're a ghoul or ghost or whatever those creatures are. Last night all hell broke loose. I've got the area cordoned off but pretty soon one of those creatures is going to wander off the green, so to speak. I wish you'd been here to help out."

"Full Moon," I said. "I was running with the Hunt to the

point of madness. I'd have been less help to you than Delilah was in her kitty-cat form. So, have the papers gotten wind of the undead brigade yet?"

Chase jerked his head in a short, grim nod. "Yeah, oh yeah. Andy Gambit's all over it."

Gambit reported for the *Seattle Tattler*, a rag that thrived on ignorance, bigotry, and yellow journalism. "What the hell is he saying now?"

"He's trying to blame the FH-CSI for the problem. And he's inciting that damned Brotherhood of the Earth-Born—the new church that the Freedom's Angels group and the Guardian Watchdogs are forming? He's inciting them to haul their asses out to the various cemeteries and pray for the souls of the dead. He's going to get a lot of people hurt if he doesn't watch it."

Delilah's eyes narrowed. "Prayers won't do any good. Not unless they contain the right spells to calm the dead. And then only if you've got a powerful enough mage or witch to cast them."

"I know that, and you know that, but Gambit doesn't believe it." Chase leaned back against the cushion and rubbed his eyes. "I'm so tired. Last night Delilah decided to play chase—and I'm not talking about me—all night long. She was going nuts, tearing around the room, knocking stuff off the nightstand, pouncing on my toes. I had to kick her outside the bedroom so I could sleep."

"I can't help it if that catnip mouse you gave me was so strong," she said, laughing.

"Sure, blame me." He gave her a kiss on the forehead. "Seriously, Camille, I wish there had been somebody around to help me last night. Menolly couldn't go out with me. She had to watch over the house."

"Next month we'll make certain you aren't alone without backup during the full Moon." I shook my head. "The trip home was insane. I'll go into detail once Menolly's awake, but last night the Moon Mother . . . she promoted me, so to speak. I'm now a priestess." I pulled down my top to show them the new tattoo.

Delilah gasped. "Oh great gods! Congratulations!" She

flew out of her chair and pulled me to my feet, hugging me tightly. "I know how much you've always hoped this would happen! But how? Why?"

I glanced around the room. "Are the wards up?"

"Still tight and active," she said.

"Okay, here's the short story. I'll tell you more tonight, so no questions till then. Talking about this is . . . difficult." The words came harder than I thought they would. They felt so harsh on my tongue. "Last night I sacrificed the Black Unicorn with his own horn. With *my* horn." And for the first time since I'd woken up, I burst into tears.

Delilah stumbled back. Even Chase looked appalled, but neither of them said a word, for which I was grateful. After a moment, Iris came out of the kitchen, holding Maggie propped against one hip. The gargoyle reached out to me and I took her in my arms. Her wide eyes glowed softly and she gently licked the tears rolling down my face.

"No sad, Camey . . . no sad . . ."

"Somebody misses her Camille." Iris gave me a long look. "You okay?"

I nodded. "Yeah, just overemotional."

"Well, then. Delilah," Iris said, holding up a roll of toilet paper that had been ripped to shreds. "I see you discovered a new toy last night."

Delilah blushed. "Oh . . . uh . . . yeah. Where did you find it?"

"The guest bathroom. I hope you had fun because you knocked everything off the counter, ripped up the toilet paper, and climbed the shower curtain."

"Camey! Camey!" Maggie interrupted.

I cooed softly as her wispy fur tickled my nose. She snuggled against me, moophing gently. She clutched my hair and closed her eyes, resting her head on my shoulder. I kissed her forehead and settled into the rocking chair, gently rocking back and forth as she fell asleep. My tears began to recede.

"She had a busy morning," Delilah said, a guilty look crossing her face. "I left her alone in the kitchen while I bathed, and she tipped over her new playpen, managed to get out, and opened the cupboard under the sink. She dumped the garbage and was eating stale pizza when I found her, though she was wearing more of it than she got in her mouth."

"Oh hell, I wish I'd been here to see that," I said, laughing and kissing Maggie again. She was child and cat all rolled into one. The best of both worlds only with wings and really big ears. "Do you think it's okay she ate pizza?"

"I got pictures," Chase said, a grin on his face. "I found her when I wandered in to make coffee while Delilah was sleeping off her escapades. I stayed here, by the way, to help Menolly keep an eye on things. And no, I do not think you should feed her pizza. She threw up on my feet right after I snapped the shot. I did *not* take a picture of that."

"Well, she seems okay now. By the way, where were Rozurial and Vanzir when you needed extra hands?" The pair had been making themselves scarce lately and I wondered what was up.

"They were scouting around, trying to dredge up more about this Bonecrusher woman."

"She's a demon," I said automatically.

"Demon. I haven't heard from them since they left last night around ten o'clock." Chase glanced at his watch. "Should we be worried?"

"Maybe." I crossed to the window and stared out at the blustery afternoon, my hands pressed against the glass. Autumn was in full swing, the rain was pounding down, and I dreaded hiking through the cemetery in this weather, in the dark of night. The Moon might reflect light through the clouds, but this wasn't going to be a Sunday picnic, by any means.

Delilah joined me and placed one hand gently atop my own. "You had a rough night, didn't you?" she asked softly.

"That's the understatement of the year. Wait till you hear the whole of it. We're in for one hell of a ride. And Venus the Moon Child is wrapped up in it all now. I'm afraid we've got some hard decisions coming up. Also, Father's right in the thick of it."

She wrapped her arm around my shoulders. "We'll make it through. We always do. The odds are getting steeper, but so far, we've lucked out."

Yeah, I thought, so far. But how long could our luck hold? How long before one of us went tumbling over the edge, onto the wrong end of a sword or in the path of a nasty spell? Shadow Wing could throw demon after demon our way, working up the ranks of his thugs until he found one that could match us, one we couldn't stop. And then where would we be?

Suddenly gloomy again, feeling lost in a very big world, I rested my head on her shoulder, wishing for once that I could be as optimistic as she was.

CHAPTER 17

I crashed for a few hours until Menolly woke up. Trillian and Morio joined me, and though it felt incredibly good to have both of them in my bed, with us all together again, I couldn't help but wonder what was going on with Smoky, but was too exhausted to dwell on it. This Hunt had been the hardest one I'd ever endured, save for the first, and my body and mind needed time to recharge. Unfortunately, we didn't have the luxury of downtime, not with the work that waited for us in the cemetery.

When the alarm buzzed, Morio silenced it, and we all struggled out of sleep. I yawned and scrambled out from under the covers. Trillian handed me my robe, while Morio headed toward the bathroom. I blinked, gazing in the mirror on my vanity. I'd forgotten to remove my makeup and now it was smudged, but with five minutes, a little makeup remover, and the M.A.C. bonanza that filled the drawers of my vanity table, I was presentable again.

Morio slipped into a pair of indigo-wash jeans and a turtleneck, while Trillian chose a pair of leather pants and a turtleneck. They both washed up good, though Trillian had a faraway look in his eye that made me pause. When I asked, he shrugged, giving me a faint smile.

"I guess we'd better get downstairs," I said when I realized I wasn't going to get an answer. I slipped into a calf-length rayon skirt and a cowl-neck purple sweater. The night promised to be both cold and bloody. I wasn't about to wear my best bustier into combat. I made sure my earrings were small—chandelier earrings were bad in battle; I'd found that out the hard way—and laced up my granny boots.

We trundled down to the kitchen where Chase had prepared dinner. Iris appeared, yawning, still in her bathrobe.

"Thank you for cooking, Chase," she said. "I was worn through from the journey."

I leaned over one of the pots and sniffed. "What's that?" Whatever it was smelled good.

"Chicken and dumplings." He spooned up one of the doughy blobs. The broth was steaming, heaven in a ladle, filled with shredded carrots, onions, celery, and meaty slices of chicken.

"What's a dumpling?" I started to ask, but then stopped. "That's right, Mother made them once in a while. Only she made sweet cinnamon dumplings in a big pot of applesauce." I leaned in and spooned up a little of the broth.

Bad idea!

"Hot! Hot! Hot!" Pressing my hand to my lips, where a small blister was forming from the scalding spoon, I still couldn't refrain from taking another taste. "But, oh, that's good. I didn't know you could cook like that."

He winked. "Oh, I can cook all right. I learned early, if you'll remember the things I told you about my childhood. It was either that or eat sandwiches all the time. Now get over to the table and I'll bring you a bowl."

As Delilah and Chase brought steaming bowls of the stew to the table, Menolly strolled in from the living room with Rozurial and Vanzir behind her. The demon twins looked beaten down. In fact, Roz looked like he had . . . shit, *he did*. His right eye was black-and-blue.

"What the hell happened to you?" I blurted out.

He shrugged. "Well, it wasn't your maniac husband this

time, at least." With a sniff, he added, "I need some of whatever that is."

"Sit. I'll bring you some." Delilah took his coat.

Vanzir straddled a chair next to the table and shook his head when Chase offered him a bowl. "Not hungry, thanks."

Menolly slipped up behind me and gave me a quick hug. "Good to see you back, and Trillian, too," she said.

"Hello, O Fangstress." Trillian waved a knife in her general direction as he slid a thick pat of butter into the soup. "How's tricks?"

"Getting trickier," she said. "Put that away before you hurt someone. And welcome home."

"We're all glad you're back," Roz said to Trillian. "We need all the help we can get."

"Good to see you." Trillian nodded back. He stared at Vanzir. "You're demon, aren't you?"

"That's Vanzir," I said. "Remember, I told you about him?"

"Oh." Trillian gave him a long look, then went back to his soup.

Vanzir coughed. "Yeah, and I can imagine what she said."

"You're being paranoid again." I let out a long sigh. "Don't always be so defensive. I gave you more than enough kudos in my description. Back to the matter at hand. Roz, where the hell did you get the shiner?"

Rozurial frowned. "Nothing we can fix right now, but nothing we should ignore, either."

I put my spoon down. He'd just yanked me away from the happy place I'd found through Chase's dinner. "What happened?"

"The Bonecrusher has spies out and about. Tregarts. Not that bright, but loyal. They're insanely strong, too. I found out the hard way. And I gather she's trying to start up a training camp in the woods somewhere."

"Training camp? For what? Demon Army Brigade 101? Holy hell. That's a disaster waiting to happen. So do you know anything else? And just what went down to net you the black eye?"

"How about one question at a time? I tried to pry more information out of our informant than he was willing to give. Damn creep sucker-punched me, then kneed me." Roz blushed and Vanzir let out a sharp laugh. "Yuck it up, buddy. You weren't on the receiving end. His knee felt like solid steel. My balls are so black-and-blue it's going to be a while before I take them out for a spin."

Menolly let out an audible sigh. I flashed her a snarky look and she quickly sobered.

I sobered, too. "So does he know who you are? We have to be discreet. We can't maul suspects and then let them go free."

"Don't sweat it," Vanzir answered for him. "He's gone. I got him before he hit the door." He gave me a little bow with a snarky flourish on the end.

"Good," I said, feeling altogether too bloodthirsty. That was Menolly's department, not mine.

Rolling his eyes—whether in disgust or amusement, I didn't know—Trillian said, "So tonight we're set for cemetery duty? We need to know what we're facing. Anybody have any idea?"

Chase frowned. "I'm not the best person to ask. I don't know what all of these creatures are, or how to differentiate ghosts from spirits from . . . whatever."

"From what Chase told me before you meandered down to dinner, we've got a mixture of walking dead and spirit activity out there." Menolly sighed. "No vampires as far as I can tell, which is a good thing. But with so much spiritual turbulence, we're going to need more than just fighting gear. We have to be able to repel them. And if there are any creatures like shades . . ." She left the thought unfinished but the conclusion was easy to reach and it wasn't a pretty one.

"Or revenants," Delilah added.

"I think we're going to need more spell power than Morio and I can provide. And Smoky's not back yet." I stared at the table. The vampires wouldn't help us, what with Wade and Menolly still on the outs, so we couldn't ask Vampires Anonymous to come to our aid. And the Supe community wasn't exactly rife with magical personnel, other than their innate powers.

"Wilbur," I blurted out, jerking my head up to stare at the others. "We'll ask Wilbur. He's a necromancer."

"What makes you think he'll help us? He's not exactly

buddy-buddy with us." Menolly grimaced. "Every time I run into him, I want to fang him one—and not for fun. He's too interested in women as cock fodder."

"Yeah, I know, but there has to be something we can offer him to help us. Maybe a couple dead bodies to play with?" I glanced around, stopping as I came to Chase's gaze. He was staring at me, almost sadly. "What?"

"Nothing," he said, shaking his head.

"No, tell me."

"It's just . . . you've changed. You're tossing around dead bodies as payment now? I know you have to practice raising the dead for your magic, but remember—these were people at one time. Living, breathing humans who had lives, loves, families."

Feeling unjustly attacked, I blinked back a sudden spate of tears. "No, *you* listen. I don't like it. I don't like desecrating graves. I don't like dabbling in decay. But if I don't learn how to work this magic, then we're at even more of a disadvantage. Maybe I am becoming a fiend. Maybe I'm turning into a monster, but if that's what it takes, I'll do it. And who said the bodies had to be human? I'm sure we can find a couple goblin corpses somewhere. He might have fun raising something else besides people."

Delilah whispered something in Chase's ear and he winced.

"I'm sorry. I know you don't like this," he said, lifting his hand to stare at the missing fingertip. "I guess this is my reminder of why you do what you do. Why *we* do what we do. I never served in the military, Camille. I wasn't brought up in a military household like you were. I had a rotten childhood, so I tried to make up for it by going into police work, but all that happened is that I encountered a seamier side of society than I ever did when I was a kid. I suppose I've had my fill of being on the front lines against creeps and losers and psychos. But there's no discharge in sight."

Menolly surprised everybody by walking behind the detective and ruffling his hair. She placed her hands on his shoulders and leaned down to stare in his eyes. "Quit sweating, you know I won't bite you. And I'm sorry you're feeling torn. But, Chase, I guarantee you, you haven't seen anything yet.

Whatever Karvanak did to you, it will be a thousand times worse if we can't stop Shadow Wing. If we have to break a few eggs in the process . . . or raise a few bodies . . ."

"Speaking of worse," I broke in. "I've got worse for you. Or it seems like it to me. I wish Grandmother Coyote was around, because we need her advice."

"What happened? Does this have anything to do with the Black Unicorn?" Delilah asked.

"Yeah, I think so," I said slowly. "I can't be sure the two events are connected, but yeah . . ." Sucking in a deep breath, I slowly exhaled and told them everything. Told them about sacrificing the Black Unicorn during the Hunt, about the fact that I was now a priestess for the Moon Mother, about the Keraastar Knights and how Tanaquar and Asteria were planning on using them to stabilize the portals, about the sorcerer's attack in King Upala-Dahns's court. And lastly, I added, "I no longer feel comfortable asking Father's opinion of things, either."

"Why?" Menolly asked, her gaze catching mine. I could see the wariness lurking within. She believed every word I was saying.

"Because I'm positive that he's sleeping with Queen Tanaquar," I said.

"What?" Delilah jumped. "But Father wouldn't . . . *the Queen*? Are you sure?"

"Yeah, I'm sure. As sure as I am of anything at this moment. He finally took our advice and found himself a girlfriend. But even though Tanaquar is a damned sight better than Lethesanar, I don't fully trust her."

"We were trying to avoid using the seals. Are they certain this is a good idea?" Menolly said.

"I have no idea. I don't seem to know anything anymore."

"Are you *sure* the idea will fail?" Chase asked. "I'm not trying to make waves, but maybe they're right?"

"How should I know? They aren't going to tell us every detail, I could see that right off." I paused, catching my breath. "Sorry, I'm just a little on edge. The problem is we don't know if this will work. That's why I want to talk to Grandmother Coyote. My instinct is screaming that it's going to upset the balance even further, but I want her take on it. Maybe I'm just paranoid."

"But suppose the plan backfires and makes them stronger? There are too many potential disasters here," Menolly said.

Morio played with his cup of tea, tapping the china lightly with one fingernail. "I think they've miscalculated the power of the demons. Think about it," he said when we looked at him quizzically. "They're just coming off a successful war. Both of them are feeling strong and victorious. Suppose it's gone to their heads?"

Delilah coughed. "Somehow the thought of a win going to Queen Asteria's head like that seems ludicrous, but I suppose even she is fallible."

Trillian cleared his throat. "There's another possibility. Suppose they're afraid of the newly risen Fae Courts and are worried that the Triple Threat might join forces with the demons? Or even that you three might join forces with the Triple Threat? You'll notice that neither Titania nor Aeval was invited to their little tête-à-tête. Or Morgaine, for that matter."

I stared at him. "You really think they're afraid we might start handing the seals over to the Earthside Fae Courts?"

"What better way to ensure that you continue taking them back to Otherworld than to invent an even greater need for Asteria to possess them?"

"Then you think this is a ruse?"

He hesitated for a moment, thinking, then shook his head. "No, I don't. I think they believe what they say. But, like you—I feel it's a double-edged sword. However, *I* don't dare say anything. Svartalfheim is still suspect in Otherworld since we uprooted the city and ran out of the Sub Realms. There's too much to lose by openly questioning their motives. And if I go to King Vodox with my concerns, he'd know about the spirit seals and that's something you *really* don't want happening."

"He makes a point," Rozurial said. "With the revelation that you girls are related to Morgaine, perhaps their fear has grown stronger."

"But our father is related to her, too—" I stopped. "Oh. Do you think that's why Tanaquar is sleeping with him? To keep tabs on him and, by doing so, find out what we're up to?"

"Tanaquar did whatever she had to in order to win the war against her sister. Blood ties aren't sacred to her. You can be sure if she had Lethesanar in custody, the Opium Eater would lose her head before she could blink. With the Fae Queens of Earthside reigning over their courts again, it potentially jeopardizes Tanaquar's sole reign as the Queen of Fae."

"But what about Queen Asteria? Is Tanaquar afraid of her?" Delilah asked.

"No," Trillian said. "Asteria's not the threat—she's the *Elfin* Queen and the elves and Fae don't play in each other's sandboxes. But consider this: We have three newly crowned monarchs over here. What do you suppose would happen if Tanaquar's people decided they want to go back to the old system—the Seelie and Unseelie courts—that was in place before the Great Divide?" Trillian finished his soup and pushed back his plate.

"But that's ridiculous. She has no reason to worry," Delilah said, starting to clear the table.

"I'll get the dishes, girl. You have enough to think about tonight," Iris said, taking the plates from her.

Vanzir leaned forward, resting his elbows on the table. "No, it's not ridiculous. Trillian's right. The more authority a leader has, the more fearful they grow of losing it. Don't forget the amount of power it took to rip apart the worlds. The Fae lords behind the decision sure as hell aren't going to want to face the newly empowered Titania and Aeval, and they *certainly* won't be welcoming Morgaine to the mix. Remember, they dethroned them, stripped Titania of her sanity, and turned Aeval into a popsicle. That sort of *diplomacy* isn't easily forgotten. Suppose they're afraid that Titania and Aeval want to repay them in kind?"

The Great Divide had been a chaotic, bloody, world-shaking event. While little was remembered among humankind—what records there were had been destroyed—Fae on both sides remembered it clearly, though from different vantage points. Aeval, Titania, and Morgaine held little love for anyone who'd had a hand in the eons-old war.

"Enough talk," Menolly said. "We don't even know where the next seal is, and there's nothing we can do tonight about this new change in plans. Meanwhile, we have a cemetery full of undead waiting for us."

I reluctantly pushed myself out of my chair. The rain was pounding harder than ever and it was going to be cold, muddy, and nasty out there. "Why don't you go talk to Wilbur while we gather up the supplies?"

"Good girl. I'll be back with our boy in ten minutes." Menolly slipped out the door as the rest of us set about gathering everything we needed for the fight. Or at least, everything we could think of.

Morio stuffed Rodney in his bag and I grimaced. "No. Please tell me you're not bringing him."

"Sorry, babe, but we might be able to use him." He gave me a quick kiss. "Cheer up. If he gets too obnoxious we can feed him to the zombies."

I rolled my eyes. I might be a priestess now—something I'd wanted all my life—but this was turning out to be the worst September I'd had in ages. And listening to Rodney's crass standup routine was the last thing I needed tonight.

Wilbur, who looked like a defunct member of ZZ Top and smelled like he hadn't touched a bar of soap in a month, agreed to come along. When I found out, I suggested taking two cars.

"There are too many of us to comfortably fit in even Chase's behemoth SUV." At least, that was my story and I was sticking to it. I made sure that Wilbur traveled with Chase, not in our car.

By the time we pulled in to the Wedgewood Cemetery, it was pitch-dark. While the Moon was just past full, the clouds were so thick they obscured even the faintest glimmer of her light.

The rain was blowing horizontally, whipped sideways by the wind. I pulled my capelet close around my shoulders. The unicorn horn was home, in a safe place along with the cloak. Sacrificing the Black Unicorn had drained it of every single ounce of energy and I wouldn't be able to charge it until the next new Moon. I didn't like separating the cloak from the horn. It just seemed wrong.

Delilah and Menolly flanked me as we headed in. Wilbur followed, Trillian and Morio on either side. Rozurial, Vanzir, and Chase brought up the rear. As we approached the gates of the lighted graveyard, the first thing I noticed was that a number of the lovely old lamppost lights had been broken. It seemed the living dead weren't too keen on sunshine or lamplight.

"Can you feel it?" Menolly asked, stopping in the middle of the sidewalk.

"Feel what?"

"The dead are walking." Her eyes narrowed and turned blood-red, and when she smiled, her fangs were showing. "Nasty dead. Not vampires, not the dead who think, but zombies and other creatures that exist to kill and devour. I can sense them, like a hive of droning insects with no thoughts of their own."

I sucked in a deep breath and closed my eyes, reaching out. And there they were, just as she'd said. A mass of squirming maggots, a swarm of ants, hungry—looking to feed. And there was something else. Something behind the energy, almost like . . . Shivering, I opened my eyes.

"They're in the older part of the cemetery. But behind them, the magical signature of the energy—it's demonic. I sense Demonkin at work here."

Wilbur spoke up. "I can sense the dead underground, too, the ones who haven't been touched by the magic yet. If we don't do something, they *will* rise. Someone cast one bitch of a spell here, and it's not just aimed toward specific graves. Whoever's behind this is using a conduit of energy—like feeding medicine into an IV drip."

"Shit," Delilah said. "The ley line."

I stared at her. "Stacia Bonecrusher. Ten to one it's her. She's feeding her magic directly into the ley line that runs through the Wedgewood Cemetery. The line connects to Harold Young's house—or the remains of it and that's where we found the goshanti devil. The line also connects to the Wayfarer where the portal is, and to two rogue portals. And if she's messing around with the ley line, then—"

"She might be able to fuck up the portals." Delilah paled. "What if she's got the third spirit seal? The one Karvanak stole from us? Wouldn't it increase her powers and let her make a shambles of things?"

"Holy crap!" Menolly whirled around. "Could she be trying to use the ley line to rip them open or twist them so that they open into the Sub Realms?"

"Who knows what the hell she's up to?" I stared bitterly at the headstones before heading for the older part of the cemetery. The others followed. "We have to disrupt this Halloween party of hers and then figure out how to put the kibosh on her ability to access the ley line. Right now, it seems like she's experimenting to see just what she can do, but it won't be long before she branches out."

As we came to the iron gates cordoning off the oldest graves, Menolly stepped forward to open them. Iron still bothered her, but she would heal from it a lot faster than Delilah and I could hope to. She swung the gates open, her hands singeing from the burn of the metal, and we darted through.

And there we found them—the living dead. There were at least twenty of them, wandering around like the random monsters on a Diablo game. Joy of joys. Most were bonewalkers—bare skeletons. A few were mummified bodies. But all of them were searching for victims. Baleful lights filled their eye sockets. As I gazed at them, I felt unaccountably sad. They'd led their lives; they went to their ancestors; they should be left to rest.

I suddenly understood Chase's repulsion to my suggestion. But I also knew that the souls that had inhabited these bodies weren't here. We were fighting shells. Dangerous shells, yes. But nonetheless, they were mere husks. It would have been worse if they'd been possessed while still alive and in their bodies.

Wilbur and Morio stepped to the front, and Morio took my hand. Delilah and Menolly edged back to let us have room for our spell casting.

The rain cascaded down, plastering my hair to my head, streaking my face and chilling me to the bone. A bolt of lightning crashed overhead as the dance of the storm played from cloud bank to cloud bank, thunder rumbling so ominously that my teeth chattered.

Morio closed his eyes and I could feel him summoning the dark power. *The power of the grave.* I fell into synch with his breathing, and as he began to chant I focused the power he was building.

"Return to dust, return to the grave, return to the night, return to the earth, return to the depths, return to the Mother, return to the womb . . ."

Wilbur fell into a cadence with him and held up his hands, palms facing the wandering group of bone-walkers. A chill ran down my spine. Just by the tone of his voice I could tell he was more powerful than either Morio or me. FBH or not, this man knew his magic and it had changed him. A gray-green energy flared in his aura, creating a nimbus of power around him, and he began to gather it, sucking it in through his breath, focusing it out through his hands, aiming it toward the skeletons.

"Dust to dust, return to the ground, cease your wandering, strip life from that which has no life, return to decay . . ."

I blinked, sinking into the energy, ignoring the droplets that trickled down the back of my neck. The compulsion to move was strong, and I began to stride forward, a trail of energy linking me to Morio.

One of the skeletons came at me and I held up my hand. A brilliant light shot out of my palm, hitting the skeleton and engulfing it in flames of purple. The creature opened its mouth and shrieked, then fell, clattering into a pile of old bones. Morio walked behind me—I could feel him in my wake.

Wilbur was doing something. What, I couldn't see. I was focused on directing the energy that Morio and I'd invoked between ourselves. But I heard another shriek and it wasn't my doing. I flashed my hands again, and again the purple light engulfed two more skeletons. They fell into dust. And then, Morio shouted, breaking the energy.

Whirling around, I saw that he was being attacked by a zombie. He let out a low growl and began to shift into his demonic form. I glanced around, quickly ascertaining my position. I was in a battlefield of living bones and had incoming on the left—a pair of the bone-walkers was headed my way. I scrambled for the dagger I kept strapped to my thigh.

At that point, Wilbur shouted and I glanced in his direction. He, too, had been taken by surprise. A zombie trundled out from behind a nearby bush, attacking him from the rear.

At that moment, Delilah leapt into the fray, leading the others, her dagger, Lysanthra, raised high. The blade was singing her name, singing her battle cry. And then Menolly raced past me, bowling over one of the skeletons as she ramrodded it to the ground, skidding in the wet grass.

And the fray was on.

CHAPTER 18

I jumped back from the skeleton coming my way. Edged weapons weren't exactly the best defense against bone, but my dagger would have to do for now because the magic I'd just run through my body had burnt me out, and I'd need a clear head to call down the magic of the Moon Mother, considering how much chance for disaster there was when it backfired.

A quick glance over my shoulder told me that Morio had engaged the zombie that had attacked him. The shouts of the others rang out as they clashed with their opponents. Hoping Chase would be okay—he was the most vulnerable of us all—I brought my attention to bear on the skeleton again. As I moved in, trying to gauge the best way to attack the creature, it sidled to the left. I didn't have any of Delilah's fancy spinkicks or Menolly's strength behind me, but I wasn't a total couch potato when it came to Bruce Lee-ing my way through a confrontation.

Sucking in a deep breath, I lunged, slicing at the bonewalker.

A hit! I actually hit its right hand. As my silver dagger slashed at the bone, there was a pale flare of light and I managed to sever the hand from the wrist. The skeleton's hand scuttled across the ground, trying to find something to attack. But now that it no longer had its body to back it up, there wasn't much danger from it. The thing would just drag itself blindly around until it ran up against something it could grab hold of. Unless somebody munched it first, or the spell dissipated.

The skeleton's eye sockets gleamed with a sickly green fire, and its jaw clattered, as if it was trying to talk. Lucky for me, it didn't have sentient magic that would allow it to speak. I danced away as it lashed out with its other hand, grasping to catch hold of me. The thing might not be wielding a sword or dagger, but it had unnatural strength and it could crush my windpipe without so much as a blink.

I heard a cackle from my left and turned to see Menolly landing smack on top of another skeleton. It fell beneath her and she began ripping it bone from bone with her bare hands, laughing all the while. Delilah was near her, her dagger singing in the night as she kicked and slashed her way through another bone-walker. Turning back to my own opponent, I made another calculated attack and managed to catch the left hand the same way I'd severed the first.

"Anybody need a hand?" I shouted, feeling a rush of excitement. The Hunt was still flush in my soul, and the exhilaration of the chase came flooding back to my tired muscles, giving me a much-needed boost.

With a victory cry, I decided to try Menolly's method and launched myself headfirst toward the skeleton. It stumbled back, but not quick enough and I body slammed it, knocking it to the ground as I fell on top of it. We landed in the mud, but the bones were hard and rigid, and it felt like I'd fallen in a rocky field. Ignoring the pain, I brought the hilt of my dagger down on the skull of the creature, smashing a hole through the forehead, into where the frontal lobe would have been located if it still had a brain.

It shrieked as I brought the hilt down again, this time cracking through the bone between the eye sockets and nose. Though it waved its arms around, without any hands it couldn't do much more than smack the arm bones against me. Or at least that's what I thought until I felt the creature embrace me, elbows wrapping me tight as it struggled to crush me against its chest.

Cripes. Obviously, I hadn't thought this all the way through!

I tried to break free but it was stronger than I, even with all the damage I'd done to it. The bone-walker was squeezing my waist like a bony python.

Pushing against the ground, I attempted to gain enough leverage to bust free of the vise grip, but my hands were too slick to manage any real purchase. Everything was starting to look blurry and I realized I wasn't getting enough oxygen.

"Relecta de mordente!" Wilbur's voice rang loud and clear and the skeleton's arms loosened. It tried to scramble out from beneath me to get away from the necromancer's bone-be-gone spell.

I rolled away and pushed to my feet, sucking in deep lungfuls of air, covered from head to toe in grass stains and mud. As we stood there, Wilbur steadying me with one hand, Menolly rushed past us. She was wielding a femur from one of the other bone-walkers, and she swung it right toward the skeleton's waist, bludgeoning the creature in half. She then proceeded to pound it to smithereens.

I glanced up at Wilbur. "Thanks. I mean it," I said, wishing I hadn't thought such nasty thoughts about him.

He grinned then—not exactly a friendly grin, but it would do. "They're tricky." And then he was off, headed toward the last group of three.

Delilah was finishing up with a couple of skeletons and I blinked, peering into the darkness. I could see something moving beside her. It looked like a large dog at first, but when I squinted, it took on the shape of a large, ghostly feline.

Arial! Her twin, long dead but still watching over her! As I watched, the mist-shrouded leopard leapt at one of the skeletons and took it down, giving Delilah the chance to attack the other. Between the two of them, they finished off the bone-walkers. Then, Arial turned to gaze up at Delilah, and within another blink, vanished.

Smiling, I barely noticed the tears streaking down my face. Arial wasn't just Delilah's long-lost twin, she was also my long-lost sister, and Menolly's. We hadn't even known about her until a few months ago and were still trying to pull together all the pieces. Father didn't want to talk about it, more than to say that she hadn't made it through her first night. So he and Mother had decided not to tell any of us about her, but instead buried her quietly in the family gravesite.

Wiping my eyes and only managing to smear a streak of dirt across my face, I glanced back. The rest of the walking dead, including the two zombies, were so much dust and ashes. We were standing in a now quiet and empty graveyard among the scattered bones.

We gathered at the center. Everybody looked worn out, dirty, and tired.

"I saw her," I said softly to Delilah.

She looked at me, another crash of lightning illuminating the gentle smile on her face. "I'm glad. I'm glad someone else besides me can see her."

"I think with all the necromantic energy here, it helps."

Menolly gave me a quizzical look but I shook my head. "Later."

She nodded.

"So, what do we do now?" Delilah asked.

"We have to break the spell that's running through the ley line or it will just keep calling them out of their graves. And if the Bonecrusher shoots more magic into the current at another juncture, the havoc will eventually travel back here. We have to find Stacia." I looked at Morio and Wilbur. "What have you got for us? What can we do to disrupt the magic she set into motion here?"

Wilbur arched an eyebrow. "There is something you can try, but she'll know what you're up to if you do it. You can polarize the energy so it snaps back at her. Like a rubber band stretched too far."

Shaking my head, I asked, "Can you think of anything else we can use? I don't want to warn her that we're onto her little tricks."

"I may have an idea." Roz squatted down, examining the soil of one of the disturbed graves. "I'm not sure how it would work, but there's a technique I once saw used long ago before I was an incubus. It acted like the knots you tie in an umbilical cord—only magically."

"Say what?" I stared at him. "I've never had a baby, delivered a baby, or even seen one born. What are you talking about?"

"I know what he's saying," Chase broke in. Delilah put her hand on his arm. He absently patted it. "I've been present at a few births—"

"Really?" I asked.

"Don't act so surprised. I'm a cop. Cops end up helping out with babies and accidents and what have you." He stuck his tongue out at me and then snorted. Turning back to Roz, he continued. "You tie two knots in the cord, leaving a central section. When you sever the cord between the two knots, it prevents the blood from draining out both ways. And from what I can figure out about magic, I suppose it would prevent the magic from leaking out. The demon might not notice it right away. And . . . won't it cause the magic in the ley line to scatter?"

I stared at Chase, stunned. "You're really picking up the jargon, aren't you?"

He grinned.

"You've got it," Roz said, giving him a hearty pat on the back. "But we don't need to cauterize the magic in the ley line—we want it to leak. We just don't want Stacia to notice."

I began to understand what he was saying. "That means we need to create a magical tourniquet. We slap it on the flow of energy, and then we bust the spell a little ways down the line. The question is, do we have the know-how to do it?"

Wilbur and Morio looked at each other for a moment. I could tell both were ruminating over their personal repertoire of spells. I stepped away from the group while they thought and put in a call to Iris, giving her a quick rundown on what we needed.

"Can you do something like this?"

She paused, then said, "Yes. I can. It's not dangerous per se, but when the magic comes pouring out of the ley line, you're going to deal with some backlash. You need me down there?"

"Yeah, but you can't leave Maggie alone."

"She won't be," she said, then sighed. "Bruce is here. And . . . Smoky just returned."

My stomach dropped a mile. I wanted nothing more than to race home and find out what he had to say. "Did anybody come with him?"

"Nope, and he won't talk about it until you get here. I'll have Bruce drive me down. He's got his car and driver with him. I'll tell Smoky you're fine so he doesn't take it into his head that he has to join us." As she hung up, I turned back to the others.

Morio was shaking his head. "I don't think I can do it. I don't know what I'd use."

Wilbur shrugged. "I'm not so sure I can either—"

"Not a problem," I said. "Iris can and she's on her way." Before they could ask, I added, "Smoky's home, so Bruce is bringing her down in his car."

As I moved away from the group, Trillian and Morio joined me.

"The lizard coming?" Trillian looked put out, but not angry.

"Not yet," I said, barely hearing my words. My thoughts were wrapped up in so many things, not the least of which was a turmoil of curiosity over what had happened at the Dragon Council.

Iris showed up before too long. She walked the perimeter of the field, feeling out the energy. Wearing a thick cape against the ever-present rain and the increasing fog, she'd brought her Aqualine crystal wand with her.

As we watched, she began using it like she would a dowsing rod, searching for the exact point where the Bonecrusher had cast the spell into the ley line. Before long, she stopped. She was standing beside a drain that had been placed in the center of an access path next to a row of graves.

"Here it is. This grate drains into a culvert that runs out to the sewer. At least, that's my guess. It keeps this section of the cemetery from flooding. The grate—and the drain—also happen to run directly along the ley line. By shooting her magic into the culvert, it got sucked into the energy of the land."

"Good going," Morio said, joining her. He leaned over, staring through the grate. "That's probably why only these graves were affected. The newer parts of the cemetery are east of here, through the gates. Far enough from the ley line to remain untouched by the spell."

"We should really map this out," Delilah said, shoving her

hands in the pockets of her jean jacket and shivering. "Tomorrow, I'll come down here with Iris and diagram out exactly where the line runs through the cemetery."

"What next? How can we help?" I joined them, closing my eyes. I was tired, but I could still pick up on the hum of demon magic as it raced near my feet, along with the low pulse of the ley line. Together, they formed an odd cadence, though twisted and off-key.

"You can help by standing back and being prepared to fight anything that comes oozing out of the drain or bursting out of the ground. This is a tricky spell," Iris added. "When I sever the flow of magic, it will pour out of the ley line and there's a good chance it's going to create something ugly. *Real* ugly, and I'm not talking about just in the looks department. I'll be too busy making certain that the lamia doesn't feel the break, so you guys will have to cover my butt."

We moved into position, ready for anything and hoping for nothing.

Iris motioned for us to be quiet as she focused on the drain grate.

I could see the energy now, the vortex caused by the Bonecrusher's spell as it intruded into the energy of the land. A swirl of winds, clashing against one another. Iris worked a few yards away from the actual juncture of energy, *pinching* the spell so it didn't suddenly bleed out and alert Stacia. She deftly wove her magic, latticing the lamia's spell in a frost-shrouded net. Then, she began to tighten it, pulling it fast.

The energy would eventually back up, and Stacia would figure it out, but if we were lucky, we'd have found her and wiped her out before she fully realized what was going on. One blessing to fighting a powerful opponent: They weren't always up to speed with all their meddling, and they ran enough magic for something like this to go overlooked for a few days.

Some fifteen minutes of intense concentration later, we were all a cold, sodden mess. Iris looked at me and nodded. She held out a short dirk that looked both sharp and ruthless. With one swift motion, she stabbed into the palpable braid of energy and sliced through it, severing the cord.

One . . . two . . . three . . . holy hell! One moment I was standing there, dagger out, waiting to see what would happen and the next, an explosion rocked the area in which we were standing, sending us all flying. Blown off my feet, I landed a good two yards back on the grass.

I scrambled up, checking to see if anything was broken, but by now my clothes were so heavy with water they'd cushioned my fall. Looking around, I tried to see if something had slipped through. Nothing . . . nothing . . . and then I saw Wilbur. He was on the ground, clawing at his neck.

"Wilbur—help him!" I raced over to his side.

Menolly got there before me. She went down on her knees and frantically started waving her arms over him. "I can't see what's got him."

"I can!" Morio shoved her aside.

Startled, Menolly hissed, but recovered quickly and crouched next to him, ready to help.

"What is it?" I knelt on the other side of the necromancer.

Morio waved his hand across Wilbur's neck and whispered something. The outline of a gremlin came into view. Originating in the Netherworld, gremlins were implike spirits. While not fully demonic, they were dangerous and fed off psychic energy. The Yodalike creature splayed its wide hands across Wilbur's head, while its feet were wrapped around his throat.

"What can we do? How do we kill it?"

Delilah motioned me aside. "I don't know *what* can, but I know *who* can. Move back, everybody." She spoke so forcefully that everybody stopped to stare at her for a second before scrambling back. As she closed her eyes, her energy shifted. And then, before we could say a word, the air around her rippled and she transformed into her black panther self, but she wasn't alone. The misty outline of a golden spotted leopard stood beside her.

"Arial!" I let out a small gasp.

"Who's that?" Morio said, his eyes wide.

Menolly glanced around, looking frantically from side to side. "Who's who? What are you talking about?"

Chase and Trillian looked just as confused, but Roz said, "I see her," and Vanzir added, "So do I."

I turned to them. "Our sister—Delilah's twin. She died at birth but she keeps watch over Delilah in her Were shape."

Trillian blinked. "So it's true."

I turned back to Delilah and Arial, who grabbed the gremlin in their mouths, one on either side. The creature was screaming, struggling to break free, as it loosened its grip on Wilbur. Menolly dashed forward and dragged him away from beneath the gremlin, who was now one big chew toy for the two big cats.

Arial and Delilah proceeded to play tug-of-war with the creature, which I really didn't want to watch but couldn't help myself—it was like a train wreck, impossible to look away from—and then Delilah let go and Arial vanished, the limp gremlin in her mouth.

Delilah padded over to Wilbur and licked his face, then gazed up at me. I dropped to my knees beside her and threw my arms around her neck, planting a big kiss on her nose. She let out a soft growl and then rubbed her head against me, purring loudly. As soon as she started her singing, I backed away. Within a few seconds, she was herself again, crouched on the ground, shaking her head. I helped her up, steadying her as she blinked.

"Is he okay?"

"He will be," Trillian said. He and Chase were kneeling by the necromancer, checking his pulse and pupils. Wilbur seemed to be coming around and they pulled him to his feet.

He rubbed his throat, wincing. "That hurt like hell. What the fuck was that critter?"

"A gremlin. I'm surprised you haven't dealt with them before, being a necromancer," I said.

"Oh, I've dealt with several beasties from that realm, but never one of those. Are they common?" He stretched his neck, rolling it from side to side. "The thing had one hell of a death grip, I'll tell you that. I feel like it was trying to suck out my soul."

"There are a number of creatures who feed off psychic energy," Vanzir said, stepping forward. "I'm one of them, but I don't have to in order to live, so I do my best to curtail the desire. But gremlins and small creatures of the sort need it to survive. And yes, they are common. People who wake up feeling tired all the time but can't find any reason, or who feel drained when they go certain places, often have encountered gremlins without ever realizing it."

"Any way to keep them out of the house? I should ward against them," Wilbur said.

"We'll talk protection spells a little later," I broke in. "Meanwhile, Delilah saved you and the thing is gone." I turned to Iris. "Was that all that broke through?"

She nodded. "Yes, I felt one rush at the gates, so to speak, and that was it. But we shouldn't tarry. We have no idea how long it will be before the Bonecrusher realizes that her spell isn't working, and we don't want to be here when she arrives, wondering why."

"Maybe we do," Vanzir said. "Maybe we should stake out the area—what better way to find out where she's at?"

"But would she have to show up? Can't she just figure it out and cut her losses from wherever she's hiding?" I frowned. "I hate to leave somebody out here like that—it's too dangerous, and it also puts us a man down."

"Not if we bug the area with a camera," Chase said. "I could have my men in here in no time with a wireless surveillance unit. They can hide it in the trees, facing the area where Iris broke the spell. Then, if the lamia shows up, we'll catch it back at the station. At least we'll be able to get a bead on her."

"How soon can they get down here?"

"Within the next hour or so."

I glanced at Menolly, who nodded.

"We have time, I think," she said. "It's still early in the night; I can wait here for them and guard them."

"Okay, let's do it. Menolly, you and Chase stay here until it's done. The rest of us—back to the house." As we headed toward the cars, leaving Chase's so he could drive Menolly home afterward, Delilah sidled up to me and pulled me off to one side.

"What's wrong?" I asked.

She frowned. "I wanted to talk to you about something . . . before we do it. This may not be the best time, but somehow I don't think we're going to get a lot of *best times* from now on. I'm not asking permission, our minds are made up, but I need to tell you and Menolly's going to be pissed when she finds out."

"What did you do now?" I turned to her, studying her face. There was a faint look of guilt in those emerald eyes, but more than guilt—fear. "You're afraid of what I'm going to say. Tell me. It can't be that bad."

"Chase and I've come to a decision. I stole a bottle of the nectar of life during the Litha festival that Aeval, Titania, and Morgaine held. Chase is going to drink it. So we can be together for a long time." She dropped her voice to a whisper. "We're planning on him doing it during the equinox."

No. No, no, no. This was *so* wrong. "Kitten, listen to me. You can't just let him guzzle it down. There are rituals that need to be performed when an FBH drinks the nectar of life. They *must* be prepared for the ramifications. You're risking his sanity if you do it any other way."

"But what can we do? Who would perform the ritual? You know nobody back home would. Even Father—even though he loved Mother and offered her the same chance, he'd never go for it. I don't think he believes any men are good enough for us." She looked ready to cry. "I just want Chase to feel like he'll have the chance to be with me always."

"Babe, you listen to me. Promise me you won't do this— it's rash and dangerous. If you give me your word, I promise to find someone who can guide you through the ritual. It won't be by the equinox, but I *will* help you. I just want both of you to come through this safe and sane."

Actually, what I wanted was for them to forget about it. Chase didn't strike me as someone who could handle a thousand-year stint very well, but then, I could be wrong. I just knew that if they carried out their plans, our detective would go bye-bye, and in a very bad way.

She bit her lip, then finally nodded. "All right. But you promised to help me and I'm keeping you to it."

"Yeah, I know," I said, thinking about all the promises we'd made over the years, and how some of them were coming back to bite us in the butt. And then there were the promises that had been made to us, the ones that threatened to shatter at our feet.

Smoky, for one. Smoky and Morio and I were soul bound, but would that promise—that oath and binding—carry through the will of his family? He was waiting for me to come home, but with what news? Would he stay? Or would his family force him to return to the fold? Would he rip apart the bond that tied our souls together?

And if he stayed, Smoky and Trillian would come face-to-face again. Only now Smoky had a claim over me Trillian didn't, and how would that shift the balance of power? Although I knew I should be thinking about our problems with the Bonecrusher, all I could think about as we climbed in the cars was the love that Smoky had offered me, and whether it would still be there when I got home.

CHAPTER 19

The lights in the house were a welcome sight as we drove up through the ever-pounding rain. Parts of the path bordering the driveway were a mud bath, and I was grateful we'd thought to have the actual drive graveled. I stepped out of the car and looked at the house.

Morio rested a hand against my back and even Trillian seemed to sense my mood. He took my other hand.

"No matter what, Camille, you belong to me. No matter who else you're bound to, you and I will always be together," he whispered.

Morio heard. He gave Trillian a long look and said, "Me, too. You go in, we'll head out to the studio and hang out until you've had your talk." He motioned to Roz and Vanzir and the four of them headed off to the shed-turned-studio apartment that we'd had outfitted. Our little family had expanded by more than half and the added space made a world of difference.

Iris, Bruce, and Delilah were still standing beside me.

"I'm going to scout the perimeter of the land," Delilah said.

"But the wards were shining strong when we came in," I said, then stopped. She was offering me privacy. "Thanks, hon."

Iris took Bruce's hand. "We'll go in the back way and have a snack, then put Maggie to bed. Smoky said he'd be in the parlor."

The parlor. Not our bedroom. That didn't bode well. I sucked in a deep breath and strode up the stairs, my footsteps firm, shoulders back. If it was bad news, I'd take it like a D'Artigo—I'd suck it up and deal with it the way I dealt with all the pain in my life. I'd push it out of the way and move on, because there weren't really any other options.

I slipped into the living room. The door to the parlor was ajar and I could smell him there. Smoky. He smelled like cedar and cinnamon and old library dust. My heart leaping into my chest, I slowly pushed the door open.

Smoky was standing there, waiting for me, his gaze fastened on the doorway. He stared at me for what seemed like a million years, then his lip curved in a triumphant smile and he opened his arms.

"Camille, my Camille. I'm back."

Not trusting what that meant, but praying it meant what I thought it did, I dropped everything and flew into his embrace. He swung me up and around, covering my face with kisses, his lips soft and passionate. I grabbed him around the neck and held on, letting him spin me at a dizzying speed.

"I love you, I love you, and I'm home," he said. "My Camille, I told you nothing would part us."

"I love you, too, but can you please put me down?" As ecstatic as I was, my stomach was beginning to shift into queasy from the makeshift carousel ride.

He abruptly stopped and dropped into the loveseat, pulling me down on his lap. I cuddled against him, resting my head on his shoulder as he gently kissed the top of my head, my forehead, my nose.

"So you're staying? You aren't going back to the Northlands? You aren't going to marry Hotlips?" My voice broke over the last one and regardless of my decision to be calm and collected, I burst into tears.

"Sweet one, oh my lovely one." He cupped my chin in his hand and gazed into my eyes. "I've made you cry. I'm sorry." Wiping away my tears, his masks dropped and the millennia passed through his eyes, this thousands-year-old beast I'd fallen in love with.

"No, I'm not leaving you. I told you I wouldn't. I'd part ways with my family if I had to. But Hotlips has been paid off. She's of no concern to us now. My mother wasn't terribly thrilled but she's . . . she's not my father." His voice dropped and I glanced up to see a cloud cross those glacial eyes.

"What happened?" I asked, pushing myself off his lap. "Are you okay? Did they kick you out?"

He shook his head. "No. No, as a matter of fact, the Dragon Council was so appreciative of the news about Shadow Wing that they gave us their blessing. Basically, they told Hotlips to take the money and shut up."

But there was something else. Something not so good. I could hear it in his voice and see it in the troubled expression playing across his face.

"You aren't telling me everything. I want you to be honest with me. No more surprises." My decisiveness returned after the little jaunt into maudlin-land and I sucked in a deep breath. "Smoky, I can't afford to be worrying about *us* when I'm facing down demons and ghouls."

He slowly nodded. "I see your point. And since you refuse to let me take you away from this war, then you're correct. I should have told you about the betrothal sooner, but I thought I had time to figure it out before it became an issue. All right. Prepare yourself. What's troubling me is this: We've made a powerful enemy and I'm frightened for you."

I frowned. What powerful enemy *wasn't* already signed up to hate us?

"Great. Whose hit list am I on now? You said the Dragon Council was on your side, and your mother may not be happy, but you said she . . . oh no." I raised my hand to my throat, a lump the size of my fist forming. "Tell me it's not your father? What happened with your father, Smoky?" Memories of Hyto's hands on my ass came racing back.

"Hyto was kicked out of the Council and my mother denied him. Not only has he lost his seat in the Council, but he's also been cast out of the family and has no rights over the children anymore. In essence, my mother divorced him and he lost any standing that we children brought him. She's been leading up to it for some time, and this was the last straw."

I could feel the fear hiding behind that impassive face. "Holy cripes, what the hell did he do? Isn't it hard to get yourself kicked out of the Dragon Council?"

"For many, yes. But he's a white wing, and white dragons hold only a moderate amount of caste and influence. When the Council put the stamp of approval on my marriage to you, he blew up and demanded the Wing Liege change his mind. And worse: When they cast him off the Council, he refuted them."

I almost swallowed my tongue. "Is the Wing Liege your king?"

"No, the Wing Liege is the lead justice on the Council. He has the authority to speak for the Emperor—we don't have a king—when it comes to matters like this. When Father refuted the Council, the Wing Liege ordered him to vacate Mother's dreyerie immediately and then proclaimed him pariah for a period of a thousand years."

Images of dragon rising against dragon flooded my mind and I was suddenly grateful that I'd been left behind and hadn't had to witness the scene.

"Hell in a hand basket. Was anybody hurt? Did it turn into a fight?"

Smoky grimaced, a look of sorrow filling his eyes. "Not for lack of trying. Father sent a blast of fire my way, but I dodged it. The guards wing-strapped him for defying the Council ruling. There shall be no flame upon the Council's sacred grounds. Ever. Only the Emperor and Empress may ignite flame in the courts."

He looked so unhappy that I wanted to take him in my arms and kiss away the pain, but nothing I could do would soften the blow.

"I'm so sorry—and I'm to blame," I whispered. If Smoky hadn't met me, he wouldn't have gotten into it with his father. Feeling responsible for tearing apart their home, I crossed to the window and stared out into the autumn night. "What can I do to make up for this? There's nothing I can do, is there?"

Smoky whirled me around, his hands firm on my shoulders. He forced me to meet his gaze. "You have nothing to apologize for. *Nothing.* Father and I would have arrived at this point sooner or later. The foundation for this was set long ago, before I first left the Northlands."

"What do you mean?" I felt so young compared to him. And in truth, I *was* so young. Fully a woman, yes, but a child in terms of the scope of years Smoky had already seen come and go.

"The reason I left the Northlands was to avoid coming to blows with him. I wanted to kill him when I was younger, I hated him so much, but dragons are raised to honor our ancestors. I thought if I left, things would get better. Maybe he'd change. Maybe he'd see the error of his ways. But Hyto got worse. He abused our servants, he threatened my mother time and again, and while she just ignored him, there was always the fear he'd act on his threats. And he loved to ravish and pillage the nearby human villages. He took pleasure in burning their houses to the ground and raping their women."

I shivered. My instincts had been right on. And then I remembered when I'd first met Smoky. He had said, "I could steal you away and no one would stop me." He *did* have some of his father's blood in him, but he was doing his best to keep it under control.

"I thought he fought alongside the humans in the wars— you told me your grandfather did, and your father."

"Hyto fought in the wars all right, but only to keep from being branded a coward. My grandfather's the brave and honorable one. At the Council, after the ruling, he actually disowned Hyto and . . . he made me his heir. So my father is truly alone. He's been turned out by all of his family. He can't be seen in the Dragon Reaches—not for a thousand years, at least." His voice cracked for just a moment. "It was bad, Camille. Very, very bad."

Very softly, I asked, "What does your grandmother think about this? Hyto's mother?"

He shook his head. "She died long ago. She was murdered by a redback."

I froze. Should I tell him what his father had said to me? Would it just complicate matters even more? But really, they couldn't get much worse. I let out a long sigh and told him everything.

Smoky's eyes shifted from glacial gray to white ice as I spelled out Hyto's implied threat. He took hold of my wrist.

"Listen to me. If anyone, *anyone at all*, ever says something like that to you again, you are to tell me immediately. If Hyto ever comes near you, I'll kill him. If he touches you, I will flay him alive. And don't you *ever* hide anything from me. If you see him, you tell me. If you hear from him, you tell me. Do you understand?" He punctuated his words with a low growl and I was afraid he was going to shift into dragon form right there.

"I hear you! Let go of my wrist, dude, you're holding me too tight."

He loosened his grip, but pulled me close. "Father threatened me—and you—before he left. And it does not pay to take dragon threats lightly. Camille, I'm serious. If you smell one whiff of that *rethoule* around, you tell me."

"Yeah," I said, burrowing into his embrace. I wasn't sure of what a *rethoule* was, but whatever it meant, it wasn't complimentary. "I promise."

His lips met mine then, in a fierce kiss, his tongue seeking my own, his hands wandering over my body. "I want you, I want you now," he said, his voice husky and low.

"You'll have to share me," I whispered back. "We found Trillian. And Smoky, so much has happened. You need to hear everything."

"Not now. I need you, I want you. I want to feel your legs wrapped around my waist and to hear you cry my name. If you want the others with us, fine, but I'm first—I touch your core first this night. You understand?"

And he was so determined, so furious at his father and pent up from the conflict, that all I could do was nod.

But before we could head up to the bedroom, Delilah peeked into the room, an ashen look on her face.

"I hate to bother you, but you'd both better come out." She glanced at Smoky's hand, which was under my shirt, caressing my breast. His hair, which had lifted up my skirt and was tickling me between my thighs, suddenly dropped to his ankles again. A quixotic smile crossed her face. "I take it everything's all right between the two of you, then?"

I nodded, pulling away from his embrace. "Everything's fine. What's wrong?"

"We have company and you both should be in on the

conversation because, from what little has been said, it's going to be a doozy. I called Menolly. The surveillance camera's been set up and she and Chase are on their way back here now." She stifled a snicker as she headed out the door. "Smoky, dude, you'd better take a moment to deflate your tent."

"Thanks for the advice," he called after her, chuckling. "It's good to be home again," he added softly.

I glanced at him. "Whoa mama, she was right." The outline against the fly of his tight white jeans left nothing to the imagination as to just where his thoughts had been wandering. "Meet you in the kitchen in a few." And, adjusting my shirt and skirt to make sure nothing was showing that shouldn't be, I headed toward the door.

As I entered the kitchen, I saw Aeval sitting there, along with Titania. Morgaine was nowhere to be seen. Another familiar face was standing near the door. Feddrah-Dahns. And Mistletoe was perched on the counter, resting his ass on one of the napkin rings. Iris was talking to him softly.

Maggie was nowhere to be seen. We didn't keep her out and about when the Triple Threat was around, or even two-thirds of the Triple Threat, nor when Queen Asteria paid a visit. Though none of us could put our fingers on why, we had agreed that it wasn't a good idea. There was some sort of threat to our little girl when they came visiting, and so we kept her out of sight, either in Iris's bedroom or Menolly's lair.

"Feddrah-Dahns!" Overjoyed to see him again, I dashed over and gave him a quick hug around that thick neck of his. "I'm surprised to see you here."

"You'll be even more surprised by what's going on," he said. There was no threat behind the words, yet they made me uneasy.

I slipped into a chair and fingered one of the thumbprint cookies Iris had set on the table, licking the jam out of the pastry to kill time. I had no idea what to say to the two Fae Queens. Smoky joined me, taking a chair on my left.

"So where are Trillian and Morio?" I glanced around.

"They're on their way up from the studio." Delilah offered me a glass of mulled cider. I accepted the steaming mug and gratefully sipped the spicy juice. "Roz and Vanzir are out getting dinner. They should be back soon. Roz called to say they're on the way."

Trillian and Morio came trudging in. Trillian gave Smoky a long look before taking his place on my right. Morio sat next to him. Smoky gave Trillian a short nod, and the Svartan returned the gesture. Oh great, were we going to have to deal with another testosterone war once we were alone? Well, as long as they didn't kill each other, I'd be happy.

Shortly behind them, Menolly and Chase came meandering in and less than five minutes later, Roz and Vanzir appeared.

Nobody said much until we were gathered around the table. Iris handed out mugs of cider and bowls of popcorn, along with more cookies and the pizzas the demon twins had brought home. Finally, we were all settled, and Feddrah-Dahns was leaning his head over my shoulder.

Aeval spoke. "We're here to talk to you about the ludicrous idea Asteria and Tanaquar have cooked up about using mortals to wield the spirit seals. This is insanity. We cannot let it happen."

"How did *you* find out about it?" I asked her, my hand freezing, another cookie halfway to my mouth.

"I told them," Feddrah-Dahns said. "I'm so worried that I thought they should know."

"Your father will kill you!" Delilah clasped her hand to her mouth, staring at him wide-eyed. "He agrees that it's the right thing to do."

"Sometimes, my youthful cat, reason must outweigh loyalty. Especially when honoring that loyalty would be to make a huge mistake." The unicorn whinnied softly. "My father will be angry with me, yes. But in the end, I hope he'll see I'm right."

"The unicorn speaks the truth," Smoky said. "Reason must, at times, prevail over blood ties."

I glanced at him. I hadn't had a chance to tell him what had happened, but he shook his head and leaned down, whispering, "Iris told me some of what went on. I know only the basics, but it's enough for now."

Titania leaned forward, her face crinkling with worry. "Camille, you were there. You saw my dear Tam Lin. Did you sense anything strange about him—or the other mortals? Anything out of the ordinary?"

Torn between allegiances, I struggled with how much to tell them. But Feddrah-Dahns had already done the damage. Whatever I said couldn't amount to more than throwing another gallon of gas on the fire.

"No. I was too shocked to even think about it. I wanted to talk to Venus the Moon Child but there was no chance."

"I might be able to find out something," Delilah said. "I do have connections with the Rainier Puma Pride."

I glanced at her, wishing she'd kept that little idea to herself until Titania and Aeval left. I scurried for something to throw them off the thought. "I did figure out that Queen Tanaquar is sleeping with our father. My guess is that she's doing so in order to keep tabs on us. I don't know how they plan on using Tom and Ben and Venus, but I was pretty damned shocked."

"So are we, which is why we're here," Aeval said. "Queen Asteria, as prim and proper as she is, has a good head on her shoulders and this sudden shift in her viewpoint is odd, to say the least. The question is, what do they know that we don't? And how did they find out about it?"

Titania let out a soft flutter of a sigh. "There is the question of whether she's being threatened into action."

"Who could threaten her?" I asked. "She's one of the most powerful beings I know."

"She would seem so to you," Aeval said, "but even the Elfin Queen must watch her back. There are powerful Fae in Otherworld. Fae who are greatly displeased with the fact that the Earthside Queens are reawakened. Fae who don't trust us. And no doubt, they know about your work over here, and your connection to the Elfin Queen. Perhaps they're blackmailing her."

I put down my cookie. Blackmail. Close to the thought Trillian had had. Another idea crossed my mind, though it sounded far-fetched. "Can she be charmed?"

Titania shrugged. "I don't know, but I greatly doubt it. I tend to think blackmail is more likely."

Menolly slowly nodded from where she hovered near the ceiling. "The lords of Fae who severed the realms during the Great Divide aren't all dead. But wouldn't they do anything and everything to keep the worlds separate? They have to know that joining the seals will only rip apart the veils and reunite the realms."

Aeval smiled. It was a smile that I did not like—cold and ruthless, and thoroughly without compassion. "Remember, they are not talking about joining the seals again—but *using* them. A whole different scenario, one in which Titania and I are perhaps the targets."

"Aeval and I made powerful enemies back then," Titania added. "The armies of the summer and winter joined to fight against the new order. We destroyed many who sought to tear our crowns from our heads. The blood of Fae ran thick for a long time. There are some who walk the paths of Otherworld who are descended from those we slaughtered. They remember, and in their memory they hate us for resisting."

"So instead of uniting against an enemy that threatens us all, you think the Fae lords have, in their infinite wisdom, decided to start a new war against you and that the Keraastar Knights are somehow involved?" The thought boggled my mind, but my father's people could be petty. And grudges lasted a long, long time.

"I think it's a distinct possibility. Look at Lethesanar. She's the granddaughter of one of the lords who fought against Aeval and myself. Tanaquar may be the picture of reason compared to her sister, but I guarantee you this: She won't willingly share the spotlight with the Court of the Three Queens."

Delilah cleared her throat. "I don't think we've ever asked this, but what happens if the portals do fall apart and the realms reunite? There was a great cataclysm during the Great Divide—volcanoes and great earthquakes and tidal waves. Legends are filled with stories of natural disasters, all of which can be traced to the dividing of the worlds . . . but what happens this time?"

Aeval frowned. She tapped one long fingernail on the table for a moment. "To be honest, we don't know. There may just be a blurring of reality—like potholes or wormholes in the fabric of the universe. Or it could be a worldwide upheaval. I really don't think anybody knows what will happen."

"As unnatural as the Great Divide was, we can't let the realms slam back together." Menolly slowly lowered herself to the floor. "We have to find the rest of the spirit seals but, before handing them over, decide if Tanaquar and Asteria are onto something. Either way, we have to fix this mess with the portals ripping apart. And on top of that, we have to deal with groups like the Brotherhood of the Earth-Born going off half-cocked."

Chase spoke up, even though he looked a little queasy at attracting attention to himself. "When the Earthside Fae and Supes stepped out of the closet, there was a honeymoon period, but now the public's getting a little bit afraid. I thought we were more advanced than this but . . ."

"Did you really?" Menolly asked. She didn't sound sarcastic. "I've seen the lowest of the low—I feed on the bottom feeders of society. You think you're wiping out bigotry in one area but up it pops again in another."

Chase sighed. "Yeah, I know. And the thing is, I really don't believe the majority feels this way. Or at least I'd like to believe they don't. But with the economic crunch we're going through, people are starting to whine about special treatment. It's the civil rights issue all over again. Only instead of blacks or women or gays, this time it's the Supes and Fae on the short end of the stick."

"That I can believe," I said. I'd heard enough grumbling from my customers about food prices and rent and medical expenses. If they thought the Fae were taking their jobs, they'd be pissed out of their minds.

Menolly shook her head. "We're good entertainment, but in their minds we aren't the neighbor next door who needs to pay rent. A lot of people think that our powers ensure our survival, and for vampires—they're not that far off base. But the other Supes—it's not necessarily a walk in the park. Getting someone who's afraid he's going to lose his job at the local grocery store to believe anything else is a Herculean task. So what do we do?"

I pulled out a notebook and began listing our concerns. "First, there's Shadow Wing. Then we have the whole business with the Keraastar Knights. And add in the potential problems brewing with the FBH community. Where does that leave us?"

"In tumultuous times." Titania stood. The Queen of Morning was brilliant and beautiful, and whatever strength she'd lost during the Great Divide was back. Her hair gleamed and her eyes were the clearest I'd ever seen them. She smiled softly at us. "And now, to the reason for our visit. We ask you to switch your allegiance to the Earthside Courts of Fae."

I started to speak but she held up her hand.

"I know Morgaine paid you a visit about this, but she did so without our permission. We do not ask for the same reason she does. It comes down to this: We cannot allow the seals to be used, whether by Fae or human hands. If Morgaine does not come to understand this . . ." Her voice lingered over the words like a threat.

Aeval picked up her thought. "If Morgaine doesn't voluntarily come around to our point of view, then Titania and I will take action to ensure she does. The fact is, as we understand the legends, *no one* has the power to wield the seals without putting everyone in jeopardy. We need your promise that you won't hand over any more of them to Asteria until we know more. We aren't asking you to give the seals to us, just hide them and keep them safe."

I stared at them. They were serious. As I glanced at Delilah and Menolly, indecision clouded their faces. I turned back to Titania. "May we have some time to discuss this in private? We'll contact you when we've made a decision."

"Don't dawdle," Aeval said. "So much hangs in the balance. And don't let familial loyalty interfere with the facts."

She joined Titania near the door. Once again, I was struck by her beauty. A walking column of shadows and gossamer cobwebs, she was cloaked in the velvet black of the night sky. Her face was pale—as pale as my own—and by her very stance, her royalty proclaimed itself.

She caught my gaze. Without warning, her voice echoed in my head, ringing as clearly as if she were speaking aloud.

Camille, you sacrificed the Black Unicorn. You did what was necessary to give him rebirth. You understand the nature of the cycle. The Moon Mother chose wisely when she picked you for the task. You will make a worthy priestess, but do not throw away the opportunity because of outworn devotion and affiliations. You can never go back to the way things were.

I glanced around, but nobody else seemed to hear her. I turned back, gazing into those brilliant eyes, and felt the magic of the night rising through my body. *I understand,* I thought at her. *We won't just write off your request. I promise you that. Too much has happened to assume anything.*

And with that, she nodded—almost imperceptibly—and sent me one parting thought. *Remember, I owe you a favor. If you align yourself with our courts, you may all call in that marker and join my court instead of Morgaine's. She may be a relative, but you are right to be cautious. She grasps for too much, too quickly.*

And with that, they made their good-byes and left through the back door.

CHAPTER 20

〜∾⊛∾〜

"Well, what are we going to do?" Menolly looked in the refrigerator and pulled out a bottle of blood labeled STRAWBERRY SHAKE. She tipped the bottle to her lips, smacking them as she drank. "These flavored bloods make all the difference in the world to me," she added. "Thank you."

"Not a problem." Morio gave her a wide-ass grin. That was one thing I loved about the man—he enjoyed giving people small luxuries.

I let out a long sigh. "So, what do you think? The Keraastar Knights—a group of mortals, albeit changed in one way or another—wielding the seals?"

"If we throw ourselves in with the Triple Threat, we'll be ostracized from Otherworld and branded as traitors. Then we'll never find out what's really going on," Delilah said.

She was right. Openly defy Asteria and Tanaquar and we'd be screwed.

"Then it's simple. We fake it. Make it look like we're going along with their plan while secretly figuring out if we think it's viable. Which may mean working with the Triple Threat." Oh, that sounded like such a bad idea, but there was nothing else we could do. "Lying to Asteria and Tanaquar is dangerous, so we'd do best to avoid contact with them as much as possible."

"When we find the sixth seal, we have to keep it secret," Menolly said. "Because I don't trust *any* of them. If Morgaine gets her paws on any of the seals, she'll use them and screw us all. I think Aeval and Titania know that, too."

"Agreed," Delilah said. "So we lie and tell everyone we can't find the next seal."

"I can't think of anything better right now. We'll have to be very careful, though. Lying to them is tantamount to cutting our throats if they find out. Any of them." I shook my head. "In the meantime, we have to hunt down Grandmother Coyote and ask for her help."

As I pushed back my chair, the phone rang.

Delilah answered briefly, then handed the phone to Vanzir. As we helped Iris clear the table, he held a whispered conversation, then hung up.

"Well, I have some good news for a change. At least, I think it's good news," he said, leaning against the counter. "Carter's got a lead on where we can find the Bonecrusher. We can go over to his place tonight, if you want."

Thank the gods, I thought. We needed a break. We'd been slogging through mud a yard deep. "I'm so tired I could spit, but let's head down there. We'll sleep afterward."

Smoky gave me a quizzical look but I shook my head. Any nookie was going to have to wait. At this stage in the game, the idea of just crashing into bed was whoopee enough for me.

Seattle was a brilliant sight during the night hours, filled with towering buildings and bright lights, but unless you were near the Opera House or some of the clubs, not much happened on the streets except for down in the Industrial District, where the vampire clubs like the Fangtabula or Dominick's were located.

Carter lived on Broadway, the home of the subculture. But the wide street also played host to the druggies and hookers who plied their wares along the rain-soaked pavement. His apartment was belowground, with a concrete stairwell running down to it. A metal railing topside kept passersby from falling in, and a magical barrier kept the thieves and lowlifes from bothering him. But overall, it wasn't the most comfortable place to visit on a blustery autumn night.

At least our cars would be safe, though. Carter's magical boundary extended curbside for three or four spaces along the building he made his home in. Rather than all descend on the demon, Delilah, Chase, Trillian, and Smoky had stayed home. Now, as we headed down toward Carter's door, Menolly poked me in the ribs and nodded across the street to where two hookers stood, watching us. Except they weren't hookers. They both had distinct demonic auras.

"Friend or foe?" I whispered.

Menolly shrugged and tapped Vanzir on the shoulder. "You recognize those skanks?"

He squinted at them for a moment, then shook his head as we trudged down to the door. "No. Once we're inside, I'll sneak out the back and veer back around through the alley. If they're still there, I'll get a better look at them."

"I'll come with," Menolly said. "I'm fast, I'm silent, and I'm deadly."

"I may not be as fast or as silent, but I'll bet you anything I'm just as fatal as you, girl." Vanzir gave her a slow wink.

Menolly let out a little snort. Hmm . . . what was this? Vanzir and Menolly flirting? I wasn't sure I wanted to ask, though. What fucking a demon was like—not Morio's kind, but a real Sub Realms badass demon—wasn't top of my need-to-know list. Especially after seeing Vanzir at work. Those tentacles shooting out of his hands were freaky.

As we knocked, the silence thickened. Then the door swung open. A lovely young woman stood there, holding it wide. Half-Chinese, half-demon, she was Carter's foster daughter. He'd saved her from life as a slave in the Sub Realms. She was also mute, and served him silently. He took good care of her and they lived a quiet, unassuming life smack in the heart of Seattle.

Carter was also unassuming, if you looked past the horns on his head that curved back, regal and highly polished. His hair was the same color as Menolly's—brilliant copper, only cut short in a deliberately disheveled shag.

The demon had a limp and wore a brace on his right knee, though he'd never told us how he'd been injured. But Carter had money. He ran an Internet research business as his cover. He kept watch over the demonic activity in Seattle, recording everything he saw or heard. A living well of local supernatural history, he straddled a fine line, doing business with us, doing business with some demons, and trying to keep under Shadow Wing's radar.

"Come in, come in," he said, waving us into the living room, then turned to Kim. "My dear, bring us some tea, please. And a good port, and a cheese plate, please?" With a glance at Menolly, he added, "And a goblet of warm blood for the *vampyr*."

The girl gave him a gentle bob, almost a curtsy but not quite, and silently slipped out of the room.

"Sit, please. Everyone."

He moved over to his desk—a mammoth oak affair—and returned with a file folder and a sheaf of papers, which he handed to Vanzir, who took one, then passed them on. I glanced at the blank papers when the stack came my way. Carter had made enough for everyone and I took several for the others at home.

"I take it this is password protected?" I asked.

He nodded. "The keyword is *rutabaga*."

"Rutabaga?" Menolly cocked her head, glancing at him.

Carter grinned. "Would that be the first word you'd think of when trying to view a demonically sealed document? You want me to change it to *open sesame* perhaps?"

With a snort, she shook her head. "You're okay, Carter."

As I whispered the word, writing appeared on the paper—notes about Stacia Bonecrusher, and a map of directions to her safe house. Her house happened to be an elaborate mansion according to the printout picture, located in one of the wealthier suburbs on the Eastside.

"That figures. She lives over in Redmond, near Marymoor Park. No wonder we couldn't get a bead on her here in Seattle."

"Close to Bill Gates," Morio said.

"No, that's Mercer Island. But he's no demon, regardless of what people think." A smile played over Carter's lips. "Stacia

Bonecrusher lives in a secure compound. From the street, it may look like a swanky gated mansion, but don't be fooled. The place has top-level security and I'm pretty sure she's got a number of demons hiding there."

"Speaking of," Vanzir said. "There are a couple of skanky streetwalkers we pegged as Demonkin as we headed in here. I should sneak out the back way and see if they're still there. I don't think they're part of the demonic underground here, so there may be a chance they're working for the Bonecrusher."

"They are," Carter said. "I know who you're talking about. I haven't done anything about them because I don't want to raise suspicion. As long as I ignore them, they won't go into hiding and I'll know where they're at."

I stopped Vanzir as he stood. "Carter has a point. If we tip our hand, we could make everything worse. Leave them alone, but make sure we check our cars for booby traps or bugs—"

"Not necessary," Carter said. "When they first showed up, I decided I needed a little more protection than the barrier spell I have out there, so I summoned an imp to keep watch. They try to do anything, all hell breaks loose."

"Great, just what we need. An imp. Let's get on with this." As I glanced over the paper, I stopped short. Stacia Bonecrusher *was* a necromancer, and a powerful one at that. Carter's notes listed her as training under Telazhar. "Holy hell, this is bad."

Menolly heard me; she looked up and nodded. "Telazhar must be working for Shadow Wing, then."

"Not necessarily," I said. "He swore never to bow to another, but that he's still alive after all these centuries and that he's training Demonkin is one big-ass sign to beware and be careful."

Morio shook his head. "Who is he? I've never heard of him."

I let out a long sigh. "If I remember my history lessons correctly, Telazhar was one of the most feared Fae to ever live. Centuries ago, he was a powerful necromancer. He raised an army and terrorized Otherworld during the magical wars that scorched the Southern Wastes, leaving them barren and rife with rogue magic."

"How did he get down to the Sub Realms?" Vanzir asked.

Menolly picked up the story. "Telazhar led an army of the dead to lay siege on Aladril. He planned on marching on Y'Elestrial after he'd taken over the City of Seers. But the seers took him by surprise. Y'Elestrial sent help and so did the elves. A powerful Fae warrior led the armies against Telazhar and they drove him back into the desert. Once they cornered him in the depths of the Wastes, Aladril's seers held him in stasis, and they sent him through a Demon Gate into the Subterranean Realms, then dismantled the spell so it could never open again."

"Apparently," I said, "Telazhar is still alive. His powers must be terrible by now." I sucked in a long breath and stared at the page. "Want to make a bet he's the one who gated her over here?"

"No, because you'd win," Menolly said.

I nodded, not wanting to think about the coming battle. "We have to be so careful and so crafty that she doesn't know we're coming. We could use some extra help."

Kim returned with our tea, and as we silently sipped the warm brew from bone china cups, and ate the ripe Camembert spread on seasoned crackers, all I could think about was curling up in my bed and sleeping for weeks. This was such bad news it made me want to retreat back into Otherworld. Maybe I should take Raven Mother up on her offer. A little house in the heart of Thistlewyd Deep, live there with Smoky and Trillian and Morio . . . it didn't sound so bad.

"What next then? And how do we cloak these notes again?" Morio asked.

"As far as how to cloak the notes," Carter said, "use the locking word. And that, my friends, is *clotted cream*. Again, I chose something that won't immediately come to mind. And as to the dilemma you're facing, I can't tell you what to do."

"We're going to have to look elsewhere for help. And I know where." I gazed up at my sister.

She groaned and slapped the side of her head. "Not the Triple Threat?"

"Suck it up. They'll have to agree—or at least Aeval will. She owes me a favor. But once I call in the marker, I'm going to owe her so big. I have the distinct feeling it's not going to turn out a quid pro quo situation."

"So we go out there tomorrow and hit up the Queen of Night to help us track down and destroy a demon general. Great." Menolly shook her head. "I really don't want to see the fallout from this one."

"Neither do I, but it's our only choice. We need more help. At least we don't have to track the Bonecrusher anymore, thanks to Carter." I held up the sheet of paper. "And we have a map."

"Yeah, we have a map," Menolly said, her eyes turning bloodred. "Big whoop. Ten to one, it leads straight to our doom."

Doom or not, we had no other choice. If we didn't destroy Stacia, she'd mangle the portals trying to rip open a gateway for Shadow Wing's buddies. And that spelled trouble with a capital *T*. I stood, feeling as resigned as I was resolved.

"Okay, let's get a move on. We've got a long day facing us tomorrow."

On our way back to the cars, we didn't catch sight of the streetwalker demons. Had they run back to the Bonecrusher to tell her we'd been at Carter's? Either way, she knew we were on the move. She just didn't know when.

CHAPTER 21

I opened my eyes to Morio sitting beside me on the bed. Squinting in the morning light, I pushed myself up and looked around. I was alone on the king-sized mattress. Last night Morio had slept on the daybed near the window, while Smoky and Trillian flanked me. I'd nixed any wandering hands, though, too exhausted to even think about sex.

"Good morning." He gave me a quick kiss and, as I slid out from beneath the covers, slipped his arms around me, drawing me close.

"You didn't get any last night, you're not getting any this morning." I gave him a playful thunk on the head.

"I wasn't looking for any," he whispered. "What I am looking for is for you to haul your lovely ass downstairs. We've got a full day, sleepyhead."

Not sure whether to be insulted or just annoyed, I glanced at the clock. Nine-thirty? Oh shit, I had overslept by a good two hours. I jumped up and grabbed a towel.

"Let me catch a quick shower."

"Iris said if you want breakfast, you'll be there in ten minutes." He laughed, then headed out the door after giving me a sharp slap on the ass. "I'll be out in the studio, cleaning and purifying our ritual gear."

Twenty minutes later, fully dressed and in makeup, I showed up in the kitchen. Good to her word, there was no breakfast on the table, but when Iris saw me coming she opened the fridge and, before I knew it, I was settled in my chair with yogurt, a toasted English muffin, a banana, and a cup of coffee. Not quite the hearty breakfast I was used to, but it would do.

Delilah came running through the back door, breathing heavily. I gave her a quizzical look and she pulled off her Windbreaker and tossed it over the back of a chair. "When Morio said you were taking a shower, I decided to get in a quick run down to Birchwater Pond and back."

I glanced around the kitchen. "Where'd Smoky and Trillian go? The house seems empty today. And where's Maggie?"

Iris answered before Delilah could. "Smoky took off for his barrow. He said he had something to do. Trillian went shopping with Roz. Vanzir's out in the studio, and Shamas is at work. Maggie's in my room having a time-out."

"Time-out? What did she do now?" Maggie had reached the stage where she was getting into anything and everything. Sometimes the only way to make her realize there were boundaries was to give her a time-out.

"She bit me," Delilah said, holding up her index finger. A sturdy white bandage was wrapped around it. "The little dickens snapped at me when I tried to put her back in her playpen after giving her breakfast. She's got to learn no biting or eventually she could take someone's finger off."

"No kidding." I stared at her finger. "How's the bite? Any infection, you think?"

"No. It's clean and Roz spread some of his wonder salve over it. So what's on the agenda today, as if I didn't know?" She slipped into a chair and grabbed an apple from the bowl on the table. "Iris, what's with all the fruit lately? The farmer's market having a run on apples and oranges?"

"It's good for you. You eat far too much junk food." Iris turned around from the sink where she was finishing up the dishes. She put her hands on her hips and stared down Delilah's irritated grunt. "If you want doughnuts all the time, you're going to have to get them yourself. You're addicted to sugar and it's not healthy."

"I can handle it," Delilah muttered, but bit into the apple anyway.

I spooned up my yogurt. "I guess today we plan out our strategy. Asking Aeval to help us with Stacia isn't going to be a lot of fun." I really didn't want to go there but we had no choice. We needed help and we needed it soon.

Delilah crossed her arms on the table and rested her chin on them. "Do you really think Father's sleeping with Tanaquar?"

She sounded so wistful and sad that I put down my spoon. "What's the matter, Kitten?"

"I just . . . he always said he couldn't forget Mother . . ."

So that was it. I reached across the table and patted her hand. "He loved Mother more than anything, but he has to move on. I just wish Tanaquar hadn't gotten her claws on him. I think she's using him and I doubt if he knows it. I think he wanted to tell me about it while I was there, but chickened out." As I bit into the English muffin, a burst of buttery goodness melted into my mouth and I closed my eyes, enjoying the flavor.

"I know he has to move on. I want him to. But . . . it just seems . . . he's sleeping with the *Queen*. That's just so wrong and I can't tell you why I feel that way." Morosely, she tossed the rest of the apple in the compost bin and rooted through the cupboards until she finally pulled out a bag of generic potato chips. "I knew we had to have something good in here."

Iris finished putting away the dishes and crossed her arms. "Fine, I give up. I'll buy the damned junk food next time I'm grocery shopping but when you break out or realize that it's sapping your energy, don't come running to me." The phone rang just then and she picked it up. After a moment, she handed it to me. "Camille, you'd better take it. Henry's on the line."

Wiping my hands on my napkin, I took the receiver. "Henry? What's up?"

"Camille?" Henry sounded shaky. "We've got a problem. I've called Detective Johnson and he's on the way. I think you'd better come down to the shop right away."

"What's going on?" I frowned. If Henry said there was a problem, there was. He wasn't prone to exaggeration.

Henry lowered his voice and it sounded like he'd cupped his hand around the receiver. "There are two men and a woman prowling around the shop. I've never seen any of them before. Camille, they frighten me. I asked if I could help them and one of the men growled at me."

Shit! My first thought was that they were from the Freedom's Angels group or maybe the Brotherhood of the Earth-Born.

"I'll be down there in twenty minutes, fifteen if traffic is with me. Meanwhile, you hang tough. And get out of there. Don't worry about anything in the shop—don't stop to take the money or anything else. And, Henry . . ." I paused, wanting to warn him but not knowing what to warn him against. We could have demons down there, or anti-Fae humans running around, or even somebody who had a personal grudge against us.

"What is it, Camille?"

"Henry—"

I didn't get a chance to finish my thought. A loud explosion of some sort echoed in my ear, and Henry cried out. The line went dead.

"Motherfucking son of a bitch!" I tossed the receiver on the table.

Delilah and Iris stared at me.

I grabbed my purse and keys. "Something's going on at the shop. I heard something that sounded like an explosion and the line went dead. Henry already called Chase—but, Iris, you get him on the phone and tell him what I said and to hurry the hell up. Let's get our asses down there now."

Iris snatched up the phone. "You want me to come with you? I can put Maggie in Menolly's lair."

"Yeah, but we're heading out now. Have Morio drive you down after you've taken care of Maggie. And tell Vanzir, if he's still here, to come with you. I have a feeling we're going to need everybody we can get. Leave a note for Roz, and Trillian, too, and tell them to stay put in the house, and watch over things." I paused. "On second thought, call them and tell them to get back home. *Now*."

As Delilah and I raced for my car, I wondered what the hell had happened. Mostly, though, I worried about Henry. Because whatever that noise was, I knew in my gut that it wasn't going to end well.

* * *

As we headed down the street toward the Indigo Crescent, my bookstore, I saw the rising smoke pluming from a half-block away. Fire engines crowded the street, and barricades stopped traffic. I screeched to a halt right behind the barricades and Delilah and I jumped out of the car, heading for the store at a dead run.

As we got within the sight line, a police officer stopped us. The rest of the street was roped off with crime tape and uniformed FH-CSI officers. Shamas was there, and he gave me a brusque nod. He was all-duty when he was working, a fact that had endeared him to Chase.

"I own that shop," I told the officer trying to keep us out. "My friend was in there working behind the counter and I'm worried about him. I was on the phone with him when I heard an explosion and the line went dead."

Just then, Chase came jogging over, the look on his face grim.

"What happened? Is Henry okay?" I took another look at his face and my heart sank. Whatever it was, was bad.

Chase put his finger to his lips and nodded us through the barricade. "They're with me, Glass." The officer nodded and waved us on.

"Henry's been taken to the hospital with third-degree burns over sixty percent of his body. It doesn't look good," Chase said, his voice soft. He put his hand on my arm. "Camille, he may not make it."

He might as well have hit me in the gut. Delilah let out a small mew, but thank the gods, she didn't transform.

"What happened?" The smoke around us was so thick it was making me sick. Of course, Delilah and I were more sensitive to smoke than most FBHs, but by Chase's expression I could tell it was bad even for them. Firemen were running in and out of the shop, their masks on, and I smelled something besides the smoke in the air. Not gunpowder, but some residue that I knew I'd smelled before.

"Someone exploded some sort of device in your shop. We aren't sure what. I've got my men working on it with the firemen, because I have a feeling the bomb may not have been of human manufacture."

My thoughts were on Henry, but I had to ask. "How much of the shop was affected?"

"The explosion was relatively localized—about a third of the shop is in ruins. The flames weren't actually the problem. It's whatever crap the bomb was made out of. Henry's burns are chemical in nature." He paused to answer his cell phone. "Hey, what have you got for me? . . . Really? . . . Okay, they're here right now. You want me to put Camille on?" He handed me the phone.

Sharah, the chief medic at the FH-CSI headquarters, was on the line. She was Queen Asteria's niece, but her ties to the Elfin Queen didn't seem terribly strong. "We've got your friend Henry here." Before I could ask how he was, she continued. "He's in bad shape. Chase told you his injuries?"

"Third-degree burns over sixty percent of his body, right?" My voice was flat. If I let myself feel anything but numb, I'd be useless.

"Right. I figured out what caused the burns, so the good news is we can try to treat him."

I didn't want to hear, but had to ask. "What's the bad news?"

"My prognosis for him isn't good. I give him a twenty percent chance—at best—to make it through the next forty-eight hours. If he makes it through two days, then I'll up it to forty percent. He took a lot of the burns on his face, chest, and stomach areas. His internal organs are damaged, and he's on a ventilator in order to keep him breathing."

Crap. I wanted to smash the phone on the ground, but it wasn't Sharah's fault. If Henry did pull through, we'd have her to thank.

"What caused the burns?"

"Alostar compound mixed with myocian powder."

Double crap. The last person I'd seen use that mixture was Rozurial. Since I knew he hadn't been the one to plant the bomb, then I had to assume that our attackers were from Otherworld. Or that they had hooked up with someone from Otherworld.

"Thanks." I didn't know what else to say so I just added, "Take care of Henry, would you? He's a good person and a good friend. I'd hate to lose him."

"Camille," Sharah's voice was hesitant. "Don't get your

hopes up. We'll do all we can, but in the long run, Henry's riding on a dark horse. If he's going to win this one, it's going to take nothing short of a miracle."

I handed the phone back to Chase without a word. He spoke to Sharah for a moment, then closed the cell and put it in his pocket.

I told him about the alostar compound and myocian powder. "Can I go in the shop? I might be able to pick up something."

Chase motioned for Shamas to join us. "Take the girls in the shop and keep an eye on them. They want to see what they can find out. Also, send the fire marshal out to me. I need to talk to him."

As we headed into the shop, Shamas motioned for us to walk in his footsteps. "We think the foundation is secure—and since there's no basement there's no chance of the floor caving in. But although the flames don't appear to have reached the ceiling, you never know if the explosion weakened the struts and beams, so no heading upstairs to Delilah's offices. Just make it quick, and be careful. And don't touch anything. Now that we know what caused it, I can tell you right off that if you touch anything coated with those chemicals bare-handed, you'll walk away with a nasty blister or worse. Remember the hellhound's acid?"

I flinched. "Yeah, right. We won't touch anything." I still had a nasty scar on my hand from where a few drops of a hellhound's acidic blood had splattered on me. The damned wound had nearly killed me.

The interior of the shop was in shambles. Books lay everywhere, charred, smelling of burnt paper. A flurry of scattered pages covered the floor. The glass case that I used to display a few rare first editions and to act as the counter had shattered, a thousand shards of sliver-thin daggers just waiting to dig into flesh. The seating area for the Faerie Watchers Club and the reading groups was burnt to a crisp. The sofa had caught fire and was now a smoldering, nasty mess of water and soot.

As we made our way through the husk that had, only this morning, been my bookstore, I noticed that most of the shelves in the back half of the shop were intact, though a few had fallen because of the blast, their contents strewn about.

By the time we got to my office, everything seemed relatively normal. I turned around to see Chase behind us.

"You said the stairs are off limits?" I asked him. Delilah ran her PI business out of the second floor of the building.

"Yeah." Shamas shrugged. "Too dangerous until we ascertain whether the stairs are safe. Not unless you've got a flying spell."

"That, I don't. Menolly could hover on up but she can't come out until tonight." I frowned, looking around the office. Something seemed off, but I couldn't tell just what it was until my attention landed on an envelope sitting on my desk. It was large—the kind invitations and oversized greeting cards are mailed in—and was beige linen. The envelope was addressed to me.

"That wasn't there before. I know it wasn't," I said, pointing at it.

"I guess we should dust it for prints," Chase said as he joined us.

"Don't bother." The words squeaked out of my throat as the overwhelming scent of Demonkin rose from the paper. "That wasn't left by any human, Chase." Over his protestations, I picked it up. Demon energy raced through my hand, so strong that I almost dropped it.

"Demons." There was no stamp nor postage mark on it. This hadn't come in the mail. I turned it over and looked at the flap. A wax seal held it shut, and a large, sloping *S* had been pressed into the wax. "Stacia. I'll bet you anything this is from the Bonecrusher."

Delilah gasped and peered over my shoulder. Just then, an officer stuck his head around the corner.

"Chief? We have two men out here who claim they're involved in this. They have a midget with them," one of the officers said. He was FBH and looked nervous.

"Iris. She came down with Morio and Vanzir," Delilah said.

Chase turned to the officer. "First, the correct term is little person. Second, she's *not* a little person. She's one of the Talon-haltija."

"Talon—whatsa?"

"She's *Fae*, damn it. Let them in, but tell them to walk carefully." As the officer turned away, Chase grumbled under his breath. "Honestly, I send these guys to sensitivity train-ing, I make sure they're up on proper procedure, and some of them still act like bulls in china shops." He caught my gaze and pointed at the letter. "Are you going to open that?"

I shook my head. "Not until we cast some sort of spell on it to detect whether it's magically booby-trapped."

A few minutes later, Iris made her way through the mess, followed by Morio and Vanzir. I silently showed them the letter.

Vanzir shuddered. "The Bonecrusher, all right. Can you feel the power emanating from that envelope?"

"Yeah. Next question: Is it rigged? Will it go boom if I open it, or is it just a polite 'gotcha' letter?" With a long sigh, I ran my hand across my eyes, already weary and wanting to run home and hide. I'd been feeling far too much of that lately.

Morio took the letter and incanted a spell. A light flared, but nothing happened. "No illusions here. And I added in a variant that checks for traps. Nothing. You can open it safely."

Hoping he was right, I cautiously loosened the flap and withdrew the letter. As I opened the folded page, I saw it was typed—Stacia was smart, all right. She hadn't written it by hand. In fact, my bet was she'd never even touched the paper, but instead, had a flunky write it. Otherwise, we could cast magic on her by having something she'd touched. But it had been in her presence, that much I could tell.

"What's it say?" Delilah asked, crowding in. I motioned her to move back and give me a little room as I scanned it. Shit, this was not good. Not good at all.

"Let's get out of here before I read it to you. Who knows if they bugged the shop at the same time they destroyed it? Come on." Pushing past them, I marched toward the front door and out into the drizzling morning. When they caught up with me, I led them across the street and leaned on Chase's patrol car, hanging my head.

"Come on, Camille, spill. What's going on?" Shamas had a worried look on his face and I realized that over the past months, he really had been working on making himself part of the family, though he still held himself somewhat aloof and his darker nature seemed to be taking over.

"Fuck and double fuck. Here's what she says." I held the letter up and began to read:

Camille, et al:

Consider this renovation a precursor of things to come. You have many friends, and we know who they are and where they live. One by one, we'll destroy everyone and everything you love. You have two choices: Return to Otherworld. Or you can fight for us. This is the fork in the road.

S.B.

Delilah let out a long breath. "Shit."

"I don't know. There's something not right here." Morio pinched the bridge of his nose, looking like he'd developed a headache. "Give me a minute."

I looked at him expectantly. "What is it?"

"Just . . . it's this. Think about it. Why not just blow us all up at the house if they wanted to get rid of us? Karvanak could have, but he chose to kidnap Chase and try to use him for ransom. He could have quietly gotten together enough cohorts to just come out and stage a private little war. So why did he—and now Stacia Bonecrusher—try so hard to get us to join them? Remember, Karvanak offered a couple times for you to switch sides and the question is, why do they want you three so badly? What piece are we missing?"

He presented a good question, actually, one none of us had really thought about. If Shadow Wing wanted us dead, why didn't he just order a mass attack on our house and blow us all to smithereens? Why go around and around, sending demon generals who, while terribly powerful, weren't using their full arsenals?

"You're right. Something's going on. But how the hell do we find out what? And meanwhile, how do we protect our friends, because I know that she means it when she says they'll start taking them out. This letter is essentially a blackmail threat."

Chase's phone rang again and he moved to the side to answer it.

"We have to see Grandmother Coyote. We need her advice," Morio said.

I nodded. "We'll head out to her woods now."

Just then Chase returned, his face ashen. "Camille, I'm so sorry . . ."

"What? What is it?" The look on his face could only mean one thing, but I didn't want to hear it.

"It's about Henry. He's dead. He had a heart attack while they were working on him and his body couldn't handle the shock. Sharah said he went quickly." He pursed his lips together, and Delilah moved into his embrace, tears running down her cheeks.

I stared at him, mutely. Morio slid his arm around my waist, but I pushed him away and walked over to the storefront. Henry had loved the Indigo Crescent, and he'd been so happy when we offered him the job. And now he was dead, because of us.

I felt a hand slip into mine and looked down. Iris was holding tight. Tears shone in her eyes.

"I couldn't love him like he wanted me to," she said, her voice hoarse. "I wish I could have, but I just . . ."

"It's okay," I said numbly, blinking back my own tears. Iris was feeling guilty—I could see it in her face. Henry had loved her, had wanted to be with her, but she couldn't reciprocate his feelings. And now he was dead, murdered in our shop, and she was taking the blame on her own shoulders. "Iris, his death is no more your fault than it is mine. He was happy, he loved working with us."

"I want them dead," she said, a fierce light in her eyes. "I want to find the bastards who did this and take them down."

"We will," I whispered, more to myself than to her. "Trust me. We will."

CHAPTER 22

Morio, Delilah, and I headed out to find Grandmother Coyote. Vanzir decided to hightail it over to Carter's to find out anything that might have come through the rumor mill over the past twenty-four hours. Iris caught a ride home with Shamas, who took her in my car.

I stared at the road as Morio drove, thinking about Henry. He'd wanted to go to Otherworld and now he'd never make it. But I'd already made up my mind to take some of his ashes there, to scatter them over the Silofel Plains, which I knew he would have loved. My heart ached for him, but yet, I knew we were lucky. We'd been very lucky so far, but that had changed. Delilah hummed an aimless tune in the back, and Morio kept his eyes on his driving until we turned off near Grandmother Coyote's woodland.

As we forged through the sodden debris that littered the ground and the thick undergrowth, I tried to imagine just what she might ask of us for this favor. Whatever it was, I'd pay it. We needed help and we needed it from someone who could see the long picture. Riddles or not, Grandmother Coyote was spot-on with her ability to see the future, even if it took us a while to figure out what her words foretold.

The birds were silent, hiding from the chill drizzle, and a thin mist shrouded the trees ahead as we silently worked our way toward the grove. Grandmother Coyote's glade wasn't that far of a walk, but in the gloom of the day and the bitter taste of Henry's death, it seemed to take forever to break into the ancient ring of cedars.

But there she was, sitting on a tree trunk, watching as we slipped out of the silent copse. The skies opened up and rain began to pound down. Without a word, Grandmother Coyote motioned for us to follow her and headed toward her tree. We traipsed along behind her.

As we entered the door against the giant tree trunk, I let out a sigh of relief. We'd found her at home. Now maybe we could make sense of everything that was happening.

As we entered the door, we also entered a magical space. There was no way to account for it by looking at the tree from outside, but then again—Grandmother Coyote lived in all dimensions, through all realms. She guarded a portal, but had her own way of creating the space she needed.

And yet, as we silently followed her down the hall, I could feel the heart of the tree around me, breathing silently. Then it struck me—this was like being inside the horn, though I was fully here rather than just in spirit. We were inside the spirit of the tree while in body.

We came to a round table. Four chairs were placed around it and Grandmother Coyote motioned for us to take our places. She sat next to me, on my left and on Morio's right.

"You wish to ask something of me." A statement, not a question.

I shivered. Whoever did the asking, paid the price. "Yes, and I'm willing to pay your fee."

"Then ask, young Camille. And listen to my answer." Her words were short gusts on the breeze that flowed through the chamber.

"What should we do? We've got this situation with the Black Unicorn horn and Queen Asteria and the Keraastar Knights and the Triple Threat and the Bonecrusher—" I ran out of breath, panting as I realized just how frantic I felt.

"Hush, my girl. So many factors. The unicorn horn and your growth into priestess is your own path to follow and wants no interference from me," she said, producing a large pouch. "We'll roll the bones again. Pick, Camille. Pick one for Asteria and the Keraastar Knights. Pick one for the Earthside Fae Queens. And pick one for the Bonecrusher." She pushed the bag across the table to me.

I slowly opened it. Delilah let out a delicate mew but one look from Grandmother Coyote silenced her. Morio sat still, his eyes closed. I reached in and the finger bones inside reverberated against my skin. I'd drawn from the bones before and knew what to expect. Pulling out the first bone, I set it on the table in front of her. It was the bone off of a human. I could tell that much.

Grandmother Coyote reached out and picked it up. Her fingers deftly raced over the surface, and she jerked her head up to stare at me, her eyes luminous in the dim glow of the tunnel.

"They are not lying. The Keraastar Knights will rise, and they will stand at the portals. Not in the way the queens might hope, but their destiny is in play and cannot be suspended. They must have the seals in order to flourish, and for good or ill—you must give them what they ask."

"But why humans and Weres? Why these three to start?" Morio kept his hands on the tabletop but I could see his gaze was fastened on the finger bone she held.

"What you were told was correct, but far, far from the full scope. Even Elfin Queens have no concept of the iceberg they've tripped over. But once set in motion, this cannot be undone. The three men already bear three of the seals—"

"We didn't see them wielding them," I said. "Or sense it."

"They possess them now and are being trained. But not by the mages, regardless of what the Queen thinks. The seals are transforming them into something new, something different. That is all I can tell you. Do not thwart this plan or you will throw the balance asunder and forfeit your own place on the threads we weave."

Great. So we were supposed to give Asteria the seals, even though it was sparking off a major shift for the future. I let out a long sigh. "Thank you."

"Next. The Earthside Fae Queens. Draw a bone."

I drew, and it was longer and thinner, the bone of . . . as I

held it in my hands a picture formed in my mind and I gasped.
A sylph. This finger bone had belonged to a wind spirit. I
slowly placed it in front of Grandmother Coyote.

She caught it up and let out a low chuckle. "Ah, so I see.
Not much to answer you, Camille, for most of this you must
learn yourself. But prepare yourself to call Aeval your Queen
for a time to come."

"What? Just me or my sisters, too?" She had to be kidding.
We were supposed to hand over the spirit seals to Queen Asteria but also switch sides to Aeval? That sounded insane. At the
very least, a recipe for getting our butts kicked.

"You, young Priestess. You won't have a choice before
long. Trust me, things are happening that will require work
from both worlds to fix. You will know when it's time." She
put the bone down and motioned toward the bag.

I silently withdrew the third finger bone and this one I recognized. Shit, it was the finger I'd chopped off Bad Ass Luke
after we took him down. It was also the first payment I'd ever
made to Grandmother Coyote. I held it up so Delilah and
Morio could see it and mouthed his name, then passed it over.

Grandmother Coyote took the bone and let out a long sigh.
After a moment, she gazed up at me. "There is dissension in
the ranks. There is a reason the Bonecrusher seeks your alliance. And it has everything—and nothing—to do with Shadow
Wing, whose attention is turned elsewhere at the moment.
Don't be fooled by her. She has her gaze fastened on a victory different than the one you think. Right now, if you strike
on the heels of her attack, you have the chance to take out the
lamia's encampment. She's expecting fear. Show courage and
offense."

"So . . . attack. Even though it seems foolhardy. Should I
ask Aeval for her help?"

Grandmother Coyote dropped the bones back into the bag
and cinched it tight. "No. You'll need her favor down the road.
You can do this, if you are smart and if you are cunning."

As she paused, I steeled myself for the last—and perhaps
most frightening—question. "What do you want in return for
the information? What payment do we owe you?"

"Oh my dear, the payment is already in motion. Trust that
the debt will be paid and the balance will be righted. Sacrifice

is the nature of duty. Now go. You have plans to make and battles to fight." And without explaining what she meant, she vanished down the hall.

We stared at one another.

"I don't like that last part. *Sacrifice is the nature of duty?* What's she talking about?" I was still smarting over being chosen to sacrifice the Black Unicorn. I knew, logically, that I'd done what was necessary—for both of us—but the memory of his blood on my hands still hurt like hell.

"Come on, we'd better get home and start planning how to take on the Bonecrusher. It looks like we have no choice," Morio said, pushing himself up from his chair. Delilah and I followed suit, and we trailed out into the day again, making our way through the forest back to Morio's Subaru. None of us said a word on the way home.

Once home, I decided to take a shower. "Meet you guys in the kitchen afterward," I said, weary and reeking of smoke from the store. "Find Trillian and Roz and tell them to get in here. Smoky, too. We need everybody's help with this." We were going on the offensive, and we had to act fast.

Delilah followed me up, needing a shower, too. "Let me come in with you. We can discuss what's going on,"

I nodded. We stripped and padded over to my shower. After adjusting the temperature, we climbed in and I handed her one of my loofahs, and grabbed the sponge puff for myself. I took the spot under the showerhead since I knew she hated it spraying in her eyes. I was using my vanilla-scented body wash. Delilah chose the tangerine. We scrubbed away at the stench of smoke and soot.

I let out a long sigh as the hot water streamed over my body. The reality of what had happened was just starting to sink in. Henry was dead. My store was in ruins. And we were about to walk into the lamia's den. A sudden bubble of tears welled up and I let out a sob.

Delilah dropped the loofahs and held me tight. I leaned on her shoulder, crying. "Shush," she whispered. "You've had one hell of a past few days, haven't you?"

"Not as bad as Henry." I tried to sidestep the ache in my

heart. But it was useless. The numbness had worn off and I
slipped out of her arms and sat on the edge of the tub, letting
the water beat down on me and splash over the side. "I can't
believe they killed him like that. He wasn't part of this—he
had nothing to do with the spirit seals and yet they came in and
deliberately harmed him and left him for dead."

"I know, I know," she said, sitting beside me. She picked up
the puff and began gently washing my back. "He was caught
in the middle. A casualty of war. We knew this could happen,
and it will be a lot worse if we let Shadow Wing win. A lot
more Henrys will die."

I let out a ragged sigh. For once, she was taking charge and
letting me be the one to fall apart and I appreciated it more
than she could ever imagine. "Everything is a mess. I don't
know what to think. The only one I trust anymore—besides
our little group—is Grandmother Coyote. I don't even trust
Father now that he's sleeping with Tanaquar."

Delilah nodded, rinsing off my back. "Yeah, I'm having
problems with that thought, too. I wonder why we're going to
end up aligning ourselves with the Triple Threat. Pretty, these
are so intricate." She fingered the tattoos on my back, then her
own on her forehead. "I wonder if there's any way out of this?.
Is destiny always preplanned? Can we avoid our fate, or is it
always fate that we meet it?"

Choking back the tears, I tried to wipe my eyes and only
succeeded in getting soap in them. "Oww! Hand me that
towel," I said, motioning to the towel I had hung over the
shower curtain rod. Delilah handed it to me and I wiped my
eyes, then dropped it on the floor.

"You're asking some pretty deep philosophical questions,"
I said. "Why? I mean . . . we are what we are. We're on the
paths the gods set us on. Aren't we?"

She shrugged. "I don't know. Was it my destiny to become
a Death Maiden? Will I have to bear the Autumn Lord's child?
Was it our destiny to fight the demons? And now you're a
priestess and have an unknown path opening in front of you.
I've been thinking a lot lately about the randomness of things.
Henry's death is just another one of them. He was in the wrong
place at the wrong time. He was our friend—which made him
a target. Was it his destiny to die today? Why did they choose

him to start their vendetta with? I guess I just hate feeling like a pawn anymore. I want to have a choice in my life."

I examined the sponge quietly, then rinsed it under the water. "Hand me the shampoo, please." She did, and I stood up and lathered my hair with the rich scent of cinnamon and apples. "I think we're beyond having a choice in the current direction we're pointed in."

"Then you think this is our destiny?" she asked, taking the shampoo.

As I rinsed the foam out of my hair, I thought about it. Did I really believe in destiny? Did I believe we were meant to walk this path? Did I believe this was Henry's day to die?

After a moment, I found my answer. "I don't know, Kitten, but what I do know is this: We're here now. We're involved in this war—hell, we're on the front lines. We're facing several tough choices and our advisor is one of the Hags of Fate. Destiny or not, I'm listening to her. I'd rather take the chance she's right—which the Hags of Fate usually are—than muck things up. Because the gods know I'm all too good at doing that. As far as Henry . . ."

My eyes watered again, but I stared into the spray of warm water and let it wash the tears away. "As far as Henry, he was a victim of circumstance. Maybe it was his time to go, maybe not. But it happened, and we lost a friend. And we're going to make damned sure the motherfuckers who did this meet the end of our swords."

"Yes," she said, quietly. "I'm right there with you on that."

We finished bathing and toweled off. She ran up to her room to dress while I found a clean skirt and bustier, and then headed downstairs. We had a battle to plan, because I sure as hell didn't want to lose anybody else.

Delilah brought up Google Earth on the computer and we typed in Stacia Bonecrusher's address. Smoky was on his way—he'd called from a pay phone to let us know—and Trillian and Rozurial had returned home while we'd been in the shower. Iris had bathed, too, and she was grimly fixing sandwiches for everyone.

Trillian was helping her, and they worked quietly at the

counter while Roz, Vanzir, Delilah, and I gathered around the kitchen table. Menolly was still asleep, but it wouldn't be more than a few hours before she was able to join us. Meanwhile, we'd map out our plans and get everything ready to go.

"There she is, right near Marymoor Park, on Oakdale Street. Just through that strip of trees that divides the area from West Sammamish Parkway." Delilah zoomed in and pointed out the house—a large, gated mansion set back from the street. From here, we could see several outbuildings in the back.

"Can we get there from Sammamish Parkway?"

"It's not all that easy. If we come in from the other direction—from the freeway, we can find access roads leading into the area. Or we could park in Marymoor and sneak across the street and through the woods. I'm assuming we're going in at night, given we need Menolly's help?" She glanced up at me and I nodded. "Okay, I'll start printing out more detailed maps here."

Trillian carried the tray of sandwiches to the table and handed them out, while Iris finished pouring the hot cider. As we all gathered around, eating, Vanzir returned from Carter's.

"Good news!" He tossed a notebook in front of me. In precise, stilted print, was a bevy of notes and as I began to read them, I realized they were about Stacia's compound.

"Where did you get these?" I pushed them toward the center so everybody could see them.

"I ferreted them out. I decided what the hell. I smell like demon—they aren't going to notice me as being that out of place. I snuck through the back to the edge of her lot and did a little scouting."

Vanzir looked so proud I didn't have the heart to chew him out, which is what I wanted to do. He could have put the whole operation in danger. Instead, I motioned for him to sit down. "Tell us what you found out."

"Hold on," a voice said from the front door. Smoky strode in and took his place at the table, giving Trillian a short nod. The two had walked around each other like they were on eggshells, but so far no fights had broken out.

He looked troubled when I brought him up to speed. "I'd better make sure Estelle and St. George have some sort of protection out there. St. George told me he thought he saw something creeping through the bushes. It was probably a cougar or even a large dog, but we can't be too careful."

Estelle Dugan was Georgio Profeta's caretaker. Georgio, or St. George as he fancied himself, had been trying to fight Smoky for years. He knew Smoky was a dragon and—in his fragile mind—he was the hero out to save the world against Smoky's fire. But the poor man was slipping further and further from reality, and spending more and more time in fugues. Estelle looked after him and cleaned house, making sure that St. George was comfortable and as happy as he could be. I figured it wouldn't be long before we heard that St. George had retired permanently from the world. At least mentally.

"That might be a good idea," Iris said. "Neither one of them are fit to defend themselves and they live way out there alone. You're not around much, so you should probably either move them into town, or hire them a guard."

"Give me a few moments," he said, disappearing into the living room. When he returned, he nodded. "Done. They'll have their protection." Just like that. I wanted to ask who he'd called but that could wait until later. When Smoky decided to do something, it got done and there was no wishy-washy mulling over the question.

"So tell us what you found out?" I said again.

Vanzir frowned. "The place is heavily guarded from the front, but they seem to feel that the barrier of the woods and the concrete retaining wall on the other side is enough to protect them. I think they have a hellhound or two running loose out there, but otherwise, I mostly saw a few scattered demons lounging around. I didn't see Stacia."

"Hmm . . . not exactly a compound," I mused.

"No. And there's another thing I found odd. There were wards around. I checked them out—and before you ask, yes, I was careful—and the wards aren't set up against Fae or humans. They're set up against *demons*. I was lucky I didn't trip any of them off and that I stayed at the perimeter of her compound." He leaned back in his chair. "What do you make of that?"

"Do you think she's afraid of rebel demons coming after her?" Delilah asked.

"No, I don't. In fact, the wards are specifically set against common types Shadow Wing uses in his Degath Squads, as well as the more sophisticated types like me."

"An odd turn of events." I pondered the information for a few minutes. "Do you think it might have something to do with what Grandmother Coyote told us? She said something about dissension in the ranks, and that Stacia's goal is aimed for something very different than we think."

"Well," Iris said. "What have you been thinking her goal is?"

"To prevent us from getting ahold of the seals. She's working for Shadow Wing—so, wouldn't that be her primary focus?"

"Not necessarily," Vanzir said, a triumphant gleam flickering in his eyes. "It's beginning to make sense now."

We stared at him. "What?" I asked.

"You say that Stacia's goal is something different than what we think. That dissension's going on. Suppose Stacia means to move up the ranks in her own way? Suppose Stacia isn't happy working for Shadow Wing and wants him out of the way?"

"What? Are you saying Stacia might be two-timing Shadow Wing?" Trillian narrowed his eyes. "Wouldn't that be suicidal?"

"Not necessarily. You'd have to be very strong, have reliable allies, and be very careful. Stacia's one of the strongest generals in the Sub Realms. She's also a necromancer and I'm pretty sure that Shadow Wing doesn't realize just how powerful she has become, or he'd have killed her already. She's a threat." Vanzir jumped up and began to pace. "What if . . . what if Trytian's father got to her? What if she's allied herself with the daemons?"

Trytian was the son of a powerful daemon—another race living in the Sub Realms—who had risen against Shadow Wing and was building an army. We'd heard of him before, and we knew that Trytian had been ordered to look for us, hoping to forge some sort of alliance. But we'd refused. Not a good idea to forge deals with any sort of demon, daemon, whatever you wanted to call them.

I caught up his idea. "What if Trytian and his group of rebels decided to go right for the heart of Shadow Wing's entourage? Suppose that the daemons mean to gather the rest of the spirit seals for themselves and use them to launch an attack on Shadow Wing. Stacia could be shifting the portals to either prevent Shadow Wing from crossing over, or for some reason that would benefit her and her alone."

"This is sounding more and more possible," Iris said. "And not at all out of keeping with Demonkin. They move up the ranks through assassination."

"Right," I said. "Her note warned us to either team up or butt out and go home. Essentially, play ball or get out of the way. I've been trying to figure out why Shadow Wing would want our help ever since I read the note, but it just didn't click. Now it does. Karvanak gave us a chance to join him, but it was just to lure us into giving him the spirit seal. He meant to kill us anyway. But Stacia . . ."

I bit my lip. "So, what do you think? Is Stacia trying to intimidate us into working with her? We seem to have a knack for finding the spirit seals and she may want to capitalize on that. And demons are notorious for using the power-over route rather than trying a little diplomacy."

Everyone looked at Vanzir. He was the expert on demons around here. He'd lived in the Sub Realms far, far too long. Now, he rapped his fingers on the table. After a moment he nodded.

"I think you're on to something. But even though it might seem like she's on our side, don't be fooled. She's just another power-hungry demon looking at moving into the top spot. The minute she has no use for you, she'll kill you." He scratched his head. "Remember sometime back when I told you that Shadow Wing is going over the edge—that he refers to himself as the Unraveller?"

Delilah nodded. "You said you think he means to unmake the worlds."

"Well, it looks to me like his top advisors are beginning to notice and are taking steps to ensure their own survival."

"So the Bonecrusher is focused on self-preservation. I can't blame her for that, but we can't work with her." I let out a long sigh and dug into my sandwich. The burst of flavor in my mouth from the roast beef and the mustard cut through my taste buds, making me smile.

Smoky leaned forward, elbows on the table, resting his chin on his hands. "We have to take her out. Even if she is standing against Shadow Wing, it's not because she loves humankind or the Fae. And meddling with the portals is dangerous, no matter what the reason. No—we have to defeat her without alerting the daemons or Shadow Wing."

"If they've guarded against demons but not human or Fae, that means we can sneak in through the back. They may be protected up the wazoo out front, but it sounds like she left a hole, thinking the demons would be her main threat." I picked out an apple from the bowl of fruit on the table and bit into it.

"This isn't going to be easy," Iris said. "But you can count me in. I want to pay her a little vengeance in Henry's name."

I smiled at her. "Count all of us in, Iris. Because we're going to need every last body we can get."

CHAPTER 23

~~~~~

Fueled by a constant stream of tea, cookies, and sandwiches, by the time Menolly awoke we'd managed to sketch out a brief plan of action. The thought occurred to me more than once that we were potentially destroying one of Shadow Wing's enemies, but I couldn't see any way to harness her help. Stacia wouldn't care about us. And who knew what she had planned once she took over his reign? And then—only if she was successful.

We cleared the guys out of the kitchen shortly before it was time for Menolly to wake up. Only Smoky, among all the men, knew the secret entrance to her lair and he was good for the secret. But I still didn't want to take a chance. The more people who knew where to find my sister when she slept, the more danger there would be of the information leaking out.

Menolly silently slipped from behind the bookshelf-door against one kitchen wall. She stared at the pile of papers on the table and the maps, then at the jumble of dishes on the counter. She was wearing a pair of skin-tight leather pants, a sky blue turtleneck, and she'd caught her mass of burnished braids back into a high ponytail, both chic and arresting.

"Okay, what the hell is going on? Something's up." She

opened the refrigerator and pulled out a bottle of blood, then popped it into the microwave.

"As soon as we brief you, we're heading out. We've got a nasty fight. Delilah's calling Chase now, asking if he might be able to join us, and Morio's off asking Wilbur to come with us. I've already called Nerissa—she's on the way."

"Nerissa? What's going on? She's not a trained fighter—not in the way we are or Zachary is." Nerissa was Menolly's girl-friend, a werepuma in the Rainier Puma Pride. While they saw men on the side, they were exclusive in that they didn't take any other women lovers. I had the feeling they were in this for the long haul, though neither would even consider the thought. But a gut feeling told me they made a wonderful pair.

"No, but she can babysit Maggie for us. She'll be here in about an hour." I let out a long sigh and waited until Menolly's blood was warm and she brought it to the table. "Henry's dead. Stacia blew up my shop this morning and killed him."

"What?" Menolly's eyes shifted from pale gray to bloodred and her fangs descended. As I told her the rest, she sipped the blood, carefully wiping the corners of her mouth, saying nothing. When I finished, she filled the bottle with soapy water and set it in the sink. She didn't mention Henry's death, but she placed her hand on my shoulder and leaned over the back of my chair to give me a rare kiss on the cheek. "What are we waiting for? Let's get ready to rumble."

Marymoor Park was on the Eastside. The Greater Seattle Metropolitan area is made up not only of Seattle proper, but of numerous suburb cities that flowed into each other, divided by manmade boundaries rather than natural divisions. Many of the bedroom communities had grown large enough to be central metropolitan areas themselves.

The GSM area surrounded several lakes, including Lake Washington, Lake Union, and Lake Sammamish, while Seattle proper was on Elliot Bay and the Puget Sound Inlet, which led out through the Straits of Juan de Fuca to the Pacific Ocean.

The Eastside was east of Lake Washington, connected to Seattle by two floating pontoon bridges, one of which—the 520 Floating Bridge—was one the longest of its kind in the world. Both the I-90 Bridge and the 520 were marvels of engineering in the earthquake-prone area, and the 520 was in desperate need of rebuilding, both to service the increased load of cars that crossed it daily, and to prevent it from going belly up during a major trembler.

We were headed for a city called Redmond, the home of Microsoft. It abutted Bellevue—a city of over one hundred and twenty thousand people—and was a little less urban but still a growing community. The two cities were divided by Bel-Red Road, short—of course—for Bellevue-Redmond Road.

As we headed toward the exit off of the 520, which had been sparsely trafficked thanks to the fact that we'd headed out shortly after eight P.M., I glanced over my shoulder to make sure that Chase's SUV was following Morio's Subaru. We'd brought two cars, considering that we had eleven people and all our gear to transport. Morio was driving me, Menolly, Trillian, and Smoky. Chase ferried Delilah, Rozurial, Wilbur, Vanzir, and Iris.

We sped along the 520 freeway until we came to the exit, which opened onto Leary Way. Straight ahead and we'd be in Redmond proper. Morio swung a right onto West Sammamish Parkway. Less than five minutes later and we were at the entrance of Marymoor Park. He eased into the left-turn lane at the light, and pulled into the park, followed by Chase.

There was some sort of event going on, and the park was still open though it usually closed at dusk. We eased into the parking lot near Clise Mansion: a community hall that had once been a country estate and now was available for meetings, weddings, and other special occasions.

As we scrambled out of the cars, I looked wistfully at the mansion. "It's beautiful. It would be so nice to have some sort of party where we didn't have to worry about all this other crap."

Trillian put his hand on my shoulder. "Perhaps for the holidays, we can throw a party here?"

I stared at him, touched. Trillian usually wasn't so keen on social claptrap, as he put it, but now the look on his face told me he meant it. I kissed him lightly on the nose. "Thank you for that."

We gathered our gear and headed out of the park. The towering firs and cedars were interspersed with maple and birch and hawthorn and alder, and numerous other types of trees and shrubs. The park was over six hundred acres. We were on the west side. A five-minute walk took us back to West Sammamish Parkway, and a few seconds later we were across the street.

Menolly looked around—nobody was on the road so she quickly hovered up to the top of the restraining wall and, perching on it, tossed down a light rope. We made light work of climbing up, even Iris, who was a lot stronger than she looked. On the other side of the wall, we found ourselves facing a shallow ravine filled with trees. It was easy enough to scramble down into the cover of foliage.

"Okay, where's Stacia's place?" It was dark, and the ground uneven. I was glad I'd traded my stilettos for granny boots. It was also cold and I was equally glad I'd worn a light jacket over my leather bustier and rayon skirt that fell to my calves.

Vanzir gauged the area, then pointed. "Up ahead. It's new. Looks like it was built in the last year or two. They cleared out another patch of woods for it." He led us under the shelter of leaves that were dripping water from the rain. At least the weather had let up a bit, and we were only facing a drizzle. But the mist was rising from the ground and, before long, it would be rolling through the area.

We silently followed him to the edge of the ravine, clambering up the embankment without much trouble. At the top, we were at the edge of the tree line, staring into the backyard of a large estate.

"You'd think with a joint this expensive, they'd have more land attached to it," Trillian said.

"Around here, land's a valuable commodity. People tend to put the money into the house rather than the yard," Chase murmured.

But *house* was a misnomer. Stacia Bonecrusher really did live in a mansion. Three stories tall, the house sprawled across the lot. Oh, it wasn't any fancier than a number of the expensive homes in the area, but it must have set the demon back close to a million. How the hell had she gotten the money to buy it? Did the demons invest in Wall Street? Whatever her means, Stacia had chosen the butt ugliest house on the block, I thought.

Mansion it might be, but it looked like one of those slap-
together houses, the siding painted a bland beige, with the req-
uisite white-trimmed windows. Like every other new house on
the block, just bigger. *Much* bigger. There were two sets of
French doors leading out into the backyard, onto stone patios,
and as I glanced around the yard, I began to sense the wards
Vanzir had told us about. I homed in on one that was about two
yards away from me, and motioned to Morio.

We slowly crept up on it, followed by Vanzir, keeping low
to the ground so the cover of night might hide us from prying
eyes. Unless, of course, they could sense the heat of our bodies. With Stacia being a lamia and so connected to snakes, it
might just be a possibility. I whispered as much to Morio, but
he shook his head.

"Too cold. It's dropped below fifty degrees. Snakes won't
be out and about in this weather. Most likely they're brumat-
ing. But once we're inside, we'll have to be careful. Bet you
it's hot as hell in there. Which makes me think," he added.
"She's a lamia, part snake. If we hit her with enough cold
magic, it should do extra damage."

Vanzir nodded. "Good thinking."

The ward was made from a ruby-colored crystal, similar
to the ones we had at home but they were definitely not Earthside or OW make. Morio and I joined hands and examined
the energy. It coiled around the crystal like a snake slithering
around its prey. And then I saw the runes magically embedded
into the energy.

Apparently Morio spotted them, too. "Vanzir's right. These
are set up to warn when Demonkin come through. They must
come and go by the front gate, or they'd be setting off their
own wards all the time."

"Unless it's set to ignore whatever kind of demons she's
surrounding herself with," I said. "Whatever the case, you,
Menolly, Roz, and Vanzir can't cross the wards without chanc-
ing to activate them, since you're all considered some form of
demon."

We crept back to the others and reported what we'd found.
There was still no one in the backyard, though lights were
shining in various windows of the house.

"So we follow our original plan?" We'd turned it around

and around during our strategy planning session and couldn't find any other solution, other than to creep in, leaving those four behind. Once the fight was on, they could charge in as a second wave, given that Stacia would know we were here already.

"Yeah, that's the only way I can see it," Menolly said. "I just wish I could go in first, but if there's a chance my being a vampire will set off the alarm, then I'd better wait with the others."

Morio pulled out the small casket Rodney slept in and I groaned. He flashed me a look that said *Suck it up* and opened the box. As Rodney climbed out of the box, Morio hissed, "You will keep your mouth shut or I will tear you apart. I am not kidding. Get it?"

Rodney glared at him, but nodded.

"You're going to go in as a scout and you'd better keep quiet when you do because there are some big bad demons in there who would think nothing of squashing you like a bug. Got it?"

Again, the nod.

"When you reach the door, you'll grow to full size. You're to take out as many of the demons in there as you can. Fight like hell because they're sure going to. And don't even think about sneaking out and running away, because I'll hunt you down and give your bones to the nearest dog. *Capiche?*"

Morio began to transform into his full demon self and Rodney stumbled back a couple of steps, nodding.

I nodded. "Okay then. Come on." I motioned to the others. "Spread out and work your way toward the back of the house."

We'd decided to come at it from several angles. That way if one person was spotted, the others might still get the drop on the action. Fanning out, we slowly began edging our way through the yard. There were assorted shrubs and ferns dotting the lawn, so we had some cover. As I darted behind the nearest huckleberry, it occurred to me that this was getting old hat.

We were good. I couldn't see the others' progress, which meant that chances were, anybody looking out the window couldn't see them either. The yard was dark, illuminated only by the light coming from the windows.

I'd nearly reached the house when the set of French doors nearest me opened and a bloatworgle came out, scratching himself as he proceeded to urinate on the grass next to the patio. I froze, hoping that the thinly trunked birch behind which I was hiding would cover me. Bloatworgles were ugly and dangerous; we'd fought several not long ago. They were among the thousands of grunts in the Sub Realms, almost caricatures of FBHs, with distended bellies and long, drooping arms and unshapely gray skin that drooped in wrinkles. But they could breathe fire and they were unreasonably strong.

The bloatworgle shook his dick and scratched his balls, then looked in my direction. He froze. Oh cripes, he saw me. I knew he could see me. As he opened his mouth, I let out a shout and dove to the side as I called down the lightning. The clouds were so thick that they responded and a ball of blue energy raced down toward the bloatworgle.

Please, please, please, don't let it backfire, I thought, but just then the energy sputtered and broke up in a shower of sparks, the flaming hot energy hitting everything in sight.

"Fuck it!" I dashed in, drawing my dagger, trying to stay out of the way of that mouth of his. Nasty blasts of fire came out of that mouth. Very nasty.

At my shout, the others broke cover and raced in. Smoky caught the bloatworgle by surprise, blindsiding him as he unleashed his claws and flew by in a blur, leaving five deep gashes across the bloatworgle's belly. The demon snarled and as he turned, blasting fire after Smoky, Delilah caught him from behind. She didn't do her usual kick-spin, but brought Lysanthra, her dagger, down on the bloatworgle's back, driving it in to the hilt between his shoulder blades. Smoky rounded for another hit and between the two of them the bloatworgle was so much dead meat. One demon—easy to kill. Many demons—chaos and trouble.

There was a sound from the doors and I looked up to see a half dozen human-looking guards standing there. Bikers on steroids?

"Tregarts," Roz said, rushing in behind me. "Demons."

Morio, Vanzir, and Menolly were on his heels. We spread out, facing the men, who were dressed in thick leather jackets and pants. Knives and chains seemed to be their weapons of choice, though it looked like one was holding a lead pipe. They moved forward, glaring at us. Mr. Lead Pipe tapped the pipe in his hand, a glint in his eye.

"Great, they look like they're enjoying this," I said, backing up to attempt another spell. Before I could summon the Moon Mother's power, they were joined by a herd of shuffling flesh-on-the-sneaker. Zombies. Or ghouls. Oh, I hoped it was zombies—easier to kill, not so much in the brains department.

There was a subtle pause as we sized each other up. They were strong. Very strong. We had a fight on our hands. I just hoped to hell that Stacia would hold off until we took care of these cretins. I grabbed Morio's hand.

"Let's try to dispel some of the zombies," I said. He nodded. We moved off to the side and Morio hurriedly pulled out a quartz crystal–beaded necklace and handed it to me. I draped it over my neck and he did the same with one of obsidian beads. We joined hands and began focusing on the spell that would turn the zombies back into worm food.

Meanwhile, I glanced up in time to see Delilah and Smoky move in on the bikers, and then they were joined by the rest. Iris hung back, shooting a shower of ice fragments at the demons. Demons generally didn't like the cold unless they hung out in the Netherworld, and considering they were working for the lamia, I doubted that there'd be any cold spots in the house at all.

Wilbur joined Morio and me, and he quickly sprinkled salt into a large pentagram, then drew a circle around it with salt mixed with rosemary. He sat in the center of the five-pointed star and began to incant something low under his breath. I pulled my attention away, trying not to focus on the shouts and screams that were coming from the fight, but on the little squadron of zombies that had noticed us and were heading our way. Great, they were drawn by the necromantic energy. Delightful.

"Concentrate," Morio hissed.

I shook my head. Why couldn't I focus? Why couldn't I ground myself? And then, just like that, the attention was there, shoving aside all other thoughts. I sank into the energy, let it engulf me as it dragged us down into the realm of shadow, into the realm of the night. Everything around me took on a faint violet glow and I knew we'd opened the door.

Morio squeezed my hands and we began the chant to release the summoned undead. Like many of our other spells, it played with a counterpoint rhythm. Morio began to open the gate.

"Devo shena, devo sherahni, devo shilak. Devo mordente, devo resparim, devo salesum . . ."

As he repeated the incantation over and over, I began to sing the counterpoint. "Walking death, wandering spirits, whispering souls, hear our command. Return to grave, shroud of death, whispering souls, you shall not stand."

The energy built slowly but steadily, a wreath of violet fire that circled around us. I watched as it circled us, a network of pulses sparking like synapses in the brain. Morio and I kept up the counterpoint and the bubble of energy expanded out. The zombies were almost to the outer border of the circle when the closest gave a shriek as it reached out to pass through the twinkling lights. Within seconds, it fell to the ground and rotted away like a time lapse photo, the final ooze from the body soaking into the ground.

One down, a half dozen to go. Another zombie shuffled up and through the border and within seconds had turned into mere memory. The others paused. While they were soulless, almost automatons, they had some spark of self-preservation built into the magical code that brought them to life.

As they hesitated, Wilbur let out a grunt and a rolling wave of light crested over the zombies. With a unified shriek, they vanished, incinerated in whatever mother of a spell he'd cast. Morio and I stared at him, our own spell dropping as our concentration broke. What the fuck had he just done? More important, could we learn to do that?

He winked at us, then turned back to the fight that was going on between the others. The demons were down a man. And . . . oh Great Mother, help us, so were we. Chase was on the ground and he looked unconscious. Wrapped in the magic, I hadn't even heard the scuffle.

I scanned for Delilah. She was slashing away at one of the Tregart demons, screaming obscenities at the top of her lungs. I leapt forward, racing toward Chase, and dropped at his side. He looked pale, and blood covered the side of his shirt. Morio joined me and I waved him away.

"Go help them. Send me Roz."

Rozurial was by my side in seconds. He frowned when he saw Chase, then pulled out a bottle of something and splashed it over the wound site, through Chase's shirt. "We need something to bind him with," he said, fumbling in his pocket for a tin of the salve he carried everywhere.

I looked up at Wilbur. "Your shirt. I need your shirt."

Wilbur shrugged and ripped it off, handing it to me. I tore it in tiny strips, trying to ignore the sounds of battle raging around me. We had to save Chase—had to get him medical attention. Roz and I bound the strips around him, after Roz slathered a handful of salve over the wound. I struggled to turn Chase long enough to get the material beneath him so we could tie it tight. He was heavy, and when I moved him, the wound began to bleed again.

"Cripes, what the hell are we going to do? We can't get him to our cars from here." I frantically looked around. "His breathing is so shallow. What are we going to do?"

Roz leapt up and raced over to Smoky, where he was fighting one of the demons. He'd almost finished the guy off and now Roz pushed him my way and took his place. Smoky hurried over.

"What? What do you need? Are you hurt?"

I shook my head. "We have to get Chase to the FH-CSI headquarters. He's been hurt, and hurt badly. I don't think Delilah knows yet."

"It's hard to focus in there. Those brutes are so tough it's amazing we can take them down at all. Here, I'll take him through the Ionyc Sea and then return to help you out." Smoky gathered Chase in his arms and—before I could say a word—vanished.

I wanted a moment to regroup but there wasn't time. There were still . . . oh hell, still five of the bikers standing and they were driving everyone back. Delilah looked like she'd been wounded, and I saw blood on Trillian's cheek, and blood spatters on Vanzir. Iris came rushing up.

"We have to do something," I said to her. "It appears these demons have skin like leather. I don't know what to do. If we retreat, they'll just try again!"

She nodded, her lips firmly set together. "I swore to myself

I'd never use this again, but . . . we have no choice. I'll take care of it," she said softly, tears forming in her eyes.

I was about to ask just what she was planning, when she yelled out, "Fall back. *Now!*"

Everyone in our party heard her—her voice echoed through the yard like she was using a megaphone. And then, she closed her eyes and I heard her whisper, "For Henry . . ." and a whirlwind of energy rose around her, a vortex of blue and white mist, and she pushed it forward with a terrible cry.

The wall of energy rolled over the demons and piercing shrieks echoed from their midst. I couldn't see what was happening, and then, as the energy began to vanish, I could see. Iris had fainted and as I knelt by her side, I looked up at the yard.

"Oh, Iris . . ." I fell silent, staring at the chaos. The Tregarts had been turned inside out. They were so much muscle and bone and raw, pulsating flesh. Without a word, I turned to the side and vomited.

"Iris . . ." Delilah dropped her dagger to her side. She looked around. "Is anybody else hurt? Chase? Chase?" A frantic light came into her eyes and she whirled around. "Where's Chase?"

"Smoky took him to see Sharah. He's been wounded, Kitten. He's still alive, but he needs medical care." I didn't dare tell her how badly he was hurt. We needed her in one piece—and not a kitten.

Her lower lip began to tremble, but she didn't go any further because at that moment, Iris groggily came to. As we helped her to her feet, there was a shout from the door. There stood a man—or at least, at first glimpse it was a man.

Vanzir jumped up, striding forward. He looked furious. "Trytian, what the fuck are you doing here, you bastard?"

Trytian! We were right. It was the daemon's son. I forced myself to march up beside Vanzir.

"Where is she? Where's the Bonecrusher?" I knew I sounded slightly hysterical but couldn't help myself. My emotions were riding high.

Trytian, who looked a little like Keanu Reeves in an eerie,

hellish way, gave me an insolent smile. "Gone. Our guards bought her time enough to evacuate. We're moving operations."

I leapt forward. "She murdered my friend and destroyed my shop!" As I brought one hand around, hard, to slap him on the cheek, Vanzir stopped me, catching my wrist. He nodded for me to move back. He spoke in low tones to the daemon, who at first shook his head and then, with a shrug, nodded.

Trytian stepped forward. "Listen, we want the same thing. Shadow Wing—dead. The Bonecrusher wanted your help. My father and I wanted your help. You prefer to work from another angle. I'll make you a promise—and Vanzir will vouch for me. If you leave the Bonecrusher alone, don't hunt for her, don't try to find her, she'll leave you and your friends alone. But make no mistake: We mean to find the seals and when we do, we're marching on Shadow Wing."

"What makes you think I won't let the information leak that she's a traitor?" I hated his smug smile, his arrogant stance. He had helped kill Henry. I knew it; in my gut I knew he was one of the men in the shop.

As I stepped forward, Vanzir grabbed me around the waist.

Trillian let out a shout, but Vanzir called over his shoulder, "Don't move. Don't even think about it."

He laughed roughly. "Oh, Camille, I not only know it, I'd guarantee it to a bookie. You're a sure bet. Because you know, in your heart, that you aren't prepared to fight Shadow Wing. And you know my father and Stacia can take him on and have a chance of winning. I know you'll still be looking for the seals, but I warn you: Don't get in our way. Because if you cross our path again, you'll lose more than a broken-down old man. You'll lose *everything*."

I broke out of Vanzir's hold then, rushing forward. I grappled with Trytian. He clearly wasn't expecting my attack but managed to grab my wrists and rolled me over as he held me down, straddling me.

"You're lucky you have friends here right now, woman. I may be out for Shadow Wing's blood, but I'm still a daemon, and some things are just too tempting to resist." His whisper was too low for anyone else to hear; he snorted. Then he let go and jumped up.

"We'll find you! We'll search the house and find something

you overlooked." Oh, to land a good kick to his balls, but I had the feeling it wouldn't hurt him in the least.

"Go ahead—in fact, I *expect* it of you. You're so obvious."

Morio lunged forward, but Trytian danced back out of his reach. "Youkai, leave this alone. It's none of your business. And the rest of you, remember what I said. You won't get a second warning. Stacia will put off Shadow Wing's orders to kill you long enough for us to make our move, but only if you don't interfere. Stick your noses in our business, unless you want to turncoat, and you're so much burnt toast."

He turned to Vanzir. "My debt to you is over . . . this more than pays you off." And with that, he vanished as if he'd never been standing there.

CHAPTER 24

I mutely stared at the empty place on the porch. Just then, Rodney came shambling out of the house. Morio moved up beside me, and Trillian flanked my other side.

"What's going on in there?" Morio said.

The flame in Rodney's eye sockets flared. "Not much. They scrammed but fast. Bitches didn't even take all of their zombies. A few bone-walkers in there, too. But—what the hell is that?" He cocked his skull, as if he was listening to something.

I frowned. There was a low humming coming from inside the house. It reminded me of the whine of a jet engine. And then, instinct guiding me, I shouted, "Get the fuck out of here—run toward the trees!"

Nobody questioned me; they all just turned tail.

We all managed to reach the tree line before there was a low rumble and then a loud explosion. The shock wave blasted us forward, but we were out of range of the flames that shot up. I hit the ground hard, landing on my knees and hands.

As I gasped, choking on the smoke, Vanzir muttered, "Cocksucker . . . he *meant* for us to be there when that happened."

Delilah coughed and struggled to her feet, then helped me up. "But he said—"

"Forget what he said. Forget what I ever suggested about working with him. He's a daemon. He was trying to kill us to make sure we don't interfere. My guess is that they decided to shift their headquarters. They must have found out we were coming and planned this little booby trap."

"How? How did they find out?" The house was engulfed in flames and the sound of sirens echoed in the distance.

"I dunno. I think we have a leak somewhere," he said slowly. "Somebody . . . someone told them. Who did you tell about this?"

"It could be any number of people. Chase's FH-CSI officers knew we were coming, Nerissa knew . . . who else?" Something tickled at the back of my mind but I couldn't wrap my thoughts around it; I was so shaken.

"Then we have a lot of thinking to do." Morio motioned toward the ravine. "Come on, let's get out of here before the cops arrive."

Delilah let out a low sob. "Chase—I need to know how Chase is."

"Yeah, and Iris . . ." I glanced at the Talon-haltija, who was staring at the flames, her mouth pinched. Her expression was one of haunting and pain. It was then that I understood that she hadn't realized what she was going to do—or that she had even been sure she could still cast that spell. Too close to her memories of her fiancé for comfort.

"Come on. Let's go," I whispered, wrapping my arm around her shoulders as we headed back into the trees. "We aren't going to wrap this one up tonight, guys."

As we slipped under the cover of the rain-drenched leaves, I wondered just what the hell we were going to do now. We had an informant somewhere—it was the only way to explain that they knew we were coming. We had the Fae Queens on our back from both realms. And I knew that Stacia wouldn't hesitate to come after us once she realized we'd survived the explosion.

I had no idea what we were going to do about any of it, but I knew one thing for sure: We'd find the Bonecrusher, and when we did, we'd rip her to shreds.

* * *

We arrived at the FH-CSI headquarters, soaked through and covered with mud and ash. Sharah was waiting for us. Delilah moved forward, her face a blank slate. Menolly and I flanked her sides.

"Chase . . ." Her voice was faint, her back rigid.

Sharah stared at her for a moment, then slowly said, "He's in critical condition. I don't know if he'll make it. We're doing everything we can."

"No . . . no . . ." Delilah wavered and Menolly pressed her hand against her back, steadying her. "There has to be something you can do to help."

I closed my eyes, not wanting to breathe, not wanting to speak. I knew the answer, but dreaded being the one to suggest it. But if it might help . . .

"I know what might heal his wounds. But it could destroy him in the long run," I blurted out. Enough heartache for one night. If it could save him now, we'd deal with the future later.

"What is it? We can't lose Chase. *I can't lose him!*" Delilah grabbed me by the shoulders. "Tell me!"

I sucked in a deep breath. "You were going to have him drink the nectar of life. The potion will also heal extreme injuries. Without the proper rituals, it might also drive him mad in the long run, but it will save his life *now*." Turning to Sharah, I asked, "Does he stand a chance otherwise?"

"There's always a chance . . . but the odds are low . . ." Her voice trailed off and I saw the glimmer of tears in her eyes.

"Then, that's it," Delilah said. "Give him this." She pulled the bottle out of her purse and slammed it into Sharah's hand. *"Do it."*

"But—but, are you sure?" The elf looked at me and I nodded.

Menolly stepped forward. "We don't have a choice. If he's going to die anyway, you might as well give it a shot, because I'm not interested in siring a son and that's our only other option."

Sharah let out a long sigh and then whirled, marching down the corridor. "Follow me," she called.

We followed. As we entered Chase's room, we saw that

he was hooked up to numerous IV drips, and he was on a ventilator.

"He was stabbed four times, and sustained heavy damage to his internal organs," Sharah said. "The knife went in at precisely the wrong spots. Whoever attacked him knew just how to inflict critical damage."

Delilah flinched, but Sharah didn't notice. She just pulled a large syringe out of the drawer. "The nectar of life will work when it's injected, as well as when it's swallowed." As she slowly filled the syringe, she glanced up at my sister. "You know this is on *your* head? I know we need Chase, I know you love him, but I'm doing this against my better judgment. Without the rituals, this could create major changes in his personality as well as his body."

"*Do it,*" Delilah said, growling.

I saw the flicker in her aura that presaged a transformation and hurried over to Sharah's side. "Unless you want a very angry black panther in here, you'd better do what she asks. We'll take responsibility."

Sharah nodded and slowly began to inject the drug directly into Chase's jugular vein. When the sparkling liquid had all disappeared, she stood back. "We'll know in a minute if it's going to save his life or not."

Delilah dropped to her knees. "Great Mother Bast, I implore you. Please save Chase. I need him. I don't know why you brought us together, but we're not through yet. We're not finished yet."

Nobody said a word, as the seconds ticked by. And then, just as I thought it wasn't going to work, Chase gasped and Sharah carefully removed the ventilator from his mouth. He wasn't conscious yet, but he was breathing on his own. Another minute and the wounds on his side started to pull together. She hurried to slather a healing cream on him, then turned to Delilah.

"He's going to live. And he'll live far longer than most any other human ever will. You have one hell of a lot to help him adjust to, once he regains consciousness. I hope you're up to the job because his life is now in your hands. Humans who drink the nectar of life usually have no concept of what it means to live a thousand years."

As she began to check his vital signs, Delilah broke down in tears and Menolly led her over to one of the nearby chairs. I turned to find Smoky by my side. He slid his arm around me and we just stood there, silent, as the steady hum of the machines monitored Chase's life.

CHAPTER 25

❦

That evening, we were still trying to comprehend what had happened. It was too soon to figure out everything we'd need to do, but when the shock wore off, we had to make plans. We needed help, and I knew that I'd be paying a visit to Aeval, to enlist her aid, whatever the cost to me.

A knock on the door rattled me. Smoky went to answer it and came back with an odd expression on his face. "You're wanted in the living room" was all he'd say.

As I peered around the corner, I got the surprise of my life. Standing there was Derisa, the High Priestess and emissary of the Moon Mother.

Derisa was tall, edging six five, and her hair was braided, hanging to her knees. With chiseled features, she looked fashioned from pale porcelain, with ocean blue eyes. Dressed in a long robe somewhere between black and indigo and covered with moons and stars embroidered in spun silver, she broke into a smile when she saw me. It was Derisa who had taken my oath the night I pledged myself to the Moon Mother, and Derisa who had taken my hand and led me onto the astral during my first Hunt.

I knelt by her side, feeling more tired than I ever had in my life, wishing only for rejuvenation, for some relief from the stress.

She leaned down and touched my shoulder. "Rise."

I stood, silent, soaking in her radiance. Derisa didn't just wield magic, she *was* magic. Her energy spiraled around me, pulling me close as she embraced me. She smelled like lilacs and narcissus, like white gardenias on a summer night, and I reveled in the scent as it washed away the tears on my heart.

"It's been a long time since we've met," she said, her lips close to my own, her gaze locked on mine.

"I never expected to see you here," I whispered, unable to look away.

"Neither did I," she said, then leaned in and pressed her lips against mine, her tongue playing gently over my own. I melted into her embrace, letting go of my aching heart. We were sisters under the same goddess, pledged to the same order, connected by a force far stronger than either of us, and her kiss melted away my tension and sorrow, leaving a luxurious and heady sense of relaxation in its wake. I could smell her fragrance, sense her power, and it made me want to give her anything she might ask of me. After a moment, she slowly pulled back. I tingled, my weariness drained away.

"I've brought your priestess robes." She handed me a suitcase.

I caught my breath. There they were—filmy spider-weave robes that only the priestesses of the Moon Mother were allowed to wear. Sheer to the point of see-through, they sparkled with silver and gold threads running through material the color of royal peacocks: a swirl of blues and purples and greens. The robe consisted of two parts—a kimono over a halter dress with a built-in bra. I lifted the dress out of the valise. Beneath it was a silver belt and a headband of silver and bronze, with a crescent, horns pointing up, atop a round moon.

All my life I'd wanted to be a full-fledged priestess. And now my wish had come true, at a cost paid with blood. So much blood.

Lifting my head, I gazed into Derisa's eyes. "I had to sacrifice the Black Unicorn's life to earn this, you know."

She smiled, kindly this time. "Do you think *any* priestess was just handed her robes? We all earned them, and earned them the hard way. What you did was not just a sacrifice, Camille. You gave the black phoenix his rebirth. Even now, he runs free, reborn as a foal the moment you struck him down, to a unicorn within the heart of the Deep. The King is dead. Long live the King."

And then I fully understood. The cycle was more than metaphorical. The Lord of the Dahns had to die in order to be reborn. He'd been growing weak and a weakened King must be sacrificed in order to live again in a younger, stronger body. Trembling, I licked my lips.

"What do I do now? Teach me. I need so much help in the battle we face. There are so many enemies, and we're starting to lose friends."

She laughed. "War isn't easy. War should be bloody. *It should cost lives and bring pain*—if it doesn't, it's too easy to take up arms without good reason. But yes, I bring you instructions. You'll train for your duties here, Earthside, since there's no way you can come home for any length of time right now."

"Train *here*? Who can teach me what I need to know?" And then a whisper in my heart shook me to the core.

"You know, my dear. You know who your teacher will be."

"No . . . not Morgaine."

Derisa gave me a sly smile. "She is a trained priestess and one of the original members of the Coterie of the Moon Mother."

"But . . . will she teach me? Queen Asteria will be furious—"

"The Moon Mother cares nothing for what the Elfin Queen thinks. You will learn from Morgaine. And you will offer your service to Aeval's Court; the death magic you are learning needs the power of the Night to be fully realized. You are truly a priestess of the Dark Moon, my dear. Not the light."

She handed me a book. "Here is your book of rituals and shadows. Show it to Morgaine so she can ascertain what she needs to teach you. And when you are done with your training, you will take your place as the first High Priestess of the Moon Mother that the Earthside realm has seen in thousands of years." Derisa turned to leave.

Stunned, unable to comprehend what she was actually saying, I was suddenly afraid. What if I botched it? What if I couldn't meet the Moon Mother's standards?

She stopped near the door, but did not turn. "Silence your fears. They steal your power. The Moon Mother chose *you*. That is the only thing you need to know for now. Everything else is immaterial."

And then she swept out of the room, out of the house, and like a living shadow, vanished into the night.

I entered the bedroom, wired from the meeting with Derisa. My world had been turned upside down so many times in less than a week, and now I faced another milestone: the meeting of my three lovers together, in my bed. And I had no idea what to expect. I just prayed they wouldn't stage a war over me.

The room was glowing softly and I gasped as I looked around. Candles lit up the room, long tapers of silver and purple and black gracing a dozen candleholders scattered around on the dresser, my vanity, and the end tables. A canopy had been erected over the bed, and from it draped sheer silk drapes, swept back to reveal a shower of rose petals covering the comforter, scenting the room with the fragrance of long-lost summer. Romance at its most seductive. But I hadn't done this so *who* . . . ?

A movement from the bathroom caught my attention as Smoky entered the room, wearing a robe as silver as the moon. He gave me a soft smile.

"Like it?"

"Oh yes, it's beautiful. Did you do this?" Once again, relief swept over me. Smoky was home, with me, and he wasn't going to leave.

"Not alone," he said, nodding over my shoulder.

I turned. Morio entered the bedroom behind me, wearing his black kimono embroidered with gold.

"My Camille . . . my lady," he said, catching my hand up and kissing it. "We thought you could use something to lift your spirits."

Grateful, I ducked my head. "It's working. Thank you."

"It was actually Trillian's idea," Smoky said, and Trillian stepped into the room, wearing a crimson velvet smoking robe.

"Trillian?" My voice caught. I'd been worried about this

moment—how they'd adjust when we were all together. How *I'd* handle the potential land mines.

He stepped forward and stroked my cheek. "It occurred to me that, since I'm going to have to share you, and since I'm going to be your alpha husband, we'd better learn how to work together. At least in the bedroom." Trillian's lip curled into that arrogant smirk I loved so much, but behind it was an offer that I knew was costing him.

I stood in silence in the center of my triad of lovers, looking from one to the other. They stared back, silent and waiting. My lovers. The men of my heart, who completed me, who accepted my strengths and my flaws, my passion and my tears. Who would fight beside me till the death in our war against the demons.

Slowly, I began to undress, one button, one tie, one inch at a time, until I stepped out of my clothes and tossed them to the side. I straightened my shoulders, standing naked before them, the tattoos on my shoulder blades glimmering in the light. The energy of the Moon Mother flowed through me, but from her dark mother phase, bloody and hidden and passionate and magical, death and sex stalking in shadows.

I moved lightly toward Trillian and he lifted his hand to caress my breasts as I stood before him, not touching him, simply letting him touch me. And then, he lowered his hand and gazed into my eyes.

"What is your will, my love? This is your night. We are your servants."

I pulled him to me and kissed him deeply, my lips hungry for his. As his arms slid around me I reached up and brushed the robe away from his shoulders. He let go of me long enough for the cloth to fall and I stepped back, looking at him from head to toe, slowly, drinking in the site of my glorious Svartan. Rock-hard abs, toned biceps, skin as smooth as silk and glowing dark under the amber candlelight. His eyes glittered—the blue of frozen lakes.

"You are my alpha, my fire and passion, always and forever," I said, and he inclined his head.

Turning, I moved to Smoky. Two strands of his hair rose to play with my neck, my lips, my hair. I breathed his fragrance, the scent of dragon, the scent of power, the scent of fire, and then I opened my arms and his hair boosted me up. I kissed him, eye level, then slid his robe off his shoulders.

He lowered me back to the floor, stark, pale beyond pale in the glow of the night, tall and strong and rigidly hungry.

"You are my dragon lord, and protector," I whispered.

And then, I moved to stand before Morio, and he reached out—not with his hands—but with a cord of energy that swirled in ribbons around me, tingling as it fluttered over my thighs, my stomach, the curve of my hips. I stepped forward, cupping his chin in my hand, bringing his lips down to mine where I sank deep into the energy that was his demon nature. His kimono opened and drifted lightly to the side.

"You are my consort, my priest under the Moon Mother, my dark demon," I said, and he knelt before me and kissed my stomach, just below my navel.

I backed away, looking at the three of them as they waited for my command. This was our night to find our united rhythm. Our night to find our place within this relationship that had expanded beyond what I ever expected to have. It was at that moment that I realized: This was *it*. These men were with me to the end, to whatever end we came to. They were my lovers and my loves. Their heartbeats echoed my own, and in our communion, we made up a powerful force. Perhaps the outside world didn't understand, but that didn't matter. In my heart, I loved each one just as much as the others, and they accepted that I had equal love for all three. And that was enough. No one else's permission or approval mattered.

"You are all a part of me." I walked over to the bed, and waited. "I want you, all . . . now . . . together, touching me, filling me full, reminding me of what it means to be your beloved."

Morio moved first, lying down on his back, his lips full and promising the darkest delights. I swung over him, straddling him on my hands and knees so that I was facing his legs. He slipped his fingers inside me, making me wetter still, then reached down and slowly lubricated his cock and slid it between my breasts. As they cushioned him, he reached up and began to bathe me, gently sucking on my clit. The steady stroke set me on fire and I moaned.

"Smoky," I whispered, letting out a little gasp as Morio seriously set to tongue-bathing me.

Silently, Smoky crawled on the bed behind me, his cock slowly teasing my lower lips, setting off every nerve that surrounded the entrance to my pussy. I squirmed, wanting him in me, deep and hard and furious.

"Please, fuck me, just fuck me." I moaned.

"Oh, have no fear, my love, I plan on it," he said, driving himself in with one strong thrust. I opened up, widening to accept his presence, thrilling to the feel of him inside me. As his hair tendriled up to clasp my waist and help me balance, a wave of dizziness rushed over me and I echoed a sharp cry.

And then Trillian was kneeling in front of me, leaning in to kiss me. His tongue tripped over mine, his gaze locking with my own. He gently ran his fingers through my hair, eyes glittering.

And then he pulled back. "Are you happy, love? Is this what you truly want? The three of us, with you, always? Fox Boy, the lizard, and me?"

The scent of their musk was thick in the room, mingling with the fragrance of my own passion. Smoky paused, deep inside of me. Morio's lips went still, hovering as his breath lightly tickled my clit. I realized they were all waiting for my answer.

I sought Trillian's face, searching for any sign that he was angry, but in the depths of his gaze I could find only understanding . . . *and love.*

"Yes, I'm happy," I whispered, tears choking my throat.

The world held so much hatred, so much fear and anger. And here—love ruled. Love and creation, for what was sex if not the opposite of destruction? Sex embodied the energies of creation and movement and life. Yet so many people feared its power, or used it as a weapon, or tried to contain it within rigid rules instead of setting it free to touch the people in their hearts.

"I'm happy," I said again, the tears starting to flow. "More than anything, this is what I want—the three of you, *all of you*, with me till the end of time. You are part of my family, you are my lovers, my husbands. You are my warriors, my comrades. I want you here, by my side in the daylight when we are fighting the demons of the world, and inside of me at night, helping me to forget the blood and the pain. You complete me, all of you, and I complete you."

"Then that's what you'll have, my love," Trillian said. "Until the end of time, we are with you, arguments, faults, insults, and all—we are yours. We'll try not to fight. Too much."

"Speak for yourself," Smoky said, beginning to thrust within me, setting up a delicious friction, but I heard the smile in his voice and his words drifted away in the haze of sex. Morio remained silent, simply setting off a riff of explosions within me with his fluttering tongue, as his cock slowly glided between my breasts.

I glanced at Trillian. He rose before me. Eagerly, I fastened my lips around him, tasting the sweet wine of his body, the salt of his skin, the essence of his being.

And then, there was no more to be said. I was complete, we were together, all of us, and for this night, the worry and fear vanished as everything except the four of us fell away in the flickering light of the candles. Under the sacred Moon Mother's light, we cemented our union in a rite as old as the human race.

Later, late in the night, Menolly, Delilah, and I sat outside, on my balcony. The rain was pounding down but the awning protected us, and we had bundled up. Feeling deliciously satisfied, I leaned back in my chair and told them what Derisa had said. They stared at me.

"You've had a lot of changes the past week," Menolly said. "How are you feeling?"

"It's going to be a long time before I sort them out. I have no idea what I'm going to tell Father—if anything. Apparently the magic I'm doing with Morio has shifted me over to the Moon Mother's shadow side. Where this all will lead . . . I don't know, although I have the feeling that Morgaine and Raven Mother are connected somehow. I'm not done with my dealings with Raven Mother, or the Black Unicorn. My gut's registering ten-point-oh on the Richter scale right now. At least the guys aren't arguing. Yet."

I let out a long sigh and then turned to Delilah. "What's Sharah say about Chase?"

She smiled, but it was strained. "He's healing remarkably fast. But now we have to cope with him drinking the nectar of life without any preparation. Who knows what it will do to him? He has some spark of psychic ability—we figured that out long ago. This might set it off . . . for good or ill." She wiped away a tear that slid out of the corner of her eye. "But at least he'll survive."

"Are you afraid it will change your relationship?" I asked.

"We were planning on doing this, but now . . . it was so sudden. There's no way it *can't* change our relationship. I don't know what to expect. I'm afraid, to be honest. I have a nasty feeling nothing's going to work out the way we wanted it to. What if something goes wrong? What if . . . what if he regrets this? So many things to think about." Her expression darkened. "And what about the Autumn Lord? I have so many years left—he might not want me to bear his child for many years to come . . . but when he does . . ."

"Don't borrow trouble," Menolly said. "Leave it for tomorrow. There's nothing we can do tonight about Chase, and Sharah's looking after him. And the Autumn Lord will move on his own time." She crossed to the railing and stared out into the night. "So where do we go from here?"

"We find the Bonecrusher again and we take her down. I pledge myself to Aeval's court. We find the next spirit seal and you two give it to Queen Asteria because once they find out I'm switching sides . . ." I bit my lip, not wanting to think of the daunting tasks that lay in wait for us.

Just then, a tap on the French doors caught our attention. It was Trillian, along with Smoky and Morio. They were dressed, looking quite dapper, actually—more so than usual. Morio and Smoky stood to the side while Trillian walked over to my chair and knelt in front of me on one knee.

"Call me old-fashioned," he said, "but I still think the man should be the one to propose. So, Camille, will you marry me and let me join with you, Morio, and Smoky in the Soul Symbiont ritual?"

I stared at him. In the midst of chaos came a glimmer of hope. In the midst of sorrow a glimmer of joy. I clasped his hands and nodded. "Of course, Trillian. You're my first love, my alpha love. I can't imagine life without you."

"You deserve a wedding fit for a queen. And we'll have one—with all of your family and friends. I'm only getting married this once—I want it to be special." He pulled me to my feet.

I glanced back at my sisters. "I'm going back to bed." They nodded, Menolly grinning like a banshee.

As the four of us headed back to my bedroom—to *our* bedroom—this time to sleep and dream, I shivered as I remembered their hands on my skin, their lips against my lips, their bodies pressed against mine. And I realized that I wanted to make them as happy as they made me. Because that's really what made life worthwhile—the giving of pleasure and joy and happiness to those we called our loves.

For whether we pledged ourselves to one person or to four, whether we were drawn to men or women or both, whether we walked the path of the priestess or the path of a witch or a bookstore owner, life without passion was no life at all.

CAST OF MAJOR CHARACTERS

The D'Artigo Family

Sephreh ob Tanu: The D'Artigo Sisters' father. Full-Fae.

Maria D'Artigo: The D'Artigo Sisters' mother. Human.

Camille Sepharial te Maria, aka Camille D'Artigo: The oldest sister; a Moon Witch and priestess of the Moon Mother. Half-Fae, half-human.

Delilah Maria te Maria, aka Delilah D'Artigo: The middle sister; a werecat, Death Maiden.

Arial Lianan te Maria: Delilah's twin who died at birth. Half-Fae, half-human. Ghost leopard.

Menolly Rosabelle te Maria, aka Menolly D'Artigo: The youngest sister; a vampire and extraordinary acrobat. Half-Fae, half-human.

Shamas ob Olanda: The D'Artigo girls' cousin. Full-Fae.

The D'Artigo Sisters' Lovers and Close Friends

Bruce O'Shea: Iris's boyfriend. Leprechaun.

Chase Garden Johnson: Detective, Director of the Faerie-Human Crime Scene Investigation Team (FH-CSI). One of Delilah's lovers. Human.

Chrysandra: Waitress at the Wayfarer Bar & Grill. Human.

Erin Mathews: Former president of the Faerie Watchers Club and owner of the Scarlet Harlot Boutique. Turned into a vampire by Menolly, her sire, moments before her death. Human.

Henry Jeffries: First a customer at the Indigo Crescent, then part-time employee. Human.

Iris Kuusi: Friend and companion of the girls. Priestess of Undutar. Talon-haltija (Finnish house sprite). Formerly one of the Ar'jant d'tel (chosen of the gods).

Lindsey Katharine Cartridge: Director of the Green Goddess Women's Shelter. Pagan and Witch. Human.

Luke: Bartender at the Wayfarer Bar & Grill. Werewolf. Lone wolf—packless.

Morio Kuroyama: One of Camille's lovers and husbands.
Essentially the grandson of Grandmother Coyote. Youkai-
kitsune (roughly translated: Japanese fox demon).

Nerissa Shale: Menolly's lover. Works for DSHS and is
running for City Council. Werepuma and member of the
Rainier Puma Pride.

Rozurial, aka Roz: Mercenary. Menolly's secondary lover.
Incubus who used to be Fae before Zeus and Hera
destroyed his marriage.

Sassy Branson: Socialite. Philanthropist. Vampire (human).

Siobhan Morgan: One of the girls' friends. Selkie (wereseal),
member of the Puget Sound Harbor Seal Pod.

Smoky: One of Camille's lovers and husbands. Half-white,
half-silver dragon.

Tavah: Guardian of the portal at the Wayfarer Bar & Grill.
Vampire (Full-Fae).

Tim Winthrop, aka Cleo Blanco: computer student/genius,
female impersonator. Human.

Trillian: Mercenary currently working for Queen Tanaquar.
Camille's alpha lover. Svartan (one of the Charming Fae).

Vanzir: Indentured slave to the Sisters, by his own choice.
Dream-chaser demon.

Venus the Moon Child: The shaman of the Rainier Puma
Pride. Werepuma.

Wade Stevens: President of Vampires Anonymous. Vampire
(human).

Zachary Lyonnesse: Junior member of the Rainier Puma
Pride Council of Elders. One of Delilah's lovers.
Werepuma.

GLOSSARY

Black Unicorn/Black Beast: Father of the Dahns Unicorns, a magical unicorn who is reborn like the phoenix and lives in Darkynwyrd and Thistlewyd Deep. Raven Mother is his consort, and he is more a force of nature than a unicorn.

Calouk: The rough, common dialect used by a number of Otherworld inhabitants.

Court and Crown: The "Crown" refers to the Queen of Y'Elestrial. The "Court" refers to the nobility and military personnel who surround the Queen. Court and Crown together refer to the entire government of Y'Elestrial.

Court of the Three Queens: The newly risen Court of the three Earthside Fae Queens: Titania, the Fae Queen of Light and Morning; Morgaine, the half-Fae Queen of Shadow and Dusk; and Aeval, the Fae Queen of Shadow and Night.

Crypto: One of the Cryptozoid races. Cryptos include creatures out of legend that are not technically of the Fae races: gargoyles, unicorns, gryphons, chimeras, etc. Most primarily inhabit Otherworld, but some have Earthside cousins.

Demon Gate: A gate through which demons may be summoned by a powerful sorcerer or necromancer.

Earthside: Everything that exists on the earth side of the portals.

Elqaneve: The elfin city in Otherworld.

Elemental Lords: The elemental beings—both male and female—who, along with the Hags of Fate and the Harvestmen, are the only true Immortals. They are avatars of various elements and energies, and they inhabit all realms. They do as they will and seldom concern themselves with humankind or Fae unless summoned. If asked for help, they often exact steep prices in return. The Elemental Lords are not concerned with balance like the Hags of Fate.

FBH: Full-Blooded Human (usually refers to Earthside humans).

FH-CSI: The Faerie-Human Crime Scene Investigation Team. The brainchild of Detective Chase Johnson, it was first formed as a collaboration between the OIA and the Seattle Police Department. Other FH-CSI units have been created around the country, based on the Seattle prototype. The FH-CSI takes care of both medical and criminal emergencies involving visitors from Otherworld.

Great Divide: A time of immense turmoil when the Elemental Lords and some of the High Court of Fae decided to rip apart the worlds. Until then, the Fae existed primarily on Earth, their lives and worlds mingling with those of humans. The Great Divide tore everything asunder, splitting off another dimension, which became Otherworld. At that time, the Twin Courts of Fae were disbanded and their Queens stripped of power. This was the time during which the spirit seal was formed and broken in order to seal off the realms from each other. Some Fae chose to stay Earthside, others moved to the realm of Otherworld, and the demons were—for the most part—sealed in the Subterranean Realms.

Guard Des'Estar: The military of Y'Elestrial.

Hags of Fates: The women of destiny who keep the balance righted. Neither good nor evil, they observe the flow of destiny. When events get too far out of balance, they step in and take action, usually using humans, Fae, Supes, and other creatures as pawns to bring the path of destiny back into line.

Harvestmen: The lords of death—a few cross over and are also Elemental Lords. The Harvestmen, along with their followers (the Valkyries, the Death Maidens for example) reap the souls of the dead.

Ionyc Lands: The astral, etheric, and spirit realms, along with several other lesser-known noncorporeal dimensions, form the Ionyc Lands. These realms are separated by the Ionyc Sea, a current of energy that prevents the Ionyc Lands from colliding, thereby sparking off an explosion of universal proportions.

Ionyc Seas: The currents of energy that separate the Ionyc Lands. Certain creatures, especially those connected with the elemental energies of ice, snow, and wind, can travel through the Ionyc Seas without protection.

Melosealfôr: A rare Crypto dialect learned by powerful Cryptos and all Moon Witches.

Nectar of Life, The: An elixir that can heal and extend the lifespan of humans to nearly the length of a Fae's years. Highly prized and cautiously used. Can drive someone insane if they don't have the emotional capacity to handle the changes incurred.

OIA: The Otherworld Intelligence Agency; the "brains" behind the Guard Des'Estar.

Otherworld/OW: The human term for the UN of "Faerie Land." A dimension apart from ours that contains creatures from legend and lore, pathways to the gods, and various other places like Olympus, etc. Otherworld's actual name varies among the differing dialects of the many races of Cryptos and Fae.

Portal, Portals: The interdimensional gates that connect the different realms. Some were created during the Great Divide; others open up randomly.

Seelie Court: The Earthside Fae Court of Light and Summer, disbanded during the Great Divide. Titania was the Seelie Queen.

Soul Statues: In Otherworld, small figurines are created for the Fae of certain races and magically linked with the baby. These figurines reside in family shrines and when one of the Fae dies, their soul statue shatters. In Menolly's case, when she was reborn as a vampire, her soul statue reformed, although twisted. If a family member disappears, their family can always tell if their loved one is alive or dead if they have access to the soul statue.

Spirit Seals: A magical crystal artifact, the spirit seal was created during the Great Divide. When the portals were sealed, the spirit seal was broken into nine gems and each piece was given to an Elemental Lord or Lady. These gems each have varying powers. Even possessing one of the spirit seals can allow the wielder to weaken the portals that divide Otherworld, Earthside, and the Subterranean Realms. If all of the seals are joined together again, then all of the portals will open.

Supe/Supes: Short for Supernaturals. Refers to Earthside supernatural beings who are not of Fae nature. Refers to Weres, especially.

Triple Threat: Camille's nickname for the newly risen three Earthside Queens of Fae.

Unseelie Court: The Earthside Fae Court of Shadow and Winter, disbanded during the Great Divide. Aeval was the Unseelie Queen.

VA/Vampires Anonymous: The Earthside group started by Wade Stevens, a vampire who was a psychiatrist during life. The group is focused on helping newly born vampires adjust to their new state of existence, and to encourage vampires to avoid harming the innocent as much as possible. The VA is vying for control. Their goal is to rule the vampires of the U.S. and to set up an internal policing agency.

Whispering Mirror: A magical communications device that links Otherworld and Earth. Think magical video phone.

Y'Eírialiastar: The Sidhe/Fae name for Otherworld.

Y'Elestrial: The city-state in Otherworld where the D'Artigo girls were born and raised. A Fae city, recently embroiled in a civil war between the drug-crazed tyrannical Queen Lethesanar, and her more level-headed sister, Tanaquar, who managed to claim the throne for herself. The civil war has ended and Tanaquar is restoring order to the land.

Youkai: Loosely (very loosely) translated means Japanese demon/nature spirit. For the purposes of this series the youkai have three shapes: the animal, the human form, and then the true demon form. Unlike the demons of the Subterranean Realms, youkai are not necessarily evil by nature.

And now . . .
a special excerpt of the first book
in the Otherwold series
by Yasmine Galenorn

Witchling

Available from Berkley!

Seattle is gloomy most any day of the year, but October can be especially rough in the bad weather department. The rain pounded down from silver skies, slashing sideways against the windows to form rivulets that trickled down the glass. The water pooled at the bottom in puddles, collecting in the depressions where the weeds had thrust through the cracked pavement. Luckily, the door to the Indigo Crescent was elevated by a slight ramp, just enough to keep customers dry as they entered the shop. That is, if they didn't manage to slip off the edge and land their besandaled foot in the puddle like I had.

I shook off the rain as I entered my shop and punched in the security code. Thanks to my sister Delilah, the alarm not only kept an eye out for thieves, it picked up on spies, too. And we needed that peace of mind, considering just who we were and where we were from.

My foot made a squishing sound as I limped over to my favorite chair and slid off my four-inch heels, picking up one of the strappy sandals. As I wiped off the designer shoe, it crossed my mind that being half-Faerie had its perks. I hadn't spent a fortune on the shoes. In fact, they'd been a gift from the local Faerie Watchers Club members who liked to frequent my shop.

When they saw me coveting the shoes in a catalog, they'd shown up a couple days later with a bag from Nordstrom. I'd debated accepting the gift about thirty seconds; then desire won out, and I graciously thanked the club for their gesture while sliding into the shoes, which were a perfect fit, I might add.

I examined the sandal, deciding that it had suffered no permanent damage. After drying my feet and reuniting them with their favorite heels, I took out my notebook and looked over my to-do list. I had books to shelve and orders to fill, and I'd agreed to play hostess to the Faerie Watchers' monthly book club meeting. They'd be here at noon. Delilah would be out on a case the greater part of the day, and of course my other sister, Menolly, was asleep.

Might as well get to work. I switched on the stereo and "Man in the Box" by Alice in Chains echoed through the store. Later, I'd switch to classical, but for early morning when the store was empty and I was alone, it was all about me. Longing for something interesting to happen, I grabbed a box of new paperbacks and had begun to shelve them when the bell over the door jingled, and Chase Johnson dashed in. *Not* the kind of interesting I was hoping for.

He folded his umbrella, then dropped it into the elephant-shaped stand by the door. As he slid out of his long trench and hung it on the coat rack, I studiously kept my eyes on the book I was sliding onto the shelf. Great, just what I needed to make the day brighter. The letch of the year dogging my tail again. Appreciation was nice. Glomming, not so much. Chase was far from being my favorite human; he didn't even make the top-ten list, and I did my best to frustrate him whenever possible. Nice? Maybe not. But fun? Definitely.

"We need to talk. Now, Camille." Chase snapped his fingers and pointed at the counter.

I fluttered my eyelashes at him. "What? You aren't going to try to sweet-talk me first? I'm hurt. You could at least say please."

"Your attitude's showing again." Chase rolled his eyes. "And can you turn down that racket?" Shaking his head, he snorted. "You come all the way from Otherworld, and what do you listen to? Heavy metal crap."

"Eh, shut up," I said. "I like it. Has more life than a lot of the music I grew up on." At least he hadn't tried to grope me, although the lack thereof should have been my first clue that something was wrong. If I'd paid more attention to my intuition rather than my irritation, I'd have packed up my gear, turned in my resignation, and headed home to Otherworld that very afternoon.

I reluctantly set Grisham down on the table next to Crichton so they could have a nice little chat and slipped behind the counter, turning the stereo down but not off. The Indigo Crescent was my bookstore as far as anybody on the outside was concerned, but in reality, it was a front for the OIA—the Otherworld Intelligence Agency—and I was one of their Earthside operatives. Lackey, if I wanted to be honest.

I glanced around. Still early. No customers. *Lucky me.* We had leeway to talk in private.

"All right, what's going on?" I sniffed, aware of a pungent odor that was emanating from Chase. At first I thought he must have just come from the gym. I'd smelled a lot of things off of him in the past: lust, testosterone, sweat from his workouts, his ever-present addiction to spicy beef tacos. "Good gods, Chase, don't you ever take a shower?"

He blinked. "Twice a day. Smell something you like?"

I raised one eyebrow. "Not so much," I said, trying to pinpoint what the smell was. And then I realized that the odor coming off of him was fear. This was not a good sign. I'd never smelled this much worry off of him before. Whatever he had to tell me couldn't be good.

"I've got some bad news, Camille." He cut to the quick. "Jocko's dead."

"You have to be kidding. Jocko can't be dead." Jocko was a giant and an OIA agent, albeit just a tad vertically challenged. He barely cleared seven three, but there was nothing wrong with his biceps. "Jocko's strong as an ox. What happened? A bus hit him?"

"Actually, he's been murdered." Chase looked dead serious.

My stomach lurched. "Well, hell. What happened? Some jealous guy find out Jocko was fooling around with his wife

and shoot him?" It had to be. No normal human could take
down a giant without a big-assed gun, not even one Jocko's
size.

Chase shook his head. "You aren't going to believe this,
Camille." He glanced around the store. "Are we alone? I don't
want any of this getting out until we know exactly what we're
dealing with."

Usually when Chase wanted to discuss something in private, he was trying to get under my skirts, but I found it easy
to resist his charms. Chase wasn't my type. For one thing, he
was obnoxious as hell. For another, he was an FBH—a full-
blooded human. I'd never slept with an FBH and had no incen-
tive to start doing so.

Dressed to the hilt in black Armani, Chase stood six one,
with wavy brown hair and a smooth Roman nose. He was
handsome in that casual way that suave men have, and when
my sisters and I first met him, we thought he might have a little Faerie blood running in his veins. A thorough background
check had quashed that idea. He was human to the core. Good
detective. Just lousy with women, including his mother, who
was constantly calling him on his cell phone, asking him when
he was going to be a good son and pay her a visit.

"Where's Delilah?" His eyes flashed.

I grinned. I knew just what he thought of my sisters,
although Delilah startled rather than frightened him. Menolly
just creeped the poor guy out, and she usually did it on
purpose.

"She's out on a case. Why do you want to know? Worried
she's going to jump out and say *boo*?" Delilah didn't mean to
alarm people, but she walked so softly she could sneak up on a
blind man and he wouldn't hear.

He rolled his eyes. "I really need to discuss this with all
three of you."

"Yeah, okay, that makes sense." I relented and flashed him a
smile. "You know we'll have to wait until after dusk. Menolly
can't come out to play until then. So have you contacted the
OIA about Jocko yet?"

Not that I expected much in the way of a response from
them. When headquarters had assigned Delilah, Menolly,

and me to live Earthside, we figured that we were one step away from being fired. While we were hard workers, our track record left a lot to be desired. One thing was for sure: None of us would ever make employee of the month. But, as the months wore on with no real word or major assignment from them, we'd begun to relax and decided that involuntary relocation wasn't altogether bad. At least we were having fun getting used to Earthside customs.

Now, however, with Jocko dead, we'd be responsible for cleaning up the mess. And if he'd been murdered, the OIA would want answers. Answers that we weren't likely to find, considering our lack of results in the past.

"Headquarters is blowing me off," Chase said slowly. His lip twisted into a frown. "I contacted HQ this morning, and all they said was to turn the case over to you. I'm supposed to help out in whatever way you need."

"That's it?" I blinked. "No guidelines? No lengthy bureaucratic regulations that we have to observe in our investigation?"

He shrugged. "Apparently, they don't consider Jocko's death a priority. In fact, the person I talked to was so abrupt that I almost thought I'd said something wrong."

While it wouldn't be the first time Chase put his foot in his mouth, HQ's reaction was strange enough to make me take notice.

I glanced at the empty aisles. Still no customers, but in a little while the place would be jumping when the Faerie Watchers book mavens arrived. Entertaining a pack of gawking, camera-happy fans wasn't on my top-ten list of favorite activities, but hey, it paid the bills and helped Otherworld-Earthside relations at the same time. And the women were nice, if a little giddy.

"Come on, let's talk. The FWC contingent won't arrive until noon, so I've got some time to kill."

"The Faerie Watchers Club?" It was Chase's turn to grin. "Oh come now. Don't tell me you finally gave in to them? Don't you just love being a celebrity?"

I snorted. "Oh sure, I *love* belonging to the Anna Nicole Smith set. All Earthside Faerie live in tabloid land, you know." In fact, yellow journalism had gotten a huge boost when we showed up, our presence infusing new blood into the *Enquirer*, the *Star*, and numerous other tabloids. "Hey, it could be worse. I could have the Guardian Watchdogs breathing down my neck."

"Heaven help us from that," Chase said under his breath.

A vigilante watchdog group, the Guardian Watchdogs considered anybody who wasn't an FBH to be an "alien." They called themselves the "earth-born" and lumped everyone from Otherworld together as a threat to society, a threat to their children, and a threat to morality in general. Wouldn't they be surprised to find out who was lurking in the shadows long before we'd ever opened up the portals on our side? Earth had its own tidy measure of vampires and Faeries, along with a few other creatures that didn't show up in the storybooks.

The Watchdogs took it upon themselves to keep track of any incidents involving the Sidhe and their kin and then exploited them for their own ends. They were a whole lot scarier than the Faerie Watchers Club, who just popped a dozen flashbulbs in our face every time we turned around and asked for an endless string of autographs.

"Say, you don't think they could have had something to do with Jocko's death, do you? The Guardian Watchdogs, that is?" I asked as I led Chase to a folding table that sat beside a shelf filled with obscure foreign novels. Pushing away the remains of my morning egg-sausage muffin and venti mocha, both of which I'd become thoroughly addicted to, I motioned for him to sit down.

"I don't think so," Chase said. "They're pretty much all talk and no action, other than their never-ending protests and picket signs."

I settled into my chair and propped my feet on the table, crossing them at the ankles while I made sure my skirt was covering everything Chase might want to see. "Do you have *any* idea who killed Jocko? And how did he die?"

"New shoes?" Chase asked, raising an eyebrow.

"Yeah," I said, not about to tell him where they'd come from. "So do you? About Jocko?"

Chase let out a long sigh. "No. And he was garroted."

Garroted? My feet hit the floor as I straightened my shoulders. That didn't track right.

"You're sure you told headquarters how he died? And they blew you off?"

"That's what I said." He leaned back and slid his hands in his pockets. "But I've got a weird feeling about this. I don't think we're dealing with humans, and there's nothing that I can tell you that would explain why. Just a hunch."

"If he was garroted, you're probably right. Sometimes the dregs from Otherworld slip through the portals. And not all of my kin in OW play by human rules." I frowned. "Maybe somebody has a grudge against giants, or got drunk on a bad batch of goblin wine? Or maybe somebody was just in a bad mood and decided to pound on the bartender? Could be this is just a case of some OW thug taking out his frustrations while he's Earthside."

"Could be," Chase said, slowly nodding. "But I don't think so."

I squinted, staring at the table. Chase was right. I knew I was howling at the wrong moon. "Okay, let's look at this logically. Nobody Earthside has the strength to garrote Jocko. At least no one who's human. Did you find *any* sign that one of the Sidhe might have had a hand in this?"

"Not that I noticed. Of course, I might not know what to look for. I did, however, find the cord used to strangle him. Here." Chase tossed a braided leather thong on the table. It was spattered with blood. "There's a feeling I get when I touch this . . . I thought you might be able to ferret something out."

It occurred to me that Chase had a touch of second sight. Picking up the braid, I closed my eyes. The faint scent of sulfur hit my nose as a dark miasma slowly began seeping out of the woven strands, oozing over my fingers like burnt oil. I jerked away, dropping the rope back on the table as I drew a sharp breath.

"Bad news. Big bad news."

"What? What is it?"

I swallowed a lump that had suddenly risen in my throat. "Demonkin. That rope has demonic energy infused into the fiber of every strand."

Chase leaned forward. "Are you sure, Camille?"

I folded my arms and leaned back. "Positive. There's no feeling in the world that even comes close to demon energy.

And this rope reeks of it." Which clinched matters. We weren't facing some disgruntled Faerie or dwarf, or any of the other numerous inhabitants of Otherworld who could easily be captured and deported.

Chase stumbled over the same thought. "I thought demons were banned from Otherworld."

"They are, for the most part. Oh, we have some gremlins, imps, a bunch of lesser vampires and the like, but nothing on the order of what it would take to produce this strong of an aura." I stared at the murder weapon. "I hate to even give voice to the thought, but there's a chance that a demon has made its way up from the Subterranean Realms and slipped through a portal."

"That's not supposed to happen." Chase sounded so plaintive I almost felt sorry for him.

"You're right, it's not." When we'd accepted our post, the OIA had guaranteed that demons from the Sub Realms couldn't get through. All the reports said that throughout the hundreds of years they'd been watching the portals, not a single demon or ghoul from down under had made it topside. But then again, the OIA promises a lot of things they never follow through on. Humans have *nothing* on the Sidhe when it comes to bureaucracy.

He tried again, skirting to find another angle. "You're positive your inner . . . magic . . . ticker just isn't off?"

"*Inner magic ticker?* Oh please, you can do better than that. Chase, you asked me, and I told you. This rope belongs to one of the Demonkin. You can believe me or not as you choose."

"Okay, okay," Chase said with a grimace. "I just don't like the sound of that. What should I do about the OIA? Tell them about the rope and what you sense off of it?"

"Yeah, give it a try." I snorted. "See if that kick-starts their butts. I advise contacting them again as soon as possible."

The Wizards Guild, the IT workers of Otherworld, had set up a communications network for OIA's Earthside contingent. Trouble was, when headquarters didn't want to take a call, they just ignored the message. Of course, when *they* needed to contact *us*, we'd be in deep shit if we didn't answer.

Chase glanced around. "Are you sure it's safe to talk here?

I can just imagine what would happen if the papers got hold
of the news that a demon's running around. It's dicey enough
with you Faerie folk and the like."

I didn't bother to remind him that I was half-human and
had as much right to be on Earth as I did to be in Otherworld.
"You're like a fussy old mother hen, Chase. Chill. I just
warded the store against snooping yesterday. We should be
safe enough."

"Uh-huh, sure you did. You positive you didn't turn the
place into a bullhorn by mistake?" He laughed so loud it
turned into a snort.

"Excuse me?" I leaned across the table and flicked his nose.
"It was bad enough back home, but now I should put up with
this crap from an *FBH*? I don't think so! I happen to be magically challenged. You have a problem with that?"

"*Magically challenged*, so that's how you're describing it
now? Hey, far be it from me to give you grief, but I'm not the
one who ended up nekkid for the whole world to see," he said,
grinning as his gaze ran up and down my body.

"Get your mind off my naked body, Johnson. While you're
at it, let's see you try your hand at a little magic," I said curtly.
"Care to show me what you've got, Superman?"

That shut him up. One thing I'd discovered since we arrived
in Belles-Faire, a seedy suburb city of Seattle, was that Chase
craved power. He couldn't wield magic himself, so he did the
next best thing when he found out about the OIA. He went
to work for them. Sometimes I thought he actually enjoyed it
when my spells backfired.

He held up his hands to ward me off. "Sorry! I didn't mean
to strike a sore spot. Truce?"

I let out a long sigh. Tactless or not, he had a point. And
with the pall on that rope, we had bigger fish to worry about
than my ego.

"Yeah, yeah. Truce. As to my warding, don't have a hissy
fit. To back up my magic, Delilah installed an electronic surveillance system. She has a knack for your technology, and
she rewired it to pick up on any bugs or other listening devices
that may have been planted around here."

I didn't tell him that she'd also blown a fuse and sparked

herself a good one. The resulting flash of electricity threw her across the room. But Delilah was no quitter. Eventually she'd figured it out and got it working.

"Good girl. I knew you wouldn't let us down."

"Girl?" I gave him a long look. "Chase, I'm old enough to be your mother."

He blinked. "I tend to forget that. You don't look it."

"I'd better not look it," I said, raising an eyebrow. I was damned proud of my looks and took pains to accentuate the positive. One perk about living Earthside: The makeup was fantastic. For one thing, it didn't stain like cosmetics made from herbs and berries. Back in Otherworld, I'd spent longer than I'd ever planned to looking like a Pict when I tried out some face paint made out of woad. Never again. When I returned home, I'd be carting a butt load of M•A•C cosmetics with me, especially tubes of Verushka lipstick and tubs of Soft Brown eye shadow. I nurtured my little vanities.

Chase coughed, and I saw the glimmer of a smile behind his eyes. "All right," he said. "Here's how it went down. This morning I took a call from one of the homeless guys who live in the alley around back of the Wayfarer. He found Jocko's body. The dude's been one of my informants in the past and was scrounging for a few bucks. So I got there first, which was a good thing, considering Jocko wasn't looking all too pretty. Of course, I immediately activated the FH-CSI."

I stifled a smile. The Faerie-Human Crime Scene Investigations team was Chase's brainchild and was a mix of human and Otherworld agents, specially trained to deal with the problem of crimes against OW citizens. Chase had initiative and foresight, I had to give him that. It was unfortunate that he had to answer to Devins, a real prick who was a few offices higher up than Chase, but usually he was able to keep his boss out of the loop.

"We're using an OIA medical examiner, and all the info has been sealed."

I slumped. Suddenly it all seemed too real. The thought of Jocko meeting his end in a back alley made me cringe. He may not have been the brightest bulb in the socket, but he made up for it in congeniality, and I'd genuinely liked the gentle giant.

"Jocko was one of the most even-tempered giants I've ever

met. That's why he got the job, you know. He could interact with others without pounding them into the ground when he got irritable. He was a good-hearted man who did his best. I'll miss him."

"He wasn't a man," Chase said, wrinkling his nose. "He was a giant. And he was crude, loutish, and made fun of my suits."

"As you said, he was a *giant*. Giants are like that, only most are much worse. What do you expect?"

Chase gave me an exasperated look. "I have no idea. I don't know any other giants. I never met a vampire or a lycanthrope either, until I met your sisters, so give me a break if I don't react with much enthusiasm. Giants and bloodsuckers and werewolves—"

"Were*cat*. Lycanthrope means were*wolf*. It's not synonymous with Were. Delilah would scratch your eyes out if she heard you lumping her with the Canids."

"Right, werecat. What was I thinking? Sorry," he said, his voice anything but. "Section five of the handbook. *Not all Weres are the same*."

"Damned straight they aren't, and don't you forget it. Some of them would slit your throat for even suggesting it." I was giving him a hard time, but better that than let Chase learn the hard way. The point of a sword or fang was a whole lot sharper than my tongue.

"Whatever. What I'm trying to say is that all of you were simply tales of myth and legend until a few years ago, when you crawled out of the woodwork. Even you—you're a witch. And half-Faerie at that. I'm still wrapping my mind around all this."

"Point taken," I said, grinning. "I guess we do come as quite a shock, especially when you've been taught your whole life that we don't exist. Okay, back to business. Tell me more about Jocko's death."

"Well, other than the fact that the killer had to be at least as big and as strong as he was, there's not much to tell. Nothing in the bar to give us any idea what happened. Nothing in the portal log to indicate that somebody new came through last night. Basically, it boils down to the fact that the Wayfarer is out one bartender, and HQ wants you to take care of it."

The Wayfarer Bar & Grill, like the Indigo Crescent, was OIA run and operated, and part of a worldwide network of safe houses and portals. The bar was also a hub for FBHs who wanted to meet the Fae. And there were plenty of admirers who lined up for a chance to see, or talk to, or screw us. The crowds were thick and the partying hard.

My sister Menolly worked night shift at the bar. She listened for gossip and rumors that might be important among the travelers who came through from Otherworld. Having her there was a good way to spot potential trouble, since the grapevine always ran faster than official channels. It was also one of the few night jobs she could find, and she was strong enough to stand in for the bouncer if need be.

Chase pulled out a pack of cigarettes but stuffed them back in his pocket when I shook my head. Cigarette smoke raised havoc with my lungs and was even worse for Delilah. Menolly didn't care anymore. She was dead. Well, undead. The only things she could smell were blood, fear, and pheromones.

I glanced at the clock. "I can't wake Menolly until dark. Delilah's out on a case and won't be back until late afternoon. Why don't you meet me here at six, and we'll go back to the house? That way you'll have had a chance to contact HQ again. And by then the sun will be set."

"Can't you wake Menolly up now since it's overcast?" Chase said.

"Chase, get a grip. Vampires and daylight just do not mix. Besides, it's rough on her to be locked in the house all day. Better for her to sleep as much as she can; it keeps her from getting claustrophobia. Menolly hasn't been a vampire very long, not by our standards. She's still learning to adjust, and we're making it as easy as we can on her. I'm doing my best to help her, but it's rough going at times. In fact, I'm working on a surprise that she'll probably hate me for, but it will be good for her."

"I see your point," Chase said, musing. "All right, I'll try to raise HQ again and tell them what you said about the rope. But if I were Menolly, I'd call in sick tonight. If there *is* a demon behind this, he might be after OIA agents. And if he had inside help, then he might know that Menolly is an operative."

An inside job? That thought hadn't crossed my mind. "Great,

that's all I need to think about," I said, grinning. "Okay, see you tonight."

Chase headed for the door. As I watched him leave, a shadow seemed to pass through the shop, and I reached out to touch it, but it shuddered and dissipated into the gloomy day. Jocko's murder had set in motion dangerous events to come. I could feel it on the wind, though any clear picture eluded my sight. I went back to my work, trying to muster up a smile for the Faerie Watchers who would be here in full force in less than an hour.

M192AS1009